Praise

"This book will do for our understanding of the Global War on Terror what Clancy's books did for our understanding of the Cold War."

Simon Barrett,
—*USA Today*

"The author is a man of a powerfully perceptive worldview of East and West. His laser targeting of the Caucasus, the Middle East, and the fractionalized world of Lebanon, specifically, speaks of firsthand knowledge of these tortured regions. His insight put forth in beautiful prose climbs into the realm of the poetic and will stir even a casual reader...Throughout it all, a rich tapestry is its own reward, seducing and pointing to a human landscape both beautiful and bawdy yet breathtakingly informative."

—Elias Abu-Ayn
Former United States Special Envoy
To the Saudi Royal Family
Author of *Operation: Snow Leopard*

"Much of Wentz's writing violates the conventions of the men's action adventure thriller. He writes at times with a poet's sensibility. This represents an unusual blend, one that suggests that Grant Chisolm himself may have the panache of the poet in him, so

i

that he is as much an American cowboy as ever but one who could sing to his friends and sweetheart if he wished to. Yes, this is a man's book but one presenting artistic sensibilities that any woman can admire and enjoy."

—Tatiana Artamanova, Ph.D.
Philogia
Univeristet Minsk
Belarus

"The author's experience and depth of research shine forth and force the reader into prickly realms of topics most Westerners do not want to enter. It is far easier to remain steadfast in the "us vs. them" mentality – to maintain that the Middle East is bad, all Muslims are bad, that Communists are bad. An adventurous and believable plot captures the reader, demanding the reader to keep turning pages. Beware if you have a busy life because the book will demand your attention."

—Rachel Blake
Military Physicist

"International in its scope and almost painfully intimate in its revelations concerning the motivation of those who exact retribution against the West for the perceived injustices perpetrated against Islam, Wentz's novel revels in its examination of the shadowy world of contemporary terrorism. The work, presented in a kind of slow-moving majesty toward a climactic finish, is likewise torturously revealing of the warriors who fight against the murderous intent of Al-Qaeda in dark spaces, dark waters, and the darkness of the human soul."

—T.D.
Office of Homeland Security

"*Zero Two Hundred Hours* is the most insightful critique of the terrorist mindset in the market today. Wentz' portrait of villainy is outstanding and something we should all find disturbing."
—Dr. Arthur M. Kunath LTC, USAR (Ret)

"*Zero Two Hundred Hours* is fact posing as fiction. Those of us who have been on the front lines of the War on Terror recognize the settings as well as the characters who people his book. They are real, the plot is real, and the truth about Guantanamo and the ugliness of war— all of this is as truthful as any book yet to deal with the mind of terrorists and their dedication to the destruction of our great nation. Wentz has performed a service for all the men and women of the United States Armed Services. Read this book."

—M.R.L.
Formerly of National Reconnaissance Office

"As a retired military intelligence professional, I am well aware of the sometimes confusing nature of intelligence collection and analysis as well as the difficulty of determining whether or not a piece of information is authentic and therefore "actionable." Wentz perfectly illustrates the indefinite and murky nature of the intelligence world. The main character is believable in his occasionally misreading— welcome to the intelligence world—of vital clues as he seeks to thwart Al-Qaeda-type bad guys. LCDR Grant Chisolm's antagonist is one of the most evil and sinister figures I have yet seen in a work of literature. He has to be someone real, someone the author has encountered firsthand. He is that believable. This is a thinking person's read."

—John Luther, Commander USNR (retired)

"The story's most interesting aspect may be reflected in Wentz's ability to connect seemingly disparate events in history to the contemporary world. As a result, the reader is cued to be mentally alert to Quranic verses from the very beginning of Islam to sultanic belligerence in the Ottoman Empire to modern cryptographic mysteries."

—W.P. Commander, USN (Retired)

"In his novel *Zero Two Hundred Hours*, Mr. Wentz shows himself to be a scholar, teacher, soldier, and storyteller, as well as an expert in political, military, and religious affairs of the modern world. *Zero Two Hundred Hours* is above all else a gripping tale of suspense. LCDR Grant Chisolm must call upon not only his martial skills but also his education in foreign languages and cultures to ferret out a terrorist plot from the slenderest clues."

—Theodore J. Slusarczyk
Former Russian Language Specialist, U.S. Army
Former Foreign Service Officer, U.S. Department of State

"Wentz rivals Clancy, Cussler, and Vince Flynn in his ability to generate excitement from one page to the next...the interrogation process was spot on. If I didn't know better, I'd say that I was a participant in some of the interviews described in the book...The enemy is real, the plot not only plausible but one we prepared for, and the characters are people we all knew."

—LCDR Richard Zuley, USN (Retired)
Former EUCOM LNO, Senior Interrogator
Special Projects Team Chief
Joint Task Force – Guantanamo

Zero Two Hundred Hours

Eric Wentz

Leaders
Press

Published in the United States by Leaders Press.

www.leaderspress.com

ISBN 978-1-63735-055-3 (pbk)
ISBN 978-1-63735-086-7 (e-book)

Print Book Distributed by Simon & Schuster
1230 Avenue of the Americas
New York, NY 10020

Library of Congress Control Number: 2021901323

OTHER BOOKS

BY ERIC WENTZ

Piercing the Veil

Iranian Foreign Policy

Preying in Iran

To my brothers Mark and Scott, and my sister, Christina.

They are the meaning of understanding, encouragement, and loyalty.

And to those siblings who expelled their last breaths without a word spoken.

Quraysh – Ancient Arabic word meaning
"shark."
The tribe to which the Prophet Mohammad
belonged.

Shurke – Old German for "villain."
Origin of the word shark.

———————————————

De Profundis Clamo ad te domine.
-Psalm 130[1]

(Out of the depths I cry to you O Lord)

———————————————

Out of the depths of the desert,
Out of the depths of the sea,
Out of the depths of the psyche,
The agony of men.

E.W.

The Prologue

Arabian Desert, AD 605

Like a dervish in a dance, death descended out of the darkness of the desert and raiders whirled on their camels and horses, striking the encampment. The Bedouin tents flapped and fell upon the slaughtered like shrouds. One man dropped to the sand, headless before his tent, as his wife screamed in childbirth and her own death.

Hours later, one rider in the moonless night held the newborn in swaddling clothes as he converged on the tented caravan. As he dismounted, he asked of the man who greeted him, "Kadisha?"

"Her labors are greater than yours or mine. What is this?" Then he paused as he looked at the sleeping child beneath the coverlet in the glow of the flickering torch. "The child will not live."

Before he could respond, a scream rang out from a tent. They entered.

In the tent and torchlight, in her pain and delirium, a woman reached for her stillborn child and forcefully grabbed at the placenta as the midwife futilely sought to wrench it from her hand.

"I knew it was a boy," she moaned.

"It is a girl," whispered the midwife as the mother cradled the stillborn and smeared its head with the placenta.

"How like his father," she moaned, and fell backward in sleep as the midwife cleaned her and took away the child.

As she slept, Mohammad, hidden in the shadow with Abu Bakr, put the sleeping child to her breast. The midwife looked away, pretending not to see. The two men walked outside where camels nibbled on a boxwood tree and the horses nuzzled one another in the near total darkness. The raiders piled their loot at Mohammad's tent.

"I would not expect this," uttered Mohammad. "This child will bring trouble."

"Not for you. No one saw me take it. She is your legacy."

"Yes, and now the relic of a vanquished tribe."

The Prophecy Of The Scepter And The Moon

> *The secrets of empires do not vanish with their collapse; they sustain them.*[2]
>
> -Mamoa Kristophorn

Constantinople, Tuesday, May 29, 1453. The year 6961 of the Byzantine Calendar.

Father Marcellus Popandreau, the last man ever to celebrate the liturgy in the Great Church, looked out over the city from the exterior of its great dome that circled the church like a crown. Within the alcove of the dome, his black robe blended with shadows. With the even temper of a saint, he sat patiently as the frenetic world around him burned off its zealotry in rape, rapine, looting, and fire. Beneath the overcast sky, the destitute multitudes in the streets far below flung themselves at and on one another.

In the distance, he spied a solitary white horse straining to advance through the crowds. As

1

horse and rider closed on the church, Father Marcellus, his green eyes wet with grief at the city's fall, receded from view into the masonry's hidden opening.

The pale rider on a white horse, like a solar eclipse, showed the pallor of his being to the dead and dying. Serene in his lunar-like ellipse, he migrated the earthly dominion of the last of the Caesars whose pagan emblem of two thousand years seemed to have melted away in an Icarian display of stupidity and hubris — the two-headed eagle.

In a slowly shrinking gyre, horse and rider moved on as he imagined the very stones beneath him in wavelike undulations of the sea, pulled loose by his very presence. In a world that to many would seem to be upside down and a precursor to the apocalypse itself, he was drawn by the ripples of the silent surge of history and the gravity of a destiny that pulled him to the center of Greek and Roman spirituality. This city, that Church, is where it had all begun, where it had been sequestered for ages. Here in this city, that Church, is where he would end it. The relics would at last be found and destroyed. In a synchronous movement of earthly ambition and celestial indifference, he advanced to the omphalos of the Byzantine world to which he felt himself tethered from birth. On this day, he would cut the cord so that he might live out his ambition as the man-child of a new civilization.

Mehmet II advanced as the city convulsed. The multitudes, like the shattered remains of a great icon, lay about in a frenzy of vibrating color and grating cacophony that could neither see nor hear in their fellow Greeks the pieces to the harmony that had once ruled over them. The remaining poor, desperate, and isolated soldiers of Byzantium, unable or unwilling to flee the city, could only cringe as they felt themselves breaking.

Mehmet II rode ahead with a green mantle worn about his shoulders, like that of the Prophet, and trailing behind him over his saddle and resting on his horse's haunches. Now and again it lifted slightly as his mount strained at the tension and smells of battle still lingering in the air. Its nostrils flared at the smell of several nearby burning houses and that of human refuse still scattered about the streets, bleeding, disemboweled, limbless, or just fearfully drenched in urine, sweat and excrement. Some of the living smelled worse than the dead. Only the rats seemed unconcerned and inured to the suffering around them.

Mehmet II, regal, resplendent, and of a harsh visage, glowered as he rode ever more slowly, his horse now and again stutter-stepping at the scream of yet another woman and child separated by their new lords. He turned at last to gaze upon the grandest structure in all of Constantinople. It was not the Hippodrome, the great raceway for charioteers, nor the emperor's palace, but the greatest structure in all of Christendom.

In a spontaneous surge of triumph, dozens, then hundreds, and finally thousands of soldiers, Turks, Syrians, and other fruits of Islam's manhood began to shout, "Is-tin-poli! Is-tin-poli! Is-tin-poli!" Mehmet II drew closer to the troops concentrated around the greatest architectural achievement of a thousand years, the *Magna Ecclesia*, the Great Church, called *Hagia Sophia* by later generations. Steadily, strongly, they engaged in an antiphonal voicing that rang like a mocking humiliation of Greeks of all classes and professions. Even the Genoese merchants and their soldiers and Venetian seamen sought refuge in the basilica that was intended as a monument to God's wisdom and the maternal affection of his earthly and heavenly mother.

Inside were the relics of untold value and a vial, it was said, of the Virgin's milk itself. Sacred objects venerated by thousands upon thousands over the centuries⊠relics which would now fall into the hands of those who might not fear to defile what they could not or would not appreciate or believe. Objects so venerated and so powerful that conquerors sought their possession as validation of their Divine right to rule over humanity.

In another surge of elation, soldiers alternately shouted "Is-tin-poli," in the city, and "Kayser-I Rum," Caesar of Rome. The antiphonal chorus sounded a reverberating presence and seismically shifted the earth and echoed in a mocking liturgy that seared into the souls of those crouched down in fear within the sanctuary of Christendom's greatest exaltation of aesthetics and faith. Completely surrounded by the Turkish army, the Greeks of Constantinople and their fellow Romans had retreated to the center of the city and then gradually into the church itself.

"Is-tin-poli! Is-tin-poli!" and "Kayser-I Rum!" rang from outside. Inside, *Kyrie Eleison* was intoned by the seemingly placid figure of the patriarch of Constantinople, or, as he was yet called, the patriarch of New Rome. Father Athanasius II repeated *Kyrie Eleison* amidst the weeping of the fearful survivors. *Christe Eleison*, Christ, have mercy.

The center of the Church, which itself lay at the center of the Eastern Roman Church, the very citadel of the faith, echoed with nervous talk amidst the incantation of prayer. The icons and the mosaics, which exalted the glory and beneficence of God in his Trinitarian manifestation, Father, Son and Holy Spirit, looked down from the walls and the great dome with indifference. Mary herself had lost her tenderness, and her eyes no longer seemed to follow those who moved anxiously about the crush of bodies in the church. Instead, they looked blankly out into space. The solace of God's abiding strength and wisdom seemed to have abandoned all. On this day, even God and the angels seemed about to submit to the Turk.

For a thousand years, prayers had wafted up to the great dome of the basilica of the Great Church, then through its mosaic firmament into the heavens themselves. From here, prayers as multitudinous as the stars themselves had sought the beneficence of God and the intercession of Mary, the mother of Christ. From this location, the imperial family from the days of Constantine, from the days of Justinian and Theodora, had prayed to God for wisdom to guide the Romans of the West as well as those of the East. But on this day, the lamentations of the vanquished mixed with prayers that seemed to hover like the heavy smoke of Greek fire beneath the dome of *Magna Ecclesia*. Their prayers had no wings. For on this day, the sun itself was blotted out by the darkness of a solar eclipse that saw the rising of the crescent symbol of Al-Lat, the ancient pagan moon goddess of the Arabs and the symbol of Islam. Green banners, the color of the Prophet Mohammad himself, and the symbol of Islam's mighty Turkish forces, appeared everywhere throughout the city while the banner of the two-headed eagle, the symbol of imperial Constantinople, lay on the ground both trampled and defiled.

Locked in the church that lay at the center of the eastern Christian world, three thousand believers called upon the Hammer of God to smite the Mohammadans upon the anvil of faith. But this was Constantinople and not Tours. On this day, there was no hammer borne by God or his minions. On this day, the Beast of the Balkans, unaware of their prayers, but ever mindful of his own, conquered in the name of Allah. Each group huddled and cringing within the Church, families and neighbors, friends and slaves, fixed upon some semblance of hope, some talisman that would offer protection or even the crass similitude of divine protection that *infidels* and the blasphemous called *luck*. Amidst their consternation, they bargained with God. If only the Turk would now be miraculously barred from the Holy of Holies where they sought solace, each would in kind offer some form of eternal thanks in prayer, supplications, or alms.

As thousands of anguished cries converged into a maelstrom, like a raging river newly born and sweeping all before it in a near climactic surge, Mehmet II was as much pushed by the intoxication of victory as he was restrained by decades of careful planning. He approached the imperial entrance of the Great Church and lighted from his saddle as his most trusted cavalier and confident, Machmood bin Ben, took the reins of his horse in hand. He ascended the steps with his entourage, his personal bodyguards now pushing aside his own wild-eyed soldiers and dismounted cavaliers.

As Mehmet II entered beneath the canopy and arched entrance, he felt the thrill and anticlimax of reality itself. He moved forward with an eye to the future retelling of this moment as he bade his warriors to stand back as he himself displayed both the mercy of the Prophet and the wrath that God might exert on those who knew not submission. But at this moment, he could not restrain his own men.

Amidst the killing, men with special gifts rushed past Mehmet II with the gaze of those who can mercilessly and precisely gauge the commercial value of human life. Even as Mehmet II shouted, the exaltation of his troops increased in volume to blend with the shrillness of mothers shorn of their legacy and their husbands, their aged mothers, and crippled fathers. Here would be the final lot of a hundred Anchises without the sons to bear them up and there the lot of hundreds more of aged wisdom that now felt the pangs of the Virgin Mary. They looked to a semblance of divine maternalism in stony mosaic that stared blankly and horribly at their pain like that which she, too, once felt and about which she on this day did nothing.

The compressed multitude now pushed and crushed breath from matrons, who had once given them life, as soldiers cut and severed limbs. And Mehmet II, ever mindful of history, called out as his cavaliers joined in the frenzy. Like the others, they cracked skulls and pulled the beautiful from among the forlorn. The majesty of the moment fell to murder and mayhem. He turned and walked back out as his chief accountant passed him to assess the price of the lovely and soon-to-be debauched, deflowered, and deranged by pain inflicted by their conquerors and the seeming indifference of God. But as he did so, one Genoese soldier who fought back valiantly, and who he was inclined to save, suddenly was struck by a sword that cleft his bearded lower jaw so that it fell on the floor. Yet he continued to fight. Mehmet paused at the novelty of a jawless warrior fighting with a severed tongue, until another blow from a cudgel from behind brought him to his knees. He lifted both arms with his sword still in hand and his body began to shake uncontrollably. It continued to shake in frightful spasms as he fell sideways to the indifferent floor.

Hours later, Hazrat Bilal, so named for Mohammad's slave, the first man ever to utter the call to prayer, sang out from the steps of the Great Church, "There is no God but God and Mohammad is his Prophet."

Throughout the city, soldiers fell to their knees and the enslaved did likewise for fear of inviting retribution while others sat numbly, too afraid to pray even in the way they already knew.

◆◆◆

The shock waves that emanated from the epicenter of Constantinople sought voice in the chants throughout Christendom imploring the intercession of Saints Cyril and Methodius or the mundane saintliness of a pope who had not galvanized the forces of the West into a wall of resolve against the *infidels*. All would tremble throughout the forthcoming days. Yet while the world shook, a small, wiry, and ascetic-looking figure, Father Marcellus Popandreau, hid well into the night in an underground lair that was a concealed repository for royal documents. With the help of two young novitiates, he finished packing away the most telling relics into several wooden reliquaries. Looking like ancient ossuaries, these were steeped in the memory of bygone intrigue and sacredness. They contained the bones of many stories and the flesh of plots yet unborn.

Bearded, hooded, and followed by his protégés, the ascetic, who himself reverberated with the holiness of a true believer willing to sacrifice all comforts to live a good life, slipped into the late night darkness. Down alleyways, through backdoors of gardens, through passageways beneath buildings and below once seemingly invincible walls into a small, unseen opening that led to a cavernous underground cistern, they tread with their treasures. There, a boat waited with two men inside.

They helped to hoist the treasured containers into the craft. The others then lowered themselves into the sturdy boat and sat against the gunwales. The boat was quietly rowed through the ancient Roman waterways toward a little known passageway that led to the sea. From there, they entered the darkness of a black sky over black water. They rowed into seeming oblivion.

◆◆◆

On the morning of the next day, all the citizens who remained now enslaved or merely deserted by all but their captors, listened and trembled – even the deaf. They, too, felt the reverberations of the morning call to prayer. Like the ever-widening circles from a stone cast into the sea, the ripples of yesterday's clash fanned out as waves that crashed upon the shores of Otranto and Messina, Rhodes, and Cyprus. Even Santorini shook again and the ashen remains in Pompey were plied to near awakening by an event felt by the dead who would be few in number who did not know the significance of the city's fall. The whole Western world would soon be forced to awaken from its cocoon of indifference at the terrible beauty of a new prayer forced upon an old city—borne here forthwith into spiritual exile. Again, for the second time, Hazrat Bilal, picked for the occasion by Mehmet II both for the melodious quality of his voice as well as the significance of his name itself, sang out,

Allahu Akbar, Allahu Akbar
Ash-hadu an la ilaha ill-Allah, Ash-hadu an la ilaha ill-Allah
Ash-hadu anna Mohammad-ar-Rasoolullah
Ash-hadu anna Mohammad-ar-Rasoolullah
Hayya 'alas-Salah [8]

All of this occurred 821 years after Mohammad's flight to Mecca, which would later become known as the *Hijra*. All of this occurred in the 856th year of the Muslim lunar calendar in which the moon's annual migration reminded men that there was a time for everything under heaven.

THE CONVERGENCE

*What immortal hand or eye
Could frame thy fearful symmetry?*[1]

-William Blake, "The Tyger"

Southern Afghanistan, Near Kandahar, Today

Lieutenant Commander Grant Chisolm remained as still as death. In the cold nighttime air in the cleft of mountains outside Kandahar, Afghanistan, his eyes remained glued to his night vision binoculars. He watched as the resurgent Taliban forces crossing over from Pakistan moved on foot through the depression below. The moonless sky was ideal for the nighttime activity of both reconnaissance teams like that of the Seals Ultimate Team, for which he had seemingly been bred, and for enemy foreign fighters bred for terrorist activity.

Four would be suicide martyrs, determined to end their lives in an explosion of glory, fell in behind a four-man advance of bearded Islamic warriors devoted to the destruction of Western *infidels.* Following at about thirty yards was another four-man team. Al-Qaeda and Taliban operatives who had successfully crossed the border only a month before, carrying the blood-spattered head of a Dutch soldier killed in a firefight, now retraced their steps. They had badly mauled a platoon of Dutch soldiers caught in an ambush on their way from Bagram. Hakim al-Hajj, Yemeni born and reared, had led the assault on the small convoy moving swiftly through the twilight, only eight miles from its point of convergence with a contingent of Canadian forces.

Hakim had bartered the head for the honor of leading a group of European youths recruited through the Brandenburg Mosque in Stockholm, Sweden. These he would take first to Lahore, Pakistan, then onto the tribal region of the Pakistani/Afghan border and into the market places of Kandahar where they would detonate an explosive belt that would sever their own spine and rip apart any man, woman, or child in their immediate proximity. In dying, these young men, one of whom could barely sprout a beard, would manifest the destructive force of Allah's committed soldiers and reap the rewards of corporeal pleasure.

Even as they trudged through the cold night air, they imagined the heavenly delight of heaving their pulsating bodies on fancifully beautiful virgins born with a knowledge of providing pleasure that might have caused even porn stars to blush. But, as they thought of the pleasures of heaven, Chisolm's six-man team, in a synchronous moment of converging wishes, imagined helping these would-be martyrs enjoy celestial bliss by inciting a premature detonation.

Chisolm waited until the entire string of enemy combatants was completely in view, entirely strung out, and utterly exposed. Each member of Chisolm's team was equipped with rifle suppressors that muted sound and minimized flash. He whispered into his wireless headset, "Repay when I hit the back boy." Within seconds of uttering that message, Chisolm fired his modified M4, and the rear guard's head splattered while the front of the line continued on, as yet unaware. Seconds later, the back three walkers went down in rapid succession. Their falling alerted the others in the procession, but not soon enough for them to respond.

As they turned toward the sound of falling bodies, each of the four would-be suicide bombers exploded from the volley of gunfire that hit them from the side of the mountain immediately opposite Chisolm. The four men in front had turned to see a flicker of light from a rifle barrel above, immediately discerning its significance. But, as they dropped to their knees in a stabilizing position to take aim, they toppled over as two men from Chisolm's unit, hidden in front of the advancing Al-Qaeda/ Taliban contingent, slammed into their backside in rapid succession. In silence, they fell in an almost surrealistic display of the effect of a well-planned and extremely well-executed ambush. Their deaths seemed a pantomime of violence with not so much as a bang to announce its occurrence. Not one of them had gotten off a shot.

Moments later, as Chisolm gave the word for the other two members opposite him to descend, he climbed down from his position, eyeing the Al-Qaeda bodies for signs of life and potential resistance. He and his men inspected each of the bodies for what they called "pocket litter," which would be sent back to headquarters for translation. One of Chisolm's men was detailed to take a DNA sample from each of the dead to match against a database of former detainees in various US and NATO detention facilities throughout Afghanistan, Iraq, Guantanamo Bay, Cuba, and elsewhere. The same man, Petty Officer First Class Travis Keen, then walked among the dead taking photographs of each.

The information gleaned could provide the identity of these men beyond what had already been discerned through NSA surveillance and interception of cell phone messages. Petty

Officer First Class Renaldo Duncan, nicknamed "Disco" by his fellow warriors, inspected the backpack on the front man among the dead.

Although all of the men carried rucksacks for supplies, the front man carried only a backpack like any day hiker or book-bound high schooler or college student. Inside, however, were three hardbound notebooks filled with handwritten Arabic script. As Chisolm approached, Disco handed one to him. Chisolm opened it, read the Arabic script with a red-bulb flashlight and said, "Phone numbers, addresses and names." He reached for the backpack that had been ripped from one shoulder of its carrier by the impact of firepower. The bag also contained a copy of the Koran, with a large hole outlined in blood and pieces of bone and flesh. Chisolm motioned for Disco to put the other notebooks back. He replaced the Koran as well, as the others approached with the rucksacks of their victims.

"Put their packs up on the ridgeline," said Chisolm. "Then we need to dispose of these bodies. There's a decline over there." Chisolm pointed into the blackness at a sharp drop, discernible only due to their night vision goggles as well as their knowledge e from having reconnoitered the area days before to determine the perimeter of the ambush.

Sweating in the cold night darkness, they retrieved each of the torn bodies and dumped them down the decline. The bodies rolled into a seventy-foot drop a good three hundred feet from the path the men had been on at the time they were ambushed.

Then LCDR Grant Chisolm said to his men, as they dumped the last body, "Keeping them out of sight and out of smell will enable us to set the trap here again when we need to." In a gesture that the men recognized from previous combat between Chisolm and their Al-Qaeda and Taliban foe, he pulled out a metal canister, and sprinkled its contents on the bodies below as he uttered, "A gift from Black Jack Pershing—pigs' blood for pigs." He emptied the flask-shaped canister and then he and his men walked back to the high ground. They continued on into the darkness, well aware that their own movement was being monitored by a high-flying drone launched from a nearby NATO facility. It relayed the progress of any fighting between good guys and bad guys in the Afghan theater to commanders in the immediate vicinity and from there to Kabul. Chisolm and his men continued walking in the slowly-lifting darkness and the colder-than-before night air. Members of the 160 Night Stalkers descended in helicopters a few hundred yards away to retrieve the Ultimate Seal Team.

But before Chisolm and his men could make the pickup point, they noticed something on their left side in the rocky terrain that hadn't been there two days earlier when they first inspected the area.

◆◆◆

Petty Officer Second Class Matt Flaherty walked ahead as the point in the general direction of the odd, and not entirely decipherable, sight. In the dimness of early morning light, the sight was amorphous and shadowy with ominous overtones. Each blink of their eyes as they approached the figure filled in the details of what at last seemed to shape itself into something vaguely human and teasingly unbelievable.

As Flaherty drew close enough to make out the entire shape of the figure, he uttered a shocked "Shit!" and waved the others to halt. Anything this grotesque and this remotely positioned was obviously placed here to draw in the none-too-frequent passerby. In this area of Afghanistan, this was likely to be either enemy combatants who would have been warned in advance of its existence or NATO Special Forces operating in the vicinity. Such a figure was bound to attract and likely to be booby-trapped.

Others kept their distance as Flaherty moved closer. There, in the dimness, he looked upon the unlikeliest of figures. The entirely naked shape of a man was spread-eagled against the fuselage of a downed Russian helicopter, a remnant of the Soviet/Afghan War of the 1980s. Flaherty held a red-bulb flashlight, going over the entire figure. The head was glossed over with some sort of whitish gook, like super glue, that had been used to seal the man's eyes shut. Duct tape had been wrapped around his mouth and head in a thick band. The head was bruised all about the face, which was puffy and distorted, and the long black hair and slight beard were encrusted with blood. The man's face, or what was left of it, suggested someone in his late twenties or early thirties.

Each arm was outstretched with ghastly perforations along the forearms through which metal wire had been passed, which was sewn into the metal fabric of the downed helicopter's nose cone. His legs likewise had perforations drilled through each foot and ankle with the metal wire passed through the flesh into and around the helicopter's metal, tied off at several different points. His genitals had been burned and partially severed so that his scrotum hung down from a piece of flesh on his right thigh. An inscription carved into his chest made clear the figure's intended symbolism. In three-inch-high letters carved with a knife was the word "AMERICAN." The author of the simple message had reached his intended audience.

In the distance, the repeated flutter and wopping sound of the helicopter picking them up was approaching. Chisolm and the others had seen enough. As they began to walk away, Lieutenant Junior Grade Rashid William, a former combat photographer, took out his camera and snapped off a dozen photographs. He had never before seen a man crucified.

Duncan then asked Chisolm, "Do you really think that poor guy is American?"

"No, but whoever did this wants us to know that this can happen to us."

"Do you think maybe he was the journalist who was kidnapped a couple of months ago in Khost?"

"He didn't look like this guy, and he was from the *New York Times*. If you're Al-Qaeda, you don't want to harm your allies."

Duncan snickered.

"Besides, if he were from the *Times,* we'd have read about it ahead of time. They like to write the news before it happens—even if it doesn't."

Duncan smiled and thought amusedly of a certain reporter who had arrived in Kabul a few months previously wearing bandoliers, two canvas belts of ammunition crisscrossed on his chest. Some things were so unbelievable that they could only be true.

Chisolm and his team waited and turned their backs as the blades of the chopper kicked up sand and dirt as it landed. Rosy-fingered dawn was now upon them.

TRAINING THE LIONS

> *Lions are never tame; it takes*
> *strategies to deal with that.*[5]
>
> -Anonymous

Guantanamo Bay, Cuba

Colonel Ramon Carlos Felix Sanchez stepped from his armor-plated Soviet-era utility van as his aide opened the door. As was his custom, he arrived early, almost always ahead of his American counterpart. Sanchez had once read that lion tamers made it a point to enter the cage into which the lions would be released for training and performing before them. This was to let the lion, or in this case the Americans, know whose turf this was and who therefore was invading whose territory. The lions must be taught to submit.

Upon exiting his vehicle, Sanchez stood still momentarily to offset the lightheadedness that seemed to accompany his anticipated meetings with the Americans. He was not certain if the lightheadedness was the result of the long car ride from Guevara Barracks or the nervousness he always felt before their meetings. Age fifty-two, Sanchez envisioned himself as too young to be anything other than healthy. Still, as he stood there, he momentarily saw spots before his eyes and caught a hint of his own mortality; a real admission for someone who wanted to live long enough to see the Revolution manifest itself upon the entire earth.

Once he recovered his physical bearings, he stood ramrod straight, impeccably attired in his dress uniform complete with ribbons. He made it a point always to be at least as well dressed if not better dressed than his American counterparts. His sartorial splendor included eight rows of military ribbons for his heroics in Angola, Bolivia, Eritrea, and parts of the world well known but unnamed. He was, however, particularly proud of his awards for marksmanship. His was a sharp eye with a steady hand.

As a much younger man, he had used that skill to remarkable effect with Cuban forces sent to defend the Angolan Communist regime in the 1970s. He had been a part of an elite group of soldiers who specialized in covert operations against South African forces operating there and in Namibia. Among the more than forty thousand Cuban troops sent to Angola, only two had received the order of Lenin, one for martyrdom in the name of Communism, and the other, himself, for remarkable and deadly efficiency against South African forces.

He walked with the assured dignity of a man who is accomplished in his profession, visionary in his aspirations, and entirely capable in directing the practical day-to-day operations of his underlings. His thin and muscular physique moved in sinewy ripples underneath a military uniform tailored to accentuate his gladiator build.

Sanchez's coal-black eyes peered out from reflexively-squinting eyelids, habitually attuned to the glare of sunlight rather than the sterility of chemically- induced lighting of fluorescent bulbs and shiny Formica office desks. He found most interior spaces depressing in their bland colors, moldy smells, and airless boxiness.

As a child, he had habituated himself to read material that would help him learn the art of war. One such book, by the American author James Fenimore Cooper, had been read in an abridged Spanish version. The hero in that novel had helped him formulate his own vision of chasing down game in a primal forest and tracking down the enemy, sticking as close to them as their own scent. Like Cooper's character Natty Bumppo in *The Deerslayer*, he could detect enemy movements with something akin to a sixth sense.

Sanchez's face bore the marks of a life inebriated with violence. From a combative youth in the streets of Santiago to the dirty business of covert operations, he had earned the decorations of near-death experiences. His naturally dark complexion had been reddened by constant exposure to the sun. Having always relished a good fight with fists as well as guns, he bore several small scars about his brow with a lengthy one that coursed down from his left temple. It added character to the pockmarked cheeks, the result of teenage acne. His smile, bleached white and winning, drew people's eyes away from the striations on the left side of his neck and head and the left ear with an otherwise conspicuously missing upper half. He was a real-life stand-in for Rambo with a Latin accent— a true military Hidalgo with a flair for living and verbalizing all the virtues of egalitarianism. He did this with a gusto that belied his questioning of its practical application, given what he saw as the predatory nature of reptilian humanity.

A cynic of exceptional charm, he lived amidst the tension of competing visions of ruthless socialism and a desire to taste the nectar and feel the ameliorating touch of a world at peace or, at least, made incapable of resorting to violence. But such would be the world only when a divinely appointed harmony would manifest itself. This could occur only after the revolution had progressed to its natural end. But that harmony, because it was good and would require the use of a militaristic abrasive to rub off its sharp edges, legitimized the use of force. Truly the ends did justify the means. Born and reared Catholic until his socialistic schooling attempted to drum this legacy from him, he still saw glimmers of this unattainable brotherhood that would come with the revolution's final manifestation. After all, he himself had said that Marxism was a more pragmatic form of Catholicism. Marx was the Messiah without the halo.

Knowing that he was, as usual, early for his meeting with the Americans, he stood outside next to his car at the Northeast Gate of Guantanamo Naval Station or, as he and the true revolutionaries called it, the gateway to the *Republica De Cuba, Territorio Libre De America.* So read the sign over the gate. He stood in the warm Cuban sun looking resplendent with his perfectly shined shoes and closely cropped hair, as well as his immaculate uniform. To maintain a perfectly coifed appearance, he would not allow so much as a pen, loose coins, or even a billfold in any of his pockets. After all, he had an aide-de-camp to carry such things for him.

During his morning reverie, his aide was sufficiently attuned to his routine to stand clear of the colonel as he took in the beauty of the Cuban landscape and its Caribbean breeze. The colonel meditated upon the meeting and contemplated his strategy. Dealing with the Americans was, even in the simplest of matters, an elaborate game of chess. And like that game, it required exceptional vision and predictive capabilities.

Suddenly he flinched and stepped back. A six-foot-long boa had emerged from a cactus squash and appeared to be headed toward the shade of the vehicle. His peripheral vision seemed as good as ever. He smiled at his own reaction and glanced at his aide to see if he had noticed. He had, but pretended not to. The snake passed within three feet and coiled up underneath the dusty green utility van.

As he looked toward the small building situated at the Northeast Gate between Cuba proper and the U.S. Navy base, he heard the vibrating sound of two more of his fellow officers' vehicles as they eased alongside his own, one to either side. In a scene that reflected the grim and simultaneously colorful impression that Americans had of their impoverished counterparts, they stepped from their polished and immaculately maintained 1961 sky blue Chevrolet Impalas. The envy of any car collector in America, these two vehicles looked like twin sisters. They were smart looking and, in their own sad way, a reflection of the virtual necessity of the Cubans maintaining the long-ago legacy of the Americans on Cuban soil. The twin cars also reflected the nostalgic outlook of many older Americans who might have thought these cars to be a symbol of better times in Cuba, in America, and in the world in general.

The two young officers, seemingly *caballeros* with their similarly slender physiques and slicked-back black hair, appeared with sunglasses that maintained their aura of mystery with a kind of chic that was almost velvety smooth. With the near dramatic hauteur of a flamenco dancer, the taller of the two walked with grace and precision while the other, although less dramatically poised, was no less beautifully coifed. Like their colonel, army captains Marquis Ipolitto San Miguel and Nikolai Victor Santiago were dressed impeccably and conducted themselves with a conscious dignity befitting their contempt and fear of the too friendly, too casual, and less-than-Latin Americans. Their drivers, at their requests, had remained seated behind the wheels of their respective cars in a display of egalitarianism that would, of course, be lost on the Americans. The Americans preached democracy, but elections were bought and sold in campaign contributions that wasted money that could easily have been better spent on the poor.

Yet, the two officers, unlike their colonel, were of the true Hidalgo class and less inured to the hardships of life than were the people for whom they continued to preach the power and the zeal of the Red Revolution. Each of the officers walked toward Sanchez who now stood looking once again at the Northeast Gate with his back to them. Silently, and in a well-rehearsed display of stark seriousness and military decorum, they stepped to either side of the colonel and moved in the direction of the small building constructed precisely on the boundary between Free Cuba and United States Naval Station Guantanamo Bay, Cuba.

In a less stern and more amicable way, Cuba vaguely mimicked the Communist-Capitalist divide of the DMZ in the Korean peninsula and the one-time dreariness of the Berlin Wall with its Brandenburg Gate or the one-time gate on the highway separating Hong Kong from Mainland China. This building, for all the seriousness that would transpire within its sixteen-by-sixteen-foot interior looked like a cross between an abridged hacienda and an extra-large tollbooth. In fact, it was the old guardhouse used to monitor traffic going in and out of the base, harking back to the 1950s, when several thousand Cubans worked on the base for the U.S. Navy. Today, unbelievably, three Cubans still worked for the Americans and were allowed to go back and forth through the fence separating the base from the rest of Cuba. The Cuban border guards still monitored their comings and goings and occasionally harassed them for their capitalistic adventurism that found little or no shame in working for the Americans. Despite their contempt for their countrymen who worked for the Americans, they were not beneath taking money from them when they got paid nor would they hesitate to punish them physically when they looked the wrong way or when they were denied a loan by the poor peasants who were better paid by the ugly Americans than were the self-sacrificing members of the Cuban military.

◆◆◆

Having captured the lair before the American lion could enter, the colonel waited in silence, knowing full well that his underlings had brought all the necessary paperwork for today's transactions with the Americans.

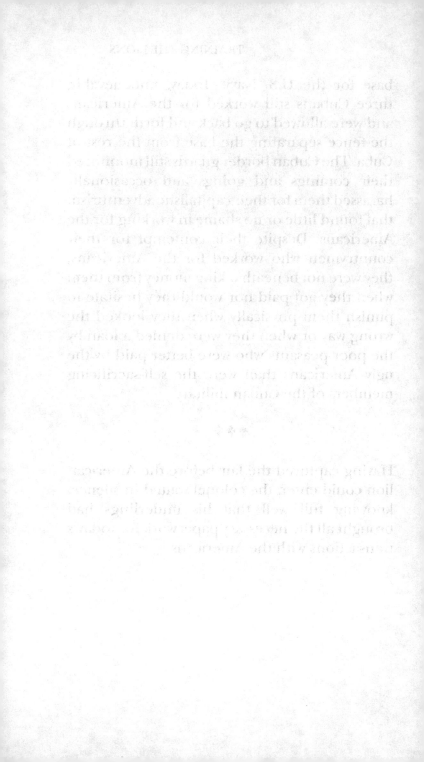

PRECIOUS CARGO

> *I don't like it when they call me a package.*
> -Detainee at Guantanamo Prison Camp

While Colonel Sanchez and his cohorts awaited the arrival of the Americans, just three miles away, on the leeward side of Guantanamo Bay Naval Station, a C-130 cargo plane circled into position to land. Inside the plane was a most precious package.

The pilot, Captain Ephraim Benton, aligned the C-130 with the mile-long runway, eyeing his console as he lowered the flaps and began to set the large craft into its final landing phase. Once the plane was properly positioned over the ocean and appropriately banked and leveled into a beeline for the landing strip, he turned on the PA system and said, "Welcome to Guantanamo Bay, Cuba, the Pearl of the Antilles." Then he added, "And to our special guest flying with us today for the first time, and perhaps the last time, may your stay at Club GITMO be a long and fruitless one."

The taunting remark did not go unnoticed by the crew or the masters-at-arms who were escorting their latest HVD (high-value detainee) from Bagram Detention Facility in Afghanistan. Detainee 9696 sat blindfolded and restrained, with ankle shackles and plastic wrist ties, in a comfortable chair latched to the floor of the cargo bay. He was asleep and began to stir only as a result of the discomfort in his ears caused by the plane's drop in altitude.

Feeling the pressure in his ears, he swallowed several times and tried flexing his jaw. Yawning didn't help either. He sat and braced himself. The plane bumped along the runway and reversed its engines to slow its massive frame. Despite his blindfold, he moved his head from side to side as if to look around. Underneath the blindfold, he squinted as if doing so would give him the x-ray vision necessary to penetrate the black cloth. His hands gripped hard at the armrests to which they had been tied and he wondered where he was. Having stopped once already at Camp Anaconda in Iraq, for reasons never explained to him, and again in the Azores, where he smelled jet fuel and therefore knew why—he wondered if this was his destination or just another refueling.

He then said in a slight accent in what was otherwise flawless English, above the roar of the engines as the plane slowly came to a halt,

"Guard, guard, if we are in Paris, I wish to buy some souvenirs, maybe some pictures of the Eiffel Tower. I need to study the pictures so I can plan to blow it up."

The guard who was closest and buckled into her own seat replied, "Sir, this is better than Paris—hot, dry, very few women, just like the desert that you're used to." The guard, twenty-three-year-old master-at-arms Army Sergeant Kolea Frazier, from a small town outside of Huntsville, Alabama, then smiled in the direction of the blindfolded man. He smiled back.

After about a twenty-minute delay, the tech sergeant in charge of the baggage area where "the package" remained, wrapped and sealed, pulled the lever to lower the rear cargo ramp. Only when the ramp was completely descended and the plane properly docked did the MAs begin to detach the package from his chair. Once the chain anchoring his leg shackles to the floor was unlocked and disconnected, and the small chains withdrawn through the plastic ties on each of his wrists, MAs knelt on the seats to either side of him and lifted him to his feet. They reshackled his wrists with sturdier, more traditional bracelets, and connected the wrists to the leg shackles with about a three-foot chain. He now stood while the guards removed his blindfold and allowed him to stand for about two minutes until his eyes adjusted to the light. The guards, each with a hand firmly placed behind an elbow, began to slowly escort him down the gangway towards the ramp. He shuffled rather than stepped to minimize the weight and noise of the chains. Two translators, one Pashtu and one Arabic, followed him to disembark while the navy's own legal team representative from the JAG, and one army doctor carrying a briefcase with documents concerning the detainee's health as well as medical bag for health emergencies, awaited him at the bottom of the ramp.

He began to descend into the morning light. Feeling more annoyed at the seemingly kind treatment of his guards as they attempted to steady his descent with their firm but gentle hold, he shucked off their hands by raising his own and twisting his arms away from one and then the other. Then in Arabic he uttered, "*Khara! An-na taaban!*" (Shit! I'm tired.) Though neither of the guards knew the language, they nonetheless understood the tone. As he took the last few steps to the concrete runway, they stood closely by and placed their hands just inches from his arms if he should stumble and fall.

Upon stepping to the bottom of the ramp, he relaxed his hands and felt the warm ocean breeze off to his right that fluffed his graying brown beard and longish curly hair. He blinked several times at the silhouetted entourage standing before him several feet away under the plane's tail. As he squinted, he made out several different uniforms similar to those he had seen in Afghanistan. Some were the tan uniforms with splotches of black, brown and white to camouflage soldiers deployed to one of the desert and dirt kingdoms of the Middle East. Others were the digitally checkered dull green uniforms with squares of bluish gray and black, like the masters-at-arms wore in Bagram Prison. *More guards,* he thought.

He watched one distinguished-looking figure with a star on the collars of his tan desert uniform sign a document presented to him by the tech sergeant responsible for all the material in the cargo bay. Though it was a navy-piloted plane, circumstances had intervened to cause the responsibility for this special package to fall to an army soldier who replaced the designated cargo specialist, temporarily incapacitated by a chest wound from an IED (improvised explosive device).

As the man looked up after signing the papers, he looked at the prisoner and said, "Welcome to GITMO." A white windowless van pulled up. The guards escorted the bearded terrorist suspect from the plane. The admiral who had greeted him, the JAG representatives, a lieutenant general, two Navy captains affiliated with intelligence operations, several aides, a short squinty-eyed civilian wearing a bomber jacket suited for a cold day—all stepped aside as the detainee shuffled toward the van. As he went by, eyeing their uniforms for rank designation, he glanced afield and noticed that the entire perimeter of the plane within a fifty-meter radius was dotted by yet more soldiers in traditional dark green camouflage uniforms and weapons which he had often seen in Afghanistan and elsewhere, M4s and M16s. Chuckling to himself, he feigned an imaginary surprise at the dignitaries who had come out to greet him. *Oh my,* he envisioned himself saying to the admiring multitude, *who could be so important to invite so many out on an early morning to greet him?*

Then he stopped abruptly, causing one of the guards to gently bump into him. He looked to his right and smiled broadly at the crew from Combat Camera that took still photographs and videotape of his arrival. Gently but firmly, the guards pressed again at his elbows as the side door of the escort van opened. Realizing that he might not see his escorts again, he turned to Sergeant Kolea Frazier and said with a smile, "I like your smell." Sergeant Frazier, like the rest of those present, had learned only half an hour before that the detainee spoke English. Never before had she received such a compliment. She smiled and said, "Thank you. Please be quiet."

At the door, the ankle shackles made it impossible for him to lift his legs without considerable difficulty. The guards inside the van grabbed at his elbows to pull him forward while the other two guards practically lifted him into the van.

Once inside, he was properly positioned in the seat, his ankle shackles attached to the floor, and the sliding door was shut. The van pulled slowly away from the plane and headed toward an asphalt road that led to *Sea Craft 92*, a large cargo-carrying water transport moored and waiting a half mile away. This van would ride onto the boat, followed by two other escort vehicles as well as the one vehicle that took the lead. Within two minutes, they had arrived at the dock. The sea transport vessels were the only means by which vehicles of any sort could be moved from the leeward side of Guantanamo Bay to the opposite windward side.

FEEDING CHRISTIANS TO THE LIONS

> *The compulsion to speak of religion is ingrained.*[6]
> -M. Tally, "The Martyr's Mouth"

After the business portion of their meeting was over, the perennially smiling American and his mercenary stooges, one army major and his wispy thin aide, an intelligent and surprisingly likeable marine captain, all relaxed. Sanchez found the Americans perplexing. Despite their arrogance and a certain naiveté, they could be tough and ingratiating at the same time. One saw this particularly at the end of the meetings when the Americans stopped negotiating and started entertaining. Though the Americans were obviously criminals trespassing on Cuban soil for over a hundred and ten years, ever since they stole Cuba from Spain when they went to war over the explosion of one of their foul coal-burning ships, they entertained with an unmistakable confidence of a well-heeled host. One would almost have thought that it was they who owned Cuba and who had therefore decided to keep Guantanamo Bay for themselves while leasing out the rest of the island to the Cubans in return for semiannual tribute of defector baseball players.

As if his thoughts were the gift of prophecy itself, Commander DiPinta poured each man a small cup of powerful espresso coffee and then proposed a toast to the best of relations between the United States and Cuba. All stood and raised their cups and took a sip of the thick brew. *Almost as good as it gets*, thought Sanchez, as he sipped. They sat, and immediately Commander DiPinta smiled and said, "And so, Colonel Sanchez, how is your family?"

Sanchez had, early on, divulged more about himself than he intended. He regretted it for to have done so was like inviting a stranger into one's house. Still, he could not take it back nor could he unnecessarily afford to offend. To do so would be to give Uncle Raul Castro, *Il Duque*, an excuse to remove him.

"Oh, my mother is fine," he replied in English. "She has lived well and enjoys the beauty and the benefits of Mother Cuba and the guardianship of Santa Barbara." Sanchez winced inside as he said the latter, for despite all his training and his belief in the grandeur of the Cuban Revolution, he felt an unmistakable urge to make a religious reference. Doing so would, he hoped, convince the Americans that Communists were not inherently atheistic. But why? Why should he care what the Americans thought? Communists like himself were opposed to the church as it was often a tool for Western imperialism and the opiate that habituated the poor to servitude and slavish devotion, not to God, but to the human exploiters of their labors.

Still, even Fidel had allowed the pope to come to Cuba. He could therefore be forgiven his momentary lapse in attempting to ingratiate himself. After all, he was merely mirroring the Americans, a well-known psychological technique. All the other officers knew their place, American and Cuban, so that none introduced a topic of conversation nor asked questions unless specifically invited to do so. Despite occasional tensions with them, he found these Americans a little less clumsy in their attempts at crossing the cultural chasm than some others he had met.

LIKE COLUMBUS

> *The most beautiful land that human eyes have ever seen.*[7]
>
> -Christopher Columbus about Cuba
>
> *Welcome to Club GITMO, the place to go when you need a break from jihad.*[8]
>
> -Rush Limbaugh

Detainee 9696 felt the van bump along the rough parts of the road even as the driver attempted valiantly to negotiate the occasional potholes or broken asphalt. Sound from the outside world was muted by the white noise of the air conditioner, and sight was blotted out by the completely enclosed space of his confinement, which had neither windows to the side nor to the rear or front. The driver remained invisible to him. The air itself had a slight scent of burned rubber and the stale smell of a moldy freezer.

His guards were purposely quiet and seemed somewhat tense. Each wore the standard issue blue latex gloves of a master-at-arms who not infrequently was forced to handle Guantanamo detainees who sometimes purposely fouled themselves in urine, excrement, spit, blood, and even their own semen. They used this "cocktail," as the guards called it, as a projectile with which to assault the guards or a means of smearing themselves in an act of spite to force the guards to have to clean up their cell and confront the smell of their fecal presence. They also wore the blue-trimmed spit shields to protect themselves from the favorite means of assault at the detainees' disposal.

After the van pulled onto *Sea Craft 92*, he barely felt the gentle dipping of the ship as each vehicle pulled onto the craft behind them. Once all were on board, he could hear a loud clanking sound as the stern gate of the ship was raised hydraulically and chained into position. The already vibrating engines engaged as the captain on the bridge pushed forward the levers causing the vessel to slightly lurch into motion, increasing the vibrations that were muted by the waters below and augmented by its own metallic structure and the steel-motorized vehicles. He could feel what he could not see or clearly hear.

Outside, the sea was tranquil. A pod of dwarf dolphins gathered on the starboard side. They splashed playfully for the first three or four minutes as the ship moved away from its mooring in the "No Wake Zone," past the mouth of the Guantanamo River and into the bay.

The detainee yawned and then drifted off to sleep. Fifteen minutes later, he awoke at the altered pitch of the ferry's engine as the captain threw it into reverse and gently glided the bow into its berth.

Within several minutes, United States Marines awaiting the ship's arrival secured the perimeter which constituted the entire parking lot, standing in a large circle flowing out from either side of the ship. Simultaneously, a three-man landing crew gathered up the ship's mooring lines as they were thrown over the side of the ship onto the berthing pier.

The engines were cut, the chains holding the bow ramp loosened, and the hydraulic system engaged, as the gate dropped onto the concrete reinforced shoreline. The lead vehicle, a white utility van with a flashing red light on top complete with driver and three armed military police, restarted its engine.

The driver, watching the hand signals of one of the ship's crew, drove slowly off, moving the van into a predesignated position where he halted. Then the vehicle with the detainee disembarked as well, followed by the two rear guard vans. Once all were in their designated positions, a military Humvee, with a soldier positioned in the rear with both hands firmly gripping a .50 caliber machine gun, pulled into the lead and another to the rear. With a signal from an army colonel standing off to the side, the caravan began to drudge through the already hot asphalt and cement parking lot of Ferry Landing and up the two-lane road past the desalination plant to the left.

As the vehicles traveled slowly through the curves and hills of windward Guantanamo, all traffic was halted for the detainee movement operation, or a DMO as it was commonly called. In the shelter of his vehicular cocoon, the detainee, though insulated, sensed and imagined the sights, the sounds, the smells, the tastes, and the feel of the world within his immediate proximity.

Outside his van, seagulls were flustered from their regal tranquility by three turkey vultures that picked at the recently crushed remains of an iguana that had only that morning challenged one of the military Humvees. They flew by their uninvited visitors and screeched their contempt in a cacophony of irritation. A rush of flowers that grew from a swatch of trees and mangroves, whose roots snuck down into the water to nourish their vegetating souls, released their sweet scent into the salty air. The morning sun set streaks of thermal glory to warm, brighten, and grow the ocean swelter of life. It bloomed along the shoreline in a burst of glitzy sparks that shook and shimmered on the water and flowed ashore in an exciting shamble of crushed foam.

Though untouched by all of this, Detainee 9696 could still imagine it, unaware though he was that the point at which his vehicle had disembarked was the very spot at which Christopher Columbus had come ashore in 1494, on his second expedition financed by the crown of Spain and the miter of St. Peter. Like Columbus, Detainee 9696 had come on a quest explicitly designed yet well beyond his ken. Though he had planned his imprisonment, his escape was yet beyond his own understanding.

CAFFEINATED DIPLOMACY

> *Coffee is the most companionable of drinks.*[9]
> -Alistaire Wilde, "The Culinary Cupid"

The business portion of the meeting had been unusually long and tedious. The Americans seemed to have realized that it would be this way ahead of time and were better provisioned than was the custom. Their bottled water was twice the usual supply. Their coffee, surprisingly strong, was also ample. Most of the time, the American coffee was weak and not something any self-respecting Cuban would dare to drink.

The agenda had included the reaffirmation of the agreement for the Americans to send back any Cubans who had slipped into Guantanamo Bay if the United States deemed them economic refugees. Political refugees, however, were welcome. *Typical American fraud,* he thought, *tease Cubans with your talk of your wealth and your opportunity on Radio Marti and then taunt them by sending them back. Only one-third were ever allowed to stay.* The others would be assembled at the gate at their next meeting and would once again swear an oath of allegiance to Cuba and be readmitted to their abandoned homeland.

Sanchez knew that those being sent back were usually less than desirable anyway. *Disloyal sons and daughters of the Revolution who would betray their country to become fat and lazy, fat and lazy like the Americans,* he thought. He wondered if the Americans knew how the rest of the world viewed them.

He had to admit, however, that his American counterpart looked trim, as did his aides. He also knew from examining the biographical file provided to him by Cuban Intelligence that the commander had run track and cross-country at Purdue University and that he loved cross-country skiing, not a skill that he could easily hone in Cuba. Sanchez smiled to himself as he thought of the commander getting his orders after finishing a cross-country skiing race, *"You are hereby ordered to report to Guantanamo Bay, Cuba, where you are not allowed to ski, sled, or toboggan. Moreover, even reading about hockey is prohibited."* No snow, no ice and no fun for the American commander.

But like all the Americans that he had met in an official capacity, they seemed to have studied baseball, especially Cuban baseball, as a way of ingratiating themselves and building rapport. He knew perfectly well what they were doing when the Americans conducted business and poured yet another coffee. They would smile yet again, they were always smiling. They smiled to disarm, to soften a person's hard resolve. What was worse was Sanchez' sense that it was working, even on him.

In their meeting two months ago, in a goodwill gesture, the commander had provided Sanchez with several New York Yankee baseball caps as well as a baseball autographed by Cuban refugee, and now star pitcher, Livan Hernandez. The gesture seemed, however, somewhat calculated, intended less to ingratiate and more to embarrass. Hernandez's betrayal of his motherland was yet one more subtle maneuver by the Americans to remind the Cubans of their inability to keep some of their finest athletes. Ball players who left Cuba, even just to play in the American major leagues, were still traitors. He accepted the baseball graciously, but wanted to throw it at the American. *When people are fat and lazy,* he thought, *they have to steal the athletes from other countries—like the Americans.*

"My friend," said Sanchez, "I have always appreciated your thoughtfulness in our meetings. You come prepared, and you have even brought gifts that speak of your appreciation of the Cuban culture. You know how we love baseball. Myself, I trust, no less than my countrymen and our leader, Fidel Castro. Today, I would like to celebrate our camaraderie and work together with my own gesture."

Sanchez motioned to his assistants. One opened a briefcase and pulled out a silver lighter and handed it to him. The other opened up a plain brown wooden cigar box that had been sitting on the chair next to Sanchez throughout the meeting. Sanchez took the box and offered a cigar first to Commander DiPinta.

"Ah, you have outdone yourself," said the commander as he reached into the box. "I assume these are another product of uncompromising quality, just like your baseball players."

"As you say, Commander." Sanchez offered a cigar to each of the other Americans in turn and then to his own assistants. Taking the last cigar for himself, he closed the lid on the box, put it down, and lit Commander DiPinta's cigar and then the others.

"I have taken the liberty of cutting the ends myself and, how do you say? I have poked a hole in the burned end. You can catch the aroma so much better."

"Thank you," replied the commander, as he drew deeply upon the cigar. The other Americans thanked him as well. They sat sipping coffee and puffing up layers of smoke in the air-conditioned and slightly cold office.

Sanchez knew that the Americans were not allowed to purchase Cuban cigars even when they traveled to foreign countries like Canada or England. His gift was tactical. Sanchez thought to himself that he had successfully countered the cynical ploy that infested the American gift of the autographed baseball. *Light up,* he thought, *you burned me, and now I will burn you.*

◆◆◆

After they parted, Sanchez sat in silence in the backseat of his vehicle, holding the baseball. As they drove back, he looked at the ball and knowingly rubbed it to loosen the seams, thereby slightly smudging the autograph. His strong hands massaged the leather hide and held it loosely across the seams with the distinctive grip that marked his slider. He reminisced about his own youth when he had thrown one baseball and then another against the steps of his childhood home in Havana. The harder he threw it, the harder it bounced back to him. His father had encouraged his efforts by telling him that someday he, too, would play baseball in America. Like Luis Tiant, like Pedro Ramos.

But things had changed between America and Cuba in ways that his father had not predicted. He had always thought things would get better. They had not. His father, however, was right about one thing. Sanchez had grown into an outstanding ballplayer, thanks in part to his father's love of the game and constant encouragement. In the 1970s, when he was playing baseball in the Cuban Industrial League and otherwise fighting in the streets of Santiago, he had distinguished himself as a teenage phenomenon. In his very first game, he had been so nervous. He was playing center field because of his exceptional speed and solid glove. No one could run on him as he tracked down a fly ball or hit singles into his domain. Many others that should have been singles were turned into outs because he caught the ball before it could bounce in shallow center. Not only could he field but he could hit. In his first year, he had led the Cuban Industrial League in triples and finished third in stolen bases with the best ratio of steals to attempts.

He knew, however, that he was better than all this. In his first year, he had even been called in from the outfield to act as a relief pitcher. In his first such appearance, he had inherited three men on base with no outs and the fourth, fifth, and sixth batter coming up. He had responded with his white-hot fastball and a slider that seemed to fall off a table and slice sideways as it honed in on the plate. Three batters he faced, three strikeouts on eleven pitches.

His glory had faded with the death of his father from untreated tuberculosis, a disease that might have been arrested if the Americans had shared their medical knowledge and drugs. *What good was free medical care for all if it cured nothing?* Then, only four days after his father's death, he was inducted into the Cuban Army, leaving his mother to mourn and his elder sister to console her. In a move that predicted his future glory as a soldier, he applied his athletic skills to the stresses of combat training. Being good at sports had resulted in his unintentional advancement to platoon leader and the first of several trips to Angola.

In the 1970s, the Cubans began to send troops to Angola to support Communist forces against the counter revolutionaries lead by Jonas Savimbi. When he finally returned after distinguishing himself as a young soldier with the stealth and marksmanship of a true Che Guevara clone, he found himself caught up in the political uproar involving thousands of his countrymen who, unbelievably, were fleeing Cuba for Florida.

The Americans and traitorous Peruvians had granted asylum to thousands of Cubans. Even the Spanish and others had allowed his countrymen to seek refugee status in their embassies in Havana. Over 124,000 Cubans had fled from Mariel Harbor on the northwest coast of Cuba. They rowed, sailed and practically swam to Florida, where many of their fellow Cubans were already living in places like the Keys, Miami, Fort Lauderdale, and other cities and towns in the south of the state.

The Americans, it was acknowledged in hushed discussions and soft whispers, had even offered money to certain Cuban officials to make sure that several Cuban baseball players would be among the refugees boating to Florida. He had hoped that it was not true, but he heard from others that baseball scouts from the New York Yankees and the Cincinnati Reds had been standing knee-deep in the ocean waiting for the Cubans to arrive. To take money from the Americans, of course, was wrong. But he could not help but wonder why no one had approached him. Why hadn't the Americans asked for him? Even after his first tour of duty in Angola, he was still better than any of the players they had signed. He knew himself to be better than any of the other Marielitas. None could throw like he could. None could run like he could. Why had they not asked for him?

He thought of so many that enjoyed the privilege of playing a game that he loved for a living. He dozed slightly as the vehicle motored along, his body inadvertently tensing as if getting ready to swing a bat at an incoming pitch. His mind wandered back in time as he relived occasions when his offensive exploits led to his being celebrated by family, friends, fans and teammates as the next Minnie Minoso, one of the greatest Cuban ballplayers who had played in the American major leagues for many years. His thoughts mixed with the half dream world of Cuban sports, fantasy mixed with fact. His heart beat faster even as he slipped into sleep and dreamed again of those who had said that he ran like Alberto Juantorena and hit like Teofilo Stevenson. Other recent stars slipped into his consciousness...Danys Baez, Jose Contreras...

Suddenly, as his driver turned sharply to avoid a child who had run to retrieve a baseball bouncing across the road, he woke fully with a start. His idle reflections were the stuff of weakness, he told himself, the stuff of foolish dreams and selfishness. After all, even Fidel himself had given up the prospect of playing baseball for the Washington Senators albeit, some say, because he simply wasn't good enough. Instead, he led a great revolution that still reverberated throughout the world.

But again, in the drowsy afternoon, he slipped into and out of the half sleep of a long and comforting ride through the countryside. He might have been the equal of any of them if only they had asked for him. Still, there would be justice. The Americans would pay. He continued to alter his grip unconsciously on the baseball he still held as he imagined himself throwing his repertoire of fastball, slider, curve and changeup. His muscles tensed as the batter swung...1980s, the war, the boatlift. Despite the passage of time, he felt every bit the toned litheness of a tiger.

"Juan! Juan!" he said, in a voice mixed with resignation and joy. "Pull over. Stop here! Pull over to the side of the road. Get the gloves out from the back. We're going to play some catch!"

JIHADIST HUMOR

> *I kill you!*[10]
>
> -Achmed the Dead Terrorist

Camp Delta, Guantanamo Prison Compound

"I am the greatest whore man in all of Europe and the Americas. So why do they send me a boy to interrogate me?"

"Well, sir," said the young man sitting opposite him, "We like to think of it as an interview, not an interrogation."

"Ah, good." The older man smiled. "Then I can do my fatherly duty and teach you what you need to know. I can teach you much."

"I'm sure you can," replied the young man. "That's why I'm here."

"Yes, yes, I'm sure, but don't patronize me. I can see through your ruse."

The older man raised his bushy eyebrows and stroked his curly brown beard streaked with gray. Then he smiled almost benignly. His teeth shone brightly against his leathery skin, dark by nature and imbued with a coppery luster from years of exposure to the sun.

"How old are you?"

"Oh, come on, sir. You know this interview isn't about me. It's about you. I just need you to answer a few questions."

"What kind of questions?"

"Oh, just some friendly get-acquainted-type questions."

The young man, a United States Navy petty officer second class, Dormel Waldrip, had been trained at the armed services interrogation school in Fort Huachuca, Arizona. In his first tour of duty, he had spent six months as an interrogator in Bagram, Afghanistan, and then four months outside Ramadi, Iraq, trying to elicit information from detained Taliban suspects, Al-Qaeda operatives, Iraqi insurgents, and psychopaths posing as holy warriors devoted to Islam.

At Guantanamo Bay, Cuba, the stories of oftentimes extraordinary breakthroughs, in sometime tedious but well-planned interrogations, were seldom the stuff that grabbed headlines but always the kind that went into detailed reports sent to those who could put the information to good use. The information coming out of Guantanamo was feeding counterterrorism operations throughout much of the world. Dormel Waldrip had been part of that success and was highly regarded by his supervisors, despite his youth.

Even at Guantanamo, however, patience could wear thin, in which case, detainees who were masterfully elusive or belligerently silent could rankle even the most experienced inquisitors. After only one month at Guantanamo, this detainee had failed to provide a scintilla of useful information – except for his accent. When he spoke English, it was with a mastery of vocabulary and syntax, precision and subtlety, and a mysterious morphing of certain "r's" and "v's" that represented a failure in childhood to grasp certain sounds of the English language. Overall, his inflection of certain words was too pronounced, something that gave him away as a foreign-born speaker. These were those who spoke the language too perfectly and who had been trained in the language but not born into it. But the precise origin of that accent remained as elusive as his answers to innumerable questions.

After destroying the confidence of his interrogators and assuring them that their efforts were futile, Detainee 9696 was, in frustration, and in a calculated attempt to appeal to his ego, moved not to the primary facility for HVD (high-value detainees) but instead to the maximum security facility for loudmouths. There, he was dressed in the white garb of a cooperative detainee. The white garb among the orange-garbed troublemakers would single him out among his peers, subjecting him to social isolation and contempt. Two could play at the psychology of baffling the other. Here he would be accessible to yet another interrogator.

Suddenly, the bearded man looked not at his interrogator but at the analyst who sat in the back of the twelve-by-twelve-foot interrogation room in the air-conditioned trailer known as the Gold Building. He asked, "Are you old enough to hear dirty jokes?"

The analyst, another young Navy petty officer dressed in a dark blue Ban-Lon shirt and a pair of jeans, equipped with the usual green hardbound notebook, sat up in his metal straight-backed chair, slightly surprised at being addressed, and said, "I think so," and then smiled.

"How old you are?"

Before the interrogator could catch his eyes with a shake of the head, the analyst uttered, "Twenty-one, sir."

"Ha! Maybe you are the same age as my grandson, do you know that? Or maybe not, maybe you are younger. So, so I have a joke. I will tell it loud enough so that even they can hear."

He pointed to the blackened observation glass, which was four feet by four feet. On the other side were an observer from the FBI and a mysterious figure from EUCOM, the European Command, and the Director of the Intelligence Operations at Guantanamo. They sat in darkness and quietly listened on their headsets to the interview that would otherwise have unfolded before them like an old-time movie from the silent era or like an Aristotelian drama distilled to its essential action by a mute button.

"So," he uttered yet again as he fluffed his white blouse and scrounged down into his seat in a confidential pose, "you are navy guys, this I know. Since Abu Ghraib, no more army guys, right?" Then he paused dramatically and slowly enunciated "in-ter-ro-gation." He smiled slyly and added, "You can 'in-ter-view' me later, after my joke.

"So, this little boy is running around the men's room, and he has a little toy gun and he making sound like a rifle, like AK-47, the weapon of terrorist. Pop! Pop! Pop! And then he sees, under the stall where the toilet is, the shiny black shoes. The little boy sticks his head under the door to the toilet, and he sees an army man and he says, 'Are you real army man?' The army man, he says, "Yes I am, boy, you would like to wear my hat?"

"Wow!' he says, 'Yes, I would.'

"Then, the boy he runs around the toilet again, and then he sees another pair of shiny shoes under the door and he puts his head down under door and he sees another man and he says, 'Are you a marine guy?'

"Yes, I am, little boy. Would you like to wear my hat?"

"Oh, yes! Yes, I would!'

"So he puts on the marine guy's hat and he runs around with his little gun shooting like a terrorist. But then he bumps into a sailor guy at the porcelain thing and he says, 'Are you a real live sailor guy?'

Yes, I am, little boy. Would you like to suck on this?"

"Oh no, sir, I just wear the hat. I'm not really a marine guy!"

Againsttheirbetterjudgmentandunconstrained by their mission or military decorum, they both burst out laughing. It was he and not they who had established rapport. It was he and not they who had established the baseline of further discussion. They might be the lions, but he was the lion tamer. The director and the mysterious observer from EUCOM smiled broadly as they attempted to suppress their own impulse to guffaw. The FBI representative had already left in what was commonly known as a "drive-by." Several minutes had told him that the session was unlikely to be of much value to him. Recognizing his success in telling the joke, the detainee pointed to the observation window and said, "I hope they liked it too." Then he added, "I like the part about the hats."

Having a few jokes of his own, the figure from EUCOM smiled to himself at the question that the Department of Defense had paid good money to find out, as in, "What makes Muslims laugh?"

At that point, after only several minutes, the young interrogator sensed that he had lost control of the interview and attempted to get back on track. But the detainee was no longer listening and even his analyst sensed that they might be better coming back another day. So the interrogator resigned himself to small talk about global developments and the importance of eating yogurt to enjoy a long life. Then the detainee ended the interview much as he had begun it. His face relaxed but his eyes were serious and he said, "Now for your lessons – next week you will come again. But you must bring coffee – Starbucks – or we cannot inter-view. I will then teach you how to pick up beautiful women and how to get laid…Say, you really like my joke?"

"Yes, it was funny," responded Waldrip.

"Okay, next time, you bring joke too – maybe a good Muslim joke. Make me laugh."

As the interrogator and the analyst got up to leave, the detainee offered his hand and said, "Good, I am here all week…maybe all my life."

The interview ended with no information surrendered and no one the wiser as to who Moustafa Arins Riat al-Haj really was – if, indeed, he really was Moustafa.

YOUR JESUS

*And there arose about this time a
source of new trouble, one Jesus.*[11]

—Josephus, *Antiquities of the Jews*

"If you really knew who he was, you would not
worship him. For he is but a Nazarene named
Joshua with a Greek writing publicist. Joshua!
Joshua! Joshua!"

The interrogator, Petty Officer Dormel Waldrip,
had made the mistake of actually engaging in
a theological debate with a man who knew
too much. He did not flounder beyond the
Koran like many of the detainees might have,
but rather, he seemed animated by the debate
and had pushed his befuddled interrogator
into a silent relenting of any pretense that
he actually knew what he was talking about.
The interrogator was nonplussed. He neither
understood the significance of calling Jesus
Joshua, nor did he wish to proceed in such a
challenging confrontation. Detainee 9696 had
a gleam in his eye and could seemingly smell
blood. He had bitten into psychological flesh
and would not let go.

As he sat opposite his interrogator, he lifted his cup of complimentary Starbucks coffee—which the interrogator had brought—sipped, and smiled. As he put the cup down, he pointed his index finger first at the interrogator and then at the opaque window to his right. He repeated the gesture several times and said, "You are my hostage. But I am willing to exchange you for my equal. You are not it. Please, do not be offended. But you are a sheep, and I am a wolf disguised as a terrorist. Which is worse? Now, please bring in the lion. I wish to fight."

He then lifted his right arm in a semicircular motion and pointed dramatically at the window and said, "Fight me if you are a lion." He kept his arm poised and smiled almost cynically at his interrogator who wanted to talk but sensed, as had happened before, that the detainee and not he controlled the moment.

Behind the opaque window sat Guantanamo's lead Islamic cultural advisor, Dr. Emmanuel Najar, and the liaison officer of the European Command. It was his job to communicate developments to Stuttgart, Germany and elsewhere concerning the events transpiring in Guantanamo and, especially, the status of the detainees who might, even against EUCOM's recommendations, be returned and freed in the European theater. This consisted of all of Europe, parts of the Middle East, including

Turkey, and all of Africa with the exception of the countries immediately adjacent to the Red Sea.

The interrogator said softly, "So you won't talk to me?"

Detainee 9696, with a sparkle in his eyes and a glint of what might have been malice, remained motionless with his arm still outstretched, responded, "Send in a lion; I want a battle."

At precisely that moment, the chief of interrogations walked into the darkened observation room and put his hand on the shoulder of Dr. Najar and said, "How's it going?"

Dr. Najar looked at him and said, "I feel like a lion today but if there are no Christians to devour, I may have to eat Wolf Man or Mohammad…"

Dr. Najar was an unusual amalgam of cultures. Born in Cairo to a Coptic Christian family, he had grown up in the shadow of a mosque and knew the *adhan* even before the prayers of his Christian faith. His education included a bachelor's degree from the American University of Cairo in biology and another in political science, a medical degree from John Hopkins, and a master's in Islamic studies from the University of Paris. Retired from the medical profession and now an American citizen, he was a devout pupil of religious studies and a man attuned to the nuances of theological debate. Grounded in metaphysical concerns and concepts, he preferred to determine the composition of the pin itself before attempting to ascertain how many angels were upon it and how many of them might actually be dancing.

As he opened the door to the adjoining room, 9696 and the interrogator looked up. The detainee dropped his arm and exclaimed, "Ah ha! A lion! At last, a lion!"

Dr. Najar's gray hair and dark, wrinkled complexion and granny glasses with bifocals let him know immediately that at least in terms of life experience this man was in all likelihood his equal. Dr. Najar extended his hand to 9696, who motioned for Dr. Najar to sit down. As he sat, he uttered, "As sala'amu alaikum," the universal Islamic greeting.

"Ah," sighed the detainee pleasantly as they shook hands. "It is nice to meet a lion. Your accent, though, tells me you are almost a countryman. Almost. Perhaps, therefore, you bring with you the wisdom of the ancients and you can tell me not only how the pyramids were constructed but more importantly to whom your Joshua prayed."

"You mean Jesus."

"No, I mean Joshua. He was a Jew. Call him by his right name. He brought the gift of faith. Will you accept it?"

Ignoring the question, Dr. Najar said, "He did not speak Hebrew. He spoke Aramaic, the language of non-Jews."

"Yes, this is true," 9696 replied satisfactorily. Then he looked at the interrogator and said, "Listen and learn. When a lion speaks, you should turn your head to speak with him or sit respectfully silent."

The interrogator smiled slightly at the realization that the detainee had once again gotten control of the interview. Thankfully, Dr. Najar would now conduct the rest of it. Petty Officer Dormel Waldrip sat back and listened.

"My lion friend, tell me, will you answer *my* question?"

"To whom did Isa pray?"

"You mean Jesus."

"We are both Arabs. We call him Isa."

"But that is a term more for Muslims. I prefer Jesus."

"Good then, tell me to whom did Isa or as you say, Jesus, pray?"

"To God the Father, supreme ruler of the heavens and earth."

"And who is God the Father?"

"He is the Supreme Being."

"So He came before Isa? If so, then the Supreme Being must have created him."

"No, they co-exist in an eternal oneness while having separate missions."

"But you said Isa prayed to God the Father. Did he pray to another god or did he pray to himself?"

"Yes, he prayed to the Father, the heavenly Father of all men including Jesus."

"If Jesus prayed to him, then Jesus cannot be God. A true god would have no need to pray to himself. It would be a contradiction."
"You miss my point."

"You fail to make it."

The interrogator, who had listened patiently, now felt the compulsion of his position and said, "Sir, I have to ask you some of those questions that you normally don't like to answer."

The detainee smirked, shook his head, and said, in a Gospel parody, "Martha, Martha, Martha, wash the dishes if you must but those who know will choose to listen."

He then turned back to Dr. Najar and said, "How can Jesus be God if..."

Dr. Najar, interrupted, "Again, Jesus the man prayed to his heavenly father that he might teach men how to pray. He himself as a man, also prayed. He himself, as divine, received even those prayers which are rendered to himself as well as the Father. It is, of course, a mystery to which I, as a humble man, must bow."

"You call it a mystery. I call it a contradiction. For no God can pray to himself."

"This is true. No God can pray to himself. However, God can receive the prayers of any man. And again, it is Jesus the man and not the divine Jesus who prays to the Father."

"Typical!"

"What is typical?"

"Your failure to understand the very obvious lack of logic in your position."

"Ah, yes, now it is my turn. Yes, I agree my position is illogical, not because it defies the truth but because it is beyond reason. What is incomprehensible and ultimately indiscernible we must take on faith."

Detainee 9696 looked at him with a smile and said, "There is one God. It is the God of Ibrahim and one to whom your Jesus and my Isa prayed."

"Surely your Isa and my Jesus and the Jewish Joshua are one and the same, three earthly linguistic reflections in one divine person."

"I like it. You confound with faith what you cannot argue."

Then Dr. Najar decided to take another tack. "Tell me, is Mohammad the voice of God?"

"Mohammad, peace be unto him, was but an instrument of God. He vibrated like some great chime that had been breathed upon. He was not himself when God's voice spoke through him. He was merely one who acted as a voice box, or a chime, for the silence that wished to speak. The Koranic utterances are but the unutterable spoken."

"Now it is you who contradict. For the unutterable cannot be spoken."

"True, but the unutterable once spoken can never truly be repeated and words are only symbols of the unutterable. They are not the reality itself."

As the two men debated, Waldrip listened patiently, fascinated and bored at the same time by a discussion that was scholarly and, at times, confusing.

"*Wa lakin shubbiha lahum.*[12] I'm sure you recognize the verse from the Koran. Yes, your Jesus dies on the tree and is buried so that you can celebrate what you call the Resurrection. We know that only the Ascension matters. This, the Ascension, this is the great miracle of his life. He ascended into heaven for Allah so loved Isa. But in the end, your Jesus, not the real Isa, is a confused individual. He imagines himself one of three gods and even his mother—she, too, you pray to as if she were a goddess. Your true followers of Jesus are really the followers of Isa. They are Muslims. Mohammad is merely the spokesman for that moral conduct that tells us that Ibrahim was no less a Muslim than Isa. And Isa was a Muslim no less than Mohammad and all just men."

Dr. Najar waited to see if 9696 were finished or not, then replied, "I have faith that supersedes all reason and this is the gift that I accept, a bequeathal from my Christian parents. And may the peace of the one true God in all his glory and his manifest force be upon you."

The detainee smiled and waited. It appeared he had the patience of an interrogator. Dr. Najar then continued, "But that would require that he deny his own crucifixion, his own resurrection."

"I can see we are getting nowhere. Each speaks from a different premise. One of the truth and the other of a corruption. Your Jesus is *of* the Word, our Isa *is* the Word. Your Jesus is *of* the spirit. Ours *is* the spirit." Both then joined the interrogator in silence.

Sensing that the lion and the wolf had each had his say, the interrogator tried again to intervene saying, "9696, I would like to ask you just a few business questions." Both Dr. Najar and the detainee looked at him.

Then 9696 said, "It must be the seventh day for I feel a need to rest."

Dr. Najar smiled at the allusion and said, as if in sympathy with the detainee, "Greater faith than this I have nowhere." Detainee 9696 then smiled slyly in return and answered, "But as I said before, I will answer the business questions only of the man who captured me. He is young, but he is a warrior. I will speak only to lions. He is one of them." Then he closed his eyes for several seconds as if going to sleep. Moments later, he opened them again, and said, "Are you still here? Did the warrior come? Is it Ramadan? I wish to pray."

The interrogator in utter frustration said, in a slightly whiney voice, "Could I get you to answer just one last business question?"

The detainee looked at him and said, "Have you finished washing the dishes already?"

The interrogator gave up the fight and rose to leave with Dr. Najar. As they did so, 9696 said, "Jesus said, 'The dinar is the disease of religion, and the scholar is the physician of religion. If you see the physician drawing the disease upon himself, beware of him and know that he is not fit to advise others'."[13] He then looked directly at the young interrogator and said, "A hadith, a sacred tradition that harbors the wisdom of the ancients."

A DAY IN THE LIFE

> *Don't do that my son or Allah will strike you blind. Abu, I'm over here.*
>
> – Muslim Joke

> *At Guantanamo we gave each number a name so we could keep them all straight in our own minds.*
>
> – Former prison guard at Camp Delta, Guantanamo

"No! No! No! I am no number 2! I am no number 2! I am wanting number 4 or number 5. You number 2! You number 2! Not me! Not me! You shit! Not me! No, not me!" Bearded and wearing an orange jump suit, indicating his overall hostility and his generally uncooperative status, "Jack" jumped up and down in his cell, shaking the metallic latticed door of his air-conditioned cubicle. Then, as the guard passed by his cell in the measured steps of a trained observer, he stopped only two feet from the detainee. "Jack" looked up at the guard whose erect carriage, blond crew cut, broad shoulders, and muscular weight-lifting-trained biceps and forearms contrasted sharply with the scrawny detainee. His black beard, which reached down to his sternum, seemed to dwarf his skinny five foot six inches of chicken-like sinew that pecked its head against the latticed door, shaking the metal as he seemingly tried to poke through the one- and two-inch diamond-shaped openings. Careful not to actually hurt himself as he bumped his forehead again and again against his cell door, "Jack" suddenly stopped as if surprised to see the guard standing there. He blinked and said, "You see, you see, I hurt. You hurted me! You torture!"

Suddenly, he stopped again and said, "Why you? Send me water!"

The guard glanced past the detainee and said, "I gave a bottle of water to number 2 as soon as I came on duty precisely...," he looked down at his digital wrist watch, "...sixty-eight minutes ago. I see you still have nearly a full bottle. When you are finished with it, I'll give you another."

"You donkey," cried another detainee right across from number 2. "You give him water and shut him up or we all give you number 2."

Before the guard could respond, the detainee in the cell next to number 2 threw a handful of excrement through the meshed wall, hitting the guard on the of neck and the back his uniform.

As the guard turned around, another guard approached the cell and asked matter-of-factly, "Why did you do that?" His emotionless tone angered the detainee beyond his current state.

"Why you talk like a robot? Be a man, come into my cell and try to beat me! You faggy pants!"

"Ha! Ha!," exclaimed number 2. "Now you number 2, not me! Not me, faggy pants! You number 2!"

The guard who had been hit by the excrement reported the incident on his walkie-talkie and waited as a replacement entered the wing and he left to change his uniform, clean himself, and in accordance with the SOP (standard operating procedure), he reported immediately to medical.

The replacement guard in similarly matter-of-fact manner approached number 2 and asked, "Why did you harass the guard? He has been fair to you."

"Because he not give me water. I want."

"You still have water. I see it."

The detainee then walked over to the plastic water bottle balanced on the metal frame of his cell, opened it, and poured the contents down the toilet. He then turned toward the guard and held it upside down to demonstrate that it was empty. "Now you get for me," he said.

The guard walked away and whispered something to another guard, a black female, who walked to a table on which there were several cases of bottled water. She picked up one bottle and approached cell number 2 with it. As she came to a halt in front of his cell, "Jack" yelled, "Look! No! I tell you many times, I not take from woman. Is disgrace. Is torture. No woman. You sacrifice me. I insulted."

The guard stood directly in front of his cell door and asked, "Are you refusing the water?"

"I want translator. No understand…translator."

"Take the water," yelled another detainee who was clearly agitated.

"No, I see she is Negro house." Looking directly at her, he flipped his beard at her and added, "You Negro house."

The female guard who was as thick-skinned as she was attractive, smiled and asked, "What's a Negro house?"

Perplexed and of limited linguistic virtuosity, the detainee said, "Is like number two."

"Okay, so I will keep the water."

As she began to walk away, "Jack" called out, "No. I want water but no woman. No Negro house."

She walked on past the other detainees who were amused but quiet.

◆◆◆

Minutes later, after a reprieve induced more by lack of anything real or imaginary to complain about, "Jack" got back up from his mattress where he had taken a brief respite and shouted, "You are pig!"

"Be quiet," replied one of the other guards.

"Jack" then turned to one of the detainees in the cell to his right and said, "I like her." Then he looked at his mattress, opened his button-down fly, and urinated on it. "She is Negro house. She now will clean for me."

As "Jack" finished urinating, the cell block religious leader called out in English, "Time to pray."

All the detainees immediately pulled out their prayer rugs and positioned themselves parallel to and in the direction of the green arrow next to which appeared the word *Mecca* painted on the floor of each cell.

The guard then placed large orange construction cones at either end of the cell wing to indicate that the detainees were praying and that the guards should be respectfully silent even to the point of minimizing their walking, talking, or opening and closing the cell wing exits and entrances.

◆◆◆

Several hours later, as the next guard shift came on, the detainee in cell 11 shouted to one of the guards whom he had attempted to assault only a week earlier, "My friend, my friend, I am so glad to see you. Sometime I am angry. You forgive me."

The guard, who was a short bullnecked no-nonsense individual, kept a straight face and self-protective demeanor marked by a certain tension in his jawline and in his slightly clenched fists. He did his job by the book and irritated the detainees precisely because of that. He never violated the SOP and kept the detainees to prescribed schedules and behavior or prescribed denial of privileges. Predictable and seemingly humorless, he kept a staunch demeanor that belied his natural affability and sardonic outlook on life. In off-duty moments, he gave vent to an ironic sense of humor, his creativity, and an ability to find solace amidst the badgering and physical assaults to which he had been subject since his arrival as part of a six-month tour of duty with the U.S. Army at Camp Justice and Camp Delta at Guantanamo. Sergeant Tito Ramirez never spoke to the detainees except in an official voice, in a straightforward way, and he never smiled while in their proximity.

In an attempt to break through his soldierly and businesslike aura, "Sinbad," one of the older detainees at fifty-four years, who had apparently been all over the world in his lifetime, decided to try telling him a joke. "Sergeant Ramirez, please allow me now to apologize to you. I am sorry for the time I kick you in recreation. So today I would like to tell you a funny story."

Sergeant Ramirez paused near the detainee's cell, and without looking in his direction, he politely listened.

"This woman, she is Bedouin. She is in the desert, and she is very hungry. She tells her husband, 'I am so hungry my stomach hurts.' The husband who is walking with her in the desert, says, 'My feet hurt from walking and maybe you are pregnant.' She says, 'No, I am not pregnant. I just ate a whole camel with two humps and now I have them too.' Her husband then said, 'Two humps don't make a camel!'" Then, to orchestrate an appropriate response, he himself laughed heartily as did two of the other detainees.

Sergeant Ramirez half smiled and said, "Thank you," and walked away. "Sinbad" shrugged, replying, "Perhaps it's better in Arabic."

Two hours later, when it was recreation time, Sergeant Ramirez along with Corporal Evan Watters, a twenty-year-old with an arm and chest expanse that typified the guards whose recreation time often included weight lifting, approached cell number 20 to escort the detainee to the recreation yard. As they did so, they each donned spit shields which covered their faces and resembled plastic welder-looking headgear.

They reached into the six-by-sixteen inch "bean hole" through which food was typically passed to the detainee. The detainee, knowing the routine, stepped to the white line in his cell and put out both hands so that his wrists could be shackled until he was released into the recreation yard. His feet were likewise shackled through another hole before the cell door was opened. As Sergeant Ramirez reached forward to grab the detainee by the elbow, the detainee, who had been silent up until then, spit on him, hitting him on the side of the head and neck not covered by the spit shield. He then attempted to head butt Ramirez and wipe his mouth across his face mask, knocking it askew. Ramirez and Watters grabbed the detainee by both arms and threw him to the floor where he flailed about wildly yelling, "They shit on me! They beat me!" Immediately, three other guards ran down the cell block and restrained the detainee, one grabbing the head while each of the others grabbed a leg and pushed the still contorting, twisting and kicking figure back into his cell. Only after he was thoroughly restrained, immobilized, and quiet did the guards relent and stand back. Each in turn left the cell with the detainee lying on his back, with arms and legs still shackled, on the mattress on top of his metal bed.

Only after Ramirez was safely standing outside the cell did he realize that the debris smeared across the spit shield and now dripping down the side of his head and neck was shit, the remainder of which the detainee was now attempting to clear from his mouth by spitting. Following procedures, Ramirez looked at the still heavily breathing detainee and asked, "Why did you do that?"

The detainee stared blankly into space, continuing to spit, and then said, "Water."

Ramirez and the others contacted headquarters to report yet another assault on the guards. Number 2 began to laugh and called out, "You donkey. You number 2, not me." "Sinbad," who had attempted to tell a joke earlier, looked at Ramirez as he passed and said, "You should laugh more. Then we like you."

As the guards continued their rounds, one of the other detainees smiled and took out his Koran and ripped several pages from it and dropped them down the toilet. As he did so, he mockingly called out, "America is God. Bush is his prophet."

At this, the cell block exploded in calls of "Blasphemy! I cut off your head, you pig!" As the others screamed at him, he continued tearing pages from the Koran and crumbling them. He then spit on them before throwing them into the toilet. He then said to a bewildered guard, "Why do you throw Koran down toilet?" Then he bowed down on his prayer rug with his back to the arrow, with his back to Mecca.

When he and the others were through, one of the other detainees spoke up. "I want *Scooby Doo!* Is the best show. Make the movie for us. *Scooby Doo!*"

♦♦♦

At the outdoor movie theater, located several hundred feet from the primary detention facilities, the off-duty personnel sat under the evening stars watching the conclusion of *Harold & Kumar Escape from Guantanamo Bay.* When the Saturday evening film was over and the lights were turned on, an assembly of civilian-attired guards leaped up on stage to the applause of their fellow sailors, marines, soldiers, and coasties all waiting to hear the latest version of "Rendition Rendition/GITMO Gets Even." The guards occasionally celebrated themselves in an attempt to salve the wounds of daily humiliation at the hands of the detainees, the American press, and "the hateful ones," as they had taken to calling those who routinely sent letters through Amnesty International belittling the guards who operated the GITMO detention facilities.

As one of the onstage members began to strum his guitar and lean into the microphone, a chorus of voices joined in to sing the oft repeated words to one of the guards' favorite songs. One which was largely kept from the ears of the higher ranks and other on-island authorities.

Hey Mr. Taliban Man

Be a martyr for me…

Blow yourself up

If you really can…

Yes, just singe your whiskers for me

And go singing…

"Rocket Man" had also had its words changed to singe the souls of suicide bombers already departed. Similarly, someone had created a modified version of a forty-year-old Sammy Davis, Jr., song, a remake of "The Candy Man," aptly renamed "The Taliban Bam." Later on in the evening, four ZZ Top look-alikes with the commensurate Taliban- and Al-Qaeda length beards, all of them female, did a remake of Ahab the Arab, complete with camel sounds and synchronized dance steps. Finally, they concluded the Guard Fest with a rousing adaptation of "Drunken Sailor," which the chorus turned into "What will we do with the *jihad* warrior, early in the morning?"

When the singing was over, the sailors, soldiers, marines, and coasties drifted off to the rectangular shipping container-type contraptions where they slept. Their comrades walked the corridors of Camp Delta where the detainees slept, taunted, and planned.

THE RECITATION AND THE ECSTASY

> *May Allah curse the Jews and Christians, for they have taken the graves of their Prophets as places of worship.* [14]
>
> – Mohammad

Al-Masjid An-Nabawi, the Mosque of Mohammad, Medina, Saudi Arabia

Shakir Amir, as he wished to someday be known, stood on the holiest of ground. Amir was the Arabic name given to one who is a leader or a commander of an army. And, like Moses before the burning bush, he had taken off his shoes. Like Moses, he wished to be a leader. Yet, this ground was defiled by the presence of idolaters, even people like himself, whose actions suggested submissions not to the good but to the heretical beliefs that compelled people to utter prayers as they stood before the tomb.

Shakir Amir, of medium stature with brownish skin and a groomed beard, stood solemnly yet skeptically before the burial site of the Prophet. Although he could not see the actual tomb, he knew it to be directly behind the gold-filigreed iron doors. The room in which the Prophet was buried lay immediately before him, while to either side were gold latticed doors to the tombs of the earliest companions, including the first caliphs, Abu Bakr, and Umar, and his beloved daughter Fatima. Next to Mohammad's remains lay another tomb, one which was always empty. This was a tomb built long ago for the prophet Isa, or Jesus, as he was known among the Romans, so that he would have a place to rest his earthly remains when he returned to earth for the Day of Judgment.

But even in the *Ahadith Qudsi*, the sacred words of Allah to Mohammad, it said and so he repeated to himself word for word: *Verily, Allah does not forgive those that set up partners with Him in worship. But he forgives only those whom he pleases, and whoever sets up partners with Allah in worship, he has indeed invented a grievous sin.* Because he knew God would understand, he stood with a group of Wahhabists who held their cupped hands at an angle so that their fingers pointed to the domed ceiling. He prayed silently and bowed his head as he did so, not because it was right but because he knew it was the wrong thing to do. *Here, even at the tomb of the Prophet, no men should be allowed to pray,* he thought. To do so was idolatrous. Yet his bowing, a clear indication of his praying in seeming earnest, was not stopped. What good were the guards if they sanctioned such idolatry by doing nothing? He had tested them, and they had failed. Truly, even his homeland was now corrupt. The Wahhabists among whom he prayed, even they seemed less pure, less zealous. The fervor of those whose hearts should have been pure had lost its luster. They no longer radiated the light of truth. The inner light, the *batin*, had been polluted while *zahir*, the outer world, seemed to be all.

Born in 1979 into a poor family in the south of Saudi Arabia near the disputed border with Yemen, Shakir Amir had witnessed firsthand the intervention of Allah in his life. Like the Prophet himself, peace be unto him, he had been orphaned early. His father, a member of the Saudi military, had been killed in one of the perennial border disputes between the Yemeni and the Saudis. In this part of the world into which he had been born, lines were perpetually being drawn in the sand to mark a boundary and blown away by the next wind.

Born in the city of Najran only several miles from the Yemeni border, Shakir's father's death had left his mother to fend for both of them. The usual bureaucratic malaise that infects so much of the corruptible world had first stalled and then denied and then reinstated his father's death benefits to his mother. Though Shakir's father had died in combat, his father's own mixed-blood heritage presented problems.

His father was the first of two sons born of a Saudi Sunni father and a mother who was of the Shi'ite Wayilah tribe. She had been abducted as a sixteen-year-old and never ransomed by her poor relatives who were only too glad to be rid of another burdensome female mouth to feed. Moreover, her reaction to the suspicions of her neighbors had been surliness and disdain which scandalized the section of the city in which they lived and caused the town's people to question everything about her son with whom she lived until her death.

Shakir's grandmother also dominated the house and the life of Shakir's mother, who never dared to fight back for fear that her husband, Shakir's father, would side with his own mother and throw her out. His mother's meekness was disheartening to the boy as it easily outlived both his grandmother and his father. The boy's soul from early on was steeped and bowed with the sins of the father, the timidity of his mother, and the Shi'ite and Sunni tribal heritage of his grandmother.

Some suggested that his father had actually died as the result of his reneging on an agreement to facilitate the transfer of munitions across the Yemeni/Saudi border for radical Islamists bent on overthrowing the Royal House of Saud. Then, in a gesture deemed symbolic and which reflected ongoing suspicion regarding the circumstances of his father's death, his mother was given only 50 percent of the usual benefits otherwise accorded a female head of household upon the death of her husband. Widowed and under suspicion, no man would have her. Though timid, she grew bitter, infecting her only child with the bile from a spleen ruptured by ingratitude, injustice, and the social and spiritual isolation that followed. Two years after her husband's death, she one day disappeared, leaving the house never to return.

Rumor had it that on that day she had been seen walking miles from home near Al Khadra on the fringe of the Empty Quarter. At the age of six, Jabal Anqawi, his real name, was alone, frightened, and begging in the streets until taken in by a kindly imam who fed the boy for the next several years. He fed his body and a soul that, for the first time, felt the heat and the alienation as of the desert slackened by the sweet waters of the Koran.

All this flashed through his mind. He remained standing even to the point of arousing suspicion among the guards. One of them finally approached him and motioned for him to leave, not because he was praying at the Prophet's tomb but because he had stood there too long. He therefore was denying space near the tomb to others who would like to come closer. Without so much as a glimmer of contempt for the guards, whom he now recognized as having done the right deed but for the wrong reason, he moved on and continued to explore the labyrinth of gold swirled into Koranic verses that embellished the interior of the mosque. Though he now trod upon that very place in time that Mohammad had, it was the verses themselves that held him spellbound. Here, as he approached the *mihrab,* the prayer niche from which Mohammad recited the Holy Koran, the walls with their sacred inscriptions came alive.

It was at that moment that his eyes had been opened for the first time. The beauty of the classical Arabic, the sound of Allah's voice itself seemed to speak from these walls. His words were inscribed in a calligraphy that suggested both the permanence as well as the sacredness of God's word. Had the awful delight been there all along? How had he never truly seen it before? His eyes filled with tears and he nearly choked as his throat swelled. On this day he was sure Allah had seen him and blessed his mission. Even the fluorescent lighting, an ugly concession to modernity, could not diminish his wonderment at feeling touched by a being who now blessed him and recognized his long striving for holiness. Though he still felt the ugly wounds of his own spiritual imperfections, he knew that his being here today was so that he might yet attain that special attunement with the divine. He had. Of this he had no doubt.

◆◆◆

"You are my Yathrib. For like that ancient city, you took me in when others would not open their hearts to an old man. For just as that ancient city changed its name from Yathrib to Medina as it offered comfort to our Prophet, so too you changed your name from Jabal Anqawi to Jabal ibn Abd al-Muttalib. You loved an old man who found you and so I was saved from despair."

Shakir Amir reflected on that moment as he stood outside the building that had once been his home. He had lived here from the age of six until eleven, taking from the old man's kindness. It was a kindness that sent the boy to school and taught him to read the Koran himself. Loved but again abandoned at the death of his stepfather Harith, he was immediately taken into the custody of yet another imam. This one was much younger and much stricter. He sent him to live at a madrassa for orphaned children near the city of Jeddah in the west of Saudi Arabia and turned the still impressionable youth over to the sternest and most frightening of taskmasters. He set the boy to studies of the Koran and English so that the boy might yet confront and convert a heathen world. Taught, beaten, reviled, praised, and abused, the child grew to love and hate Allah and to repeatedly ask why he had twice been abandoned.

Despite the harshness of his new surroundings, and even the too fond touches from the fire-breathing imam, he settled into a life of study and soccer. He excused the abuses that he suffered to his own shortcomings and, in many ways, blamed himself for being too kind, too inviting. For he was, as the old imam had said, like Yathrib, the ancient Medina, too kind to strangers. He would, however, force himself to change. He would cover up his heart and learn of Allah's justice rather than his mercy. When he finished his schooling at the madrassa at the age of eighteen, like his father before him, he entered the Saudi armed forces as a foot soldier.

He was merely average in terms of his physical prowess, making him only a relatively competent figure during his basic training. His love of soccer never translated into athleticism or sinewy vibrancy. Moreover, Shakir had nearly failed in his marksmanship. He scored the lowest possible ranking in pistol qualifications and did only slightly better with the AK-47 and other rifles with which he was expected to acquire at least a rudimentary competency. However, his familiarity with the English language, a gift of the old imam as well as a necessary part of his madrassa's expectations for his eventual proselytizing among the heathen, gave him respectability among his peers. Moreover, his periodic bursts of sarcasm that invited all the others around him to laugh, including his superiors, made his companionship desirable. In the most masculine of communities, the Saudi military, he found the solace of being wanted and of being purposely driven. Slowly, but with increasing certitude, his view of himself changed from that of a studious but forlorn orphan to that of a man with the scholarly and personal bent ready to bequeath his insights regarding the world, politics, and especially religion to those who sought his companionship.

Not long after his enlistment, he found himself assigned to an infantry element that trained and operated out of Camp Faisal in the Empty Quarter, an expanse in southern Arabia. Its vastness and isolation made it an ideal place for all kinds of training, including the kind that should not be readily observed by outsiders, such as nosy Yemeni or intrusive Americans.

He learned to use, despite his shortcomings as a marksman, such weapons as the Belgian and the Austrian made rifles. Like the AK-47, these two were durable and could be dropped in the sand and would not foul up like the more precise but less reliable American M16 or M4, whether the older or the new and improved version.

He met a young officer whose job it was to weed out the less reliable, the spiritually unawakened, and, therefore, untrustworthy. This young officer who simply went by the name of Achmed, even among those enlisted, sought out quiet conversation to find those to whom the others looked for guidance because they were deemed the purest of heart. It seemed that when the men were puzzled, despite his age, they came to Shakir Amir. By Allah's mercy, he had been made into an instrument, albeit an unknown one, of His will. Achmed, who really was Captain Khalid bin Kassan, a member of the Saudi Royal Guard whose job it was to guard the royal family and recruit certain other devotees to "special projects," saw in the young Shakir something he could bend, something that would yield, and something at the same time that seemed implacable – anger. But it was an anger mixed with an appealing and good-natured humor, filled with rapturous zeal of an increasingly uncompromising sort that self-censored even that which he thought to be funny but somehow injurious to promoting respect for Islam. Achmed realized that in his subtle way, Shakir was suggesting that he saw himself no less a child of Allah than was Mohammad.

One day, after a three-hour interview, the keen-eyed captain extended his hand to his young recruit as he offered him a full scholarship to an American university of the royal family's choosing. They had already selected for him, before the deal was finally struck, a school to which they had donated hundreds of thousands of dollars in order to create a chair of Islamic studies. Once established in the American heartland, they would promulgate their beliefs and assert their presence amidst the unbelievers. They chose the University of Arkansas at Fayetteville.

In America, it was said that anything could be turned to gold. But after four years at the university, living in an off-campus apartment and finding no semblance of the life he had left behind, and finding no solitude but only loneliness, he felt his religious zeal slipping away; it was they who were converting him. He could feel the alchemical effect of American culture as it began to transmute his golden soul into tarnished brass. In a final surrender to the venial nature of college life, he dove headlong into abasement, its frivolity, its moral relativism, and as well, its scholarship. He did much of this as a means of endearing himself to the prevailing culture and as a means of teaching the ignorant Americans the unrequited affection that Saudis and others from the Middle East had for a culture that, at first, they believed promoted virtue and not vice. But what the Americans considered virtue, he considered nothing more than a hedonistic love of liberty without regard to the morality of the choices it promoted.

His trips with his newfound friends to strip clubs, beer bashes, and even experimentation with certain drugs – all these he rationalized as playing the part of the *taqiyya,* a Muslim who accommodates himself even to the excesses of another culture to blend in until he can become an instrument for its reform. However, as in Saudi Arabia, his actions did not go unnoticed. And while he knew that Islam itself could never be reformed but only refreshed, he knew of himself that he needed to be reformed as well as refreshed.

THE SOUND OF THINGS

> *The almost unapproachable intricacies of their faith: revelation within revelation, divergence within divergence.*[15]
> —V.S. Naipaul, *Among the Believers: An Islamic Journey*

Red Sea Coast, South of Medina, Saudi Arabia

Shakir waited in the courtyard that adjoined the mosque. Its eight-foot-high walls of cement and plaster were bleached white and offered the protection and privacy for small audiences wishing to hear this young imam who studied the Koran assiduously and who spoke with eloquence and beauty that could captivate, intrigue, puzzle and inspire. His credibility was already assured as he had served in the Saudi military and climbed to the rank of captain once he had completed his college degree. His bachelor's degree from the University of Arkansas in philosophy had furthered both his understanding of America's culture and his contempt for its scientific rationalism which debased Allah and elevated man to a self-idolatrous status.

An elder man approached and Shakir said to him, "Ishmael, you and others that we will meet with today, we must be firm with them. We will begin here in the courtyard of the mosque. Bring them here to me."

His young recruits were first vetted and brought to him through a figure that he had met in America, a graduate student in American Studies who had an uncanny knack for showing up at the same parties as he did. They had gotten to know one another better after Abu Ibrihim had offered to drive him back to his apartment after he had become intoxicated to the point of passing out. He had awakened the next morning to the smell of hot coffee, a glass of water in the face as he lay in bed with a monumental headache, vomit caking his bedspread, and the trash can at the side of his bed stinking with the sour smell of partially digested food. Worse followed. A stern lecture complete with a slap to the face on the risk to himself, his military aspirations, and to the Saudi people who were paying for his education. Amidst the swollen eyelids and self-disgust, he apologized at his kitchen table where Abu had warned him of his wastefulness, of his profligacy, of his sinfulness. He had then handed him a cigarette and said, "This is the one and only thing you smoke from now on, nothing else."

He then slammed his fist down on the table and added, "I have left you twelve lectures on CD about the Islamic Brotherhood by Sheik Rachman. You have one week to listen to them. I will visit you again next Sunday. We will discuss them. Here is the mosque you will attend from now on. You will be there on Saturday where you will meet the imam. Here is his address and his phone number. He is expecting you. You will discuss none of this with anyone else. Do you understand?" He handed Shakir the piece of paper with the information.

Shakir looked up almost tearfully and nodded in acknowledgement. "Yes, I understand," he whispered. As Abu got up to leave, he looked around the kitchen and grabbed hold of a bottle of Jack Daniels and then one of Grant's Smooth Whiskey and emptied both of them down the sink. His leaving was loud and punctuated with the severity of his instructions. Shakir's instructor's knowledge of the details of his life convinced him that Allah saw everything and worked through the eyes and ears of the Mabahith, the Saudi secret intelligence agency. Strangely, Shakir also knew that the pain in his head and the humiliation at the hands of this man were a sign that Allah had heard his prayer for help and forgiveness.

On this morning, as he sat beneath the shade of the umbrellas and amidst the cooling effect of the palms swaying in the easy breeze, the former soldier and fervent student of Islam, Shakir Amir, spoke his first message to these young men from all over Saudi Arabia. All had been brought to him by his recruiter, the same man who had recruited him, Achmed or Ishmael. No one was certain of his real name.

Twelve young men now sat sipping from Evian water bottles as Shakir began.

"Which of you is a good Muslim?"

All were silent. So he asked again, "Which of you is a good Muslim?"

Hesitantly, one young man sitting in the back of the others smiled faintly and raised his right hand.

"How do you know this?"

"I don't know. I just try to live a good life. I love Allah and I pray five times a day."

"Did Allah speak to you?"

"No, but I do what I must do and know how to study the Koran."

"Do you know that there are *infidels* who study the Koran? Some of them know the Koran better than you. Are they good Muslims?"

Feeling himself being led into an ambush, the young man put his head down and said nothing.

"No," said another. "No, an *infidel* is still an *infidel*. If you study the Koran but do not live the Koran, you are still an *infidel*."

"Anyone else?" He waited.

"So if you study the Koran but do not love it, you are not a good Muslim. And if you say you are good, but abase yourself with hedonistic pursuits, then you do not love Allah. For you are loving another god—sex, drinking, or some other perversion. Then you are an idolater as in the Age of Ignorance, before Mohammad.

"So if you wish to be a good Muslim, how can you know that you are in fact a good Muslim? How did Mohammad know that he was a good Muslim?"

None spoke. "He knew, he knew!" he said emphatically as he wagged his pointer finger.

"He knew because he heard the voice of Allah. He listened in silence. In this very land, he sat in silence and he listened. Everything you study grows greater and stronger when it is absorbed in silence. He sat in the caves and he listened when Gabriel spoke to him. Do you listen?

"If you would hear his voice, you must go to the desert like Mohammad, peace be unto him, and there sit in silence after you are given instruction. For if you truly, truly wish to hear his voice, you must recognize it even when it is spoken through others. Listen!" He spoke the last word with an exaggerated whisper.

He paused, and then as his eyes took on a hardness, he slowly closed them. Then his lips moved as if mouthing words. All were silent and slightly embarrassed. Then he opened his eyes again and looked directly at the young man who thought himself a good Muslim.

"You will know that you are good when Allah speaks to you through those he has ordained to speak for him. But today I wish to ask you, which of these is good and which is cursed?" He paused again as he gathered himself to make certain that all were listening and that he would be simple, direct and clear.

"Which is good? Yathrib or Medina?"

At first no one spoke. But then one said, "Medina is always good, so Yathrib must be cursed."

"Which is good? Shia or Sunni?

All knew easily how to answer this one. "Sunni."

"Which is good? Takfiri or apostate?"

"Takfiri," they replied.

"Which is good? Allah or Satan?"

"Allah."

"Which is good? Rome or Mecca?"

"Mecca," the chorus continued.

"So which are you? Are you a child of the Age of Ignorance, as before the Prophet was born, or are you a child of light?"

"I am not a child," uttered a young man off to his right.

"We are all children in the eyes of Allah. The only question is whether or not you are a child of ignorance or a child of light?" He looked hard at the young man who had spoken and then smiled as if to say, "I know you mean well, but you are missing the point."

The others spoke momentarily in order to break the tension, "The light, the light."

Taking his eyes from the young man who had interrupted the flow of his cadenced query and answer, he continued, "Consider why I first asked you of Yathrib and Medina. In the time of the Romans, who would not listen to Isa, Allah punished not the Romans, but the Jews who rejected the prophet who spoke of the one who would come after him. So Allah punished them by allowing the Romans to take Jerusalem from them. A holy city was ripped from them because they could not hear.

"Some, they fled and went to the desert so that Allah could again teach them to hear. So Allah in his mercy gave them a place in the desert where they could live and listen. But again, as before, Allah sent his prophet among them and while others would listen, they would not. So the same instrument that spoke for Allah was the same that delivered his justice. As it was in Jerusalem, which they had lost to the Romans, so too they lost Yathrib to the sons of Islam. So that city which we now call Medina was once the city of the Jew who was of *The Book* but who lived as an *infidel* because the Jew would not listen.

"Then later, those same Romans would not listen also. For a thousand years, Allah called out to them to listen, to hear his voice in the beauty of the Koran. But the Roman, he could not hear because he stuffed his ears with the coins of dirty commerce, preferring the voice of the marketplace to the voice of Allah. So they, too, lost their city to the faithful. Istanbul fell and Allah sent the Romans into exile."

"But the Jews have taken back Jerusalem. They own it again even though it is not theirs," offered one of the disciples.

"Yes, the Jew, the Jew who has allied himself with Satan, he has again taken the city. He did not do this because he was strong but because those who are of Islam have shown themselves to be weak. Allah's punishment is for all, *all* who will not listen.

"Today," he continued, "today, even as we sit here, we have a brave brother in the city near Jerusalem who fights for all good Muslims. He does not compromise. His name is Yunis al-Astal, and he tells us that soon, very soon, even the city of the Catholics, the Romans, the Crusaders will fall just as Constantinople did. He tells us this must be so for the pope himself is like the Jew. Those defiled by their own deafness cannot love Allah or his sacred word.

"So which is better, the call to prayer or the Jew at his wall praying for the destruction of Medina because Allah has taken it from him?"

"The call to prayer."

"So which is better, the call to prayer in Jerusalem itself or the cry of the pigs who eat their own flesh as they defile one of the holiest cities on earth?"

"The call to prayer."

Then, lifting his voice with angry intensity, he continued, "So which is better? The call to prayer in Hagia Sophia, the Great Mosque in Istanbul, or the sound of Christians and Jews who today invade the city and the mosque to desecrate it with their prayers, and their cameras, and with their archaeologists who chip the plaster from its walls and once again expose the images of false gods?" He did not wait for an answer but continued, "Today the truth is that the pope and his followers—each is like a child who worships trade as once did the Romans of Constantinople. They are apostate. Even their city must fall again to the true followers of Islam. The Turk!" He uttered the last word and spat.

"Rome today is a whore among nations that preaches the destruction of Islam. It promotes

the very destruction of our own holy cities.
There was once, however, a noble Turk who
tried to slay the pope. But he can only be
slain through a bullet to the heart. We should
learn from that man who tried to kill him. We
should learn from him how to act. Remember
his name: Mehmet Ali Agca. Mehmet...Ali...
Mehmet Ali Agca. He is the first to attempt to
deliver Rome and the pope to us. He is to us an
exaltation. He is our salvation. He is our model.

"So which is better? The sound of the pope
who denounces Islam or the sound of a gun
that sings like the call to prayer itself? For, like
Islam, it too is a call to *submit* as all must do.
Someday, Allah willing, we will all be martyrs in
his name."

Then he paused again and looked skyward as
though drawing inspiration from an unseen
force. Placing his hands to either side as if
he were about to pray, he continued, "Allah
knows that no force on earth can stop a good
man. Be a good Muslim, and someday even the
American White House will be ours. That time
is not so far off."

Then yet again, he paused as he took the time
to look into the eyes of each of his disciples.
There he found acceptance, there he found
the willingness he desired and required for the
mission for which they would soon be trained.

"So which is better, my friends, to surrender to the *infidel* or to carry out *jihad* against the sons of darkness?"

With clenched fists, one and then another, softly but firmly, so as to not draw undue attention to themselves if others should be within hearing range, they uttered, "Jihad! Jihad…"

Then, as if teasing them with the prospect of action that they might be instigated into taking because of his promptings, he held up his hands to indicate that they should desist from saying another word. Knowing already that they were firmly with him, he began again.

"Today all good Muslims weep for the apostates. For they will burn everlastingly in God's wrath. But none—I tell you none—none will burn like those of the Great Trivializer who desecrates the holy and turns men into pigs like the Jew. Have you ever wondered why there is sorrow and confusion in the world? Have you ever wondered why the most powerful nation on earth is filled with sin, hypocrisy, and greed?

"I will tell you why. Some of you already know that I was sent to America to learn its ways. This I did. For I was a member of the Saudi military and I wished to be an officer. So I traveled to the University of Arkansas.

"At first I was in awe of the power of America. Never had I seen such buildings, such wealth, and such sin. But I was quiet and shy and there in that land, they are filled with constant chatter. They can hear nothing but the sound of their own voices.

"But why? Why do they wallow in such filth? Why are they so deaf? I will tell you. They are proud of their sin. Yes, like the Jew, they are proud of their sin. Let me give you an example. When I was a student at the University of Arkansas, I was shocked. I attended for four years and even in the midst of my most sinful state I could not bring myself to take the name which all the students there take once they attend. Do you know what they call themselves? Do you know what animal they are named after? Do you know what their school emblem is? Huh? Do you know?

"Shall I tell you? It is the pig. Yes, it is the pig after whom they are named. They call themselves Razorbacks. This is a type of pig. Yet they are proud of it."

Shakir was sweating. He paused and took a drink from a bottle of Evian.

"In America I saw this. And these Americans they see me too. And they think, what is this? Another follower of Allah? Let us ply him with drink until he vomits. And I was weak and so I sinned. But Allah saw the misery in my heart and the tears in my eyes. 'Allah! Allah!' I cried out. And as Allah had sent Gabriel to Mohammad, he sent me a very special brother from my homeland so that I could return to Him. So I did and now I am with you.

"Let me tell you yet another example of the sinfulness I encountered. In America they love the Jew. Think of how they attack the Arabs throughout the world and help Israel even as it drinks the blood of our children. And why is this? Because the Jews are clever and they rule America with their clever disguises. Think on the names of their presidents—Ibrahim Lincoln. He was a Jew. Good that he too was shot although not by a Turk but by another Jew. Then hear the names of still others—Roosevelt. He was elected once as a young man, but then he fell from his horse charging up a hill and so Allah punished him by making him a cripple. Still the Americans would not listen. It is for this reason he went to war to save his people from extermination. Or so he said. But they never could prove any Jews were really killed by the Germans. The Jew gets his way because he is clever and deceitful.

"When Allah finally punished Roosevelt by killing him an even worse Jew came. His name was Hiram Truman. It was a good name for a

Jew. Almost all the American presidents are Jews. Even Clinton. That is why he had sex with Monica. She was a Jew and he wanted her."

He took another drink and paused dramatically, looking with emphatic fervor at a young man who sat to his right. He glared at him until the young man lowered his eyes. Having forced him to submit, he began again, but this time in a hushed whisper, forcing his disciples to lean in to hear him.

"Look. Look," he said as he reached for a stone that he had planted there an hour earlier. He lifted it and withdrew from underneath an American one dollar bill.

"What is this?"

All were silent. So he asked again.

"What is this?"

"It's money—American," volunteered the young man whom he had assailed with his eyes only a short while before.

"Yes, yes it is," he said slowly and in an otherwise normal tone of voice.

"Now look at this, look closely. Do you see these words?" he asked as he pointed to four words that appeared on the backside. He then passed it around. Most of them could read some English. As they each looked at it in turn, he asked again, "Do you see it? It says, 'In God We Trust.' But the Americans do not believe in God. No, you see, their god is the money itself. They even say it. Their god is money. May Allah forgive them. No people are more arrogant. They worship money. In this they are like the people of Constantinople. They put their money in their ears to stop the voice of Allah. So you see, there is hope. There is hope because the Jew will, for money, cut even his own throat.

"The time is coming when Allah will speak to you through one whom you already know. Be prepared to listen. Now, before we continue your education, we have yet one more story to tell.

"In America, where does the president live? No, no," he said as he waved for them to put down their hands. "It is a rhetorical question. He lives, as we all know, in the White House, does he not?"

They nodded affirmatively.

"But let me tell you something. What is the color of the Kaaba Stone? This one you can all answer, for I am certain that you know.

They answered, "Black."

"Yes, it is black. But as you all know, when it first fell from heaven in the time of Ibrahim, it was pure white, whiter even than the whitest dove. But because of man's sins, it turned to black and so it has been ever since. So it will be with the White House. Soon, very soon, one who is *taqiyya*, one who conceals his true beliefs, he will emerge as their leader. The Americans will follow him because he will fool them. Once he is their leader, the deceit shall be removed. He will show the White House for what it truly is, a house of shame. It will be black as the Kaaba Stone. "This I know," he added as he raised his index finger for emphasis. "The Kaaba itself and the White House have almost the exact same dimensions for their foundation. The White House is bigger, but the sides in relationship to the front and the back have proportions to one another that are almost exactly the same as those of the Kaaba.

"Now why is this?" he asked as he placed the dollar bill that he was still holding in one hand back underneath the rock. "Did their presidents design it that way through their own ingenuity? I tell you that they did not, they weren't that smart, clever maybe, but not that smart. No, not that smart, for no prophet has ever lived in the White House. If he did, the Americans would kill him anyway. *Taquiyya.* That is the key.

Yes, deceive them if you must, as I myself have once done, and then, when they do not suspect, you will strike! In doing this, there is no sin. Remember what it says in the Koran: 'Say to the desert Arabs who remain behind: You will be called upon to fight a mighty nation, unless they embrace Islam. If you are obedient, Allah will enrich you. But if you run away, as others have, He will punish you severely. And if Allah punishes you for your failure to call out his wishes, better that you had never been born."

Immediately upon completing his remarks, he stood and walked away, dramatically, silently, and purposely. As he did so, an older man who had been listening inconspicuously slowly rose from his place in a latticed chair and moved to the group of young men, and said, "Others will attend to your needs. For now, wait here and think on what he has said. You will speak often with him hereafter, if you are selected."

A CLASH OF CULTURES

Ferry Landing at Piraeus, Greece

Musa al-Akim approached the ancient ferry landing on the outskirts of Athens. He was a lanky figure with a shaved head, a dark, day-old growth of beard, and severe eyes that remained hooded beneath jet-black eyebrows. Sunken with dark circles beneath them, his venomous eyes looked down disapprovingly at the slight Greek hostess. His distain was palpable as he looked at her slightly exposed cleavage and then directly into her eyes. He paused on the gangplank and asked, "Are you hot?"

"What?" she asked.

"Are you hot?"

"No, why?"

"Then button up your blouse."

She blushed as another passenger handed her his ticket and Musa walked on.

As he moved to the interior of the ship's dining area, he smiled at a familiar figure seated inconspicuously at a small table in the corner. Said Dukayet, a good-looking Lebanese of mixed Arabic and French descent, partially stood and embraced Musa and kissed him on either cheek.

"You'll not get too many women with that stubble," Said laughed. "They like something a little gentler. You must have too much iron in your system."

"Humph," replied Musa. "The kiss of a true friend is preferable to the whores on this boat."

"Perhaps, but they smell good. And they can do things to pleasure a man that our women could only imagine—did you say something to the girl? I saw you talking. She did not seem happy."

"Yes, I told her she was hot."

"Ah! So, you are making progress. At last you talk to them in such a forward way. Good! We'll get you a girlfriend yet. You know the European girls really are so stupid. They love us because they find us mysterious. If you want to take them to bed, you just tell them. If they say 'no,' you pretend to be hurt and you say, 'It is because I am a Muslim—you hold this against me.' The girls will protest that they are not prejudice and to prove it, they will do it with you. Then tell them you believe that they are different from the other Westerners who harbor bad feelings about us. She will do *anything* you ask."

"Perhaps, but let us talk about our mission. Then you can tell the women how soft and aromatic you find them."

"Ah, Musa, soft and aromatic! You are a poet. You must be the child of Omar Khayyam."

Said Dukayet was in many ways the antithesis of his recently assigned partner. While Musa was a child of the deserts of Saudi Arabia with present-day links to wandering Bedouin, Said was a child of urbanity with its commensurate skills of survival, dissimilation, education, and sweet and charming loquacity with an indifference to moral absolutes and an appreciation of the hedonistic and corrupting influence of Western culture.

Musa felt the occasional friction between them as Moses must have once felt between himself and the apostates who had fled Pharaoh. While he could always imagine himself leading his people onto the righteous paths in a desert kingdom, he could only see Dukayet as the ungrateful Israelites and children of Isaac who would betray Allah and his prophet Moses for the comforts and pleasures of Pharaoh's palaces. He still thought of him, however, as a friend, although one with whom he really was at ease primarily for his nonjudgmental disposition, the very characteristic he otherwise found disturbing if not appalling.

Despite this conflicted attitude, he had to admit that Said's ability to speak French, Arabic, Turkish, and English would prove invaluable. These skills as well as his authentic passports and long-standing relationships and friends, both Arab and European, throughout the West as well as North Africa and the Middle East, made him an invaluable asset. A one-time soccer prodigy while growing up in fractured Beirut, he had a plastic plate permanently embedded in his left thigh that helped hold his leg together, the legacy of a car bomb detonated by Shia militia men when he was sixteen. This wound had frustrated and embittered him to those who took away his opportunity to fully embrace his first love, soccer. He forever walked with a painful and noticeable limp.

Said also represented the splintered iconography of Lebanon that at once praised and worshipped one political figure and then another in its search for salvation, deliverance from an endless succession of Iranian, Syrian, Israeli, Jordanian, French, British, Egyptian and American interlopers. These were the transnational children of the Sunni, the Shia, the Roman Catholics, the Maronites, the Jews, the Orthodox and the Reformed, the Palestinians, and the non-Palestinians, the occasional Greek or Armenian Orthodox, Hamas, Hezbollah, as well as the Druze and Ismaili Nazari. Said was the bastard child of them all, a stranger in his own land. He hated what others had done to him and embraced the excuses it provided to reenact old grudges on anyone's behalf from centuries gone by. Doing so provided him with a subliminal means of revenge on a society and a world that he would prefer to burn down and start over. *All* his countrymen were guilty, and if they were part of the collateral damage his actions created, it was deserved. *All* the world could therefore be his ally as well as his enemy. To him, there seemed little difference between them to him except as he gravitated toward one and another as his whim and feelings dictated. His country was broken and he along with it. Extremism in one cause or another seemed only natural, a means of making a certainty out of at least one thing in his life.

Said the urbanite was the embittered and fractured child of modern and ancient grudges, real and imagined, while Musa the desert child was an ascetic as abrasive as desert sand, as antiseptic as its bakingly hot winds, and as righteous and morally uncompromising as the equatorial sun on wet clay. Both could burn, destroy, and still create delusional utopias of quenchable waters amidst the mirages of a world yearning for Koranic certitude.

"Tell me, my friend," asked Said, "why did you insist on taking the ferry when we could have flown?"

"We wish to leave no trail. Tickets and passport identification are increasingly scrutinized at all the airports. Not so on a ferry where you can still pay cash without arousing suspicion."

"Still, I would have preferred a short flight, more time to party. A lot of British girls in Cypress. When you meet them, remember what I said...You get anything you want if you convince them that they are acting like racists."

"Humph. What if they really are racist and they really don't care?"

"Then you must *take* what they will not give. You are a man. It is your right."

Unseen by Said, Musa's face blanched at the suggestion and then darkened. He remained silent and then smiled embarrassedly at Said's expectant look. Musa felt the revving of the ship's engine. The vibrations impeded small talk and gave a welcome reprieve from any further discussion regarding women.

Though quite different from one another, together they could do what each individually might not otherwise execute. Together they could also restrain at least some of the less enviable vices of the other. Generally, each looked upon his partner as an untried virtue and intriguing vice that each could select and absorb or work to excise from the other.

Each perceived the vices of the other as a kind of infection to be avoided or, simultaneously, as a playful reprieve from the more familiar and less exotic appeal of those vices he already possessed. Moreover, Musa's view of the world was essentially static. He took people as they were and assumed that they would never change. He viewed childhood as the crucible of formation from which a man might not reform but only renew. Still, while he understood people to be unchangeable, he viewed himself as a dynamism ordained by Allah to model virtue and to slay the already damned.

Musa looked upon humanity in general and individuals in particular as preternaturally opposed to change, all except himself whom he viewed cynically as tethered to vices that he could not break except in some explosive self-sacrifice that could endear him to the severity of a deity that knew his actions but not his heart's desire.

As the ferry moved pleasantly and forcefully through the deep blue waters of the Mediterranean, each thought of his purpose in this life and the means by which he would fulfill a mission that both ascribed to God.

A CHATTY REBUKE

> *She was a Frank, she crossed herself*
> *with four fingers. The priest will not*
> *bury her like everybody else.*[17]
>
> —Alexis Zorba, *Zorba the Greek*

Larnaca, Cyprus

Larnaca, one of the most beautiful cities in all of Cyprus, is small by the standards of European metropolises. Its beauty is wrapped up in its eternal conviviality, its seeming indifference to the ongoing Turko-Greco dispute over governance of the island, its immutability amidst the passage of time, and the sunshine that makes the city sweetly Mediterranean. Its deliciously exuberant and tantalizingly mysterious tranquility and affability are steeped in a reservoir of the artifacts of ancient antiquity and a contemporary assemblage of *bon ami* residents. Here, an archaeologist might well meet up with tourists from Italy, Greece, Tunisia, or with a dark brown fisherman repeating the labors of his ancestors, buried here long before the cross and crescent, the

Pater Noster and the Shahadah, the Arab and the Greek, had ever converged in tumult upon its shores.

On this particular Thursday, the harbor was placid. Sitting outside the coffee shop, Musa once again pulled out a hand-drawn map of a site that had attracted him as well as thousands upon thousands, if not millions, to it. Next to the map, he placed a postcard that showed an ancient building with a domed roof and two minarets. Built in the 1700s, the building on the postcard was one of the oldest shrines in all the Islamic world, the Hala Sultan Tekke. The location's significance related to an event that occurred in 678, the year that the Arab invaders first set foot on the island.

While Musa and Said examined the floor plan and looked at the postcard, they waited expectantly for the guide who was soon to arrive. As they finished their morning coffee, a diminutive gentleman, who acted as a guide for the guests of the Sun Shine Hotel at which they were staying, appeared, walking enthusiastically down the planks of the harbor pier.

Catching sight of them at a distance, he waved and smiled as if they were long-lost friends. Said stood, smiled in return, and shook hands. Musa nodded and stiffly reached out to shake hands with this overwhelmingly friendly fellow.

Their guide, a fiftyish, sun-darkened Greek, with the wrinkled look of a desiccated black olive, continued to smile enormously. From the moment they met, his loquacity was inviting. Having already paid for his services at the hotel, it was only left for their guide to drive them to a nearby shop to buy some trinkets and then their ultimate destination.

"Where are you from?" Nicholas Thermopolis queried them in English, the one language islanders most often shared with tourists.

"I am from Lebanon and my friend is from Saudi Arabia."

"Oh good, good. I afraid you from Persia. You look maybe Persian but not so much."

"You don't like Persians?" asked Said.

"Oh, no, no, no, no. I like all. Everybody. But sometime they don't like me, maybe because of my name." He stopped talking, his silence inviting them to ask how his name could offend Persians.

Knowing that he was being set up, Said smiled at Musa and nudged him, urging him to do the obvious.

Musa, who was less certain of his English than Said, hesitantly asked, "Okay, okay, so how your name is problem?"

"Okay, you, I am Greek."

"Wait, wait," responded Said, "maybe you do not like the Persians because they are Muslims." He looked at Musa knowingly, expecting their guide to squirm apologetically. Instead, he smiled broadly, and opened the door of his recent model white Subaru Forester. They climbed in the backseat of his immaculately clean vehicle. Once he was seated behind the wheel, he cranked the engine, grabbed at the gear shift and drove off. Then he looked at them in the rearview mirror and sighed pleasantly.

"I like you," he said. "With you, I can share a secret." He paused with the invitation to once again engage him as if he were a professional storyteller, which he knew himself to be.

"Okay, okay, so what big secret?" asked Musa, feeling a real desire to know despite the transparency of Nicholas's set up.

"I like you, too, so I will tell you. I am a humanist. Like Aristotle. Like Justinian. Like a true Church Father. I know that all men are brothers. So I did something no other Greek on this island would do."

Said looked again at Musa and said, "You are tickling us, but it is you who are laughing, I think."

"Yes, I am a humanist who loves God. So I love all women too. So what did I do? When we were fighting the Turks on this island, back about thirty, forty years ago, I went one day to talk to my neighbor who lives on the same side of the green line that I do. Do you know the green line drawn by the United Nations to keep us from killing each other?"

"Yes," replied Said, "we have something like it in Beirut."

"Then you know you are to love who is with you on your side of the line and hate the others. So I think I will love a girl who is a Turk. I tell my neighbor, 'You give your daughter to me. Then I will marry her. You stay with me on this side and live. You keep your house and I keep your daughter. What you think?' He say, 'No, you are Greek, but I like you.' Then, like a big surprise, he say, 'You would marry a Turk?' Then I am sly and I say, 'Maybe. What you give me for dowry?' He smile at me and he say, 'Istanbul, you want it back, I give you.' But maybe I say I want instead something. 'You can keep Istanbul,' I say but instead I say I want something else. He think and he say, 'What you want?' I say, 'I want Constantinople.' He say, 'It a deal.' So now I have Constantinople and beautiful Turkish wife and five boys."

Musa asked, "What religion are the children?"

"Ah, remember I am humanist so I made another deal. He give me his house too so no Greek can take it from him. A house, a girl, and five boys."

"So what religion are they?" asked Musa again, with a certain intensity. Said reached over and placed his hand on Musa's knee as if to say, "Easy, easy."

"My deal is this. If the child are girls, they will be Muslim, if boys, Christian. So five boys. We try for girls but God has spoke. He must want more Christians."

"But who would marry you?" asked Musa. "Was a priest or imam?"

"Ah, good question. So we go to priest and he say, 'I cannot marry you in church. She is Muslim. She must convert.' But if she convert, she thrown out of house by women. So he tell me, 'Go to imam and see what he say.' The imam we visit and he say, 'No.' He say I must convert. If I convert, the Greeks who know me will kill me and call me a dirty Turk. So I go back to the priest and the priest give me a letter for the imam. Then he tell me take it to him. He say, 'Ask him if he love his grandmother.' He smile when he say this to me.

"So I went by myself to the imam and I say, 'Here is a letter from my priest. He says he know you well and for me to give you letter.' He opens the letter and smile. He look at me and he say, 'No.' Then I say, 'Do you love your grandmother?' He look at me and then he smile again and say to me, 'This is blackmail. I know who told you.' Then he look at me and say, 'It is done. Tell him. It is done. She is not renounced. She is not apostate.' Then he look at me and he say, 'You are sly but I hope you are happy and that you have many girls.' So we are married in church—quiet, no one come, but we married."

"I see," replied Said. "So you like Persians?"

"Yes, but because of my name, they do not so much like me. Not because of Nicholas but because I take my last name from where my ancestors were born. They born near the great battle, Thermopylae. You know Thermopylae?"

"I think so."

"Yes, it is where Spartans all die but they kill so many Persians they cannot defeat my people. The Persians know my name so they don't tip."

Said took the hint and made a mental note to distinguish himself from the Persians.

"This, I think, you will enjoy more than any of the other sites. It is a holy place with beautiful palms and gardens by the salt lake." After several hours touring churches and shops throughout Larnaca, they arrived at the real purpose of their visit to the island. Not wishing to express too much interest in it for fear of arousing suspicion, Musa, who really did want to see it out of genuine anger and disbelief at its mere existence, would observe all about it in critical detail. Said was mercenary enough to recognize the necessity of visiting the musky world of museums, mausoleums, or shrines. They were largely one and the same to him and this one, despite its beauty and the esteem in which it was held, was still a dimly lit world that was sufficiently free of life to convince Said he himself may have already died.

They entered. Here they were immediately immersed in the quiet and the reverential world of one of Islam's holiest sites. Only Mecca, Medina, and Jerusalem were held in greater esteem. The atmosphere was not only tranquil but almost languid. It was as if the sun and ease of the gardens and the palms had drifted into the world of the dead and revived it to a kind of dream world where the dead and the living could yet commune. Here it seemed that an Odysseus might have shared blood with the dead or an ancient crusader and some Janissary could have discussed with the Turk and the Arab invaders of the 600s how they came to be buried next to one another as they sipped the dark bean coffee of Ethiopia.

"Musa, you know that in 647 the Arabs invaded Cyprus and attempted to take over the island. But the Cypriots—ha! They fought hard. They come again in 649 with his uncle, Mohammad's uncle—I mean aunt. I get them mixed sometime. Sometime I get the year mixed too. She was Mohammad's aunt who nurse him. Because of this some call her a saint."

Musa bristled at the mere equating of yet another companion as a saint. There was only the Prophet. For a Greek Christian to suggest otherwise was sheer impudence.

Said raised his eyebrows and smiled at Musa reassuringly. He then whispered in his ear, "Pretend that you are *taqiyya* and smile at him. He means no disrespect. He is only ignorant. Remember, he likes you." Musa exercised a half smile as he glanced again at Nicholas who continued, explaining that Umm Haram, the woman who wet-nursed Mohammad, lay buried here after falling from a donkey and breaking her neck.

As they approached the actual crypt in which her remains were entombed, Musa was struck by its ostentation. This was man's vanity, not a reverence for Allah. The marble inlays and the pretense of holiness with inscriptions from the Koran embossed and engraved all about struck him as blasphemous. Still, he found it interesting but little different from the pagan Egyptians who mummified the remains of their dead and planted them beneath grand pyramids.

"When I was a boy, I come here just to see it and to play about. But it was not so much then. It was not cared for. The mosque was crumbling. The roof leak and there were insects, many of them throughout. But then the Americans come. They spend millions of dollars to fix it. I wish they give me some of that money. Now it is clean and maybe like was long ago when the Turks first built it after they find the tomb. They find it only a thousand years after she buried here."

The Turks, thought Musa, were like the Americans, imperialists who ignore religion when it is convenient. The Turks are pagans who like Muslims but who want to be Europeans and who are allied with the Americans. They will give back Istanbul so they can learn to be Europeans. As he looked at his guide, he was simply confounded. Said smiled and continued the tour, noting the dimensions of the crypt, the doors behind which it was contained, and the exact location of any lights, light switches, the alarm system, the windows, and of course, the location of the relics themselves.

ARABIC NUMBERS
AND MAPS

Farasan Island, the Red Sea

"There are three things you must know: one, the terrain; two, the enemy; and three, yourself. The first you must study through books, maps, observations, intelligence of any sort that enables you to learn the lair of the enemy. Only when you know his home better than he does can you attack with confidence."

As Shakir spoke, seated at a veranda overlooking the Red Sea, he clicked on a laptop computer. As it clicked and whirred, he reached into the briefcase that sat on a chair immediately to his right at a round table that seated comfortably five of his disciples with the others seated behind them. He clicked on one site and then another, delving deeper and deeper into his archived material. Finally, he stopped at a site that was designated "GPS—Where Am I?" and manipulated a map to a 1:25,000 scale whose accuracy included contour lines of the hills and valleys as well as water depths of bays, inlets, and rivers. He invited everyone to look at it, knowing that the oceanic blue and the contour lines were all but indecipherable to all but one disciple who made a mental note of certain numbers he saw at the bottom of the site. It read, "19 degrees, 54 minutes North Latitude; 75 degrees, 9 minutes West Longitude."

While the others conceded their ignorance at the map's revelations, the one disciple smiled and raised his eyebrows questioningly and feigned appreciation at this teacher's presumed mastery of geographic esoterica that was intended to secure his authority and their subjugation to yet more of his presumptions of wisdom.

Several hours later, all of the disciples sat on the edge of a swimming pool with Shakir. All were being ably instructed in the art and adventure of scuba diving. Their instructors included one Moroccan, whose thick accent made him at times difficult to understand, and two Dutch-born Turks, whose commitment was not to the nation of their birth but to the religion and warrior ethos of their ancestors.

Despite the language difficulties, they were experienced PADI-certified instructors who were able and entirely willing accomplices in an enterprise that they felt to be extraordinary and knew to be dangerous. Their passports had been confiscated upon entry into Saudi Arabia. They were well-paid and well-secreted employees of an unseen hand that recruited them, paid them, and virtually imprisoned them. They were here for as long as Shakir and others deemed necessary.

In the course of the instructions, Shakir's own temper burst forth on several occasions on any who dared to question what they were doing and why they were doing it. Six weeks of a course of instructions took them from PADI-type instructions of a "level 1 beginning open water diver" to "advanced open water," to "rescue diver," "navigation expert," and "enriched air diver." In the course of forty-two days of instructions, they logged over sixty dives, some of them as deep as two hundred feet. Shakir himself dove with them. Seemingly a novice at diving who just happened to be a quick learner who frequently grew exasperated at their slow pace of instruction and his disciples learning, Shakir cloaked the fact that he had taken the exact same diving instructions at Ishmael's urging in the United States. He had taken the same courses again through a private series of instruction from a dive master while vacationing in Qatar. The ease with which he seemed to master the instructions, both written and performance, cemented his authority with the men. They saw him increasingly as an imam with a penchant for adventure who would soon lead them as the light of revelation was granted to him. Only one seemed willing to question the purpose and nature of their instruction. But the questioning of the imam's authority was revealed more in furtive glances, furrowed brows, and occasionally an odd tilt of the head that revealed a questioning mind. Haban al-Amur nonetheless continued the training, quietly mastering dive techniques, the explicit purpose of which had not yet been revealed to him or the others.

Late in the evening when the moon was full, Shakir and his group along with their instructors were assembled on a solitary beach where a yacht moved parallel to the shore from which various lights splashed their luminescence on the water, mingling the flinty sparks of moon dust with the harsher glare of incandescence. The yacht was close to fifty feet long and had on its bow two men, one of whom Shakir knew, watching as the team of disciples stood questioningly on shore.

In the last two weeks of instruction they had performed no less than seven night dives. But on this occasion, Shakir informed them that effective immediately all would dive exclusively at night for the next several weeks and that the ardor of their training would intensify. Now, with moonlight sprinkling silver all about the water, they donned their diving equipment, which for the first time, included not one but two air tanks connected by a manifold tied to their regulator and mouthpiece. For this dive, each had an allotment of air that was double his usual amount. Their wet suits were their usual neoprene light for warm water diving. The divers were also equipped with fluorescent chemical sticks that they snapped to ignite so that each diver's whereabouts could be readily discerned both on the surface and below the water.

After they had their gear on and had checked each other in a last-minute safety inspection, Shakir advised them to try out their whistles, their underwater flashlights, and their compasses. Each person wore a SeaQuest Buoyancy Control Device (BCD) appropriately weighted to help him submerge when he was at the designated dive site.

As they approached the calm waters with mild surf, the instructors advised each to put on his flippers as they entered the water and to inflate their vests. All eight, plus Shakir and the instructors, put on their masks and snorkels, flipped over on to their backs, and gently kicked their legs. The flippers propelled them through the warm evening water of the Red Sea.

Once they arrived at the boat, each of the disciples were helped aboard at the stern diving platform that protruded ten feet. As the last man crawled aboard, the yacht sped off for five minutes in a southerly direction. Then, as they approached a predesignated position already entered into the ship's positioning system, the yacht slowed and the captain turned off the engines. As the boat quieted, the men looked to Shakir for instructions.

"Each of you will be tested tonight as you never have been before. Look at your compasses. Once submerged, you will set your heading to thirty-five degrees northeast. If you do this, and you follow the course, all of you will end up back at the beach in approximately one hour. Stay shallow. This way, you will not use too much oxygen."

He waited as the men adjusted their compasses to the appropriate heading. "If you tire, remember, the tide is moving toward the shoreline. You can drift dive part of the way with the tide and currents pushing you to shore."

Shakir looked at the still silent men reassuringly and then added abruptly, "It is twenty-three forty-three hours. If all goes according to plan, the first man will arrive ashore at zero forty-three hours, twelve forty-three in the morning."

At first the men seemed confused when Shakir mentioned the "first man."

"We are not diving together?" asked one of the men.

"No, no, no," responded Shakir. "You will not dive in pairs tonight. You must reduce your dependence upon one another. You are not children. Some of you depend too much upon the better navigators among us. So you will depart the boat in ten-minute intervals. Then, after the last man departs, the yacht will drift forward but not so fast as to overtake you but to be alongside. Again, stay shallow, no more than six meters. If anyone gets lost—and you shouldn't, just rise to the surface and use your whistle and flashlight to get our attention. The boat will come for you."

Unbeknownst to the disciples, Shakir had already dived twice from this exact same location on the team's off days during daylight to be assured that his own performance would once again be exemplary and inspirational. He therefore indicated that he would go first. As he fell backward into the water, gripping his facemask and regulator mouthpiece tight against his face, he turned over and resurfaced and deflated his BCD by depressing the air valve. He sank slowly to about twenty feet. He stabilized himself briefly at this depth, turned on his flashlight, checked his compass until the north arrow was aligned with the bevel, and set the lubber line to 35 degrees northeast. His bearings established, he held his wrist compass directly in front of him and pointed his right arm in the desired direction and began to kick. The others, in ten-minute intervals, followed suit, their luminescent chemical sticks and flashlights marking their position sufficiently clear in the waters of the Red Sea that the crew of the yacht could actually monitor each diver's descent and direction for the first couple of minutes. Moving farther from the yacht, each diver in turn disappeared.

The sixth diver, Said Abdullah Zemmeri, moved about in relative comfort for the first fifteen minutes. Then, he noticed below him a kind of fleeting surge of waters, not one stirred by his own movements but by something else. At first, he dismissed it and continued until his right flipper seemed to hit something. He checked his depth gauge to see if he had inadvertently drifted toward the bottom. But it still read six meters, moreover, he flashed his light all about and could not penetrate to the bottom.

With a slight trepidation, he continued until he again kicked something with his right flipper. He felt a slight quick tug on it.

Convinced that he was being followed, perhaps, he hoped, by one of the instructors, he nonetheless kept kicking with greater speed and shallower and more frequent breaths. He began to perspire even below water. Momentarily losing his bearings, he again flashed his light all around only to feel a cringe of waters immediately above him. As he jerked the flashlight straight up, the light's penetration stopped, bouncing off a shiny white oval passing over head. He froze, dropping his flashlight into the abyss, forgetting that his backup flashlight was packed tightly in his right vest pocket.

Now in near complete darkness, he looked up to see the light of the moon, and he kicked hard. As he did so, his head bumped a sandpapery surface that scraped its entire torso across his forehead and flicked its tail against his face nearly dislodging his mask, snorkel, and mouthpiece. He reached for the knife on his right leg, hands trembling, and yanked on it repeatedly as he again began to sink. Despite his yanks on the handle, he could not dislodge it from its scabbard. Panicky as he was, he forgot to depress the safety latches that prevented the knife from falling out.

He was sweating profusely and breathing shallowly, turning from side to side, as he felt the pressure on ears, face mask, and chest as he drifted downward to nearly fifteen meters. Suddenly he felt something grip his left flipper, pulling him even farther downward. He felt pressure on his foot as well as he grimaced and kicked and twisted violently, surrendering his denial as he bent his body and hit his fist three times hard against the snout that now seemed attached to his flipper. The creature jerked his head from side to side, shaking and tearing off the lower half of his flipper and part of his big toe. Temporarily free, and despite the pain, Zemmeri kicked and stroked rapidly, suddenly remembering to inflate his BCD. He felt for the valve and went flying to the surface.

He popped the water, spit out his mouthpiece, and began screaming. Off to his left, he spotted the yacht at about two hundred yards. As he yelled, something bumped him from behind as it latched on hard to his tanks, gripping both of them in its jaws, teeth scraping hard against the metallic cylinders, pushing him forward in the water. He was choking, flailing his arms, and trying to yell for help. Propelled inexorably forward by a muscular torpedo almost nine feet in length, he relented and pulled his regulator back into his mouth as he was pushed under.

Moments later, he saw the flash of several searchlights on the waters above him and saw two splashes ahead of him as the boat eased into position about three meters above and six meters off to his left. The powerful grip that held him let go in fear as the other two divers from the boat flashed their lights at him, temporarily blinding him and frightening off the predator. The shark turned after letting him go, and Zemmeri floated on the surface, his vest still inflated, paralyzed with fear and bleeding from his left foot. His only movement was an involuntary shaking. The other divers grabbed him on either shoulder and pulled him backward toward the stern diving platform. A sash of blood flowed from his foot, blooming into a bitter red rose in the nighttime waters of the Red Sea. Fortunately, his submergence at significant depths had not been long enough to inflict the bends.

Though traumatized, Zemmeri was frightened more than hurt, other than the missing big toe. Within a month, he would again join his comrades for further training. Such is the zeal of the truly committed. Thereafter, all night dives were conducted in groups, each man in turn leading the group with Zemmeri packed securely in the middle.

◆◆◆

Shakir moved to a chair under the awning of the Farasan Hotel and sipped a morning cup of coffee. Dressed in the traditional white robe and ghutra, Shakir glowed with pleasure at the wind ruffling his attire and casting a morning shadow that fluttered like a black flame on the ground. The beauty of the moment seemed a reflection of Allah himself smiling upon his efforts. His shadow diminished in length as the sun rose higher and, as the morning sea breeze sent its salty fragrance to mingle with the scent of dark coffee, Shakir felt his own presence so strongly that his shadow lightened the ground which it otherwise darkened. Such are the contradictory powers of a prophet whose presence reconciles opposites and restricts the ultimate source of spiritual illumination by casting shadows and inciting a maelstrom of golden and silver words as precious as the sun and moon flakes that gild them. Little he saw in the contemplation of his own shadow that was less than a symbol of his bequeathal to others mandated by the very laws of nature, and He whose divine breath set all in motion. And yet, if his self-referential way of seeing his position in the world of nature could be plotted, Ptolemy would still rule the heavens with himself at the center and Copernicus and Galileo would be forced to submit. The laws of physics could be overcome by divine will working in concert with a receptive vessel unrestrained by time or space. Shakir watched, stationary, as his shadow slowly moved and as his disciples circled about him in reverential and perfect yearning to be manipulated into the embrace of his gravitational pull. Their submission was to be their release from the void of heretical thought and blasphemous venality. With faith, even time and space could be bent to the will of the divinely ordained creatures of the Word.

Once all were seated, Shakir began with the routinized quotation from the Koran that invited *jihad* against the unbelievers.

"As Allah has told Mohammad, 'When you proclaim your call to prayer, they take it as mockery and sport; that is because they are ignorant.'"

But on this morning, there was, as yet, no harangue following the recitation. Instead he stood and invited them all to walk with him through the morning beauty. He commented that Eden itself must have been a marvel beyond their comprehension. For even this place, as beautiful as it was, and which did indeed take his breath away, could not compare. Then he commented on the small herd of miniature gazelles that still dwelt on the animal preserve that surrounded them. The liquescent and opalescent luster of the sea within walking distance of any part of the island cast its morning iridescence before them as heavenly signs of approval of all that they would design, bless, and execute.

On this morning, Shakir would at last reveal to them that which he had hidden. As they walked and talked and smelled the fragrance of the flowers, the sea and the sun itself, each in turn recalled all that they had learned. Then he stopped them and said, "You have worked hard for more than four months. Imagine your brothers in the Netherlands. There in the city of Amsterdam, yet another group of divers is being trained. They, like you, have a divine mission that awaits them. In fact, their mission and yours are one and the same. They, unlike you, have no such beauty as this. They, unlike you, have no such warm waters to swim and train in. They swim in the cold waters of the North Sea in a pagan land. Yet the breath of Allah warms their flesh against the cold and the ardor of their efforts. They know of you, you know of them. Through them and you, Islam will overcome all obstacles and conquer and rule the world as it should."

Relaxed and almost soft and gentle in his demeanor, Shakir joked and commented frequently on the beauty about them and the fine qualities that each man possessed. As they talked, he eventually led them back to a small conference room at the hotel where Ishmael was waiting. There, for the first time, Haban al-Amur, a reluctant warrior, had his suspicions confirmed as once again they were shown a map thrown up from his computer on a large screen. However, the geographic coordinates were fully visible for the first time and mentally he took note even as the others looked at a map without any place or name references. Then, after showing the map and pointing to the water depths and the inlets and bays as well as several streams and rivers, he gave each man a folder inside which was a miniature version of the same map. Each man would have a test on it tomorrow. Then, he walked to a door, opened it, and inviting all of them to enter, he flicked on the lights. The adjoining room had a long conference table around which were twelve leather chairs. The table itself was covered by two lengthy linen sheets.

He invited all to seat themselves as he walked to the head of the table and Ishmael stood at the other end.

"What you are about to see will help prepare you for your mission. Over the next several weeks, you will memorize each contour of it."

Ishmael and Shakir removed the two long sheets, revealing a clay and plaster mockup of a harbor facility; two of them immediately recognized it, one of them gasping as he did so. Softly, he whispered the name. Stunned, the others were wide-eyed and silent.

After a two-hour session during which they discussed the model before them, he again walked with them to the beach. As they did so, he once again pointed out to them the miniature gazelles, the rock doves, and others of the natural world. He did so in a kind of rapturous mood. Looking upon each of the various creatures they saw before them, verily he blessed them. Verily he addressed them. And verily he assessed them. Verily. For each, he told them, had greater value than even these various creatures did. As dumb animals, they but followed the will of Allah. They too had submitted and in doing so they led perfect lives. All men, however, were sinners. Their submission, though required, had to be cajoled, coaxed, or coerced. Yet again he closed his eyes and extended his right hand and said aloud even as his disciples, all but one, closed their eyes in concert. "Like Moses who crossed this sea to deliver his people, like Moses a perfect vessel for Allah's will which turned its waters against Pharaoh and his children, and like Moses you and I will cross a great sea to deliver our people from Pharaoh through martyrdom as we strike down even Pharaoh's children. Allahu Akbar."

He who had not closed his eyes, Haban al-Amur, did not do so for his had been opened. He had already eaten of the Tree.

SPHERES OF INFLUENCE

> *What would the seemingly perfect sphere of humanity look like. . . ?*[19]
>
> —Mark Hastings, "Poet of the Sphere"

Chisolm slipped in sideways from the aisle to the third seat which was next to the window. He winced slightly as he squeezed by the rotundity that embellished the L-shaped seat next to his with a fleshy spheroid with large elbows and trapezoidal forearms that seemed loosely attached to biceps that had long ago lost their elasticity and power of motion. Instead they shook with exertion to push their mistress against the backrest to let Chisolm pass. Once this embarrassing and irksome exercise had passed, like a tidal movement that must return, her fleshiness cascaded to fill the voided spherical ideal. Her shape was a strong indictment of Aristotle's postulate that the sphere is the symbol of perfection. However, her presence then metastasized into an unbounded exhibition of genuine joy and

163

flirtational exuberance. "Hi!" She winked as Chisolm slid carefully into his seat, hoping to avoid pinching her overextended abundance between the armrest and himself.

"Hi," replied Chisolm. He was tired and had just nearly completed another combat tour in Afghanistan when he was unexpectedly called away from his command and practically forced onto a military transport outside of Kabul. Receiving verbal commands without corresponding written confirmation was not unprecedented in the U.S. military but it was still highly irregular. LCDR Grant Chisolm felt more than he knew that his transit to Sigonello, Sicily, then Avian, Italy, both U.S. military installations, was a precursor to another adventure that he wasn't sure just yet that he wanted. Having served three four-month stints with U.S. and Coalition Special Forces in Afghanistan, he wanted a rest before the strain of more untold adventure. But, as always, it seemed that invisible hands were working hard behind the scenes to transfer him from one flight, and then to an inconspicuous presence on board a commercial KLM airliner from Florence to London Heathrow Airport.

The lady's presence, that of a sweepstakes winner of a Travelocity promotion, reminded him of the affability of his countrymen. They smiled indulgently at nothing and were themselves the carbon life-form that the warm earthers despised and whom Chisolm viewed, at least at this moment, as a reminder that at times life seemed to be closing in on him. He squirmed uncomfortably at her good-natured friendliness and pretended to fall asleep.

◆◆◆

Chisolm walked through customs at Heathrow as he cued in the line marked "Non-EU Members" and then to Passport Control where he was asked the usual questions.

"What is the purpose of your visit? How long will you be staying? Where will you be staying?"

He then moved with two suitcases toward the corridor when he spotted a familiar face. They recognized each other simultaneously. She beamed a smile of utter delight, and he walked toward her with the slightly awkward gait of a man hauling luggage. They hugged and kissed. Chisolm had written to Blanche DeNegris for more than two years once he had left England after his last visit and adventure to that sceptered isle. She had responded with affection and sincere desire to see him again. The niece of Dennis Stallard, a friend and elderly mentor, Blanche was the epitome of womanly grace and intelligence. Working for the British Museum, Blanche had a sharp eye for detecting and assessing archaeological finds, plus a keen interest in ancient languages, making her a companion both respected and insatiably curious about everything. Ever cautious in his personal relationships, Grant nonetheless saw in her the virtue of his mother in the girl-like vivacity that could be as startling as it was refreshing. She smelled like lilac and, to Chisolm, she moved with virginal sweetness that he yearned for yet, respectfully, dare not touch.

"Goodness, Mr. Chisolm," she chided in her English accent. "Why so long, Yankee? Afghanistan," she whispered, "is closer to England than to America." Chisolm smiled at the insinuation that she might have seen him at least once during the past two years if he had made the effort. She wasn't getting any younger, and she longed to be, however secretly, the mother of his children and the maternal guardian of his soul; she saw in him a man of gallantry, cunning, and at times caustic repartee that could leave her in tears without his even knowing it. There was also a steeliness about him that was at times hidden but which when surfaced made him as menacing as he was kind. She sensed even in their first few minutes together that Afghanistan brought that steeliness to the fore more than any other of his features. Still, she loved him. Instinctively, intuitively, she had recognized in him the possibility that his man's heart was great and yet burdened at the same time. It needed a gentle touch lest the grimness of his personal confrontations with its dark elements and those of his combat foes cause him to misinterpret the world. The steeliness within, however, had manifested its sheen with an armorial bearing that seemed honor bound to desensitize itself to pain and, in the process, to the subtle charms and grace, and feelings offered to him from when they had last parted. The differences in him from when they had last said good-bye were alternatives to the soulful fabric of a good man.

Immediately upon his arrival, Blanche and Chisolm went to her car where they threw his luggage in the backseat and then sped off into the cool August night, a slight mist sprinkling the windshield. An hour and half later they sat in the lobby of the Union Jack with an old friend and mentor of Grant's, who happened to be Blanche's great uncle, one Dennis Stallard.

Dennis had, over two years earlier, met Chisolm in the T. E. Lawrence Reading Room at the same club. This gentleman's long-time connections with Chisolm's family dated all the way back to WWII when he had befriended Chisolm's grandfather, one of the first members of an elite fighting force that fought alongside their British counterparts. That family connection had led Chisolm to the nether regions of silent contemporary elites in armed conflict with insidious forces. Chisolm had, almost unwittingly, been recruited into a force of sometime shadow warriors who worked beyond the glare of headlines, in the anonymity of seismic indifference that allowed tectonic shifts of political import. These shifts, if orchestrated correctly, occurred at a depth of intrigue that caused mere ripples and slight vibrations on the surface of the political landscape that were as yet all but undetectable.

"My friend," continued Dennis, "it is such a pleasure to see you again. You know, when you are my age, you become forever preoccupied with visions of one's own mortality. I was concerned once you left for Afghanistan that I might not see you again – such are the concerns that come with the degradations of old age."

"Oh, uncle, stop," added Blanche. "You shall live longer than you know."

"Hum, longer than I know? Sounds like someone with Alzheimer's to me. But, fortunately or unfortunately, as some would have it, I have already – that is, lived longer than many might have expected.

Chisolm noticed that Dennis had grown considerably older in only the last two years.

His gestures and even speech seemed slow. But there was still one constant in his being that was unmistakable. His affection for his niece was transparent.

After several minutes of conversation in which Dennis attempted to elicit some of the particulars of Chisolm's latest training, he smiled resignedly at his cryptic responses and then turned the conversation to the as yet secret excavations in Scotland of the archeological site that had brought both his niece and his protégé to a near-death experience in Chisolm's last visit to the United Kingdom. Then, he looked smilingly at his niece and said, "My dear, there is as yet one thing more I truly wish out of life."

She blushed knowingly and said, "Uncle, no more, please."

"Ah, but it's true. If I should see you happily married, I could make a blessed departure to the next life."

Chisolm sat back in the comfortable lounge chair rather stiffly and looked fleetingly at Blanche and then down at the coffee table in front of him. Dennis waved to a waiter to bring two sparkling waters for the blushing niece and the sober Chisolm. As the evening wore on, the conversation eventually shifted to the borderline of classified information and hovered there momentarily as Blanche gracefully made her departure. Chisolm's room had already been arranged at the Union Jack until tomorrow when he and Dennis would meet yet again the mover of the worlds, another old friend by the name of Regis MacArthur.

KINGS, KHANS, AND CUPID BY THE NUMBERS

Soulful men and lovers do not understand the zero; they think it is an egg.[20]

–T. Chin, "A and B=C"

On the evening of the next day, Chisolm waited quietly in the lobby of the George Inn and Free House about thirty miles northeast of London. Traveling with him was Dennis Stallard who had directed Grant as he drove. Upon arrival at the George, Dennis told Chisolm to pull around the back on the gravel-strewn driveway. Upon parking the car, a backlight flicked on illuminating the area. As Dennis and Chisolm approached the door, a tall and slightly stooped-shouldered individual opened it, smiling as he extended a hand to his old friend and then to Grant.

"Sir," said Chisolm, as he shook the hand of one of the most intriguing and quietly powerful men he had ever met.

"It is good to see you, son."

Regis MacArthur seemed, despite his large frame, physically diminished from the last time they had seen each other over two years ago. Their meeting this evening would confirm Chisolm's perception.

As they entered the private conference room typically reserved for business meetings, two men rose from a large couch and stood to greet Dennis whom they already knew. Each in turn shook hands and seated themselves again as Regis led Chisolm to a chair between one end of the couch and two other velvety and slightly worn but comfortable lounge chairs, all of which were situated around a dark walnut hewn rectangular coffee table.

"My sons should also have joined us this evening so that we might all once again delight in our fellowship and hear your recent deeds of valor, Grant."

Chisolm remained quiet despite the invitation to extol those present with tales of his most recent experiences in Afghanistan. He was reluctant to speak of anything that bordered on classified information in the presence of those whom he had just met and even with Stallard and MacArthur who were not involved in those enterprises and didn't therefore need to know.

With the invitation to speak unfulfilled, Regis smiled slightly at Chisolm's taciturn disposition and began, "Lieutenant Commander Grant, to date whenever you've needed equipment and supplies for your mission associated with us, you've no more than called one of your colleagues back in the United States. Those contacts and our contacts work in concert. It is now time to meet at least part of the team that will assist you hereafter. Allow me to officially introduce you to one of the captains of our enterprises, Dr. Zaghast Deimcho. Dr. Deimcho has been our lead accountant for the past several years."

"Doctor?" Chisolm asked.

"Yes," replied Deimcho. "I have a doctorate in mathematics from the University of Warsaw. I have another in advanced accounting from the University of Prague. It's a habit of mine, I'm afraid."

"As you may have detected, Dr. Deimcho is Polish, a long-time friend, and a man who speaks several languages with a fluency exceeded only by his facility with numbers. And you will observe, Lieutenant Commander, that I said, 'numbers,' and not 'money.' Dr. Deimcho is indeed our lead accountant, but he is much more interested in numbers than he is money, which is, I suppose, why he works for me...or rather us." The latter he said with a wry smile as he glanced at Dr. Deimcho who remained quiet though attentive at his introduction.

"Dr. Deimcho," he continued, "possesses a kind of mystical connection with numbers that I find absolutely baffling. The ability to yoke together the columnar precision absolutely essential to accounting with the spiritual significance of zero and the symmetry of nature and manmade clericalism raises the mendacity of his tasks to the realm of Platonic idealism that few can duplicate and fewer appreciate. However, this should not fool you. For in the end, his name is Deimcho and not Gandhi. He can make numbers dance on the head of a pin and he can, in more mortal form, scare us all with a kind of clerical scrupulosity that he finds sinfully delicious and which I find just plain sinful. He knows the difference between numbers and money and can guide you when I should depart."

"Depart?" asked Chisolm.

"We all have our time," replied MacArthur.

After a slightly embarrassing pause, Dennis said, "Before you leave, you will have the necessary contact information."

"And now our final introduction of the evening," continued MacArthur, "Mr. Shamar Khan. Mr. Khan is one of the great benefactors of society. These benedictions that he provides to society are unique, and Mr. Khan, I should note, is one of the most perceptive men I have ever known. Be careful what you think in his presence, he can dissect your thoughts and perceive the condition of your soul even better than you can. Mr. Khan has, through his long-time generosity, benefited hundreds of scholars and entrepreneurs directly and thousands indirectly. He can do all this because of Mr. Khan's unique vision of the world. He has an intense appreciation of history and of current events. He can, better than anyone I know, catch the reflections of distant mirrors in contemporary society. We have worked together for years. This evening I've asked Mr. Khan to meet with us so that he can inform you of a matter of some import to those of us here. My sons, both of whom you know, will continue to consult with Mr. Khan regarding this evening's matter."

Mr. Khan was a brown-skinned man with a trimmed, thin moustache that was pencil perfect. His black eyes were friendly and forgiving. As he spoke during the next hour, his gestures were firm but almost kindly. His English was flawless with no trace of his Pakistani origins but much of his English private schooling. There was a depth of feeling about him as if he himself had tapped into a font of wisdom that emanated from his bones, his flesh, and his motions. It gave him an aura of quiet authority that could trace its origins back to the ancients. The tranquility of his being seemed oblivious to time or to space. As he spoke, as he walked, the wells of wisdom were always where he was. The others all felt his concerns in each of his utterances and the soundings of his own penetrating questions.

"As you may know," said Khan, "my own sources and contacts are scattered throughout the world. They inform me that of late they have detected a movement to orchestrate what might be a series of terrorist attacks." He paused, waiting to see if this one point would invite questions. But all were silent, content to let him proceed.

"Among other matters of interest and concern is the unusual interest that my own countrymen, as well as others from certain regimes in the Middle East and in enclaves of their brothers in Europe, are now showing in scuba diving classes. Before 9/11, you may recall that a number of individuals took it upon themselves to enlist in flying classes. They did so without arousing much interest but at the world's peril. We would not like to see such occurrences again."

Khan then walked over to a rolled-up map leaning against a chair and unfolded it on a coffee table for all to see. He pointed his finger at Amsterdam. "The largest group so far that we know of is training here. But there are other groups as well. He then pointed in turn to London, the south of France, Hamburg, Alexandria, the Red Sea, Miami, Florida, and Trinidad. "I am fearful that my brothers who have yet to learn the true meaning of *jihad* are gathering again to perpetrate yet another attack on the innocent and unsuspecting. Regrettably, gentlemen, they misinterpret Islam."

Everyone in the room was respectfully silent as Khan continued. "Only yesterday, I received yet another warning from a contact in the Caribbean, Puerto Rico. He tells me that the virulence of the preachings coming out of the mosque in the city of San Juan is alarming. A recent visiting imam from Saudi Arabia seemed to have come for no other purpose than to stir up ill will against the country's Christian population. And so, so it is also true in Jamaica, Venezuela, Trinidad, and Barbados."

"Sir, just how virulent are these preachings that you are alluding to?" asked Chisolm.

Khan looked at Chisolm kindly, slightly smiling and offered, "These are the preachings of the most radical Wahhabists and Salafists who would, if they could, destroy the West entirely, as well as any Muslims who are not in accord with them. I know that I have already been listed among their enemies. I therefore fear for you and all good soldiers who will continue to be called upon to defend the rest of us against them."

As Mr. Khan continued to speak, Chisolm noticed his attire, a dark tweedy suit that seemed very English and a red rose in his left lapel with a dark blue shirt and a simple red silk tie. Although the accountant and MacArthur each sipped on a tawny port in the course of the evening, Mr. Khan and Chisolm retained their abstemious ways. Dennis Stallard held a pint that was only half empty and warm at the end of the meeting.

Finally, Regis turned to Chisolm and said, "You have now met yet one more individual who shares an interest in our brotherly concerns. Think of them as *your* brothers. When I am no longer here, you will consult with them as I and, dare I say, Dennis recede.

Perplexed but not troubled, Chisolm could infer that his own observations regarding Regis's health and constitution showing the ravages of age were indeed on target. He then glanced at Dennis who looked back with a knowing smile. Chisolm looked again at Khan who seemed to anticipate his questions and who therefore volunteered, "Mr. Grant, we all work together for a greater good. Even in your government, there are those who work quietly with us, free of the too-intrusive eyes and guidance of government bureaucrats."

◆◆◆

At the end of the evening, the conversation turned to a discussion of the upcoming America's Cup. "I like the Australians this year," insisted MacArthur. "I know two of the chaps. Their skipper's exceptional. He can detect wind movements and their changes better than anyone I know. He also doesn't tolerate monkey business on his yacht. His crew is in superb shape, very knowledgeable. They can practically navigate blindfolded. How I wish I were a younger man, I would join them—even as a Brit."

"You still can, I suspect," said Dennis.

"Oh, I may have a few voyages left for I do so yearn to know." Then he paused and raised his port glass as if to toast and said in a grandiloquent voice that was at once sincere and mildly self-parodying, "I wish to follow knowledge like a sinking star beyond the utmost bounds of human thought until I die." Then he looked at Dennis who likewise raised his pint and joined him with a depth of feeling which was louder than their voices which resonated in the chests of all present like the tolling of a bell, "Come, my friends, 'tis not too late to seek a newer world. You and I are old. Old age hath yet his honor and his toil. . . To strive, to seek, to find and not to yield."

Chisolm smiled at Dennis and MacArthur and thought to himself, *Tennyson.* All then raised their glasses spontaneously, the accountant his port, Khan and Chisolm their glasses of water. Recognizing the toast as the appropriate time to depart, MacArthur raised himself up with a measure of difficulty and said, "We shall be staying the night. Your room is arranged, Commander." As the others stood to say goodnight, Dennis placed a hand on Grant's shoulder and whispered, "A moment please." Once the others had departed, Dennis said, "Grant, you'll forgive an old man's taking liberty concerning the personal life of a much younger man, but there is someone who has missed you a great deal and who hopes you'll call her yet again. You'll have time to visit while you are here. At least allow her to share the details of what she has found near Ben Nevis. The findings are incredible and not yet released to the public. She's a good girl."

"I know that, sir. I'll call tomorrow."

"Not for me, Grant. For her, for you."

Then he added, "Tomorrow we will consider further the implications of our findings. Afterward, you'll have several days off and, oh, by the way, yes, you are still in the U.S. Navy. Your pay will continue as usual. Your status is that you remain permanently attached to CENTCOM (Central Command), but you'll travel where you need to and be free of the bureaucratic red tape."

Then Dennis stretched out his arms in a gesture of fatigue and said, "I must be getting old. I must be getting on in years. . . and on to bed." He smiled and added, "In the morning." Chisolm, mentally fatigued, but physically rested, went to his room, put on some running shoes, and went for an evening jog through the country lanes in and around the village.

A WARY INTERVIEW

*Intuition is a knowing, a sensing
that is beyond the conscious
understanding—a gut feeling.*[21]

—Abella Arthur

*International Red Cross Headquarters,
Geneva, Switzerland*

"You understand that this is the Red Cross and not the Red Crescent, of course." Though stated as a matter of fact, the remark was really a question.

"Yes, sir, I understand," replied the interviewee.

Monsieur Yves Delgado, the newly appointed bureau chief for the Red Cross International, home based in Geneva, Switzerland, eyed his prospective employee with a mixture of concern for the well-being of his agency's reputation and suspicion over this man's avowed desire to be a boon to the suffering of humanity. The concern and suspicion were already irrevocably yoked together but somewhat offset by the man's aplomb and fluency in English, French, and Arabic. His passport bore all the appropriate markings of his Moroccan homeland. If it were in fact a forgery, it was masterfully done and obviously executed with a craftsman's skill and with the cooperation of someone working on the inside for the Moroccan government.

Abdallah ibn Machmood's mosque affiliations were innocuous in that they were practically nonexistent. His references were all good albeit somewhat surprising. Even though most of them were individuals from various Muslim relief organizations, organizations in which Delgado had personal friends and other affiliations, none of these people were among his references. Perhaps, he thought, I've been in the office too long. The price of being a good manager. Personal discomfort and sacrifice over the glamour, danger, and personal rewards of fieldwork. He therefore trusted that the letters of recommendation were genuinely sincere.

Delgado looked again at the application with the accompanying photograph. Beardless, that was a good sign. The beards themselves were often a telltale sign of affiliations out of keeping with the Red Cross International's avowed political neutrality. Looking up at the applicant's red hair and blondish-red-eyebrows and dark green eyes, he could not help but think back to his college history classes at the University of Geneva. He recalled specifically a map of the waning days of the Roman Empire with various arrows pointed toward the perimeter of the empire's expanse with names like Huns, Goths, Lombards, and Visigoths. Surely, he thought, this man's coloring and aquiline nose recalled the Visigoths' penetration of North Africa in the fifth century more than dried ink on parchment scrolls and illuminated maps. Either that or the Spanish and French colonialists of more recent centuries had planted seeds in the fecundity of the poor and willingly penetrated.

The conversation dawdled. Delgado could not easily bring himself to confirm a position with the Red Cross. His own hesitancy might be the reason for which Machmood would walk out the door, a prospect whose departure would irritate those who had first sought to bring him into the Red Cross International. He had impressed those who conducted the initial interviews. Discounting his own feelings, he reached across his desk to shake hands and said, "Congratulations, my friend. You will begin work for us immediately." Machmood smiled and his eyes flashed a gleam of intelligence and then immediately clouded at the too-long handshake and too-steady-a-discerning look that told him that the man was assessing his very soul. He nonetheless continued to smile as he loosened his hand from Delgado's grip and thought momentarily of what he had heard about gypsies who engaged in palm reading. He doubted that this was the way it was normally done. But the gypsies, like the *infidels* of the West, were called Romans and therefore not to be trusted.

◆◆◆

Exactly two months later, after some classroom instruction on the history of the Red Cross and indoctrination into its mission, Machmood, because of his language skills, was selected for an unusual but important enterprise. He, along with six other members of the Red Cross International, would fly from Bern, Switzerland, to Jacksonville International Airport in Florida. From there, they would proceed by bus another twenty miles to Naval Air Station Jacksonville, located on the banks of the St. John's River, where they would board a Continental Airlines charter to their final destination.

◆◆◆

Sitting by the window, watching the city of Jacksonville disappear as the plane turned south over the ocean, he snickered at the irony and thanked Allah for his wondrous opportunity. Truly he was blessed and truly Allah had opened before him an opportunity that few could have foreseen. The hands of the Almighty were upon him and would, as it seemed, even hold back the waters to assure his safe arrival at his destination. Moses himself could have asked for no more than he was now receiving. This blessed flight he knew must somehow be the prelude to a divine destiny that would allow him somehow, someway to smite Pharaoh and his folly. As he passed over the azure waters of the Bahamas, he chuckled as he looked at his ticket on which appeared the words "Round Trip." Then he thought of the old saying, "What goes around comes around." *If they only knew.*

THE PRODIGAL SON

> *Your prodigal son has left again to exorcise some demons.*[22]
> —John W. Hinckley, Jr.

Abdallah ibn Machmood disembarked from the military charter from Jacksonville, Florida Naval Air Station to Guantanamo Bay, Cuba. He, along with more than two dozen other members of the Red Cross International, walked from the tarmac to military customs where they were greeted by an array of military police and members of the Public Affairs Office. While they stood in line to await clearance to the badging office where the necessary passes would be issued, two military police handlers in green and black camouflage walked their German shepherds up and down the line sniffing at shoes, camera packs, and computers. Trained to detect even hints of illegal substances from explosives to drugs, they stopped each in turn at the handbag of one of the female members who looked a bit like a disheveled Tina Fey from *Saturday Night Live*, her brown hair fairly unkempt and her eyeglasses slightly askew and her cargo pants and Disney World T-shirt wrinkled and baggy. Forced to open her handbag on a table in front of the others, she dropped a wallet, feminine necessities, and several coins. The MPs looked at the innocuous items and were satisfied that the dogs in all likelihood had sniffed out the telltale signs of marijuana or some other such substance, the residue lingering from who knew what contacts, asked her if she was carrying any illegal or contraband items. She insisted that she was not.

While the MPs questioned her, Machmood tried to maintain a look of complete innocence and composure. His eyes, however, darted from one military policeman to another, looking for signs of recognition. One of the officers looked hard at him as if trying to bring focus to a kaleidoscope of faces. He remained calm until a member of Combat Photography began taking pictures. Though the pictures were intended to validate the safe arrival of the Red Cross members, the fact the Machmood stood right in the middle of the line made it appropriate and unnerving for him that the camera was focused right on him. Dead center, he thought of himself as a target and his heart skipped a beat as the photographer looked directly at him. He realized it was the same combat photographer who had taken his picture almost one year ago to date.

Eventually, with visitor badges in hand, the entire group was escorted to the baggage claim area where the German shepherds were once again busy sniffing the luggage for signs of contraband. As the animals and their handlers left, the members picked up their single piece of allowable luggage and boarded a white school bus and headed to the ferry landing.

THE VOICE

Can it be you that I hear? Let me view you.[23]

-Thomas Hardy, "The Voice"

A voice can be the finger print of the soul.[24]

-J.H.D., "Speaking of Angels"

Petty Officer First Class Christina Tabler walked into Bulkeley Hall on the hilltop overlooking much of Guantanamo Bay on the windward side. She was alert and ready for a full day's work as lead petty officer in the Special Security Office.

Base security identification facilities were situated on the first floor of a pre-World War II building that had weathered the decades with an unmistakable ardor. Its exterior, though still maintaining its bright whiteness, was peeling, its roof was looking old, and the interior had the unmistakable mildew scent of wet wood and stale air. Still, for some, the mahogany railings and hickory floors and the ten-foot-high ceilings and black-and-white photographs of various events and vignettes of Guantanamo's history dating back to its beginning in 1903 were part of the charm. To some, like the chief petty officer walking in the door, even the stale air had an appeal. He liked to think of it as the embalmed breath of his predecessors who were still present and lingered in the hallways and the twenty different rooms in the building. Oddly, the bathrooms with their near-the-ceiling screened rectangular windows were the only rooms in the building with a constant flow of fresh air.

Chief Sean Hawser was a salt of the ocean whose current shore leave for three years at Guantanamo provided him with an opportunity to bring his family to Cuba before his next at-sea assignment. As the head of the Identification Division, constantly working in concert with the SSO, he was well informed and proud of his achievements as a dynamic chief who had worked his way up and through the ranks.

"PO Tabler, good morning. Good to see you. Back from leave, huh? Is America still where we left it?"

"Yep, Chief, still there. Still fun and still home."

"Good. I bet ya had a good time with your family and all."

"Sure did, and…" She paused and held out her left hand.

The chief looked perplexed and then a wide smile crossed his face.

"Does this mean what I think it means?"

"Yes," she said. "We're getting married next year as soon as he comes back from Iraq!"

Others, overhearing the news, surrounded her and offered their delight at her good news. After several minutes of expressions of joy, congratulations, and semi-humorous, "When's the baby due?," the chief called an impromptu meeting.

"We have a plane load that'll be here this afternoon. They're in processing on the leeward side and then they'll boat over to here. They probably won't get here until tomorrow morning for their IDs and checks to make sure they're actually supposed to be here.

"I need all of you to get prepared for tomorrow morning —badges, camera, action!," he exclaimed as he used his hands to snap an imaginary director's shutter.

◆◆◆

The next day, the nonmilitary personnel were escorted in white vans from their rooms at the Bachelor's Officers Quarters to the ID office. PO Tabler greeted them as their base escorts walked the eight members of the International Red Cross to a desk at which they were handed the various processing information that they were required to fill out, including name, affiliations, and nationality.

The first two men to be photographed for the creation of their IDs were familiar faces. They had been to Guantanamo a year earlier. The third man approached her with his paperwork, and she was about to ask him if he thought Cuba would actually be this hot when she caught herself and instead asked, "Have you been here before?"

"No, no." He laughed. "This is my first time. I will translate for the others."

His reddish-brown hair and the telltale signs of faded freckles suggested a European background. But his accent and the fact that he would be translating the English, which most of the Red Cross members spoke, into Arabic for the benefit of the detainees struck Petty Officer Tabler not only as odd, but the voice itself seemed familiar. Most of the translators were themselves Arabs and looked the part. He did not.

She furrowed her brow even as she smiled at him and waved him over to the cameraman.

◆◆◆

An hour later, the members of the International Red Cross walked out of the ID office with their plastic picture badges on blue lanyards with the words *U.S. Navy* imprinted repeatedly along the length of the nylon cord that hung around their necks. With these badges, they would be escorted into Camp Delta where most of the terrorist suspects from the Global War on Terrorism were kept.

Later the same day, Petty Officer Tabler logged into the computer and went to the site of her Non-classified Internet Protocol Router account and tapped into the bank of more than nine hundred unclassified photographs of the former detainees of Guantanamo Bay. As she touched the keys going from one photograph to another, Chief Hawser came over to her desk and said, "What ya lookin' at, people to invite to your wedding? I don't think they'll come but they might send a card."

At first, Tabler did not respond and instead looked flustered.

"Chief, there's something here... something here... I know it. I just can't place it."

"Place what?"

"That Red Cross guy—the one with the red hair. Here, look at his picture."

She navigated to that day's photograph entries, double clicked on his picture to enlarge it, and pointed at it.

"What about him?"

"Do you remember I told you about my other life?"

"You mean when you were an army cop, military police?"

"That life. When after Fort Lewis in Washington, after I finished my training, I was sent to Fort Leavenworth for a stint and then a year later I was sent here. That was 2004. That's the same year we released a number of detainees to their home country. They were repatriated. But then there were several hundred more of them here. But there was one I kind of remember because he just didn't look like the rest. He looks like the Red Cross guy that was here today. But that guy, the detainee…the one I remember had long hair and a long beard."

"But today's guy didn't," replied the chief.

"I know but it's the voice."

"The reason I remember is 'cause a couple of times he would call me names. You know, the usual. But I only saw him for a few weeks and then he was repatriated. This guy…"

Suddenly she stopped. "Look, I'm not going to go over all of these. I just need to know who was repatriated in the summer of 2004."

"We should have that. Combat Photography was required to take pictures of every detainee when they were brought here and again when they left. Look through the data files. It's all public domain type stuff."

As Petty Officer Tabler clicked through the repatriation files associated with detainees who left in the summer of 2004, she began humming the Shaker Hymn to herself, "It's good to be simple, and it's good to be kind. . . "

She stopped humming. "Morocco!," she exclaimed. "That's him!" She then extracted the photograph of detainee 5211 from the Repatriation Review and split the screen to show the photograph of the Red Cross member next to it.

The name under the photograph of the clean-shaven Red Cross member read, "Abdallah ibn

Machmood." The Repatriation Review report read "Idris Ibn Abdallah."

The Red Cross member had a pleasant, almost disarming and beautiful smile, while that of the former Moroccan detainee had a glowering expression.

"I knew it!" Petty Officer Tabler exclaimed triumphantly. She saved both documents, then sent them to the printer.

"If you're sure, we need to get this information to the colonel in charge of the camp and to the intel chief, Rusty Peppers."

◆◆◆

Three hours later, Colonel Winston Bradley, who was in charge of the prison camp, Petty Officer Tabler, and Chief Hawser were sitting behind the door of Rusty Pepper's office.

"Of all the balls. Even I can't believe it. Detainee 5211 coming back as a reformed member of Al-Qaeda."

"I don't know how reformed he is," said the colonel "but I'll give you that, it is ballsy."

"Just when you think you're lucky and one of these killers leaves you, he comes back. He'll deny it, of course."

"Worse, Rusty, we can't stop him even if this is 5211. He can join the Red Cross if he wants. Hell, for all we know he's now a humanitarian."

"Gee, PO Tabler," said Rusty Peppers, humorously, "you must have thought it was my birthday to bring me a present like this one."

Chief volunteered, "She is that way, especially since she got engaged this week."

"Well, that's wonderful," said Peppers. "I hope it's not to this guy."

"No, sir," she laughed. "But he used to work here—he's army. That's how we met."

"Well, GITMO is romantic. Certainly more so than places like Paris. I guess that's why 5211 is back. He misses us and playing hard to get hasn't exactly worked. I never ever wrote him a single letter," he concluded sarcastically. "When they write the musical about this place, I hope we can give him a little song and dance routine. He was such a special guy."

After an awkward pause of nearly a minute, Peppers said, "By the way, thank you for bringing this information to us. It's very helpful. Chief, thank you as well. I'm going to ask that you not share this information with anyone including your coworkers or your mommy and daddy or even that lucky guy that just got engaged."

"Yes, sir," acknowledged PO Tabler and the chief.

"Chief, I'm counting on you."

"Will do, sir."

Peppers stood up to indicate that the meeting was over. He shook both their hands as did the colonel. As PO Tabler was about to depart, Peppers added, "By the way, send me the date for the wedding. I'd like to send a gift. It's the least I can do."

Tabler smiled in response.

After they left the colonel closed the door and sat back down with Peppers.

"Winston," said Peppers, "give me a list of every detainee the Red Cross wants to see as well as the translator for each session. If 5211 now has access to his former buddies, he may be acting as the liaison between them and Al-Qaeda. It's bad enough with the attorneys coming in here. They get 'em to shut up and then they, I've no doubt, share illegal information with the detainees."

"Rusty, I agree. I just wish there were some way to get the attorneys in here with them."

"Some of them, especially the American ones, I wonder how they sleep at night."

"Well, sir, they are lawyers."

"Yeah, maybe we'll get lucky and they'll get attacked by an irate American citizen. Damn sharks. . ."

"Maybe, sir, but first they'll have to know the kind of stuff some of the attorneys do. Then, the . . . well, maybe, who knows?"

"You mean like the fact that one of the law firms representing the victims of 9/11 is also representing a number of the detainees here on base? If the American public, if the victims of 9/11 knew that, they might actually question the motives, the actions, the integrity of these lawyers. I wonder if they eat their young."

SPEAKING IN TONGUES

> *Something enormous is always lost in translation.*
> *Something insidious seeps into the gaps.*[25]
>
> –Amy Tan, "The Language of Discretion"

Wearing a green sport coat and a pair of off-white pants, the translator momentarily forgot himself and began to lead the three-man procession into a cell where Detainee 9696 was already waiting, his right leg shackled to the floor and both of his arms comfortably folded across his chest. As the translator was escorted into the room by the guard, he blanched at the sight of the detainee and froze, causing the two experienced International Red Cross aides to bump into him.

The guard stood aside waiting. Finally, Machmood recovered himself and walked to the table and chairs seated next to the detainee. The guard left the room, shutting the door behind him. The detainee looked up, unconcerned, and puzzled by the peculiar demeanor of the translator.

The two regular aides, one of whom was English and spoke no other languages, were completely dependent upon the translator. The other, an Argentine, spoke halting English and fluent Spanish. Their waiting after asking questions to first hear the detainee's response and then again for the translator's interpretation of the reply made them his dependents.

The first several questions were perfunctory, little more than cordialities concerning the weather, the detainee's general comfort, and the questions that he himself might have concerning his own detention. At first, the detainee eyed the Red Cross members warily, wondering if they were in fact who they claimed to be. He wondered, in particular, at the smallest of the three-man team who was only five feet six inches tall, but whose biceps belied an obsession, supposedly helping the suffering masses of humanity and individuals wherever they had the misfortune to be. His somewhat sly smile only added to the detainee's suspicion. That he was being questioned in English with an Arabic translator told him that his own indiscretion on board the plane of replying in English to one of the guards had apparently not found its way into the report provided by Guantanamo indoctrination authorities to the International Red Cross. He played along, answering each question in Arabic despite the discomfort caused by the translator who seemed to be glaring at him.

As Machmood began to translate, Detainee 9696 noticed for the first time that his "g" and "k" sounds were distinctly North African, Moroccan, or Algerian. Relieved that he could once again conceal his true identity, he replied with a mixture of Arabic dialects that would have befitted the construction team responsible for the Tower of Babel.

Twenty minutes into the session, the translator began to ask questions of the detainee that were beyond that of merely translating into Arabic what the other two Red Cross members had been asking. None of them knew that the detainee already understood the questions, which they conveyed to the translator.

Once the usual pleasantries concerning his health and general treatment were answered, the Red Cross team leader said, "The Americans tell us that you are not who you say you are."

"Who do they say I am if I am not me?"

"The say you were picked up near Kandahar, unconscious, after a firefight with a group of Taliban and Al-Qaeda members."

Feigning ignorance of the English in which the man addressed him, Detainee 9696 looked at Machmood for translation before responding. "I did somethings a while ago, but I cannot remember so well. My head hurts. I cannot always remember."

As Machmood translated the comment from Arabic into English, the lead man for the Red Cross asked, again and again, "Are you ill? Do you think you have a concussion?"

He then asked, "Have the Americans offered to x-ray your head? Maybe . . ." Before he could finish asking the question, Machmood was squinting at the detainee as if trying to discern something buried inside the man's body. Suddenly his eyes brightened and he looked at him with the same jaundiced expression with which the combat photographer had viewed him as he was being photographed after first landing at Guantanamo. All the while he continued translating until a midsentence epiphany occurred. His eyes narrowed in an accusatory glare as he ignored the lead man's remarks and said in Arabic, "You are a dead man."

At one point, the detainee listened not to the translator conveying a question in Arabic, but to Machmood's dismissal of the first several answers to some of even the most innocuous questions. The translator, taking full advantage of the ignorance of his Red Cross aid workers, slipped in several of his own comments.

"Why don't you tell us the real reasons you are here? We thought you were dead. One of your own told us they had killed you. The drone that hit was planned. Someone had to tell them our location. You betrayed us."

The detainee was at first confused but merely furrowed his brow in response, and then relaxed and replied as if he actually understood what the translator was alluding to. "Sometime we do what we must."

"So do we, and I must tell you, we have access even into the camp. Before we leave here, we want more information. Who did you talk to? Did you bring the Predator drone into our camp?"

Detainee 9696 then smiled at Machmood and sat silently. Finally, the other two Red Cross members assured 9696 that they were concerned for his well-being and would remain in camp for several more days if he wished to speak with them.

As they were leaving, Machmood turned once more and said in a low voice while smiling at 9696, "You are a dead man. Redeem yourself."

Since he spoke it in Arabic, the other two men thought he was merely extending yet one more message indicating their willingness to help.

◆◆◆

Machmood continued to translate through the next two days but, in fact, was ready to leave Guantanamo. He had learned something in the interview with 9696 that his past associates would want to know and who would look upon him with new respect because of his current status as a plant in the Red Cross International and his access to his former comrades. So far, he assumed he had carried out his responsibilities without arousing the suspicion of his superiors. Each day he walked from Camp Delta to the Sea Side Galley with his team. There, in the presence of numerous U.S. military personnel as well as contractors from the Department of Defense, he had breakfast, lunch, and dinner. He smiled politely at guards who sometimes came directly to the chow hall still wearing the shin guards and other paraphernalia of those involved in what was known as an FCE, a forced cell extraction. A procedure required by guards to remove hostile detainees from their cell, it was a technique perfected by guards that made it very difficult to get a good kick or punch to the body of the "custodians," as the guards sometimes called themselves. If not for their green and black camouflage uniforms, one might have mistaken them for catchers in search of a baseball game. Many of the accoutrements were worn for a similarly protective function. Machmood grinned as he ate. In the evenings, he walked from his room at Bachelor's Officers Quarters to Sherman Avenue, the only major road that ran through most of the base on the windward side, and settled in with other members of the Red Cross at the Tiki Bar.

One of the oldest continuously existing bars at any U.S. Navy base outside the continental United States, it looked like a re-creation of the setting for South Pacific with an outdoor bar, a large open-air tent for protection from sun and rain, and several other tables and chairs situated under the warm Cuban night. He was Daniel in the lion's den. Only now the lion was asleep.

He looked out over the quiet of Guantanamo Bay and the twinkling harbor lights and the distant necklace of lights that stretched the seventeen-mile perimeter of the base and wondered. He was seeing it with new eyes in a new way. For the first time, the tranquility of the nighttime ambiance of Cuba's affability with its Jamaican bartenders and Filipino waiters and waitresses seeped into him, muting, briefly, his hostility and massaging his tense body. For a moment the chatter of revenge that constantly beckoned ceased, and his body relaxed and the near headachy tension of his neck and shoulders fell away. For a moment, imaginative nature with its warm breath of evening breeze held a finger to the lips of destructive demons. Momentarily silenced by peace, Machmood looked about to hear, as if from a distance, his own name spoken. His reverie ended, he laughed at a joke he had not heard and caught a glimpse of a lifestyle to which he might have surrendered in a moment. If only Allah had not called to him. If only *jihad* were not everlasting.

◆◆◆

That evening, several miles away at the Joint Intelligence Center, FBI personnel and a member of the Criminal Investigative Task Force (CITF) were examining the latest report from the Fort Belvoir DNA Center in Virginia. Perplexed at the findings which had been e-mailed to each, they had immediately sought out the other in hopes of finding an explanation. Confounded, they agreed to seek a meeting with the Joint Intelligence Group director first thing in the morning.

THE DAY OF SORROW

Then something in me moved to prophesy
Against the beloved stand-offishness of marble.[26]

-Seamus Heaney, "xxxviii"

Grounds of the Former Jannat Al-Baqi Cemetery,
Medina, Saudi Arabia

With several days off merely to observe the holy
sites of Arabia, Haban al-Amur drove not to
Mecca but to Medina, a place devoid of shrines,
devoid of vegetation, devoid of mosques or any
place where a man might be inclined to seek
out the spirit of Allah. But Haban knew, he
thought, as much by a presence that lingered
in a wavy motion above the asphalt as by the
road map and the Wikipedia description that
he held in his hands. Here in this hot and
seemingly nondescript area of desolation had
once dwelt the most important of men. Here
in this parking lot, beneath its surface, lay the
mortal remains of Imam Hasan al-Mujtaba,
Imam Mohammad al-Baqir, and even Lady
Fatima Zahra, among others.

As he gazed upon the liveliness of a parking lot that represented the nondescript and intimacy-destroying touch of revolutionary zeal and the Lethe-like forgetfulness of modernity in all its seduction, as well as the crippling effect of secularity, he shuddered at the minds that had done this. He wondered at the true lack of reverence, the lack of regard, the lack of insight, and the lack of tenderness that seemed to want to destroy anything that was not of its own image. Here might have been the dwelling place not of a prophet but rather of Narcissus, constantly seeking out his own image even as he simultaneously asserted his desire to destroy it and anything else that might have even hinted at idolatry. These zealots would destroy all so that life itself would be as severe and as barren as the desert from which their god was created. He wondered at those who had done this. Could their god truly be his god?

From Buddhist shrines in Afghanistan to Hindi temples in Pakistan to ancient pagan cave and rock paintings in North Africa, they felt compelled to deface and destroy the telltale signs of humanity's ancestors. The severity of their presence was always the same, the abrasive sweep of sandblasts against tokens of man's spiritual aspirations until they were granulated, powdered, and wind gone. For men such as these each year was the year zero, each year was the beginning again of man's triumph over the past by means of destroying any semblance of its being. For them, each moment was an eternal now with no connection to the past and no need for a future. For them, life was not continuous, only an everlasting and utterly futile attempt to attain perfection by denying man's imperfectability even as they sought to squelch all corruption through violence, egotism, ruthlessness, and the inherent duplicity of their own desire for power. For them there was only *is* without a *was* or a *would be.*

As he walked, he knew that here may once have been the delights of ancient families who loved one another. And here may have been the remains of those who listened to the Holy Prophet as he spoke. And here were the remains of his children, his aunts, his uncles, and friends. As the scalding desert hovered above the asphalt, he imagined the heat waves that wavered and distorted his vision of the worldliness all about him as a sign of the spirits of the dead who yet lingered. Some were anonymous and, he thought, endearing in their facelessness, once sun-browned people who blended almost artfully if unintentionally with the sand until they stained it with their blood and lingered as if to cultivate their own remains. He heard and felt their presence as a soft and most faint whisper of saintly folk who strove in obscurity to live in submission and wisdom beneath the gaze of a god who he hoped was as forgiving as he was demanding. Then, in a spontaneous gesture of affection for those whose names he did not know as well as those he did, he bowed his head and brought his hands to his face and whispered a blessing on their behalf to the god who he knew could hear his voice before his prayer was even uttered. Then he wept softly to know what had been done and at the knowledge of what he knew he himself must soon do.

He turned to Masjid al-Nabawi, the mosque in which Mohammad himself is said to be buried. Looking at a distance upon its grandeur and the pilgrims that came and went, he wondered at a Salafist regime that could construct such an edifice devoted to Allah, but which could crush the bones beneath its soil of the son of the Prophet whose remains lay within. Such a regime was anathema and killed and pillaged in the name of Allah and vanquished its foes with an acidic burn of the uncompromising zealot, who could subdue others but not his own appetite for power, oil money, and the lust for Western excesses. The excesses defiled the soul and turned praise of Allah into a mockery, a kind of urbane blasphemy that tempered true mercy with hostility, self-righteousness, and pitiful consumerism. They were lost.

THE PLEASURES OF THE TAKFIRI (OR THE VEILED THREAT)

> *They have no power, they do not produce children;*
> *They are strangers to benevolence. . .*
> *They are agents of vengeance.*[27]
> Francois Lenormant, *Chaldean Magic:*
> *Its Origin and Development*

Grounds Outside Topkapi Palace, Istanbul

"What do you want? You hate the Americans. You hate the British, and, of course, you hate the Israelis. In fact, you hate all the West. But you also hate the Muslims," replied Adnan al-Katani.

"Bin Laden said that if we must kill ten million Americans, it is permitted in the name of Islam."

"I don't care about Bin Laden."

"You should!" Najar said angrily.

"He is not out here risking his life as we are. Besides, you should know, I should tell you, I almost refused to work with you. I was afraid you might be like your cousin."

"My cousin is *takfiri*."

"Your cousin also has his head up the donkey's ass. Besides, unlike you, I have actually met Bin Laden."

"You have? Where? When?" He asked with his eyes wide open.

"It was in the 1990s not long after he declared *jihad* against the Americans. I was a guest of Tariq Aziz, the former prime minister of Saddam Hussein. I was staying at the El Rashid Hotel in Baghdad. I was introduced to the man. When I shook his hand, I saw how he was tall, soft spoken, and very gentle. Very gentle. We are here, he is not."

"Yes, gentle, but firm, I think."

Katani said nothing in reply. Najar took his silence as an opportunity to continue.

"In my world, sacrilege will be forbidden and even the Turk will be brought back into the *umma*."

"My friend, I know you are sincere, but let me tell you something. I do what we are about to do because I want my life back. My father is Palestinian. But because of this marriage, I am welcome nowhere. I cannot live in Jordan. I am unwelcome in the actual place of my birth in Lebanon. Only in the Bekaa Valley can I live—there in a tent where the Syrians and the Iranians use us like stooges, cannon fodder against the Israelis. So I suppose, like you, I must hate them too. So you see, between the two of us, I suppose, we hate them all, everyone, including ourselves."

At this remark, Najar smiled ever so slightly and the almost imperceptible nod of his head suggested that he actually understood. But before another remark could be uttered, Najar again interrupted and said, "Yes, I hate in the name of Allah and for this I am willing to die."

"As are all *takfiris*, but I think it may take more courage to live."

He then glanced up at the expanse of the Hippodrome Park where once charioteers of various political factions of ancient Byzantium raced before the emperor and thousands of others. There, standing beneath the height of a great stone and mortar obelisk of Constantine the Great, stood four women completely covered in their black burkas with nothing showing except their eyes. Yet another wore a veil that covered even her eyes. As Katani and Najar watched, they each in turn had their pictures taken before the monument. When the last of these was finished, the one who was completely veiled, Katani turned again and said, "Look at them and tell me, what is the point. Sometime I think they are like you and me. They should have one picture taken and four copies made. For no one can tell one from another. Their dress is as anonymous as their pictures are stupid. Maybe, I think, they are like us." For once, Najar had no reply.

AT THE GATE OF SALUTATION

> *If one had but a single glance to give the world,*
> *one should gaze on Istanbul.*[28]
>
> –Alphonse de Lamartine

The Courtyard of Topkapi Palace, Turkey

The one-time palatial estate of the sultan who ruled over the expanse that once was the mighty Ottoman Empire is situated on a hill that overlooks the Golden Horn, the five mile expanse of water that splits Istanbul in two. From here looking to his left, the sultan could survey the merchant ships and vessels of war plying the waters of the straights of the Bosphorus. These waters which lay to his right squeezed the Mediterranean and Black Sea into a narrow channel that in turn squeezed merchants from other nations for tribute to ensure safe passage. And from here the sultan squeezed out the will to resist among the Christian nations, Muslim insurgents, Kurdish rebels, and Balkan Slavs who were compelled to traverse these waters.

Outside the Gate of Salutation, through which one passed into the Topkapi complex of several courtyards and hundreds of individual rooms, stood a figure in a maroon business shirt with a droopy black mustache, black hair, and black morning stubble that caught the sweat of his face and neck. His pants were also black and had the peasant worn look of rural Turkey, somewhat faded, slightly shiny, and threadbare. From the bottom protruded the distinctly pointy-toed shoes worn by men in much of Eastern Europe and the eastern Mediterranean world. His dark eyes were succinct in their gaze, turning away immediately upon meeting the eyes of his suspected contacts, as if a brief glimpse sent a coded message, which a longer look might negate.

As Katani and Najar passed by, this figure, who had stood like a natural impediment in the rush of people moving upstream against the steady and pronounced incline that led through the various courtyards with their gardens, turned and followed without a word.

Finally, as they each stopped to purchase the ticket into the palace interior with its various rooms and museums, their contact motioned for them to step to one side near a tree not yet infested with the tourists. There they sat down on a low wall that outlined flower gardens of hydrangeas, the windflower, the crocus, and the tulip, the national flower of Turkey.

In hushed conversation, he offered that they would soon enter on their left the Chamber of the Sacred Relics in which the objects of concern were on display. As they cued to enter, a gang of Japanese tourists, led by a guide holding up a cardboard red and white Rising Sun flag of imperial Japan, burst in front of them, slowing their entry and delaying their observation of the sacred. At last they entered the hall in which they gazed in turn upon the sword of King David, which the Israeli Prime Minister had recently tried to purchase, the swords of the Four Righteous Caliphs, and finally the most revered objects in the Islamic world, objects of the Prophet himself. These included a sword, a bow, his seal, strands of his beard, his tunic, and even a tooth. With the exception of the seal, all were housed either in ornately designed scabbards, boxes of gold, silver, and gems, or by some other means completely concealed. It was largely on faith that the observer looked upon each object as truly holding the remains referenced. The sacred were veiled.

As they slowly moved past the objects, Katani wondered at their authenticity while Najar simmered in anger at yet another display of idolatry against which he, as a true *takfiri*, a

Salafist, and Wahhabist, had been reared to despise. And so he did.

Their contact merely looked on impatiently as he once again measured the steps from one corner of the room to another. Najar continued to brood as he noticed the chatty Japanese tourists and their constant indifference to the incantatory singing of the Koran by the muezzin in an adjoining room who recited from the morning until the museum's closing. He also looked upon the letter that Mohammad had written urging the leaders of Egypt to submit to Islam and to himself as Allah's Prophet. How he wished that this one object could be released to him alone so that he could unleash these words again upon an unrepentant world given to the sins of idolatry, materialism, and arrogance. Then the caliphate might reemerge and the imam, whether hidden or apparent, would once again lead the armies of Islam in victory over the *infidels* and the apostates.

HONORED GUESTS

> *We are privileged; this medal that I wear around my neck is for all service members.*[29]
>
> —Colonel Robert L. Howard (Retired),
> Medal of Honor recipient

Guantanamo Airport, Leeward Side

As the Continental 737 came to a complete stop at the end of the runway, the captain of the plane came over the intercom and reminded everyone to take all their possessions as they disembarked into the 100 degree Cuban air. He then added, "As we prepare to leave, please allow the following military personnel to disembark first. Congressional Medal of Honor Recipients...and LCDR Grant Chisolm."

Chisolm winced at this inclusion, thinking that these gentlemen should be allowed to disembark alone, without the distraction of his presence. However, he left his seat as the fully loaded plane of passengers watched silently and respectfully. He moved in behind the last of the three gentlemen who walked out onto the gangway and descended the ramp, the sun glaring, and their smiles beaming at the welcoming committee of the base commander and the usual array of flight mechanics and others standing by to minister to the plane's and the passengers' needs.

The base commander, dressed in his summer whites, shook the hand of each of the Medal recipients and handed them a Guantanamo honorary coin. As Chisolm stood facing him, the commander extended his hand and apologized for having no more coins. Chisolm smiled and shook his hand, recognizing the commander's consternation at having nothing to give him. Chisolm offered, "Sir, I'm here on orders."

"Oh, oh, thank goodness. I didn't understand how I could have been misinformed. Of course, you're very young. But maybe you received the award in Afghanistan or Iraq—who would know?"

"Sir," replied Chisolm, "I'm not one of them. I'm the new liaison officer to GITMO on behalf of CENTCOM."

"Finally," said the commander. "We've wondered when they'd send someone. How can they not take advantage of the intel we gather here!"

Chisolm smiled and walked toward the hangar and an array of military and civilian personnel who waited to pick up the luggage and the people from the aircraft. A white Explorer van pulled up just outside the doors of the hangar. The Medal of Honor recipients and Chisolm got in. The driver shut their door, hopped back in, and pulled away.

Minutes later, the van arrived at the pier where a car and ferry were waiting to take them across to the windward side of Guantanamo Bay. The *Sea Crest 92* was moored with a steel gangplank already lowered into place to allow on and off traffic.

The ship departed, and within several minutes, the inlet on which the ship traveled converged with the Guantanamo River. The river immediately tugged at Chisolm's sense of curiosity. It was populated with mangroves on both sides so that land itself was completely hidden beneath a world of vegetation. As he looked at the quiet waters now being agitated by the ship's wake, he wondered what lay beneath.

GREETINGS AND SURVEYS

> *How fiercely, devoutly wild is Nature in the midst of her beauty-loving tenderness.*[80]
>
> -John Muir, *The Yosemite*

That evening, Chisolm found himself in his new quarters just off Sherman Road, the only major highway on the base. The housing complex was primarily for contractors and guests but housed military personnel when billeting was at a premium. At Windward Loop, Grant found himself sharing quarters with a lieutenant commander from Dallas, Texas. Their hacienda-like structure consisted of imitation adobe and earthquake and hurricane-resistant concrete and steel with a nod to the prospect of artillery and tank bombardment from communist Cuba and its one-time guests, soldiers, and sailors of the former Soviet Union. It was as sturdy as a bomb shelter. Despite the solidity, the interior plaster and exterior gave off an ambiance of warmth and friendliness consistent with the festive atmosphere that Cuba still rendered in the minds of earlier generations of Americans.

Chisolm immediately unpacked his running shorts, shoes, T-shirt, and a fluorescent safety belt, so as to be seen by passing motorists. As he stepped outside into the still shining sun and its intense heat, a car pulled into the driveway. A woman in a U.S. army sergeant's desert camouflage uniform immediately got out of her white SUV.

"Good evening, sir, my name is Sergeant Sherry Mumford."

She saluted Chisolm and offered, "I am your immediate contact and your assistant. I work for you. I'll be taking you around the base tomorrow to help get you situated and work through the various security provisions."

Sherry Mumford was a five feet six inch dynamo with thick wavy auburn hair that she tucked deliberately and stylishly beneath her army camouflage cap so that tantalizing curls unfurled over her temples, giving her a slightly cavalier coquettishness. Her movements were lithe, limber, and almost girlish. She was in her middle twenties and her personally hemmed and reconfigured Battle Dress Uniform (BDU) did little to conceal a figure that was well honed by a daily routine of running and calisthenics, as well as swimming and pickup volleyball games. In an official and forward way, she indicated, "Zero seven hundred, sir, we'll head over to the Hill Top Galley for breakfast and then onto the various stations. You'll need all your paperwork. We'll get you all set up to do your job, sir."

"Thank you, Sergeant. I look forward to working with you."

"I'll see you tomorrow morning, sir."

As she backed her SUV out of the driveway, Grant followed, down the hill, toward Sherman Road, and onto the sidewalk that paralleled the several-mile stretch of highway. At the bottom of the hill, Chisolm turned right and continued jogging, not knowing exactly where he was going but feeling the need to percolate his blood with an hour run. As he coursed the highway, he spied a tarantula stepping out from the brush along the sidewalk. At his approach, the brush moved excitedly as the ever-present and abundant banana rats and an occasional iguana sought to put distance between themselves and Grant. Ten minutes into his run, Chisolm saw a sign that said "Restricted Area." Ignoring it, he continued along Sherman Road.

The road traversed low-lying marsh on his left and brush and cactus to his right as if he were crossing over the divide between ocean surge and a desert. A mile past the sign, as

Chisolm began a long, slow climb, heading in a northeasterly direction, off to his right was another sign. This one, like the other, warned passersby to stay clear of the immediate vicinity and "No Photography." A football field away was a dilapidated complex of wooden frames and corrugated metal roofs of open bay housing surrounded by barbed wire enmeshed in creeping vines that all but obliterated from view entire sections of the complex.

Chisolm glanced at yet another sign that warned that by an act of Congress "this complex is off limits" to all but select personnel. Since the complex was entirely deserted, Chisolm wondered at the restrictions. Despite his curiosity, he continued on his run, remembering the numerous occasions in which he had seen photographs of this facility on various news broadcasts. Covered by vegetation and blasted by heat and sun, it lay tired, old, diminished, and unworthy of further attention.

As he crested the long hill, he looked up at a pair of large rectangular stone pillars, twice a man's height, on either side of the road directly opposite one another. *Tank traps*, he thought. Something capable of being detonated and collapsing across the road. They stood as solitary sentinels, the legacy of the Cold War in which the US military awaited a Russian-Cuban invasion of U.S. Naval Station Guantanamo.

To either side were signs warning of the dangers of leaving the highway to walk in either the tidal basin waters on his left or the desert on his right. The area had once been heavily mined and the fear was that even after its de-mining several years earlier, some of those mines had moved because of the softness of the soil. Those never found might yet explode from even the slightest pressure of the unwary passerby.

Chisolm slowed at the top of the hill, a three-Humvee convoy of U.S. Marines approaching him from the rear. He stopped and watched as they passed, one of them in the rear car pointed at Chisolm and then made a gesture with his thumb indicating that he should head back in the direction from which he had just come.

Chisolm watched as they passed and then looked off into the distance at the mountain on the Cuban side of Guantanamo that overlooked the entire base. He turned and headed back toward his housing, wondering about the various buildings to his right that stood isolated on occasional peninsulas that thrust into the otherwise swampy terrain. Here and there stood tan buildings with an array of antennas and windowless walls—only mortar, cement, and the bleached-out sand surrounded them.

As he crossed the street that led up hill to his apartment, he again spied a tarantula, this one converging with the brush and about to disappear. He looked up and saw two vultures circling overhead as well as a *lignum vitae* tree in full bloom. He considered briefly but poignantly that at that moment he was surrounded by nature in all its lethality and beauty, a blend that sent a shiver down his spine.

MEETING THE MOVERS

> *...Our brotherhood speaks in deeds not words...*[31]
> -Thomas Gluzinski, "Brotherhood of Silence"

The next morning, Sherry Mumford picked up Grant promptly at 0700 and escorted him through the variety of inductions and indoctrinations required of all military and civilian personnel coming to GITMO. By the time they had finished, Grant was equipped with a car, a meal pass, and all the necessary information to make him a member of the GITMO Joint Task Force, the entity that dealt with enemy combatants housed at Guantanamo. The Global War on Terrorism had long ago reached Cuban shores, but here, the lethality of the encounters was lessened by the confinement of the detainees, the separation from their military arsenal, and the constant vigilance of their captors.

In the early afternoon, Chisolm and Mumford, for the very first time together, passed through the checkpoint manned by members of the Puerto Rican National Guard. Several soldiers in full combat regalia guarded the to-and-fro gateway of the Joint Task Force. Sherry and Grant showed their military IDs and their special access passes for the compound. To their right, as they passed the guard booth, stood a military Humvee with a .50 caliber machine gun on top. At that moment, it was being held by another soldier also suited up in a helmet, bulletproof vest, and other gear deemed essential for someone who might be attacked or forced to confront deadly enemies. As they passed the gate area, Chisolm eyed the shrubs and desiccated vegetation on either side. If he did not know that he was in Cuba, he might have mistaken the area for Texas, Arizona, or New Mexico. But where the highways there held signs warning of illegal immigrant traffic, here they only warned of the $10,000 fine for killing an iguana.

Only a few hundred yards beyond, at a Y in the road, Chisolm saw the camp itself, the primary housing and recreational yard of several hundred enemy combatants from the war. Here detainees from Afghanistan, Yemen, Saudi Arabia, Iraq, Morocco, Tunisia, as well as a number of other countries in Europe, including England, and France, as well as numerous countries in Central and South Africa passed the days, the weeks, the months, and sometimes the years far from their homeland and near the intelligence gathering facilities of the United States military.

Mumford turned her van right at the Y, the camp to her left and parking lot for guards, translators, interrogators, and a variety of auxiliary personnel on the right. A half mile down the road, she pulled her van into the Sea Side Galley where she and Chisolm stepped out of the air-conditioned vehicle into the forever-hot Cuban sun. The Galley itself was a Quonset hut airplane hangar converted into a kitchen. Spacious, and looking like the eviscerated remains of some giant insect, the exterior corrugation reminded Grant of a beetle's abdomen. The Sea Side Galley was bright, well ventilated, and aromatic in its daily presentation of the military staples of garden salads, potatoes, rice, a meat or two to choose from, and sweets for dessert like pudding and pie. Chisolm grabbed a burger and salad along with a cup of coffee and a glass of water. Sherry selected from the salad bar and covered it in fat-free Italian.

The side doors of the galley were open to a vista for which tourists and beachcombers might have paid a premium, the deep blue of the Caribbean as it swarmed in majesty and beauty against the rugged rocks and concrete reinforced buffer that prevented erosion and kept the Galley poised permanently, even if in an unlikely place. As Chisolm and Sergeant Mumford discussed their backgrounds and the whys and wherefores of military careers, Grant almost reflexively kept looking out to sea. On the horizon, were two large passenger ships, possible cruise line vessels that seemed to be heading in their direction. Mumford, noticing his gaze, offered, "They come here quite a bit. They get as close as they can without causing trouble. The tourists want to see the detainees, the camp, us. We're all celebrities these days."

"Who else watches us?"

"Well, if you take a good look around, you'll notice that many of the hills, ours and theirs, have buildings on top. The ones on the Cuban side are thought to be peopled with Cubans, of course, and Chinese. The Commies listen to us and we listen to them. That's one reason we don't all wear our name tags all the time. With the binoculars they have they can probably read ours. At the very least they know what we look like. Besides, the ChiComms want this base and are hoping to generate enough ill will against us that they and the libs in Congress will pressure us into moving out. Then they'll take over. Just like the Panama Canal. We gave it up. Now the Chinese run it. That was stupid."

The last comment was intended to enlist Chisolm's support before she went off on a tirade against bleeding heart liberals. But Chisolm remained silent as he again stared out to sea amidst bites of his burger.

◆◆◆

Late in the afternoon, Chisolm was escorted to the security officer in the primary facility for intelligence gathering and evaluation of the threats to the United States and its allies posed by the various detainees at what the guards derisively referred to as Club GITMO. These were the detainees captured primarily as a result of U.S. action in Afghanistan with its British and other NATO allies.

This was a two-tiered brick building with a cantilevered metal roof to fend off the occasional torrential downpours and the perpetual glare of the Cuban sun. Situated within walking distance of the Sea Side Galley and just off the main prison compound road, it was poised directly opposite one of the base's three outdoor theaters. Here, film viewers were treated nightly to first run movies from the United States that gave a sense of normalcy to the otherwise occasionally isolating and claustrophobic world of Naval Station Guantanamo. The building backed up to a ridge that was marked off by a fence and the occasional warning signs. Several outlying barracks, gymnasiums, administrative quarters, and a small exchange for purchasing the assortment of products one would normally expect to find in a cross between a 7-Eleven and a pier-side bait shop were clustered together. The area beyond them, beyond the fence line, was off limits to all but a few select personnel. To ensure restrictions were maintained, the guard compound, named Camp America, lay adjacent to an area not far from the ocean. Here the prison guards and staff were housed in an assembly of prefabricated green ship container-like boxes equipped with air conditioning and showers.

Inside, Chisolm showed his badge to the watch officer situated behind a large desk console immediately opposite the main doorway. Along with Sergeant Mumford, he climbed the stairway to the second floor. As he stepped out of the stairwell, he approached a cipher lock which required that he punch in his newly acquired PIN as he slid his badge through the scanner.

Upon entering, Chisolm and Sergeant Mumford walked down a corridor of walls decorated with black-and-white photographs of Guantanamo's picturesque past, going back more than a hundred years. The door to the security manager's office was closed. The door, however, had a sign that read "Edward DeMolay, Security Manager, Keeper of Secrets." As Sergeant Mumford was about to knock on the door, it opened.

"Hi, I knew you were coming. That's my job, to know things—I'm the keeper of the hidden knowledge," the security manager said playfully.

"Hello, Edward. This is Lieutenant Commander Grant Chisolm. He's here for the indoctrination brief. I'm sure you'll fill him in."

She then turned to Chisolm and added, "I'll come back to get you in about an hour."

"Okay."

"Lieutenant Commander Chisolm, Edward DeMolay, former U.S. Army, former U.S. Navy, and currently DIA and Keeper of the Keys."

DeMolay was big, loud, and friendly. His mop of black, unruly hair, goatee, and Fu Manchu mustache seemed to be an elder's rebellion against more than thirty years of military regimentation. Now a civilian worker for the government, he sat back in a relatively plush chair of his own provision. Grant sat and listened as DeMolay filled him in on the do's and don'ts while working behind the wire at GITMO.

Ten minutes into DeMolay's spiel, another civilian walked in with some paperwork. He laid the forms on DeMolay's desk and then turned and exclaimed, "Grant! Grant Chisolm! How the hell are ya? I didn't know you were comin' here. I've been on leave. Man oh man. Hey, waz up?"

DeMolay looked on for a moment and said, "Grant, I got a meeting to attend. Later."

Chisolm stood up and was about to shake hands when the other man put his arms around him and patted him on the back.

"I didn't expect to see you, either," replied Chisolm as he returned the hug. "The last time we saw each other was at the debriefing in Fort Benning."

"Yeah, that's where it was. You and a few other squids mixed in with the few leathernecks training with the true warriors—go Army," he chided playfully.

"Remember, I'm a SEAL, a sea, land, and air guy. So yeah, we can drop out of the sky right into Club GITMO. You know, before we drop into the sea, we can even pull an Eighty Second Airborne stunt and land in the dirt. You're not the only people that like to jump out of perfectly good airplanes."

"Guess not, buddy."

Max Dolchyk was a sandy-haired six-footer with a thick neck and ruddy complexion perched atop a slope-shouldered torso with long gangly arms protruding from a short-sleeved blue shirt. His khaki cargo pants were de rigueur for half of the base's intelligence officers and FBI types and any other would-be-assassins, daredevils, and government contractors wishing to create an aura of authority greater than their actual fit and responsibility. Few, if any, were actually licensed to kill.

As he moved to sit down, Max Dolchyk limped noticeably.

Chisolm asked, "What happened? Your leg?"

"Well, yes. Since last we saw each other, while you were glorifying yourself in the deserts and the mountains of bad places, I was spending my winter in the mountains of Bosnia. Jesus, is it cold up there! I suffered frostbite and permanent injury. Hard to believe, huh? I lost one toe and part of my left foot. Frostbite! Who woulda thunk it? I'm on a disability, no more warrior stuff. Just government spooky stuff now. How about you?"

"I'm coming on board as the Liaison Officer for the Central Command. I'll be working closely with our intel units in Baghdad."

"So, Grant, what do you do for recreation these days? There's a lot to do here. Our little base in the sun may only be forty-seven square miles of a tropical paradise, but we have the best Morale, Welfare, and Recreation (MWR) this side of Greenwich."

"I hear the diving here is challenging and fun."

"Spoken like a true SEAL. Why don't we hook up later? If you've some time this weekend, we can go to the dive shop, grab some tanks and gear, and head out to one of the reefs."

"I haven't been diving in almost a year, and I don't have any of my own gear."

"The base dive shop has everything you need. And that includes masks, snorkels, neoprene suits—you name it, they got it. It's even got water and salt for the ocean. I think they've got the iodine too. And they're open until twenty hundred hours on Thursday. We can go over and pick up your equipment then."

While Chisolm and Dolchyk reminisced and made plans, Sergeant Mumford again entered the room.

"Well, it's time to meet the big boss."

Dolchyk gave Grant a thumbs up, winked at Mumford, and said, "Listen to her, she knows her stuff."

Chisolm and Sergeant Mumford walked down the hallway past a series of cubicles housing various analysts and administrative personnel. As they approached the door, Sergeant Mumford offered, "He's expecting you. I've made the appointment. I'll wait out here. Go on in."

On the semi-closed door was a sign that read "Rusty Peppers, Director of Intelligence Operations, Operation Greenland. Warming the globe with you in mind."

Grant knocked on the door causing it to open a few more inches. The director looked up from his desk.

"I've been expecting you. Have a seat."

The director then mumbled something to himself as he glanced back up and to his left at a computer screen filled with a list of e-mails. He shuffled some papers on his desk, stacked them neatly, and placed a cover sheet on the top that read "Secret." As he was about to get up from his desk, his phone rang.

"Dear Lord, make them go away. I'm not doing this for fun." He started to reach for the phone, looked at the LED that gave the caller's number, and said, "I'm too damn busy. Call the pope. Maybe he'll have answers for 'em."

Then he got up, walked past Chisolm to the doorway, and said, "Jackie, hold all my calls for the next hour."

Rusty Peppers. His name was appropriate. At five feet six inches tall, he was not someone that would easily attract attention at first. But as Chisolm would soon learn, and as others already knew, he had a wry sense of humor, a gruff exterior, a fiery temper, and a genuinely keen insight into matters political, ethical, and logical as they pertained to his profession as an intelligence officer. His insights into human psychology had made him a superior interrogator.

His longish sandy brown hair seemed like the legacy of a surfer's past that might at first have made him more a candidate for Malibu than Guantanamo. But at sixty-eight years of age, he was more apt to reminisce about his days in the U.S. Army while in Vietnam, Grenada, Panama, and Iraq than about rolls, pipelines, and hangs.

As he turned around to face Chisolm, who was now seated at a round conference table with four chairs, Peppers asked, "Did you choose to come here or did someone make you?"

"Combination, sir. I was in Afghanistan when I got the word that I was to assume another assignment."

"Yes, well, that is peculiar. CENTCOM hasn't had a liaison officer here since GITMO prison opened. Why now? Or at least that's what I was inclined to ask at first. But now I understand that a particular detainee is of interest to you."

"Yes, sir. I believe his name is Moustafa."

"We refer to him as 9696."

"Sir, what can you tell me about him?"

"Not much, but you'll get a chance to meet him soon enough. He tells me that he will only talk to you. He's been saying that for several weeks. I think he might just be the biggest con man we have in the camp. But he says he has secrets. Of course, they all do. But we gather intelligence here. We'd like to have more of it. If he'll talk to you and not the rest of us, then so be it. You be his nanny and maybe you can get him to suck on your teats. You think you can do that?"

"Maybe, sir. But if this man, 9696, is the fellow I recall, I don't know why he wants to talk with me. He's not the only Taliban or Al-Qaeda guy I helped capture."

"Well, you must have made an impression. He remembered you. He even described you in detail at one point. Said you were a big man with green eyes and good teeth. Did you kiss him?"

Grant smiled sardonically in response. "I don't recall it, sir."

"Ha! I guess flossing works." After a fairly long pause, Peppers added, "Look, I'm not entirely certain why you're here. The fact that CENTCOM sent you over is curious. Why now? CENTCOM has its hands full with Iraq—but why now? Why not two or three years ago? From what I know, you're not even permanently attached to CENTCOM. I understand a SEAL being wanted in Afghanistan but now you're here filling a billet that's been empty for several years. Somebody likes you…But that might not be a good thing. Take care…"

The phone rang and Peppers stood up to indicate that the interview was over. Chisolm stood as well.

"Thank you for your time, sir."

As Chisolm was about to leave, Peppers added, "And, oh, by the way, I hope you can handle the truth here. It's the pursuit of it that keeps this place open."

THE DARKNESS IN WATER

"Aqua, my friend, aqua."

Grant looked up from his desk at which he was reading e-mail from his CENTCOM commanders seeking specific information about detainees held at GITMO.

"Ah, Max, how are you?"

"Well, now I have another diving buddy."

"What? You want to dive? I told you. I don't have my scuba with me."

"Grant, this is GITMO! We're on the ocean! Our dive shop is excellent. What if we head down there at seven sharp and pick up some tanks and we'll rent whatever equipment you need? They've got everything. I assume Afghanistan didn't purge you of your saltwater blood? What do you think? You blew me off yesterday because of all your work but not tomorrow. What do ya say"?

Max's boyish enthusiasm would have convinced even the most stalwart landlubber. Grant's love of the sea needed very little prompting. He nodded his assent to Max.

"I'll pick you up a bit before seven. I'll bring some extra equipment just in case we need it. I've got a couple spear guns. If you want to get some fish, this is one way of knowing they're fresh."

"Sounds sweet."

As quickly as he had appeared, Max disappeared into an adjoining office and burrowed into his tasks as assistant security manager.

No sooner had Chisolm turned back to his computer screen than his phone rang.

"Hello, Lieutenant Commander Grant Chisolm, CENTCOM liaison. This is Commander Avery

Shinini, *almost* your base commander. I'll be taking over as soon as the current officer leaves. I didn't have a chance to personally welcome you to the base. But I was hoping our paths might cross. I understand you're a SEAL."

"Yes, sir, I am."

"Well, do you still have webbed feet?"

"Yes, sir, I still do. Why do you ask?"

"I like to get my morning exercise, whether in the pool or in the ocean. When I can find a fish as foolish as myself, I like to go splash into the ocean. I've about a half-mile stretch of the bay I occasionally swim in the early morning. I'm inviting you to take your chances with me. I get into the water by six."

"Well, if I can get a bathing suit today at the exchange, you're on. Where do we meet?"

◆◆◆

Next morning, with barely a glimmer of sunlight on the horizon, Chisolm and Commander Shinini stepped into the warm Caribbean waters until a wave hit them chest high and then they both dove in. Chisolm and the commander stretched out their arms to slice through the salty broth and against a slight breeze in a relaxed freestyle, each lifting his head alternatively to the left and then to the right to breathe in a synchronous movement with the water, the wind, and the air itself.

As he coursed through the waves, Chisolm felt the joy of one who tastes the saltiness of his lover with each kiss, his lips expelling the life he sucked from the wind that played the ocean into curls, whirls, and a surliness that crested and sank before being allowed to splash into those that slipped into its mystery and penetrated its depths. Still dark and eerily inviting, the sea caught a fading glimmer of moonlight even as the distant sky glowed with the first rays of an as yet unseen sun.

Ten minutes into the swim, the commander looked up at Chisolm and spit, "Hey, you all right? Isn't this great?"

"Yeah, what a way to start the day." Chisolm and the commander then flipped over onto their backs to quietly take in the emerging beauty of the early morning skies and the last of the fading stars. But as the fading moonlight and the first iridescence of the sunlight dappled the waters, Chisolm noticed, as he raised his head and looked behind him at the shore he had just left, two dark fins protruding above the water and heading in their direction.

"Look!"

"Shit!" said the commander. "That can't be good. Back to back, buddy, 'til we see what it is."

Beneath each fin, a set of luminescent eyes caught the flickering moonlight and their bodies moved as effortless as breath through the clear water. Grant and the commander remained facing each other, half expecting an attack.

"If they circle, back to back is right. Otherwise we just stay close."

Two creatures approached. One of them swam right into Grant, its snout scraping his side even as Grant momentarily reached down with both hands to fend off an attack and allowed himself to sink under the water to get a better look at his adversary. His goggles enabled him to see with clarity underwater as opposed to a naked human eye. The other creature passed between Grant and the commander, its scaly body brushing lightly against his outstretched hand.

The scaliness came as a shock and a relief. "Shit, it's a fish," gasped the commander. "Damn it! Big un. Fish—what the hell!" Chisolm popped to the surface in time to see the two fins disappear a couple of body lengths away.

"I wondered what they were—had my attention, sir. Tarpon. They're tarpon, sir. Big but not bad. Let's keep going." Catching their breath, and their pulse somewhat quelled with the realization of their being followed by fish as opposed to the unspoken dread, they both coursed through the waves in smooth strokes at a slightly faster pace than before.

Minutes later, Chisolm and the commander were holding on to a ladder that descended from a rock and concrete pier that jutted from the shoreline into the water. First the commander and then Grant ascended. Wet but still warm from the smooth-flowing Caribbean breeze and the early sun, they looked at Petty Officer Second Class Boyle who was standing there waiting to drive them back to their quarters after they dried off.

"Sir, you had me worried. I was afraid you might not make it. I was about to call the coasties."

"Fortunately, it was only a couple of tarpon. But it scared us, too."

"Tarpon, sir?"

"They were big," offered Chisolm.

"Sir, that was no tarpon."

"What do you mean?"

"Sir, I was up above on the cliff to get a better view. I don't know about any tarpon. I was watching you. At first because it was still dark, I couldn't see much. But as the sun came up a bit, I could see you. I noticed a shadow surfer, sir. It was behind you and below. I was about to call the coasties but I wasn't sure if you had called in a float plan. If you hadn't, they might not have liked it since you were swimming in a dive park area."

"So you're saying something followed us beside the tarpon?" asked Grant.

"See!" replied the petty officer as he pointed out to sea. "There it is again."

No more than fifty feet from the pier, the shadow reappeared heading back out to sea, its dorsal fin barely breaking the surface and then it was gone.

"Maybe it wasn't the best idea I've ever had for a morning swim."

"Still, Commander. I appreciate the invitation. Still up for breakfast?"

"More than before. I think I may have left some of me in the water."

As Chisolm and the commander finished drying off, Petty Officer Boyle put the Humvee into reverse, spun it into position, and headed up the hill from Phillips Landing back toward the commander and Chisolm's quarters. The morning swim would provide even more food for thought than the breakfast itself.

PREPARING FOR NIGHT DIVES

> *Recreation is the great equalizer.*[33]
> —Carmine S., "Utopia"

A flurry of butterflies, exclusively white and what as a kid he had been taught were "cabbage butterflies," engulfed the parking lot of the GITMO intelligence center. Chisolm at first stared in disbelief at the snowfall as the creatures came to earth on the gravel and hot pavement, cars, rock gardens, cactus, and the trickle of water that lingered in a ditch that lay to one side of the building, separating it from the three rectangular boxcar-like constructs established as the "Camp America" fitness center.

Chisolm stood just outside the entranceway of glass doors in his navy blue mid-thigh length running shorts with half-inch golden seam margins and a gold-colored T-shirt with the word *Navy* in stylized silver letters across his chest. Other than his basic Duomax white and black running shoes, dark sunglasses, and a white baseball cap, he was wearing the official Navy physical fitness training gear. It was a small concession to regulations after a year of near native-like existence in Afghanistan in which Chisolm and his team of Special Ops crew went unshaven and, at times, unkempt in order to blend in with the locals and the dirt.

Chisolm walked through the parking lot, carrying a workout bag toward the first of the three boxcar-like buildings. Crossing over the bridge of 2x4s and plywood that traversed the ditch others had come to refer to as Santa Barbara's gulch, Chisolm nearly stepped on a small but deadly creature of Cuba's arid terrain, a scorpion. He picked up a twig and touched the tail of the scorpion, which raised it claws in response. Then it struck at the twig. Chisolm stood, threw down the twig and was about to step away when the scorpion, instead of retreating, moved toward him. Thinking that others might come upon this creature unawares and suffer the consequences, Chisolm stepped on it, crushing it into the ground. *It's not them that I hate, it's their poison*, thought Grant.

He stepped to the first rectangular building, opened the door, and felt a blast of cold air that immediately began to wipe away his sweat from the "Cuban bakery." After several miles on the treadmill, Chisolm was surprised to hear a familiar voice behind him.

"I should have known. You're a creature of habit. You should have been a Ranger, buddy. None of the sissy SEAL stuff for you."

"Hi, Max," said Chisolm without turning around. In between controlled and measured breaths, as he continued pounding the treadmill at a brisk eight miles per hour pace, Grant gasped, "Why join...when I have...men like you...to cover me...I like water...more than dirt."

"Spoken like a true squid."

Max immediately got on an exercise bike and adjusted the setting and pedals. "I'll race you, Grant. First one up the mountain."

Chisolm glanced over, turned up the pace to 10.5 miles per hour and said, "Slow, but steady."

Noting the increase in Chisolm's tempo, Max offered, "I'm game, buddy."

For the next two minutes, Chisolm and Max engaged in an imaginary race until Max yelled out, "Beat ya! Now you have to go diving with me."

Chisolm laughed, slowed back down to an eight mile per hour pace and wiped his face with a towel.

Half an hour later, the cardio portion of their workout over, they both headed to the last and largest of the three workout buildings. Inside they were immediately greeted by a Jamaican attendant who asked them to sign in and take a towel. After a blend of muscle toning and upper body strengthening, Chisolm alone finished off with several sets of chin-ups and pull-ups. As he dropped himself gently to the floor, Max walked over drenched with sweat and said, "Remember, tomorrow at zero eight hundred. We'll fit you out at the dive shop. I'll pick you up, we'll get something at McDonalds, then go over."

◆◆◆

After a cup of black coffee and some pancakes and syrup, Chisolm and Max headed to the dive shop. Recreational as well as professional divers and underwater warriors like the SEALS found the dive world a kind of earthly, if not watery, paradise. Guantanamo Bay itself had ample opportunities for the novice as well as the experienced divers. No one place on the base was more than twenty or so minutes from the dive shop unless a person were billeted on the leeward side of the island. Then a person would have to come over by one of the ferry boats and hitch a ride to the shop. Still, the controlled military environment made the base and its confinement an attribute to be envied. Seasonal spearfishing was adjusted to keep all species of fish and shellfish off any endangered list and the Coast Guard required that all dives and recreational boating itineraries be phoned in ahead of time and at their presumed successful conclusion. Moreover, outside the mouth of their harbor to either side lay Hidden and Chapman beaches to the leeward, Cable, Cusco, and Kittery beaches to the windward—beautiful and rugged at the entry points and deep. Each was mysterious and filled with sea life that could be breathtaking, especially the huge sea turtles floating about like Volkswagen Beetles testing their buoyancy and watertight seals at over a hundred feet before dropping off into the Cayman Trench, which stretched out on either side and then descended to several thousand feet.

At the dive shop, Chisolm explained that, no, he didn't have his PADI-certification card with him, and he did have the appropriate qualifications to scuba dive. When he explained that he was a SEAL, the dive shop manager accessed the PADI-certification list on the PADI homepage and confirmed that Grant was qualified in open water, advance open water, and well beyond. He was in fact a master diver.

In less than an hour, Chisolm and Max were loading their vehicle with eight full tanks of air, an extra-large BCD, water shoes, flippers, face mask, and snorkel as well as the appropriate weights, underwater compass, depth gauge, and mouthpiece. Other than the tanks, Max brought his own gear.

As they finished putting the equipment into the truck, Chisolm asked, "Why all the fishing gear?"

"Because, my friend, we're going to introduce you first to the superficial pleasures of the island environment by giving a Venetian tour of the bay surface. On the water, not in it. We're going to MWR. I've reserved a pontoon boat for today. We can use it, give you a grand tour of the bay, and then the Guantanamo River. They're both worth your while. Also, I've brought along some sandwiches and plenty of water."

Several minutes later, they were heading down a steep hill to the harbor recreational boating facility. Arrayed with sailboats, various motorized pleasure crafts, canoes, and kayaks, the MWR facility was the envy of most Caribbean tourist facilities. Hanging out to dry and for easy display and grabbing, on a long wooden fence, were a slew of life vests from the traditional orange to fluorescent green, purple, and other surreal colors. No doubt anyone falling into the water with one on would immediately be seen from a distance as something unnatural and to be scooped out of the water or as a giant lure to attract the deadliest of prey.

Chisolm and Max walked into the bait, boat, and fishing equipment shop where a person could sign out the various seafaring equipment needed for a foray into GITMO waters.

As Max came through the screen door behind Chisolm, a black man with broad muscular shoulders smiled from behind a glass counter and said in a thick Jamaican accent, "Hey, man, it's the captain coming for his boat."

"Morning," chimed Max. "As always, I'm Captain Bligh, and I'd like you to meet my sidekick, the venerable Fletcher Christian, otherwise known as Grant Chisolm."

"Nice, man, nice," said the Jamaican.

"And this, Grant, is Jaimee Street, captain of the boathouse and all around raconteur. He loves to sail and kayak, sometimes fish, and he speaks English so strangely that not even the other Jamaicans can understand him. I know, however, that he always understands me since I adhere to the age-old motto of world travelers throughout history. I think it was Julius Caesar who first said that there's nobody in the world who can't understand English if you speak it loud enough and slow enough."

Jaimee smiled and said, "Dat's wot he tinks. Nobody understands him—he's crazy."

Chisolm smiled at the good-natured bantering as Jaimee reached under the glass counter and handed a clipboard to Chisolm's friend, who signed and pulled out his Guantanamo Bay skipper's license, and copied down his certification number indicating his skill and familiarity with all things nautical and about small craft boating.

"You need one of these, Chisolm. It's the card you get when you demonstrate what a cool sailor you are."

"Ya man, he had the worst score on the whole island. But we feel sorry for him and give him his own special boat," Jaimee teased.

"Yeah, at first I wasn't allowed to take the boats with motors. Just the old ones in the boathouse where there's no water and most of the boats have no bottoms. But I learned, didn't I, Jaimee?"

"He's a fool—be careful, Mr. Grant. He likes to go fast even in a pontoon boat." He paused and said, "Number twelve. You have it for Saturday and Sunday. Bring it back in one piece."

"That we will."

Chisolm and Max went out onto the dock where one of the dock hands was maneuvering the number twelve pontoon boat into position after gassing it up.

"She's all ready for you," the dock hand said as he tied the mooring line to a cleat.

Max walked over to an empty wheelbarrow. "We'll take this to load up our stuff."

Minutes later, the gear stowed safely on board the boat, Max called in their itinerary to the Coast Guard. Chisolm and Max uncinched the mooring lines at the bow of the boat, pushed the vessel off the plastic flotation squares on which it rested and jumped on. Max immediately jumped to the back of the boat and shifted the already running Mercury outboard motor into reverse, pulling the vessel clear of the dock and the other half dozen pontoon boats, plus several sailboats and an assemblage of serviceable if somewhat worn fishing boats.

The morning stillness evaporated in the sound and movements of Max shifting gears as he pitched the drive into forward, slowly moving out of the no wake zone past the unofficial marker of mangrove trees with their spider roots delving into the four-foot deep waters of Guantanamo Bay. Clusters of mangroves in the immediate vicinity of the no wake zone floated like vegetation buoys, marking the shallow waters. Once past them, like a child suddenly free of parental restraints, Max threw the gear shift into full bore and the pontoon boat flew across the waters, forcing both men to hang on to their baseball caps.

"Whores galore!" shouted Max. "Ain't nothing like a roasted critter on galvanized steel! I'm the wave crusher!"

Euphoric and given to a kind of literary license that was cryptic, obscure, and at times meaningless to even himself, however colorful, Max seemed like a Viking who had just discovered the combustible outboard motor. He was in heaven and at first Chisolm felt as if he were merely along for the ride. But Max had served sixteen years with U.S. Special Forces before a foot injury in the Balkans resulted in a medical discharge with benefits. That he could no longer trek up mountain sides with an eighty pound rucksack was regrettable. He still had a wild streak as well as the mental wherewithal and the wariness of an experienced warrior to be dangerous to his adversaries. Those qualities also made him an excellent security manager and a man who might still take calculated risks even when it was not completely necessary.

"My friend, you are in for an interesting two days," yelled Max above the din of the motor and the rushing sound of the bow pouncing on the small waves. He was a boy in heaven.

"Two days?" queried Chisolm.

"Yep, fishing, diving, and exploring."

"Okay, but I thought we were diving this morning."

"We can, but you'll notice I brought along underwater flashlights with our equipment. Thought we might even get in some night dives."

"Somehow I think there's more happening today than meets the eye," replied Grant.

Max laughed in response.

"I've had plans for some time. I just needed the right accomplice. After all, squirrels don't bob for nuts when acorns abound."

For a moment, Chisolm thought the latest Maxism almost made sense. But that was just for a moment.

SINUOUS WATERS

> *I come into the peace of wild things who do not tax their lives with forethought of grief.*[34]
>
> —Wendell Berry,
> "The Peace of Wild Things"

Fifteen minutes later, Max and Chisolm pulled into the no wake zone on the other side of the bay near the mouth of the Guantanamo River. Max eased past the "Go Slow" warning signs perched atop the metal poles anchored in concrete blocks that sat beneath a mere five feet of brackish water. Near the confluence of the black waters of the Guantanamo River and the back waters of the bay itself, Max brought the boat to a near standstill as he eased it past some Filipino contract laborers, along the south short of the opening, who were fishing and enjoying a leisurely day. They waved at the boat as it turned north up the river past a mouth that was drenched in mangroves to either side, thick, lush, green, and foreboding despite the bird life that hovered in its branches, the sparrow hawk, the wild canary, and the turkey vultures.

"Got to go slow through the river," said Max. "A lot of manatee. Big old roly-polies. They love to play with people. They even tipped over a kayaker in here one day. Fortunately, a boater was behind him and picked him up."

"Are we here to fish?" asked Chisolm.

"We could be, but I need to get your opinion on something. The fishing gear is just a ruse to keep the Coast Guard and everyone else off our tail and to keep us above suspicion as we go quietly up the river."

Chisolm smirked and asked, "Have you ever read Joseph Conrad's *Heart of Darkness*?"

"You asked me that once before in the Balkans. Why? Do I remind you of someone in the story?"

Chisolm was silent.

"But when you asked, I told you no, I hadn't read it."

Chisolm sat back waiting for another Maxism to come forth.

Then Max added, "Mistah Kurtz —he dead. I ain't."

As they slowly meandered up the river, Max entertained Chisolm with his only recently acquired knowledge concerning the flora and fauna. Then, as they approached a grove of trees whose limbs hung over the water, casting deep shadows over the already dark water, he slowed the boat once more and pointed beneath the branches and whispered, "Look there."

At first, Chisolm could see nothing, but then the waters suddenly exploded with a ferocity of flailing appendages and a sudden submergence beneath the waters that created a current that ran perpendicular to their boat and then under it.

"Hell, I've never seen that before. Wonder what it was. Sharks don't move like that."

"Danger number one," replied Max. "Or maybe I should say the stuff that says never swim in this river. There's a reason it's not allowed."

As they watched and waited for something to emerge from the depths in hopes of catching a glimpse, Chisolm and Max suddenly looked behind them at a quickly approaching twenty-foot Coast Guard vessel with a .50 caliber machine gun, sufficiently powerful inboard motor, and slender wave cutting ability to thrill the helmsman with a feeling of near flight capability. The boat sped rapidly toward them, slowed for several seconds as it closed, and then launched forward again at full bore as the coasties waved teasingly and one yelled, "Hey, old man, it that a pontoon boat or a tampon boat?"

"Get close enough and I'll show you which vessel has the blood on it, you pussies."

They laughed as Max turned to Chisolm. "They're kids with a hard-on. They're not supposed to run their guns through here. If they hit the manatee, they'll kill 'em. I'll have to have a talk with the commander. They're wild asses, but I'd want 'em with me in combat."

"Looks like they scared off the creature."

"That creature may be the most dangerous thing in these waters, worse than anything else I'll show you."

"You mean there's more?"

"These waters are infested."

"Why?"

"Because the Cubans dump waste from a chicken processing plant into the river as well as into the bay itself. Because of the currents, the chicken guts flow to this side and not to the side you went swimming on. For guys like us who hope to dive, let's hope it stays that way. . . I'm chicken enough all by myself. I don't want to go swimming in that stuff and be mistaken for just another piece of white meat. After all, no chicken ever crossed the road for a fish kish."

Chisolm wanted to ask what that could possibly mean, but then the boat rocked hard and lifted up and down as the full backflow from the Coast Guard vessel washed alongside the pontoon boat, splashing and pushing it hard to one side.

"They'll be back in a little while. We're less than a mile from the Cuban section of the river. Even those crazy asses won't go there. The Cubans monitor everything on the river. And their guards are armed."

The sun was already creating enough heat to force both Chisolm and Max to break out bottles of water from the cooler. As they were sipping water, the Coast Guard boat returned. Only this time the vessel eased alongside theirs and the helmsman said, "Hey, Daddy Max, watch yourself up river. There're some big logs just touching the surface. We may have hit one or two."

"Thanks, crazy man. Are you sure they were logs and not manatees?"

"What else could it be?"

"Yeah, what else could it be?"

"Who's your friend?"

Before Max could respond, Chisolm reached across the gunwales and introduced himself.

"Are you a civilian type, sir?" asked the helmsman.

"USN," replied Grant.

"And you each address him as lieutenant commander, you swabbies," responded Max.

"Sorry, sir. I didn't mean any disrespect."

"Be kind to animals, and I think we can forgive you," responded Chisolm.

"Yeah, he's a Navy SEAL, fellas. He doesn't like it when people hurt his manatees. Slow down. You know, brake for animals and all that stuff."

Then he pointed his finger at the helmsman and said, "Remember, if pigs flew like chickens...'

Before he could finish, Chisolm chimed in, "We'd all have eggs in our face."

Max turned to Chisolm with a mild look of disbelief and said, "Damn, you're stealin' my lines."

The helmsman then looked at Chisolm and said, "Sir, any time you want to ride out with us on our wild bronco, just let us know. The ocean is our prairie."

"Yeah, cowboy, but you scared away all the fish. Better get goin' before Max here calls the Indians."

"Oh, you wouldn't want to do that, sir. We protect these waters from infiltrating Cuban terrorists."

"Okay, cowboys," replied Max, "but the next time we go out with you, it'll be our beer money."

"Right on, sir. We accept. Well, we gotta go. More bad guys to catch, more women to save, and more roads to travel."

They sped off once again, leaving the splash of their wake hitting the pontoon and rocking the boat.

"Good kids, but that's it—kids. They're all from the West Coast and they think their boats are surfboards."

"Should be SEALs, not coasties," replied Chisolm. "We like 'em a little bit wild."

Several minutes later, they approached the bridge that marked the northernmost extremity of the U.S.-governed waters in Guantanamo. Chisolm read the sign on the bridge, "HALT. You are entering Cuban waters."

"As a security manager, I like to inspect the various parts of the base for possible enemy intrusions. The water here is shallow enough that a man could ford these waters and maybe even float down the river undeterred at night, slip across the bay quietly, or even walk across the bridge. But the bridge has sensors that detect motion and the bridges are watched. The Marines come through routinely. On the way back, talk to me about how you would infiltrate this area."

A HOLE IN THE WATER

> *I'm only on the other side of the water.*[35]
> -Kibzy 786, *"Ripples in the Water"*

Chisolm threw the mooring line overboard and then stepped on the plastic flotation pads that composed the shore side dock. He cinched the rope to the mooring ring and the stern rope to an anvil-looking cleat, pulling the boat parallel to the pier.

"Okay, so why exactly are we here?"

"To give my friend, Grant SEAL Chisolm, a little Guantanamo history."

"Is this in lieu of diving?"

"Not really, but that'll be up to you. Grant, I want to show you something."

They walked through the dirt and nearly lifeless vegetation already browned by the Cuban sun. Over two small hills they came again upon the seaside where a scarf of birds unfurled abruptly from the rocky beach and several decaying pieces of metal, rusty and protruding from the salty water, like obstructions against some amphibious assault.

As they stood upon the shore, a seagull hovered and squawked nearby. Max picked up a rock and made a throwing motion at the seagull, but never let the rock go. The seagull at first dropped down several feet closer. Max cocked his arm again. Only this time he let the rock go, bouncing it off the water—the gull diving to catch it before it sank into the surf.

"Deception," said Chisolm. "It thought it was food."

"There's a lot of deception goin' on around here, buddy. Look."

Max pointed toward several pylons protruding a couple of feet out of the water in a relatively straight line, along with several concrete-and-iron blocks of enormous size that stood amidst thick, solid, metal fencing, each strip at least a foot-and-a-half wide and driven into the seabed, flush with one another. A metal picket line, that was really an unfinished wall on one side parallel to the coast, stood helpless as the waters flowed around this vertical display of strength.

"Do you know what this wall or what's left of it is here for? Do you know why it's so complete and tightly sealed at one end so that, more than a half a century after its construction, we still can't sneak through even with a surfboard?"

"What? Another result of climate change?" asked Chisolm facetiously.

"Ah, you are a cynic, Grant, and that is why you need me to explain."

"Before World War II, this was one of the busiest military ports in all of the U.S. and its possessions. Those manmade islands we passed earlier were mooring facilities for coal and oil replenishment. This place was quite busy and hopping. So, shortly before the war, the second, this place was so busy and I guess it made sense. Plenty of ships but no repair facilities."

"What happened? Why wasn't it finished?"

"It was. It was. That's the mystery. It was finished. Imagine that, a dry dock. How hard can it be to build one?"

Max smiled. "The Navy dredged this entire area and built the enclosure and then pumped the water out. Then they found the day after they had nearly drained it down to the last few feet of water that it filled up again. In fact, the Navy pumped out almost all of the water three times. After the first two times, the commander set about reinforcing the walls in an attempt to make damn sure that he had made them so that nothing, or at least no water, could get in."

"No water? But something else?"

"After the third try, he showed up the next morning and found the enclosure flooded again and there was a six-foot shark in it."

"How did he get in?"

"Exactly. He figured that if a shark that big could get in, then the very bottom of this area must be so soft, so permeable, so filled with underwater springs or caves as to make the whole engineering project futile. It was abandoned."

"Anyone ever find out how the shark got in?"

"Nope, but the next day it was gone. And that, buddy, was enough to convince the commander that the base of the facility was too soft, too porous."

"Has anyone ever gone underwater to check it out?"

"Nope, not allowed to dive in this area. Too strong a current, too close to Cuban waters. And, even if you want to dive, you'd have to dive at night when the guards in the tower can't see."

Max then paused dramatically, raised his eyebrows, and said, "But I'll betcha it would be interesting to find out what's down there. If there are underwater tunnels…"

"Where do they lead?" finished Chisolm.

"Mia compadre, as the assistant security manager, I cannot insist that you consider such a thing—that would be wrong."

"Yes, no moon to speak of, it'll be pitch-black. We'll pretend to fish."

Chisolm picked up a handful of dirt and sand and said, "Yes, that would be wrong."

◆◆◆

Late that evening, a guard in one of the two towers on either side of the water gate to Caimanera, Cuba, looked out over the quiet waters of Guantanamo Bay. In the distance, he noticed several constellations of red, green, and white lights suspended on the water. He watched as occasionally one cluster moved cautiously through the darkness like a slow-moving meteor shower, the boat itself remaining invisible to the naked eye.

"It's dark enough. Now's the time. Let's get our gear on."

In the subdued light of their motor console for the outboard motor, in which their gear was barely discernible, Max and Chisolm slipped their wetsuits on over their swimming trunks, their wet boots, and then helped each other with their BCDs and their air tanks. "We'll go in quietly, no splash."

"So we go in the dry dock area and explore the perimeter. Will the guards catch a glimpse of our flashlights? asked Chisolm.

"Not if we stay close to the metal pylons. Their angle of sight makes it almost impossible to see anything moving on the side opposite them. I'll lead."

Max slipped in with Chisolm right behind him. They inflated their BCDs and then he raised his hand with the button end of the regulator up and said, "I'm going down, Grant, stay close."

On hearing the hissing sound from his regulator, Chisolm followed suit, submerging beneath the pitch-black waters. Moments later, both men turned on their flashlights. At twelve feet, they touched bottom. The sandy bottom stretched off into the darkness, several species circling about them, triggerfish, bonefish, snappers, and a great barracuda. Chisolm and Max then swam slowly, deliberately, along the wall of the metallic enclosure. The rusted but still-standing pieces of metal and concrete held the currents of Guantanamo at bay. Max and Chisolm reached out to pick up pieces of shells, rusted-out utensils, several Coke cans, a large metal container that lay half buried in the sand. The lip was help shut by a snap and piece of yellow rope. Oddly, the condition of the container and the rope itself indicated that they were new, not something that had been lying on the bottom indefinitely. The container, battleship gray, was the size of a large ice chest. On either end were metal handles for lifting.

Chisolm immediately noticed, on the front, some letters mostly concealed by the sand. Scraping the sand away, he discerned one word written in the Cyrillic alphabet, VZRIVCHATI. Chisolm translated the Russian word for "Explosives." Just as Chisolm was about to signal "Danger" to Max, he pushed Chisolm away from the container. Max then jerked hard on another long piece of yellow rope tied to the handle on top of the container, forcing the heavy metal lid open on its hinges.

Chisolm, relieved at no dire occurrence, kicked back to it and flashed his light to get a look at its contents. Max let go of the rope and came abreast of Chisolm.

Together, they discovered from top to bottom laid out in neat rows of ten by four and four rows deep, blocks of unidentified material triple wrapped in heavy plastic, waterproof containers.

They gently examined the blocks and then put them back. Max motioned to Chisolm to close the lid and follow him. He picked up the yellow rope attached to the lid of the chest and pulled himself hand over hand along its length, as Chisolm swam alongside, shining his light on it. For almost seventy feet, they swam through the sandy bottom and several pieces of metal and concrete until the rope led downward into a large hole, wide enough for a man to swim through with his full array of scuba equipment.

At first, both men hesitated to enter, instead slashing their lights back and forth in the abyss. Their lights revealed a myriad of near microscopic creatures that floated about in the quiet dark water like dust particles reflecting the sun's rays. As Max moved to enter the downward-sloping opening, Chisolm grabbed his arm, holding him back and pointing toward a momentary flicker of light in the distance. Both Chisolm and Max watched as the flicker of light, something reflecting the illumination from their own light, came closer and then disappeared. Grant then motioned that he would enter and held up his hands to indicate that Max should stay there and hold onto the yellow rope. At first Max shook his head "no."

But Chisolm, the more experienced diver of the two, shook his head up and down and then waited a moment and raised his right hand putting his thumb and forefinger together to form a circle, the universal symbol for "OK." It was as much a question as it was a statement. Max hesitated, then returned the symbol. Chisolm again lifted the rope leading into the passageway and handed it to Max who took it resignedly. He would stay behind for safety reasons.

Chisolm entered the cylindrical opening, pulling himself forward on the rope that remained taut, both from Max's pull on it as well as the fact that it was anchored onto something else at the other end. Two minutes into the passageway, Chisolm felt the pressure of his ears increase to the pain threshold, forcing him to pinch his nostrils together as he attempted to expel air while he closed his mouth tight around his regulator, pushing the air back up into his ear canals, equalizing the water pressure. He looked at his depth gauge. In only two minutes, he had gone from about twelve feet to forty-five.

Still behind him, Max tugged on the rope, as if testing to see if Chisolm were still in touch with it, jerking it from his hands. Chisolm in turn picked up the rope and jerked hard twice as he continued his descent. At over fifty feet on his depth gauge, Chisolm swam up to a huge concrete structure that at first blocked his way. But his air bubbles floating upward and around it indicated an opening above. Chisolm slowly and carefully ascended over the block, still following the rope. Continuing to move forward at a thirty-degree angle, Chisolm noticed the hole widening when a flicker of something white streaked suddenly by, catching his light. He stopped momentarily and flashed his light all around and behind him. He stopped again to assess his situation and then ascended more slowly to thirty and then to a mere twenty feet when the tunnel disappeared. He emerged into a desert landscape, with a few crustaceans and pieces of metal scattered about, along with two small wooden craft almost completely buried and, bewilderingly, a mannequin standing upright in the water. Its feet were planted firmly in a half metal barrel of cement that kept it anchored to the bottom.

The mannequin was a life-size figure of a man with black features wearing a faded camouflage uniform, and his right arm extended, as if pointing to the opening of the tunnel out of which Chisolm had just emerged. In his left hand, at its side, the figure held a small red, white, and blue flag—Cuban. Tied to its feet was the end of the yellow rope.

Chisolm wanted to explore more, when suddenly, his flashlight again caught just a flicker in the darkness and then a shadow that disappeared. Alone, Chisolm decided it was best to turn back. He turned and again descended into the tunnel. Minutes later, he reemerged into the sunken dry dock. Max was gone.

SILENT WATER

Fear me, I have taken your eyes with the night.[36]

—M. T., "The Water Witch"

Chisolm looked about in the eerie silence and still water. A lobster poked its head out from beneath two pieces of rusted steel that lay next to a block of concrete with a piece of galvanized tubing protruding from the top. The metal container lay undisturbed.

Chisolm's anxiety rose as he ascended, kicking gently to the surface, turning off his own light to mask his ascent from anyone else in the vicinity. As he crested the surface, he looked to his left beyond the pylons and the wall of rusted steel, the pontoon boat was still there. But as he expelled his regulator, a flash of light blinded him.

"Max?" he asked.

"Come here," said a gruff voice.

"Max's gone," replied another.

"Who are you?"

"Your salvation. We need to talk with you, Grant Chisolm. Come aboard."

Perplexed as well as anxious, Chisolm continued toward the steel wall.

"Take the light off my face. Put it on yourself so that I see yours."

The flashlight was brought upright to illuminate the face of a man with a full mustache that drooped to either side, longish blond hair that covered his ears and eyebrows that accentuated a pair of grey eyes. The radiance of the light cast just enough brilliance to reveal that there were two other men on board, one on either side of the man with the flashlight.

But even as he was looking at this man, he could see just a few feet away the silhouette of another boat, which, peculiarly, had all of its lights off including the rear and side navigation lights, which are required illumination throughout the world. Slowly, as Chisolm's eyes adjusted, he realized that there was at least one man on that boat as well, maybe more.

"We'll help you up if you can get over to us."

"Who are you?"

"Friends of Max. We need to ask you some questions."

"He told us you'd be here. He wanted us to follow. Get out of the water so we can talk."

Chisolm put his regulator back into his mouth, flipped his face mask into place, deflated his BCD, turned on his flashlight, and once more descended to the bottom. Finding the opening in the wall of steel, he once again crawled through and surfaced at the rear of the pontoon boat, momentarily catching the valve of his air tank on a wire rope tied to the foot of the railing that encompassed the deck. As he reached to untangle it from the valve, it suddenly went taut pulling him backward with malicious force. The force pulled the line clear of his air tanks allowing him to grab onto the diving ladder attached to the stern.

As he stepped onto the bottom rung with his left flipper, pulling himself up by the flimsy gate that followed the stern's contour, two pairs of strong hands reached out to help lift him on board. Chisolm asked, "Who tied the line to the stern?"

"What line?" asked the man with a gruff voice and the flashlight.

"This one," said Chisolm as he reached down clumsily over his flippers and lifted the twined wire line which was once again slack.

"You?" asked the man.

"Max and I didn't have any line attached."

There was an awkward pause as Chisolm let go of the line and then took off both of his flippers.

"Well?" asked the mustachioed man.

"Well what?" replied Chisolm.

"Where's Max?"

"Who are you?"

"Name's Whiskers. What about Max?"

Before Chisolm could answer, the boat lurched, the stern gate rattling and cracking as something began pulling it.

"You're anchored, aren't you?" asked one of the men who had helped pull Chisolm up. "Of course."

"Then why're we moving?"

First, very slowly, then in a couple of fits and starts, and then with a firm pull, the boat began to move away from the other boat.

"Grab the line," whispered one of the men, as he tossed the bow line to the man on the other boat.

As the pontoon boat pulled away, the man on the other boat tied the mooring line to the stern, causing its rear to turn on its anchor line, as the rope connecting the two boats grew taut.

Again, both boats stopped as their combined weight created a heavy drag on the invisible force beneath the water. Then again, they moved slightly, almost imperceptibly, then by inches, then by feet. Suddenly, a violent jerk on the metal line and then another.

"What the hell?" said one of the men.

The boats stopped moving, the line connecting the boats to the unseen force drifted, and everyone was silent as if in expectation of some revelation.

Bursting from the water, a flailing sound and then, moments later, another explosion of water only thirty feet from the stern of the boats, and then a momentary silence. All of the men braced themselves against the railing or on some fixture, anticipating even worse.

A minute went by and nothing. Then, as the men began to relax their grip, a crash occurred at the stern as a black and white form slammed through the stern gate and landed onto the deck, snapping at air, causing the pontoon boat to rock and tilt violently under the extra weight.

All three men in the pontoon boat jumped to get out of the way, as Chisolm flashed his light directly into the creature's face. As its jaws opened, the metal wire appeared wrapped around several of its razor sharp teeth. Then, as if in demonstration of its killing force, the jaws snapped shut again and the creature slipped back into the sea, one end of the now-severed wire still lying on the deck.

"Whoa, whoa," said one the men, gasping. "What the hell's goin' on?"

The man on the other boat cracked, "Damn, I've never seen anything like that before."

"Few have," said Whiskers.

As they expressed their relief at the creature's disappearance, they watched as Chisolm picked up the metal line and began to pull it in. His slow, deliberate heaves, required to reel in whatever was at the other end, told everyone that more menace may yet be in store. As Chisolm pulled hand over hand, something jerked on the line again. It pulled the line taut, causing Chisolm to let go. But as he did so, the line again went slack. He immediately picked it up and again began to pull.

Within two minutes, he was straining to bring in the weight at the end of the metal wire, tangled around a mangled BCD and mash of bleeding flesh and bones. Headless, the corpse now lay at the feet of the three men and Chisolm.

"Oh my God," said Whiskers. "My God."

"Oh, Max," sighed Chisolm. A fluorescent yellow glow light attached to the BCD still burned.

The torso remained wrapped in the badly torn and shredded BCD and air tank, minus both legs and his left arm.

◆◆◆

"How is it you knew we were here?"

"Show him, Yuri," said the big man with the yellow mustache.

Yuri, who was at the stern of the larger boat, pulled alongside Chisolm's. He had a laptop computer open and turned it so that Chisolm could see the screen.

Yuri explained, "He had a transmitter device connected to his left arm. See here, the beacon is still transmitting. It's moving. Poor guy. Life is shit. I'd like to kill that beast that got him."

"Shit, Tom," said one of the men, directing his comments toward Whiskers. "What're we gonna do now?"

"Eric, Steven, there's some plastic tarps in the port bow locker. Get it out. We'll wrap the remains. We'll have to get this back before anyone notices. Grant, we're going to bring you in on this but not just yet—but things seem to be moving more quickly than we anticipated. Someone knew or suspected you were here. That means that someone had to have information on the two of you."

"Two of us? I just got here a few days ago."

"Someone else is in these waters. We also knew about you. Max told us. Grant, I'll need you to come with me. I'll explain things on the way back. But we'll be going into the Coast Guard facilities. They'll be empty this time of night. The boys 'er out on the ocean. We'll get the body to the morgue. The hospital—I'll explain everything to you. The others'll help. They'll keep your boat until you come back. Your fishing trip ain't over. Everything'll go on as was planned."

"What do you mean? We're not reporting this?" asked Chisolm.

"Grant, there's more here. You just lost a friend. So did we all. But nothing more needs to be shared with anyone just yet. And by the way, Max's not dead. He just had a family emergency forcing him to leave immediately. I'll handle all the details."

Chisolm's head was reeling. But he also felt that he was once more caught up in a maelstrom that he could fight or one with which he could flow. He decided at least for the moment to drift with the tide.

MAKING NO WAVES

You can't handle the truth.[37]
—Colonel Jessup, *A Few Good Men*

"NIS is to stay out of this. They're not to know anything." Rusty Peppers had heard enough to know that the degree of difficulty of this particular case outweighed the stress of anything that he had encountered as the head of intelligence operations of GITMO.

"Max was divorced and his only child was retarded. I know he paid child support. We'll make arrangements so that it continues until death benefits kick in. This can only happen after his death is acknowledged—something we'll have to stage at a later date.

"It's three a.m. The body has been temporarily frozen at the hospital morgue in a drawer that is locked to all but two people. Hospital personnel were deliberately kept uninformed, including the hospital commander."

Peppers then looked at Grant and said, "Well, Grant, for a newbie on base, you've certainly had an impact—good or bad, I don't know."

"Yes, sir, but before we go further, I think this situation dictates my informing superiors at CENTCOM."

"CENTCOM? Damn, do you think we're all fools here? You may pose as working for CENTCOM but you've got other backers. A liaison officer does not get clearance to participate in interrogations, but you have."

"You'll have a chance to speak with them later today," Peppers immediately relented. "All your communications have to be done on a secured line or on the JWICS (pronounced Jay-Wicks) The Chinese have high ground listening and observation posts all around GITMO thanks to our commie Cubans next door."

"What have I gotten myself into?" asked Chisolm.

"You're now part of Operation GAR," interrupted Whiskers.

"GAR? Like the fish?"

"Could be. But Guilt and Redemption is more what we had in mind."

"Who picks the names?" asked Chisolm.

There was an awkward silence.

"I did," said Whiskers. "We didn't stop 9/11 and some of us still feel guilty about that. Now we intend to redeem ourselves. We'll stop this, whatever it is that's unfolding now."

"Grant, Max came to us to discuss base security on several occasions over the past six months. He thought, and with good reason, that sooner or later Al-Qaeda or someone would try to attack and possibly free the detainees. Together with the base commander, we took a tour, ya might say, examining all possible points of entry to the island from the sea. We tried to think like the enemy. What are the weak spots on the base? How would we attack?"

"So what are they? The weak spots?" asked Chisolm.

"Foremost is the desalinization plant. Without its operation, we'd be out of tap water in two or three days. We could bring it in by barge and by plane, as we did when Castro first cut the pipeline in 1964. But that's cumbersome, expensive, and a real pain."

"But the water near the plant is shallow, and all the ships that dock there have net protections as well as electronic sensors. It's pretty difficult to get by them undetected. Besides, the bottom of the harbor also has sonar buoys, a feature of island security that is quite effective. No one seems to have given it a second thought, but it's something an enemy incursion would have to take into account," said one of the men sitting on either side of Peppers.

"Besides," added Whiskers, "an attack on the water supply would only be a diversion. The detainees are about the only objective for attacking Guantanamo and the water plant is nowhere near the prison camp."

"And," added Whiskers, "at our request, the navy has already laid down some new ultrasensitive sonar buoys throughout the harbor. They'll detect any subs, even mini-subs trying to enter the harbor."

"What about divers with sleds and other motorized carriers?" asked Chisolm.

"They'll detect most anything. Unfortunately, if there's a lot of traffic from recreational boats, it's difficult to sort one boat from another. On weekends there're several dozen recreational boats out on the harbor at any one time, including at night. We just hope that they don't attack on a weekend."

"Yeah, it's difficult to detect and to distinguish bad guys from the usual harbor traffic," said Whiskers.

"Besides, two weeks ago three refugees, supposedly from Cuba, attempted to come ashore near Camp Delta. All three spoke Spanish fluently, but the fact that they floated on their raft all the way to the windward side makes no sense. If they were just trying to get ashore in GITMO, they should have rowed as quickly as possible to shore instead of rowing directly to Cable Beach. That's doing it the hard way."

Peppers interrupted, "They're now posing as economic refugees. If they're economic refugees, the agreement with Cuba says we have to send them back. Only political refugees have the right to stay at GITMO. It's as if they're *begging* to be sent back. Strange for the tired refuse of Cuba to escape only to give us information about their desire to come to America to make a lot of money. We think that this was sort of a dry run to test our security. Once we send them back, they'll know more than they did before. Something's up."

"Yeah, there's more. The current flows from west to east past the base. Anyone who misses an opportunity to come ashore on the airport side runs the risk of being carried past the base all the way back into Cuban waters. Their actions don't make any sense," added Whiskers.

"There's more."

"Wait, wait," interrupted Chisolm. "What about these men? Where are they now?"

"We're holding them in the detention facilities on the leeward side. If they're Cuban, we'll repatriate them at our monthly meeting with the Cuban military. But one of our translators is suspicious. He says their accents are more those of people from Central America, maybe, say, Nicaragua. He doesn't think they're Cuban."

"Yep, there's something suspicious about them all right, they talk like they're Cuban, but when the translator started talking baseball with them, they didn't know much. Couldn't even name the latest defectors from the island to the big leagues. They only seem to know one, Dennis Martinez. He used to play for the Cleveland Indians—he's not Cuban. He's Nicaraguan. One of the men even referred to him as El Presidente. That's what the Nicaraguans called him, because he used to say that he wanted to return to his homeland and run for office. Most Cubans wouldn't know who he was and certainly would not refer to him as El Presidente. That's the way of getting yourself in trouble in Cuba. Something, as you can see, doesn't quite make sense."

"Something's up, I can feel it in my bones," added Peppers. "Max's death only makes it more clear."

"We suspect that whoever killed Max intended to get you too, Grant, and then dispose of the bodies in such a way as to make it look like a shark attack," added Whiskers.

"We came along too soon. They couldn't finish the job."

"Someone must have had an idea of what you might be up to. The fact that the explosives were still there when you got back makes us think that they ran off in a hurry. There are lacerations across the torso. They wanted a lot of blood in the water. And with all the other boats fishing the harbor late at night, how could they tell yours from the rest unless they tagged it somehow?" asked Whiskers. "We'll inspect the boat when it's daylight. But they may have already removed the tracking device."

"Look, Grant, you're already part of GAR whether you want to be or not. You know too much. It's true you haven't been formally read in, but you'll be once we get to your handlers. I've worked with them before. We go way back I think. That is, I think I know who they are. You work for them and we all work together. This is a mess, but we think whoever set you and Max up had to have easy access your boat.

"Yeah," added Whiskers, "And our prime suspects have to be the people working the docks. None of them are U.S. citizens. They're all Jamaicans."

"How's that affect things?" asked Chisolm.

"They only make about four or five dollars per hour. They're contract employees. It wouldn't take much to bribe 'em to plant something on the boat of a particular individual. Offer 'em say two hundred dollars per month to keep them informed when Max went out and make certain his boat was always tracked."

"Aren't they government employees? MWR? DOD?" asked Grant.

"Not really, they're employees of SAT, Sea and Trade Company. They're out of Norfolk. They're currently doing construction and maintenance at several U.S. bases around the world. They have the contracts for GITMO. Their manager, Randy Martinson, runs everything on base. On both sides. Yep, he's not the head man of the company, but he does most of the managing of personnel, hiring, and firing."

"So, what's the problem?"

"Are you aware of the construction on the other side the base?"

"Hardly," said Chisolm.

"Well," added Peppers, "we're building housing for several thousand people."

"Military?"

"It's a military base so someone might think so, but no, that's not the case. It's for an anticipated flow of Cuban refugees once Castro dies. The contract went to the lowest bidder. The company, SATCO, recruited laborers from Pakistan. Most of them are dirt poor, so they'll work for next to nothing."

"You mean the base has a number of laborers from a suspect country."

"Hard to believe, I know," replied Peppers. "But that's the lay of the land. To make things worse, contract employees do not—I repeat—do not require a background check. We could be infiltrated already by Al-Qaeda or members of the Taliban. Only we won't know it until we have our own 9/11.

"Two nights ago, we also had some suspicious activity outside one of the camps. One of the contract employees was running past Camp Delta at two a.m. It's perfectly legal. Still it's suspicious. It's the third or fourth time this individual has been seen near the camp at a time of night that seems suspicious."

"But those who killed Max—where would they have come from?"

"Perhaps Cuba, perhaps from much farther away. But Uncle Fidel doesn't want to provoke a response from the U.S. He knows he'll lose. But there's talk of the Cuban military's perhaps growing disenchantment with Castro's relative indolence. They're chafing at the bit, and they don't seem to have anything to do. Restless armies are dangerous for governments."

"But what to do about this?" asked Chisolm.

"For the time being, you and Whiskers need to find out how the attack or attacks will occur. The area closest to Camp Delta is right next to the Cuban border. You're going back to your boat tonight. You'll fish, just as you were planning. Your diving gear is still stowed. Then, as part of your orientation, you'll do some diving at Kelly Beach. It's pretty rugged there and maybe we'll find more. If there's an attack, then there's a good chance it'll come direct. Perhaps from open waters. We need to find out. You'll begin by talking with this man."

Peppers handed Chisolm a picture. "This man may be able to help us. He works up on Marine Hill and he is quite well informed. He's been here since 1953. He's Cuban and he carries the retirement pensions across the border every month. Hundreds still depend on them for their livelihood. You'll need to talk with him. He knows the history of the base and always seems to have his ear to the ground."

"Look, it's almost four a.m. We're all tired. Go fish."

Peppers got up from his chair to indicate that the meeting was over.

"Grant, make sure you call in the Coast Guard to tell them you finished your fishing trip. Close out the itinerary. We don't want anything to seem out of the ordinary."

"Yes, sir."

THE SHADOW OF FATHERS

> *His son, in my house! How I loved the man.*[38]
> —Menelaus, *The Odyssey*
>
> *I am your father.*[39]
> —Darth Vader, *Star Wars*

Monday morning, Grant sat opposite Rusty Peppers for breakfast at the Sea Side Galley in Camp America. Peppers said, "You'll need to come with me for dinner this evening. We'll meet at the Bay View Club on top of Deer Point Hill. Normally, they're not open. But I'm sure that Larry Harp will be glad to meet with us. When you go into work this morning, you'll also need to explain to your sponsors what happened. They already know some of it. I spoke with one earlier this morning. They want to hear from you as well. Remember, a secure environment. We're surrounded by Cuban and Chinese listening posts."

"All right, I've already turned in all the equipment yesterday at MWR. But one of the guys at MWR, the boat people, one of them asked me quite a few questions about my fishing. He also took an unusual interest in things. Asked me more questions than I would normally have expected. Also, he was just too friendly. Something wasn't right."

"As we told you last night, these guys only make about four dollars, five per hour. They're bribable and I wouldn't be surprised if they—well, if they were less than loyal to their employer. Let's eat, your eggs'll get cold and I'm grumpy and hungry."

◆◆◆

Late in the evening, Chisolm and Whiskers sat in the Bay View Club, GITMO's only truly elegant dining facility, along with Peppers who excused himself after only a few minutes. Setting at an outdoor table that overlooked the tranquil waters of the bay, they quietly expressed their disquiet at the weekend's events.

"We've gathered up all the explosives—high-grade stuff. Soviet-era technology but more recently manufactured. This kind of stuff, unfortunately, still flows out of the Ukraine unchecked."

"We know more than this?" asked Chisolm.

"Not yet, but we'll look further into it."

As they sat talking and looking out to the sea, an old man, black, wrinkled, and shuffling deliberately, approached their table along the veranda looking from the restaurant to the outdoor pavilion eatery. He wore black pants, a short-sleeved white buttoned shirt with a collar and black socks that shone through his brown sandals. Chisolm was in his desert camouflage uniform, the everyday attire for Navy personnel who worked behind the wire, the prison camp at Guantanamo. Whiskers was dressed casually in shorts and T-shirt and sockless sandals.

"Hello, hello," he said as Whiskers and Chisolm looked up at him from their chairs. "Good to see you, good to see you." Whiskers and Grant rose.

"My friend," said Whiskers. "Come and sit down. This is Grant Chisolm. He's a curious man and you're a wealth of information. So, we wanted to talk to the man who knows more about the place than anyone else."

"Bless you," said Larry. "A friend of a friend is always a friend."

Chisolm and Larry shook hands. Larry's grip was somewhat weak and almost breakable.

"I'm having the kitchen make some pulled pork sandwiches. Normally they don't work today, but I told them it was a special occasion. So the kitchen, really my wife, is preparing us dinner."

"You're doing more than we might have expected. We just wanted to talk to the man who always has his ear to the ground. The man who knows what has happened on this island and what will happen before anyone else."

Larry smiled and looked at Chisolm. "He's very good, isn't he? He should run for president. He makes everyone feel *so* good," he chided.

Chisolm smiled and then he noticed Larry looking not at his face but his chest, especially at his Velcro name tag. Larry reached across the table and touched it.

"Your tag, can I see it? You said your name, but it is something I want to see and not hear. Let me see."

Chisolm slipped the name tag off his chest and handed it to Larry. He held it only inches from black eyes that floated in a milky white sea, the brow, eyes, and eyelids straining to focus on the letters. "C-H-I-S-O-L-M. Chisolm," he said. "Come closer."

Chisolm moved his chair closer. Larry put the name tag back on the table. He examined Chisolm's face and smiled knowingly and then patted Chisolm on the cheek. Chisolm blushed at the endearment, wondering at the gesture.

"Do you like baseball?" Larry asked.

"Baseball?" Chisolm asked.

"Yes, do you like it?"

"Yes, I do, I played it in high school. It wasn't my best sport."

"Ah, but you should love it."

"Why?"

"Your father did. He loved it."

"You knew my father?"

"I know everybody. I used to be the manager here and in the other club on base as well. When the Cuban Club was very progressive—I was the manager there too."

"Wait, wait—my father."

"Yes, the name and the face. You look like him. I played catch with him. He should have been a Cuban. When we had the leagues on base, he played. Everybody wanted him on their team."

"But how did you know him? Are you sure?" asked Chisolm.

"Your father was a digger and" —. He stopped abruptly and looked at Whiskers as if asking permission to continue.

Whiskers nodded as if to say, "Go on."

"Yes, he was a digger."

"What do you mean?"

"Your father, he was a Seabee?"

"Yes, he was."

"And like all the Seabees during the Cold War, he was always digging."

"What can you tell me about the diggings?" asked Whiskers.

"Ah, they go back even before me. But maybe I should not talk about these things. I'm old, I want to live in peace. I want to become a U.S.

citizen. That would make me happy. I don't want trouble."

"Larry, we just want to know if you can help us."

"How?" Then before Whiskers could answer, he added, "I liked your father. I heard what happened."

Larry Harp then reached into his shirt and pulled out a gold medallion with a female's head in relief. He kissed it.

"St. Barbara, patron saint of Cuba. I prayed to her for your father's soul. He was not Catholic, but all prayers are good for all good people"

Chisolm dropped his head, involuntarily closed his eyes, caught himself, and looked up, embarrassed. Whiskers noticed, as had the old man. Both were looking directly at Chisolm.

"I was the only one the Americans trusted. I would prepare meals and bring them water. Sometime beer when they were digging. But your father would never drink beer. He would let some of his men sometime. But only after they finished their work."

"Larry, do you think that if other people knew about the digging, they could use the information to invade the island?"

Larry paused. "Sometime, I think they dig too far. Maybe onto Cuban soil."

"Did the Cubans—Castro—the Communists—did they know this?"

"Whiskers, I am old. Trouble, huh?"

"Not for you. No one but the two of us will know," he said, pointing to Chisolm and himself.

Larry leaned back and closed his eyes and asked again, "Was your father a Seabee?"

"Yes," said Chisolm. "He was a digger."

"I knew it. What a ballplayer."

"Larry?"

"Yes, I know, the diggers, the Communists."

"Please, Larry."

They were interrupted by an elderly woman with a dark complexion, holding a tray with pulled pork sandwiches, french fries, and lemonade.

"Consuela, do you remember Chief Chisolm? He was a digger. He was here. You remember. Look, he's back."

"Oh, my goodness," gasped his wife as she almost dropped the tray of food. She then put it down next to Grant.

"You've come back to us." Without hesitation, she grabbed the arm of Whiskers as she looked at Chisolm. Letting go, she then grabbed Chisolm's face with both hands and kissed him on the forehead. Grant grinned awkwardly as Whiskers beamed at the incident. Her effusiveness caused him to blush. She continued holding his face as she backed away to look again.

"You look just like him."

"Enough, Consuela. He is…he is…"

"We loved your father, what a baseball player," said Consuela.

"Yes, so I understand. I never knew. I don't remember much. We never played ball together."

Consuela smiled at her husband and said, "I'll leave you men to talk."

Almost two hours later, as Chisolm and Whiskers walked away from the restaurant, he turned to Chisolm and asked, "I don't understand—what happened? What did they mean about praying for him?"

As they walked toward the parking lot, Chisolm took a deep breath and said, "My father is the reason I do what I do." Chisolm paused and stopped walking. He looked at Whiskers and asked, "What do you know about me?"

Whiskers smiled and said, "Maybe a Christian in Action. But then, we know less than you might imagine."

"My father was working in Lebanon, Beirut. He was attached to the Marine contingent. My dad was there to help with securing the facility. I have been told by others that he had only just arrived the day before. And then the bombing happened. Several hundred died. My father among them. The man who helped plan it was allowed to walk free."

Chisolm looked directly into the eyes of Whiskers and said, "You guys didn't do your job before the bombing nor after the bombing. They were allowed to do it, and they got away with it. I have scores to settle."

THE INFIRMARY

"So, based on what Larry told us, the infirmary has a metal grating that appears to be an outlet for steam generated by the motors that ran the cooling and refrigeration units beneath everything," said Whiskers. "But the infirmary is built into a hillside just beyond the outdoor movie theater. It was intended to withstand multiple blasts. The legacy of the Cold War."

"So we're going there. Can we get in?" asked Chisolm.

"The answer is no. But you and I have prerogatives associated with security issues. If we need to go there, we can. However, the infirmary itself is locked tight and has not, as far as I know, been open for more than twenty years. To get in, we'll either have to break the locks or we'll need to find someone with a key and I think I know who has one. Let's go."

Twenty minutes later, Chisolm and Whiskers turned off the main drag and into the driveway of the Guantanamo Bay History Museum. A World War II vintage structure with white wooden exterior and red-trimmed doors and window frames, it displayed the archival material and photographs of the first U.S. Navy base outside the continental United States. The exterior grounds consisted of several acres of semi-grassy and always dusty flats that extended to the cliffs that overlooked the juncture of the mouth of the harbor and the deep blue waters of the Caribbean Sea. A graveyard of weathered and dry rotted boats, the legacy of desperate Haitian and Cuban refugees who had risked all to find asylum on the base, or in Florida, littered the chain-linked, fenced-in yard.

Whiskers and Chisolm got out of their tan Humvee, the bronco of choice of FBI personnel and other operatives, affectionately and derisively referred to as a BT or Butt Tickler..

As they approached the front door of the building, a bespectacled man with a look of amusement gazed out one of the windows. He disappeared for several seconds and then reappeared as he opened the door.

"Welcome. Are you here for a tour?"

"You don't need to give me another, Rock. But my friend here, LCDR Grant Chisolm, might need it once he gets some leisure time. But not today. We need to exploit your history knowledge and your access to parts of the island that are otherwise off limits."

"You want a tour of the island battle sights?"

"No, no, nothing like that. It's just that we have some security concerns, and we need to address them—with your help."

"Like you said, let's sit down—inside. It's cooler."

After twenty minutes of discussion and revelations concerning the diggers, the Seabees, Rock volunteered he had something that he had discovered six months earlier when he was investigating the infirmary out of his own sense of curiosity. He pushed himself away from the table where he was sitting, got up from his chair, and said, "Gentlemen, follow me."

They walked into the back room of the museum where a map and blueprint-storage desk sat. Made of hard maple and having eight drawers running parallel to the floor and the complete width of the desk front, it dominated the entire room. Too big to be inconspicuous,

Rock himself had refinished its exterior to a high gloss to make the desk itself the subject of admiration as a beautifully preserved remnant from the navy headquarters at Guantanamo in its pre and post-World War II heyday.

"There," Rock said, "I found this in one of the operation rooms of the old infirmary. What they're doing there, I have no idea. But all of these were rolled up and tied with some string."

He opened the top drawer and pulled out a stack of paper one-half-inch thick and nearly three feet wide by five feet long. Once he had retrieved the entire stack from the drawer, he pushed it shut with his stomach and smacked the stack down on the top.

With Chisolm and Whiskers on either side of him, he rubbed his hand across the smooth, dry, slightly dusty from the degeneration of its own fiber paper. The top layer was still slightly apt to curve up lengthwise from years of being rolled up. Chisolm and Whiskers held down the corners at the top and bottom.

Before them lay a nautical chart complete with intricate details of the eastern most Cuban waters, including those of Guantanamo Bay. The chart itself was a pinkish-white with a compass rose in the lower right-hand corner and the various latitude and longitude markings running the entire length and width of the chart and the legend indicating the length of a nautical mile and its ratio to the measurement of the chart itself.

In the area depicting the waters off the coast of Guantanamo harbor, several swastikas had been penciled in. Nearby were red-penciled circles. The circles had a strike through them. As he looked at the legend, Grant noticed names next to several red marks: USCGC Aacaci, USCGC Dow, UP-405, YF-487, and at least a dozen more.

"What do you think, gentlemen?"

Whiskers replied, "Look at the dates next to the circles. And the date at the top of the Chart, April 7, 1942. Wolf Packs, German Wolf Packs. These are German subs, I bet."

"I've been thinking the same thing," said Rock. "The ships with numbers would be patrol crafts, the others are cutters, a bit bigger."

Chisolm merely lifted up his end of the chart and said, "Let's look at the next one."

Together they lifted the first chart and placed it on the floor. The second one was more of the same only the date was April 15, 1942. There were more swastikas and more red circles with strikes through them.'

"This looks like a kill chart," said Chisolm.'

"I wondered if it might be," said Rock.

"But what was it doing in the infirmary?" asked Whiskers.

"I have a theory," said Rock. "Bear with me. I'll lift and you two peel off the bottom two charts."

As Rock lifted the entire stack, Chisolm and Whiskers separated the bottom two charts and lifted them over Rock's head. He then replaced the stack on the desktop. They placed the other two on top.

The two sheets were blueprints. The first appeared to be an overhead view of three long pen-like structures. The measurements, marked to one side of the three pens and running parallel to one another, were 480 feet by 82 feet with a 42-foot divide separating each of the identical pens from one another. The area marked with the north arrow was an additional 344 feet of clearance from the pens to a wall. The other end had three arrows, each pointing down from the words *water gate* and toward the southern end of each enclosure. The rest of the sheet was crammed with detailed measurements for cranes, rails, hydraulics, storage designations, and electrical wiring diagrams.

Chisolm lifted the top sheet at one corner. Rock and Whiskers pulled the second blueprint out and placed it on top. They flattened it, smoothing out a couple of wrinkles and squaring the corners flush with the entire stack. It took them several seconds to recognize what they were looking at.

Rock offered, "See here," as he pointed to the measurement near the top of the sheet, 344 feet. "And here." He pointed to a lengthy bracket that ran nearly the width of the paper and read 116 feet. "This, gentlemen, I think, is a trough. It's a water compartment, a kind of lock for, I think, a ship. This is the side view. A hell of a trough, 116 feet deep."

"These are submarine pens," interrupted Chisolm. "Here—sea level markings. This thing is beneath the ocean."

"But what's it got to do with GITMO? There are no subs here," responded Whiskers.

"None now," said Rock, "but I have old photographs of submarines that moored here during the war. The problem was that the Germans patrolled these waters heavily from here to Key West during the Second World War."

"The kill map?" asked Chisolm.

"I think so," said Rock. "The Germans sank plenty of ships near here. It's only ninety miles from Cuba to Key West."

"Ninety miles isn't a particularly wide span for a submarine to patrol," said Chisolm.

"Well, I think it was a lot more than one. The Germans were all over these waters. Key West to Cuba was a kill zone—a choke point where the Germans waited to intercept merchant ships leaving from the Gulf ports."

"When I was going through training at Great Lakes Naval Station near Chicago, several of us drove up to the maritime museum in Manitowoc, Wisconsin. I learned that over 10 percent of the entire US submarine fleet was constructed there. They'd float the ships down from Wisconsin, then eventually down to Illinois to the Mississippi, and then out to the sea. Several of them were actually torpedoed by their German counterparts before they could squeeze through to the Atlantic or to the Panama Canal."

"But I'd like to know what this design has to do with GITMO. They're no pens here," said Whiskers.

"Well," said Chisolm, "what exactly were the diggers, the Seabees doing here?"

"Diggers?" said Rock.

"Seabees. Do you know Larry Harp?" asked Chisolm.

"The old man at the restaurant?"

"Yes, he said there was a ton of digging going on around here, and I understand Larry's been here since 1953."

"That doesn't help us, Grant, unless we can tie these plans to something at GITMO."

"Maybe we can," offered Rock. "I know this island well enough to tell you this, though. There is no way these pens could have been constructed anywhere but in this vicinity."

"Why?" asked Chisolm.

"Because there's no shoreline anywhere in or around GITMO deep enough to have something of this kind of construction. Look at the diagram. The markings here indicate that these pens have an underwater entrance at a depth of sixty feet below mean sea level. High tide or low tide, no such entrance has ever been seen. No area of the bay is deeper than sixty feet. In fact, most of the bay is only about thirty to forty feet deep."

"What about the shoreline areas of the ocean itself?" asked Chisolm.

"No, not even there. You'd have to go a couple of hundred feet more at least to exit into deep enough water, except on the Cuban side."

"What do you mean?" asked Chisolm.

"Well, look over here," replied Rock, as he pointed to an adjacent wall where a large map of Guantanamo Bay hung.

"See this area, Kittery Beach? If you go there to dive, you'll see that until you're well out to sea, there's very little really deep water. But after that there's a ledge that goes down to about one hundred feet. Then after that it drops again to several hundred feet. But to open a sub pen would require too much extra digging. You couldn't do it."

"But what about the Cuban side?" asked Chisolm."

"Well, see this area right beyond the beach? It's like I described to ya all the way to here. But then as you approach the fence line, the underwater sands disappear. Then beyond the fence line all the way to the Cuban part of Kittery Beach, you have a sheer drop off—in Cuban, I repeat, Cuban waters. Americans aren't allowed there today, and they wouldn't have been allowed to dig there even in the good old days of President Fulgencio Batista, the little sergeant who could, or at least thought he could, the son of a b—."

"But how is it you seem to know so much about this area if it's off limit to Americans?" asked Whiskers.

"Well, gentlemen, I too like to dive and am deeply interested in oceanography. Sometimes, let's just say, the current can carry a person past the fence line right into Cuban waters. Of course, if that were to happen, a person would have trouble getting back unless he had a jet scooter with some pretty good amperage. Otherwise, he'd get exhausted trying to fight his way back."

Rock then looked to the ceiling and was silent. Chisolm and Whiskers waited for him to say more.

"Gentlemen, I've already said too much. Besides the lat and long marks on the blueprint—that's highly unusual. Since when would a person put them on a blueprint? Unless, of course, they held an exceptional significance. Besides, they couldn't possibly be right. And of course, we don't know that these blueprints are for a project that was ever really implemented."

Rock paused, then looked at Chisolm and Whiskers knowingly, and then made the motion offering each of them imaginary wine glasses. Each responded with a smile and reached over to accept the invisible glass of wine.

Rock then raised his glass and offered, "To El Presidente, Fulgencio Batista, staunch ally of the United States and the man of uncommon loyalty and willful ignorance."

"Rock?" asked Whiskers as he raised his eyebrows along with his imaginary glass.

"I know you dive," responded Rock. "But what about your friend here?"

Chisolm smiled and said, "I'm a SEAL. I dive."

"Well, of course, if we did dive, we'd just go and look around, ya know. And we certainly wouldn't cross over to Cuban waters. That would be wrong."

"That's right," said Whiskers, "and we never ever do anything wrong."

Grant paused, still holding his imaginary drink, taking in the full implications of what both of them were so readily suggesting. He then looked at Rock and asked, "Will this help us? Will it help explain anything—anything else that seems to be going on?"

Rock look puzzled since he knew nothing about Max's death or about any other unusual activities going on. Then he smiled and offered, "I have two jet scooters in my garage, and I know one of the dive masters who's on vacation. He wouldn't mind if I borrowed it for a day or two."

"Rock, let's keep all this on the quiet side. Wild Bill Donovan may still be watching over us."

"I'll do all that is necessary as quietly as I can. No need to worry. By the way, would either of you like a real drink?"

"Grant and I have to work for a living, not like some other people I know."

"Ha! I'm just smarter than the rest of you."

As they walked toward the door, Chisolm turned and said, "Next time, the drinks are on me."

DEPTHS OF THE COLD WAR

Early Saturday morning, Chisolm, Rock, and Whiskers gathered at McDonald's for coffee and scrambled eggs. They then headed out to Kittery Beach which was east of the Guantanamo prison camp and immediately adjacent to the fence line that separated the base from mainland Cuba.

The beach housed a picnic facility complete with grills and a long rectangular-shaped cinder block building, with open bay seating for any would be picnickers, and a roof intended to ward off the sun and thwart the torrential downpours that marked the Cuban winters and summertime hurricanes.

As the three men disembarked from Rock's van, he pointed to the steep, rocky cliffs that shot out from the shoreline, blocking the right side of the beach into a kind of cove. After they off-loaded their equipment into the shelter, Rock pointed again, this time to a guard tower that sat atop the rocky cliffs at their farthest extremity, the corner that was buttressed on two sides by the ocean.

"The guards are supposed to keep an eye out for intruders from the sea and any Cubans who cross over the fence line. They might also spot refugees who follow the current past the mouth of the harbor and past the prison camp. But they can also see people like us in the water. If they see us headed to the left, toward the fence line and Cuban waters, they'll report it."

"What about the scooters?" asked Chisolm.

"They're a definite no-no. They're not allowed, especially this close to the fence line. They'll call the Coast Guard and have us pulled out of the water." Rock paused, smiled, and then went on, "And this is why, gentlemen, we shall approach by moving toward our right and then toward the beach. We'll be at such an angle to the guard tower that we won't be able to see them and they won't be able to see us."

"Rock, you're a man after my own heart," responded Chisolm.

♦♦♦

Several minutes later, Rock led the way along the bottom of the cliffs toward the beach, invisible to the guards, and into the rock-infested surface. The pounding of the waves against the rock outcroppings assaulted their ears as the pervasive saltiness imbued the air and sent the saline smell into the taste buds. Chisolm followed Rock and Whiskers as they plunged into the water. The roughness of the water, at first, kept them perilously perched on the rolling waves that pushed them toward the rocks that shot up all along the surf, until Rock and then Chisolm and Whiskers flipped over on their backs and kicked out to the deep water. They signaled "okay" to one another, and dropped down to a depth of about forty feet, aligned their compass bearings and turned left away from the still hidden guard tower and toward forbidden Cuban waters.

They flowed easily with the current, swimming over occasional beds of sea grass, past coral reefs with their displays of sea anemones, and the convolutions of brain corals. The bright displays of fish, sea turtles, and an occasional green eel were sprinkled like spice upon the otherwise tranquil and sandy bottom with its ridgelines running parallel to the shore and acting as underwater navigation markers.

The threesome dropped another several feet as they entered Cuban waters, marked distinctly by the disappearance of the sandy bottom and a display of a wall of rock and coral on their left which dropped off into invisible depths. At a little over fifty feet, they cruised until Rock suddenly slowed as he signaled that they explore the area. He hand-signaled that this general area corresponded to the location of the pens marked on the maps.

The area seemed ill-suited to provide any kind of portal to a submarine pen or any other kind of underwater facility. The area cascaded from the surface in a coral display that descended to the still foggy depths below.

At a depth of nearly sixty feet, Chisolm let loose of his depth gauge and turned off his scooter as the recoil from the surf above gently nudged him into a crevice between protrusions of brain coral and a gradually curved object that lay perpendicular to the wall of rock blushing with coral. As Chisolm maneuvered beneath it, he reached up to touch it. The encrustation of sea life could not conceal the object's metal base. He then realized that the protrusion, however encrusted, had a cylindrical opening through which a man could ascend into the darkened chamber. Strangely, the interior was without encrustations as if it had recently been scrubbed. Chisolm ascended several feet into the tunnel, Rock and Whiskers glancing up at his protruding flippers, the two men hanging suspended just below him.

Chisolm was gripping a large turning latch protruding straight down from a double-hung hatch of solid metal. To his surprise, he was able to easily spin the wheel latch in a counter-clockwise direction. On its third full turn, it lifted slightly, Chisolm then opened it completely with a firm push.

Rock and Whiskers, still lingering below Chisolm, flashed their lights into the hatchway and watched as he slowly lifted himself into a dark space. He then pulled out his own small flashlight and shined it above him. The area was dark, but as soon as Chisolm ascended several more feet, his head popped into an air chamber. He felt a rush of cool air that suggested a type of decompression chamber with air pressure used to keep the sea waters at bay.

As Chisolm flashed his light around, he realized he was in the middle of a circular chamber with a perimeter seating area, presumably for divers. But as he breathed in the air, he experienced a slight headache, going from the water pressure of sixty feet to a virtual vacuum. Still he lingered, flashing the light in all directions, noting pumps and valves on all four sides. He then looked straight up and noticed a ladder that went from the rim seating area to the top of the cylinder where another large hatch was visible.

In an impromptu decision, Chisolm climbed up onto the ledge and sat quietly, still slightly headachy, and moments later, Rock's head popped up. Rock pulled out his mouthpiece and said, "Jees, Grant, what is this place?"

"Looks like some sort of decompression chamber."

Rock crawled out and sat across from Chisolm. Moments later, Whiskers popped up and joined them.

"Well," said Rock, "this may not be a submarine pen but this is one interesting discovery."

"What's above?" asked Whiskers.

"That," said Chisolm, "I suspect leads to the pens. Otherwise, there's no explanation for this chamber. It has to be connected to something else. I suggest, before we explore, we stay here for a few minutes and adjust to the air."

◆◆◆

As Whiskers crawled up from the chamber, he saw Chisolm and Rock already aiming their lights to illuminate the area around them. They stood on a smooth concrete floor, and, shining their lights to one end, saw several rows of switches against a wall. Rock walked over more than a hundred feet and held up his flashlight to read the names alongside each toggle switch.

Chisolm followed and, without hesitation, began to flip the switches. At first nothing happened, the darkness remained. Then a slight flicker came from a row of lights farthest away from them, and then another, and another. Row upon row of lights gradually lit. Within two minutes, the submarine pen was entirely illuminated.

"A subterranean submarine world," said Rock.

The threesome deposited their flippers and took off their vests and tanks to lighten their load. They slowly walked the entire perimeter of the first pen, looking down into its vastness. The pen was empty except for about an inch of water that covered the bottom. All along the sides were valves and hatches to flood the concrete and steel rectangle. At the end, closest to the ocean itself, was a huge portal with a double-hinged door that opened inward like the massive lock gates of the Panama Canal. Its seal was watertight and triple reinforced with vulcanized rubber and pumps that hummed to keep any seepage from the ocean from subverting man's attempt to keep the sea at bay.

"How did they get the subs out of here?" asked Whiskers.

"If in fact they ever got them out," added Chisolm. "The thing is, we don't know that the facility was ever used. The equipment here is definitely post-World War II. It's more like Cold War era."

"What I don't get is the condition. It's as if it's actually been maintained," added Whiskers.

Rock's eyes were wandering over the top of one of the submarine pens. He seemed not to have heard what Whiskers said. As he walked to the edge of the closest pen, Chisolm and Whiskers followed.

Without saying a word, Rock pointed to the indented area along one entire side of the pen.

"It's a seal," he said, almost to himself. "Before flooding the pen—look there—they're drain holes all along the indentation."

Then as he walked quickly to the other side of the pen, he pointed again. "Hydraulics. They sealed the sub inside, filled the pen with ocean water. The roof of the pen sealed all around the edge. It's a perfect rectangle. The sub was already submerged. Once the gate opened, the sub was free to exit into the ocean."

"Three pens," added Chisolm. "Enough to cause the Russians to worry if they ever knew about them."

"I'd like to think they were fat, dumb, and happy," said Rock.

"What I'd like to know is if the Cubans know about this," added Whiskers.

◆◆◆

An hour later, after exploring most of the facility, Chisolm wandered off by himself and opened a door to a room that had a sign, "Electrical—High Voltage—Danger— Authorized Personnel Only." He tried the door. It was unlocked. The inside was pitch-black, and oddly, he couldn't hear even the slightest hum of an electrical instrument of any sort. He felt to his right and touched a light switch and flicked it on.

There was an immediate crackle of several incandescent lightbulbs, one of which immediately blew out, the bulb bursting into pieces and spreading itself on the floor. The remaining bulbs were sufficient for Chisolm to see that he was now standing in an enormous metal box with vents on all sides and another door to his right. The room looked like the inside of an enormous furnace. As Chisolm tried the door to his right, he found, once again, that it was unlocked. Moreover, the door was a half-inch sheet of metal that had an electric wire attached to the bottom.

Attempting to open the door caused another light to flicker on and off before it finally flared fully and revealed the door's details. The door itself was at least eight feet in width and seven feet high. Chisolm pulled on a handle and the metal shook and moved slightly. Only then did Chisolm realize the door was on a glide. Using both hands, he slid the door to his left and saw more darkness. The air smelled stale and dusty as if it were a sort of long sealed mine shaft. While he contemplated going in, Rock and Whiskers appeared behind him.

"Curiosity kills cats," said Rock. "I say we've seen enough. Time to get back. People might miss us. We want no surprises."

As Chisolm flashed his light into the darkness behind the open door way, Whiskers said, "I wonder where it leads?"

TORTURED TALKING

> East is East and West is West...[42]
>
> -Rudyard Kipling, "The Ballad of
> East and West "

Malones Lookout, Guantanamo City, Communist Cuba

Colonel Sanchez handed a pair of high-powered binoculars to Mr. Walter Delgado, the Nicaraguan ambassador to Cuba. "You can use these as well as the permanent binoculars," said Sanchez as he pointed to his right where a uniformed individual already stood with his back to them both.

His jet black hair beneath his military brimmed cap and his bronze neck belied his country of origin.

"Buenos dias, Captain," uttered the ambassador to the figure.

"I'm afraid I do not speak Spanish," replied the man in the dark green uniform as he turned around. "Only English and, of course, my native tongue."

"This is Colonel Chou Liu of the People's Republic of China. Like you, he too wished to see the American base for himself. In time it will, of course, return to us," said Sanchez.

"Perhaps then you will consider renting it to us, your socialist brothers."

Beneath a barely controlled anger at the prospect of Cuba being again subject to foreign power, Colonel Sanchez replied, "Yes, of course, but then the listening posts that you have established all around Guantanamo Naval Station would not be necessary. Do you agree, Colonel Liu?"

Sensing that he may have gone too far in suggesting another long-term Chinese acquisition on Cuban territory, Colonel Liu, slightly embarrassed, smiled in feigned sheepishness and responded, "Yes, of course."

But Colonel Sanchez, despite the subtle apology or perhaps because of it, could not relent. He felt flinty and ready to ignite at the information he had received only minutes earlier from one of his aides. At this moment, any foreigners, including the Nicaraguan ambassador or a Chinese military official were equally likely to invite his wrath.

Colonel Sanchez looked again at Colonel Liu and said, "You already control the Panama Canal. It would be a shame for Cuba to replace one imperialist with another, especially one that thinks that ping-pong is a sport."

Colonel Liu blinked several times in consternation over the comment about ping-pong and then excused himself, saying, "I must return to the listening post. Others await me."

Sanchez turned without saying goodbye and walked to the fence that surrounded the observation post.

The Nicaraguan ambassador, in an obvious attempt to ingratiate himself with Sanchez said, "You were a bit hard on the colonel."

"No harder than I would be on anyone who would attempt to undermine Cuban sovereignty."

"If you are not careful, your words, if you don't mind my saying, could result in repercussions. President Castro and Uncle Raul may exact an apology from you."

"There shall be no apology."

"Then," replied the ambassador, "if you ever need to flee Cuba, you will have a home in Nicaragua."

"Ah, but not likely. You have not made Victor Martinez your president."

"Victor Martinez, the baseball player?"

Looking at the ambassador through a forced smile, Colonel Sanchez responded, "One could do worse. He is retired from baseball and would be better than some of the others I know."

Realizing that Colonel Sanchez's testiness was not likely to abate soon, the ambassador offered his own solicitation to ameliorate the edginess that was proving more than a little awkward.

"Please allow me to buy you a drink."

"I do not indulge," responded Colonel Sanchez, maintaining his flintiness. "In this climate the heat only combines with alcohol to dry out a man and burn him up on the inside."

The ambassador scrunched up his shoulders and opened his palms skyward at his sides as if to say, "What have I done to so offend you?"

Colonel Sanchez then looked out over the base again and offered, "The Americans know we are here. We know that they are there. Sometimes it is necessary that both pretend that neither of us is here or there. Sometimes we watch the Americans but pretend not to. Sometimes they watch us and pretend not to. Their guards have orders not to look directly at us. They are not even allowed to look directly at our guard towers so that they do not accidentally provoke an incident. Our guards are told to do the same."

He paused and then looked directly at the Nicaraguan ambassador.

"Sometimes it is necessary to look directly at your adversary and let him know that his presence has provoked you," continued Colonel Sanchez.

"Yes?" queried the ambassador.

"Within the past hour, I have received a message. One of my aides informs me that a man has been arrested this morning while returning under cover of darkness near Caimanera next to Guantanamo Naval Base. He was in scuba equipment. He had a car waiting. Inside the police found a Nicaraguan passport. Strangely, he spoke only broken Spanish. My men have questioned him, and they think he is an Arab, maybe from Saudi Arabia. Tell me, what is he doing here?"

"I'm certain I have no idea," replied the ambassador.

"It is a well-known fact that the Nicaraguan government sells its official passports to anyone who has enough money. Is your government doing this again? Even Hugo Chavez has complained about the illegals who enter his country with passports supplied by your country."

"Colonel Sanchez, I accepted your invitation to spend a collegial and leisurely afternoon discussing the usual depredations of Yankee imperialism. But you strain even the bonds of cordiality that an ambassador feels obliged to extend. So, I shall call my driver. Good day."

Colonel Sanchez remained stoically focused on the ambassador as he strode away, thinking, *Well played, well played, but you are lying.*

◆◆◆

Two hours later, Colonel Sanchez stood before the prisoner. He was over six feet tall, slender, muscular, and with two glaring yet fearful eyes from beneath a bruised and scratched forehead. His wrists still bore the marks of the handcuffs which a guard had taken off only moments earlier. Pretending that he knew more than he actually did, Colonel Sanchez returned the glare. Then he softened his look for just a moment and said, "*Salam wa a lei e cum.*"

The prisoner did not answer.

Then, in Spanish, Sanchez said, "Did you think you could break into Guantanamo so you could be with your countrymen, heh? The Americans don't really need any more jackasses like you. They have enough."

The man's silence stirred an anger in Colonel Sanchez that even he could not explain. If the man were planning something against the Americans, he could understand the hostility. Sometimes he too felt that way against the Yankee imperialists. But that he should attempt to do this against the Americans on Cuban soil was another example of foreign intervention and adventurism that amounted to an assault on Cuban sovereignty. Whether the intervention was sponsored by the Chinese, the Nicaraguans, or some Arabs from who-knew-where was more than he could bear.

"If you are Al-Qaeda, I understand your hate. But, like the Americans, I too despise you. For I am not a Muslim, and I, therefore, assume you wish to kill me. And, years ago, your brothers fought against the socialist government of Afghanistan. You fought with the Taliban alongside the Americans. That you should attempt to kill Americans while a guest in my country makes you most unwelcome. And to think you should do it after stealing a Nicaraguan passport."

"I did not steal it."

"Tell us more."

He returned to silence as Colonel Sanchez pulled up a chair and sat opposite the prisoner who remained standing. As he glared at Sanchez, two others rolled up a heavy metal table that was little more than a frame on casters. On top of it sat two car batteries with jumper cables. The prisoner saw the display as he looked past Sanchez at the two men who stopped behind him. His left leg began to shake uncontrollably, and his throat sealed shut.

Colonel Sanchez turned to look behind him and said, "Show him the pictures."

As the prisoner stood naked before them, Sanchez was handed a large brown envelope with a rubber band around it. While still looking at the prisoner, he slowly opened the envelope and pulled out a stack of black and white 8 x 10 photographs. The prisoner's eyes darted to them as Sanchez held up the first one. It was a close-up of a smashed-in head of a teenage-looking male, so battered that his nasal cavities were exposed, which caused the prisoner's abdomen to constrict spasmodically. Moments later, Colonel Sanchez produced another photograph and smiled as he turned it to the prisoner. He nervously looked away and began to move his lips in quiet prayer.

"We are not the Americans. Here you will have no attorney. Maybe we can get an imam to pray over your body. But there aren't many in Cuba. And if you have no country, and you don't seem to, then we will have to dispose of your body in the sea. There it will be food for the fish."

The prisoner remained silent. Colonel Sanchez smirked and said, "Connect the batteries and select the voltage, enough to thrill him but not to kill."

"It will burn, but not kill," replied one of the men behind the cart.

The scene was well rehearsed.

"Tie him to the chair and put the cloth in his mouth. We don't want him to bite off his tongue. They often do. Get the hoses ready.

We'll need to wipe his shit and piss off from the floor. It's always such a mess."

"I have something to say, maybe," said the prisoner.

"Good, but we'll keep the batteries ready just in case you're stalling. After the batteries comes the waterboarding. It always works."

◆◆◆

"It always works," said Colonel Sanchez. "I don't know what we'd do if the pictures aren't convincing."

"What is their origin, sir?"

"Photographs left over from the Batista regime. Autopsies. You know, the things from the police homicide files."

Within two hours, Colonel Sanchez and his team had uncovered startling information that marked collusion with foreign entities even within the Cuban government and military itself.

"The wheels are already in motion. He told us much, but he doesn't even know the names of the others. They've compartmentalized information most successfully. They know what they are doing."

THE REVELATIONS
OF PRAYER

> *Say "Shibboleth" (תלוביש). If anyone said,
> "Sibboleth" (תלוביש), because he could not
> pronounce it, then they would seize him and kill
> him by the fords of the Jordan.*[43]
> —Judges 12:5-6, NJB

"I see the green flags flying over the camp. You are honoring the Prophet. Will you answer the call to prayer?"

"Why do you ask?" replied the interrogator.

"Because green is his color, peace be unto him. And even *infidels* such as yourself will be forced to honor him."

The interrogator responded, "In the Koran we have the story of a cow that is red. So why should the color green be that of a prophet?"

"Ah, you are goading me. This I like. I accept the challenge. Yes, in the Koran the cow is red—perhaps like a newspaper."

The double entendre did not escape the interrogator. "You are playing now."

Joseph Walid had a background as rich, as confusing, and as contradictory as that of anyone he himself had ever interrogated. Reared in a Palestinian village in the West Bank, he had grown up with an antipathy toward all things Western. Taught from his youth to defy all that the Israelis, the British, and the Americans had stood for, he nonetheless felt an odd kinship with the West. As a Melkite Christian, he had long recognized his heritage as being inextricably linked to those crusaders of the Middle Ages and even modernists who provided the earthly sovereignty of the Roman Church. The pope was a Roman, and he himself was an Arab, once living under Israeli authority. In revering the one and defying the other, he was constantly conflicted. So much so, at the age of sixteen, he had enlisted in the Palestinian Liberation Organization and even converted to Islam over the vehement objections of his parents and elder brothers.

But in the aftermath of the Palestinian atrocities and his learning of the Holocaust, he attempted to renounce his Islamic faith, only to be threatened with death if he did so.

As a twenty-year-old, he was captured by Maronite Christian militiamen in a raid in the Bekka Valley—militiamen who helped him to complete his reconversion to Christianity. Two years later, he was an Arab student enrolled at the American University of Beirut where he turned his academic strengths into a scholarship to Texas A & M University. There he studied pre-med on the long road to medical school and eventual enlistment in the U.S. Army.

Now a major and hereafter a medical doctor, an eye, ear, and throat specialist, Dr. Walid had, over a period of years, renounced both his Islamic and Christian faiths, as he embraced American positivism in an attempt to be purely optimistic and decidedly patriotic. Oddly, a social conservative with an evolving affection for his American fellow citizens, he had offered his fluency in French and Arabic to the U.S. Army as a way of solidifying his anger against the world of which he had once been a part.

"They say you are a mysterious man, but you should know that the green flag is what the Americans fly on the days when it is not so hot that they can't work out. Other days, when it is too hot, they fly a black flag."

"One flag for the Prophet and the other for Satan," the detainee insisted.

"Your Arabic is not like mine. You should know my speech is the traditional dialect of my people. You should recognize it."

"I do recognize it but that is of no matter. I don't care where you are from but you care where I am from."

"Yes, your accent is peculiar. So will you tell me?"

"I am from Detroit. Many Arabs are there. Soon we will take it over. We will own General Motors, and we can build the car bombs right on the assembly line. It will save time later on."

"So you have worked there. You seem to know a lot about it."

"Do they still have gambling in Windsor and the whores?"

"In Canada? I wouldn't know about that."

"No, of course, you are a good Muslim like me. Together we can deceive anyone."

"Perhaps you are deceiving me even now. You are a Muslim?"

"There is one god and Mohammad is his Prophet."

"You are a jihadist?"

"In the true sense of the word."

"In what sense is that?" asked the interrogator.

"I pray five times a day. I also agree to see you. But now it is time to pray and your Star Spangled song disrupts my daily prayer. I wish it to stop."

"Then don't pray."

"No, don't play. I wish it to stop."

"The Americans will not stop. We are relentless."

"We? I thought you were an Arab."

"I am an Arab American. I love my heritage and my new country."

"Why have they sent you to me? I liked the boy."

"Yes, you liked him because you could play with him. I am more your age. Maybe you will play with me."

"We jihadists never play with our enemy. We merely kill or die trying."

"Once again, your accent is peculiar, neither Saudi nor Egyptian nor entirely Iraqi. You are a deceiver. Your Arabic is perfect, like that of a foreigner who speaks by all the rules. It is not your native tongue."

The detainee smiled. "Perhaps I reveal too much. I shall speak in English. But first I wish to pray. I shall speak again after I answer the call to prayer."

The interrogator got up and left the room as the detainee looked about in an attempt to ascertain the direction of Mecca. In the windowless room, he was slightly disoriented but recounted the position of the sun as he was led from his regular cell to the interrogation room. He surmised correctly the east and lifted his hands to either side and began to pray.

The interrogator and two other individuals stood in the adjoining room, hidden from view by a one-way window. They could watch him, but he could neither hear nor see them though he faced them directly.

As he stood before them, his prayer beads were dangling from his right hand. Quietly, with his eyes closed, he mouthed the words of exaltation:

Assalamu Alayki
Assalmu Alayki ya Maryam Ya Mumtalia Ni'matan
Arrabu Ma'ki Mubarakaton anti bayna nissa was
Mubarakon Samratu batniki sayidina yasu'l masih
Ya kiddisa Maryam ya Walidatal lah salli liajina
Nahnul Khataa al ana wa fi sa' ati mawtina. Amin [44]

As the three men, the interrogator, Chisolm, and the liaison officer from the European Command, watched in silence, the detainee began yet again in prayerful solemnity, his eyes still closed and his lips still mouthing the presumed reverential entreaty to Allah.

In a sudden revelation, the interrogator half whispered, half gasped, "He's an imposter! In several weeks of interrogation, nothing and now this!"

Glancing at Chisolm and the liaison officer, he uttered, "Wait here!"

He left the room. On the opposite side of the window, the door opened and the interrogator walked in and immediately began to recite the prayer along with the detainee.

Their lips moved in unison, "*Araabu Ma'ki Mubarakaton anti...*"

The detainee paused, opened his eyes, and looked directly at the interrogator. As he looked away to begin again, the interrogator preceded him from the beginning, "*Assalmu Alayki ya Maryam...*"

Their thoughts moved in unison even as the detainee's lips ceased to move. But he bowed his head and looked away from the window and toward the wall as he continued his prayer. When he finished it yet again, Walid once more began, "*Assalmu Alayki ya Maryam...*" and the detainee joined him, this time aloud.

Upon finishing this same prayer once again, the detainee dropped his hands to his side, still holding the prayer beads in his right and said, "You have interrupted my prayer."

"I have a sister named Mary," offered Walid.

"And I usually say one decade of the rosary five time a day like any good Muslim."

"I'm sure Mary will intercede on your behalf as she would for any Christian who has the misfortune to live in a prison camp with hundreds of radical Muslims."

"Peace be unto her," replied the detainee with a wan smile of resignation.

Chisolm looked on with frustration, wanting more than ever to talk with the man he had captured in Afghanistan and who had requested his presence as a condition for what he knew. The European liaison officer looked on, perplexed, and asked Chisolm, "What just happened?"

"We captured this man twice, once in Afghanistan and now here."

THE RAZOR'S EDGE

"Give this to those who are most expendable." Machmood handed two double-edged razor blades to the lawyer. "One of them must be the newly arrived detainee. He is the one who must die."

"But," objected the lawyer, "the Americans will search his cell. They'll find these."

"Not if they use them the right way. True, the Americans call this contraband. The Americans may not search a man's hair, his beard, or his groin. They may not offend Islam. Their policy helps us. Once you make clear their obligations to carry out *jihad*, show them the best way to cut. Best to cut the forearm length-wise from elbow to the wrist. This will embarrass the Americans yet again. Three suicides in four months."

"What if they refuse?" replied the lawyer.

"Warn them that we have contact with their families. I myself have taken the letters that they wish given to their children and their wives. It is nothing for the Red Cross to visit them and for our friends to kill them. Believe me, they will cooperate."

◆◆◆

The lawyer, Nadal Mahmet, a Turk with extensive connections throughout the Arab world, had a brow marked with deep creases with a crink in the middle. When he was worried, concerned, or thinking hard, the entire brow lifted directly over his nose into three large v's that extended to either side, the creases running parallel to one another, ceasing at his garishly black and wavy hair. His large and meaty hands seemed those of a butcher that could break bones with or without a butcher's tools. Those same hands were professionally manicured and extended the beneficence of Anatolian hospitality to all would-be clients in the form of women and even illicit drugs and the delight of shooting weapons on a private reserve outside of Istanbul.

His broad shoulders and thick torso were slightly stooped with a Neanderthal gait that could not belie the, at times, charming and reassuring manner that could bedevil his courtroom adversaries and win over even the seemingly virtuous with an unctuous obsequiousness. But once lured and lulled, his victims were thoroughly devoured and digested. A man of few principles, he could not easily be bought for any enterprise unless a considerable sum was offered. A child of privilege, educated at the University of Paris and Georgetown University, he was thoroughly secularized, evangelically apolitical, and ascetically irreligious. Nonetheless, he delighted at the irony of defending religious fanatics from certain Middle East countries, which quietly succored his pro bono work on behalf of the unfortunates held in captivity at Guantanamo with large sums of money that were undeclared, unclean, and which he found undulatingly sensuous. The scene made him an amorous devotee of commercial piety. He would, therefore, do as bidden by his contact. Moments after the guard shut the door behind him, while wearing his slick gray suit and a blue tie with a tie clasp all of red with a crescent moon like that on the Turkish flag, he sat down as detainee Achmood Karazai looked up from the table on which his shackled hands rested. Both feet were chained to the floor.

Nadal Mahmet smiled broadly as he greeted Achmood Karazai. "*As sala'amu alai'kum.*"

"*Walaikum as sala'am.*"

The detainee was dressed in a white pair of baggy trousers, an equally long white pullover linen shirt, and ordinary brown sandals. His beard was almost a foot long and seemed fake, framing as it did a long and boyishly young face.

Mahmet reached across the table to shake hands. The detainee extended a hand that was partially black and which had four fingers but only a stump where his thumb should have been.

Mahmet held the detainee's hand in both of his firmly, warmly, gently, and trustingly. Looking at Achmood sympathetically, he pressed his left hand down on the hand that he still held and asked, "The Americans, they did this to you?"

"No, no, the Americans, no." Both spoke in their native Turkish.

"How then?"

"I was making a bomb, it went off too soon."

"Ah, was it to be used against the Americans?"

"Yes, but they captured me. The sound gave me away. They heard it go off and surrounded the house."

"So you would agree, of course, the Americans must be at fault. They did this to you and the world must know. Do the Americans know how angry you are for the injustice they have inflicted upon you? Huh? I think the world would want to know how you have suffered. Your wound? Is it a black powder burn?"

"Yes, but..."

"It is terrible. The Americans can be so smart, but their torture is really quite primitive. They are not worthy of the company of a fine young man like you. Your presence here flatters them. Your enemy should not be so long entertained by the holiness of men like you. You, who worship the one true god, must punish the *infidel* in ways he cannot imagine. . ."

It took Achmood several minutes of being effectively led before he could retell his story in such a way as to convince himself and, perhaps, others of what the Americans had done to him. Within half an hour, he was crying and ashen.

Nadal Mahmet explained how he could exact revenge against his American tormentors. Within another several minutes, Mahmet convinced him that *jihad* was to be carried out most effectively from within Guantanamo by means that would justify him among his fellow warriors. He must bring the world's attention and sympathy to their plight. He must not waste away here. His younger brother was still fighting somewhere in Afghanistan. *Jihad* was required sacrifice but only for those who are truly worthy.

After several minutes of whimpering and quiet crying, Achmood looked up pitifully at Mahmet.

"What you will do, you will do for others. You are *shaheed*, the martyr who bears witness to Allah."

Mahmet then turned and walked to the cell door, opened it, and called, "Guard, I wish for you to unshackle this man."

Looking over his shoulder, he smiled at the still whimpering Achmood and said, "You won't hurt me, will you?"

Achmood shook his head from side to side.

Once Achmood was unshackled, he lifted up both of his arms as if pleading for an embrace. Mahmet hugged him vigorously and said, "Yes, you are a man, yes, a man, and one who will be honored hereafter."

As they both sat back down, Mahmet took out a white handkerchief from inside the breast pocket of his gray sharkskin suit and slid it across the table. Achmood opened it and dried his tears as he realized what lay before him.

"I have represented many men. But truly—truly I tell you—none like you. When you go before Allah, you will go as a martyr. You must clean yourself. You will bathe. Allah will see you as one who is pure as the snow of our mountain. On the mountain in our homeland, Ararat, Noah is still honored for he brought hope to all people. You too will be honored. For in your own way, you will be like the prophets of old. It will be for you to strike at the Americans. In so doing, you shall kill Pharaoh. And you, you are a hero to your people already. Others will speak hereafter of your greatness. Others will sing of you as well and your parents shall weep for joy. As it is said of the Prophet, peace be unto you, my son. For already it is written."

He then paused purposely and looked directly into the face of Achmood and said, "Strike at Pharaoh! Strike at Pharaoh! Remember the

Americans are not allowed to touch you in your groin area. Hide this in your new pair of underwear. You can put these on even now. I will not look. Hide them in between the two pairs."

When Nadal Mahmet left, the detainee at eighteen years of age was at peace in his newfound manhood and determined. The day had been set. Pharaoh would be punished. He would indeed be *shaheed*.

THE MOURNING INTERVIEW

"You are not who you seem to be," said Chisolm.

"Few of us are," replied the detainee in English.

"Shall we continue in English or Arabic?"

"Which do you prefer? I am fluent in both."

"In Arabic so that I can practice."

Chisolm spoke in the harsh guttural language of the classical Saudi dialect. The detainee smiled and said, "Your dialect is different from mine. You speak as a Bedouin of the Arabian desert. I speak as the urbane merchants of Damascus and Baghdad. You are a warrior so that it is only appropriate you speak the dialect of the Wahhabist. I am, on the other hand, one who sits before you as a poor, humble merchant with my life to trade in return for your trust and your confidence."

Chisolm was silent. The front of the 10 x 13-inch white envelope on the table separating him from the detainee had the words "DNA Results."

The detainee read the words as they appeared to him, upside down, and smiled again. "You wish for me to see this."

"It's nothing."

"Then why bring it with you? And the words are in Arabic. You meant for me to see this."

Chisolm paused and said, "You, sir, are a stranger in a strange land."

"Indeed, for I am a man much older than you, and yet I have asked for you. I want you to be my personal interrogator. If you know anything about culture, you know that this is not normal. You see, your first interrogator was too young. He was a boy. You I have chosen because of your demeanor. You are a forceful man. You too are too young but have the gravitas. You speak little but are listened to when you do speak."

Chisolm smiled and said, "You speak like a fortune cookie."

"At least I do not tease by withholding what I would surrender to the one I have selected. But perhaps you wish to play the interrogator's game with me. You will ask me questions about things which you already know. You will therefore determine if I am telling the truth. So stop playing and I will tell you much. I do not wish to dance. But I can teach you. But no one else. You are my fool."

"Why me?"

"You are my captor. You could have killed me, but you didn't. I owe you my life."

"I merely followed orders."

"No, you did more. As I was regaining consciousness from the blast, I opened my eyes. One of the others who I think was wounded moved. Your men shot him."

"The wounded are often booby-trapped. We touch them or they touch a switch and the bombs go off. You should know that."

"But one of them stepped toward me. I think he might have shot me too. But you did not let him."

"So what is it you wish to share with me?"

"First the envelope. I know it is for me. That is why you have brought it."

Chisolm lifted the envelope and opened the flap and pulled out several white sheets with charts, graphs, and a series of notes. He ignored them and flipped immediately to the back page under "Conclusions."

"This comes from the DNA testing center in Fort Belvoir, Virginia. According to this, you have a DNA profile, a fingerprint, almost identical to another man we killed in Afghanistan. The DNA suggests that you and the other man are brothers. Is it possible?"

"You have the DNA from this other man?"

"Yes, he was found nearby."

The detainee hung his head and then a tear fell, and he was silent for a long time.

"I'm sorry," said Chisolm.

"He was my Jacob and I his Esau. For I am the eldest. Yet he stole my father's affection. For he is reared in the faith of my father and I in the faith of my mother."

After another long silence, the detainee asked, "Are you sure? I did not know he was so close even though I was looking for him—to bring him back."

"His body was found in one of the buildings maybe two hundred meters away. We hit them simultaneously."

"I do not blame the Americans. I blame the others. Our own people. Maybe even God."

"The name you gave us. It is not yours. It is his, isn't it?"

"Maybe."

"But we just received the translation of the items confiscated from the raid. The name you gave us is the same as that found on the other body, your brother. Why did you use his name?"

"I know you and others were looking for him. I thought if you found me, you would stop looking for him. It is well known in some circles he is still one whom you would like to kill."

"In fact, we thought you were your brother. That is why you are here. He would be regarded as someone we would most want to interrogate. Had his DNA results not come back, we would still think you were your brother."

The detainee sighed and said, "You know we are only one-and-half years apart. We are as much alike as twins. Even our eyes and our hair. Everything is the same."

"But your brother was a Muslim, a radical Islamist. Yesterday's interrogation suggests that you are not any kind of Muslim at all."

"True, but perhaps I am no less radical. After all, I could even be *takfiri*. In that case, I could even pretend to be a Christian long enough to deceive you and others."

"It would have been quite insightful in that case to calculate that someone would lip-read your Hail Mary's as you were posing as a Muslim in prayer."

"What kind of Muslim would I be if I were one? Sunni or Shia?"

"Sunni."

"But why would I be one as opposed to the other?"

"Now it's my turn. You're engaging in counter-interrogation techniques right now. You're screwing with me."

"No, I only do that with women, I assure you."

Chisolm remained serious. "How is it you speak English and Arabic and for all we know other languages as well?"

"If you know who my brother is, then perhaps you already know. But while you are attempting to learn more about him, let me say, yes, I am quite facile in languages. If the time comes, you'll see how facile."

"What were you doing in Afghanistan?"

"My washing machine broke. I needed to find the parts."

"What were you doing in Afghanistan?"

"Looking for my brother. I had time to do this after I found the washing machine parts."

"Does anyone in the camp know that you are not who you claim to be?"

"None. No one recognizes me. There's no one I recognize either. Only, only the translator from the Red Cross. He thinks he knows me. He thinks I am my brother."

"Did he know your brother?"

The detainee paused again and said, "Your Arabic is very good, but I wish to practice my English."

"That makes it easier for me."

"That is my wish, also. But as for my brother, there are things you do not know of him. His dilemma. His background. You do not even know his real name."

"And yours?"

"In good time."

"Now would seem to be a good time."

"*Taman, taman.* But now I wish to mourn and to think of the parts for my washing machine."

SPEAKING THE TRUTH

> *The noblest thoughts that ever flowed through the hearts of men are contained in its extraordinary, imaginative and musical mixture of sounds.*[48]
>
> —Professor Henry Higgins in *My Fair Lady*

Wednesday Morning

"When he speaks English, it's maddening. His accent isn't British. It's at times though almost BBC. At other times it's more like an American. And when he refers to America, he speaks like someone who's been there. And his Arabic, it's perfect. It's as good as mine but with a blend. It's Iraqi but it's something else as well. I can't figure him. His guttural sounds—there's something in them, not just Arabic and not something I can identify," said the interrogator and translator, Joseph Walid.

"But you did a good job with the Hail Mary. You detected that."

"Only because he chose to pray in my own language, my own faith."

"We'll have to keep this quiet. We don't want anyone in the camp to know we have a Christian posing as a Muslim. His being Christian is bad enough. If they find out he's a poseur, they'll try to kill him. They'll accuse him of apostasy or of mocking their religion. Our fellows here aren't exactly the tolerant kind," said Rusty Peppers, as he leaned back in his office chair.

"Lieutenant Commander, what's your impression?"

"I'm not an interrogator by training, sir."

"But he's willing to talk to you. He asked for you. He must trust you."

"That's the problem, sir. He says he's not sure yet. He said he needs to know more about me."

"Classic counter-interrogation methods, sir," offered the translator.

"He says he needs for me to trust him and for him to trust me. Then he says he'll tell me everything."

"Everything? He told the first interrogator nothing. I think he's playing again."

"Go on," replied Peppers, looking at Chisolm.

"He wants to know all about me, including my parents. He wants to know where I live. If I'm married, do I have children? Why did I join the Navy? And finally, he wants to know my real name. He knows that none of his interrogators use their real names."

Peppers responded, "And of course, it would be against protocol, policy, and procedure, to give him your real name, especially your last name. Still, he may be telling the truth. Maybe he really does need to know if he can trust you."

He then looked at Chisolm and asked, "How do you feel about being up front with him: It's up to you. I'm not going to force it on you."

"I'm willing, sir, but when?"

"How about tomorrow?"

"That could be a problem, Mr. Peppers," offered the translator. He's scheduled to meet with Nadal Mahmet, his attorney, or at least the man who has volunteered to be his attorney. He says he won't need a translator. He would like to be his appointed attorney, you know, making it all official."

"Appointed, heh? I'd like to know who would appoint him and who's paying for all of his so-called pro bono work."

"Just look east, sir, as in the Middle," offered Colonel Winston Bradley. "There are a lot of wealthy Arabs who are willing to pay for the legal fees. Some of them are even funneling the money through banks in the Bahamas and Canada just to make it more difficult to detect who's paying for it."

"Maybe the next day, sir."

"Yes, Thursday it is. The arrangement will be made," confirmed Colonel Bradley.

GRIEVING HEARTS

> *Grief is the consolation that unites
> those who go on living.*[49]
>
> —A.T. Koenig, "Teasing Life"
>
> *It [Pain] is God's megaphone
> to rouse a dead world.*[50]
>
> —C. S. Lewis

Thursday Morning

"I am surprised you have returned so soon. You must trust me or you wish to know the secrets I have," said the detainee in English.

"Perhaps it is both."

"You wish to know who I really am."

"Yes."

"Then first you must explain yourself to me. Who are you?"

"Chisolm reached into the right pant leg pocket of his desert camouflage uniform and pulled something out. His hand moved to his left breast pocket and he attached his name tag to the Velcro pad.

The detainee smiled and answered, "What is you first name?"

"Grant."

"Hmm. Very Scottish."

Behind the one-way viewing window, Rusty Peppers with more than thirty-five years of experience as an interrogator had keen insights into the psychological phenomenon that made people talk. He also knew when they were lying. So far, he hadn't seen enough to know.

"And yours? Your real name?" asked Chisolm.

"If you have the DNA of my brother, you should already know the answer."

"Others might. I don't."

"Ibrahim Joseph Iskandar Saroyan Ayub."

"That's quite a name."

"My parents were ambitious. And you, you can call me Moustafa. That is the name by which those in camp know me. And you, your real name?"

"Grant Chisolm, as I said."

"It is brief."

"As my father's life."

"Tell me."

"In 1983, my father was deployed with the U.S. Marines, part of the peacekeeping force sent to Beirut, Lebanon,"

"I remember that. Many were killed. Was he a Marine?"

"No, he was Navy. He was gone much of the time. I hardly knew him."

"He died there?"

"Yes."

"I am sorry. This day, your grief is mine. And I think—I fear—my grief is yours. My brother. Your father."

"So, like my father before me, I am in the U.S. military."

"You have children?"

"No, I'm not married. Do you?"

Detainee 9696 paused. "Another time. A man should not grieve beyond his capabilities in one day. He will go crazy."

"What more can you tell me today?"

"Perhaps where I was born. My father wanted exceptional children. I was born in Iraq, Baghdad. My brother and I were only one-and-half years apart. I am the oldest. He is always my little brother."

"You were born in Iraq, yet you are a Christian?"

"My father is Muslim. My mother is Christian. The agreement was that the firstborn would be reared in the faith of my mother. She is Assyrian Christian. She is also Armenian."

"Your brother?"

"Reared in the faith of my father, a Sunni Muslim. You might say we were a house divided. Still my father was ambitious. He wanted the best education for both of us. So he sent us to

Kuwait. I was nine and my brother was only seven."

"Why Kuwait?"

"A Muslim who rears his children—even one of them—as a Christian, he will have troubles. He is going to attract the attention of the local imam. He already had—it was urged that he cast my mother out and that I be sent to the madrassa. My mother, as you would understand, objected. My father lost business—he was a merchant—because the imam spoke out publicly against him."

"What happened?"

"My father sent us away with the permission of my mother. It was a school in Kuwait. It was a very, very good one. Very strict. Even today, my heart jumps when I think of how strict they were."

"They? The imams at the madrassa?

"One would think so. But they were not imams. They were nuns."

Chisolm was stunned. "Nuns in Kuwait? Running a school?"

"Strange, isn't it? But, yes, they had a special school. It has been there for a long time. Wealthy Arabs, even Muslims, sometimes send their children there."

"This seems strange to me."

"The best educated Arab Muslims in the Middle East are educated by the Rosary Sisters. They still scare me."

"Then what?"

"My father was a merchant in different things. Some legal, some I think not so legal. So, when we were older, he branched out into many things. He made a lot of money. My brother attended Cambridge. I attended as well. But later, I taught Islamic studies and world history at the University of Finland."

"You speak Finnish?"

"The classes were conducted in English. Then, I went looking for my brother. The nuns did not squash his spirit. He went to Chechnya. For years, he worked against the Russians. For a while, I did too. But after the Beslan school siege, I left. I could not kill as they did. But I left as well to join a friend. He was a priest, Greek Orthodox. Together we worked to uncover a mystery."

"A mystery? Is this why I am here?"

"I have said enough."

"But I still don't know why I should trust you or even if I can trust you."

Detainee 9696 reached into his beard and pulled on an imperceptible string and momentarily struggled as his fingers sought to extricate something hidden. He then cupped that something in his hand and held it out to Chisolm.

Chisolm cautiously reached across, palm up, to receive the item. Detainee 9696 immediately dropped two double-edged razors into his hand.

"A gift from my attorney and the International Red Cross."

Chisolm stared at 9696. "How? Why?"

"Last night I heard someone crying. You should know him perhaps—the boy who is new. He is to cut and kill himself. A form of *jihad*. It is a strange and ugly way. But I talked with the boy. He told me that he does not wish to die. I asked him for the razor. He gave it to me. I give you mine as well. Our deaths are to embarrass you and all the Americans—to send a message—better death than life at Guantanamo."

"When were you to do this?"

"Friday night, when many of the guards are off duty or relaxed. There may be others."

"Who knows of this?"

"I think the leaders of the camp—some of the Yemenis, the Saudis. They are the worst. There are several who look at me severely. I think they know. You need to get the boy out of here, me as well. If we do not kill ourselves, they will."

"Thank you."

"As a dead man, I cannot help you. I asked for you. Now you must ask for me."

Chisolm, anxious to convey this information to Rusty Peppers, rose to call the guard to again take 9696 to his cell. Chisolm reached across the table and shook the prisoner's hand.

"I am old enough to be your father. Take care of me and I will bless you."

Chisolm could say nothing in reply.

"Tell your friends behind the window to act quickly. I'm getting old here." He smiled at Grant's stoic demeanor and added, "I trust you. You don't smile so much like the other Americans and you listen—I can hear your silence."

THE HUMILIATION

Port of Spain, Trinidad – Friday Morning

Major Thomas Patel, age thirty-two, sat quietly on his haunches listening to the imam. His prayer rug beneath him depicted a series of beautifully ornate interlocking geometric patterns in a calligrapher's flair against a dark green background. With his dark complexion and, of recent weeks, fully-bearded and mustached face, along with black hair that curved slightly out above his ears and on the back of his neck, he blended in quite inconspicuously. Beneath his loose-fitting attire, a baggy shirt and traditional peasant pants that came up above the ankles, white and wrinkled, were two powerful arms that he hoped to keep concealed so as not to arouse suspicion or admiration.

His near anonymity was as designed as the calligraphy that enveloped the exterior as well as the interior of the mosque in which he now sat. Whenever he spoke with his fellow Muslims, he did so in a sort of choreographed mumbling to disguise his British accent and his otherwise perfect diction and hard to conceal repertoire of words that revealed a background in travel, reading, and experience that might bring him unwanted attention. He lived in a house that he supposedly came recently to claim from a deceased uncle that was within sight of the mosque. The location provided him with an opportunity to watch the comings and goings while nonchalantly drinking tea in his bedroom window that overlooked the street between them. Part of his disguise was a slight limp from a shrapnel wound in his left ankle that still ached from an IED he had encountered in Basra a year earlier. There he had walked the streets of the city as a supposed native, observing the activity of several Al-Qaeda suspects after the British forces had left.

From the minbar, the imam spoke in English with a Yemeni accent. Although he had been in Trinidad less than a year; he had already cultivated a bevy of followers who wished to execute the veiled threats against the *infidels* that imbued each of his lectures.

"You are children of the one true God. Yours is the God of Ibrahim, the God of Moses, the God of Isa, and the God of Mohammad, peace be unto him. Yet your grievances are unabated. You suffer daily the insults of those who despise you. Even here, even in a land to which you came many years ago. Yes, I too know of your suffering. Your ancestors left India and came here more than a hundred and fifty years ago and, like you, they wished only to be respected as human beings. They came as indentured servants, hoping for a better life. But they were humiliated when they arrived. They were little more than slaves to their Western masters, the British, and their overseers who took them to work on the plantations as pieces of dirt. The humiliation. Always, always, the humiliation. But we should not be surprised. For the Western crusaders have sought to spit upon us and show us their feet upon our faces for a thousand years. Yet, there is always hope if you believe in the one true God. For like Moses, Allah shows you the way through the desert of your suffering. If you do not doubt him and you but strike the rock upon which you are cast by the *infidels*, not with your doubts, but with your faith, the water of justice shall quench your thirst. Justice and mercy shall be yours.

"For once they took Jerusalem from us, but the great Salahuddin returned it to us. They sought to subdue us with the armies of the Romans, but we took Constantinople from them and taught *them* the meaning of humiliation for their heathen ways. And remember, when the Polish Roman declared himself the pope and sought to humiliate us by calling himself the champion of Isa upon earth, it was a Turk, a Muslim who struck him down and nearly killed him for the idols that he worshipped.

"Here you live in a land like so many others that has felt the boot of the British. Remember what they did to your ancestors when they mocked them in India. You know of what I speak. They sought to make Hindu and Muslim alike strike at one another by forcing them to use bullets covered in pig's fat so as to humiliate them. But the sepoys struck back and butchered the British who still today not only eat the pig but who are of the pig and so they remain unclean. Still, they could not tame us, for we are the children of the righteous and merciful Allah. And we struck again and again until we created a truly Muslim country. The *umma* was carved out of the world, out of India to give us Pakistan and Kashmir and Afghanistan. Countries in which your brothers now fight not only the British but their pig brothers, the Americans, and the even the Dutch who sleep with other men in sin and call it freedom. Is that the kind of liberty you want for yourself and your children? Do you wish to be pigs who sleep in filth with other men?

"No, no and yet today the humiliation continues and your brothers cry out to you from the Temple Mount where the Jew attempts to take Muslim land and turn it into a western house for whores and always, always, it is a Jew or an American who tells you he does this for your liberty. There can be no liberty for those wrapped in the sin of idolatry. This you already know.

"I have lived in the West, and I have gone to their schools. I can tell you how they attempt to strip us of our faith and make us dress like pigs. Their women are whores, and they wish for ours to be the same. They rape our lands in Iraq, in Afghanistan, in Gaza, in Jerusalem, in the land of the Turks, in the mountains of China where they kill your Muslim brothers, the Uyghurs, to make them submit so they can rape our women as well. Always, always the humiliation. But there is hope. For you are men and men can be warriors, men can carry out *jihad* and bring justice to the *infidel.*

"In your lifetime, if you are the sons of the one true faith, you can strike back at them and turn their own liberty against them. You can be merciful and save their women from being whores. Some of you have seen their women, and some of you may have been with them. For they use what God has given them to seduce us and make us like them. If you have done this,

you can still change your ways and come again
into the embrace of the one true God. But you
yourself must be holy. You must renounce their
whores and truly, truly, I tell you that this is what
they are. For their women have sex with many
men so that they do not even know the fathers
of their children. And if they do not wish to
have the children even of their husbands,
they abort them. Yes, did you know that the
American woman will abort five children in
her life? She will kill the innocent and shed the
blood of her own children so that she does not
have to share her food with them. This you will
not find in the *umma*. This no Muslim would
do, no Muslim would tolerate this.

"Even here, even now, you suffer the humiliation
as the Westerners come from all over to make
fun of you when you attempt to honor Hussein
and Hassan, the grandsons of Mohammad,
peace be unto him. Your commemoration is
now little more than another festival where
they line the streets, not to honor the beloved
grandsons of the greatest man in all of history,
but to drink wine and beer and to have sex with
women and even other men. Like so much else
that they fear and reject, the Westerners spit
upon the holy. They cannot understand what
a good Muslim does for they are ignorant.
Their books are filled with filth and lies. They
cheat all that they deal with, even one another.
And your Hosay to them is just a parade to

be despised and filled with drunkenness and humiliation of good Muslims. But if you are among the good Muslims, if you are truly part of the *umma*, you shall deliver your brothers from their wickedness.

"How can this be done? For there are many Westerners throughout the world. But Mohammad was just one man and yet he forced both the Jew and the Roman to submit or die. You can do the same. For you are his children and you, I believe, have faith and that is why you are here. And if you are silent, you can hear your brothers crying to you for justice and for mercy. They cry to you for you are of them. You are of their blood and they know that you are an instrument of the one true God and that you will carry out *jihad* in his name. Yes, they cry to you for deliverance from the Jew in Jerusalem. They cry to you for deliverance from Beirut. They cry to you for mercy in Kandahar. They cry to you from Mumbai. They cry to you for mercy from the wickedness in New York where the Jew steals money from people all over the world. They cry to you for mercy in Grozny where the Chechens fight for their very lives against the Orthodox Russians. They cry to you for mercy in the streets of Paris where the Franks beat them, for they are still the old crusaders who invaded our land a thousand years ago. They cry to you for mercy in Switzerland where they cannot even build a minaret. They cry to you for justice in Rabat where the pagan king pretends that he is one of us while he defiles Islam with his Western ways.

"But soon, soon, some among you will strike in the name of *jihad* and your brothers and all true Muslims will praise you. Then they will be truly free, free again to live in the peace of the *umma*, in London, in Paris, and even in Washington DC where we shall one day rule. And once again the caliphate will stretch not just from Mecca and Medina to the land of the Romans, but even again into Granada and Cordova, Vienna and Sicily. And finally, even our brothers in Guantanamo shall be free, not indentured servants, not slaves to Western masters, but free Muslims to embrace the *Koran* and the *Hadith*. And all this and more will come to pass when brave men, like we have here today, embrace the teachings of the Prophet and cleanse themselves of sin by committing themselves to *jihad* and the beauty of surrender to the teachings of the one true God. The caliphate will come again to all lands in which it once was and stretch across all the waters of the world into Brazil, Venezuela, California, Texas, and even to the Communist land of Cuba and all of Trinidad and Tobago."

He paused and looked down at his hands, and then as he looked up again, he held his hands before him and said, "My blessings upon you for you are the instrument of your brothers' deliverance."

His face glistened with sweat and his mouth quivered slightly from the exertion of what was a heartfelt and spontaneous address, or at least one without notes. He stepped down from the minbar and was immediately given a glass of water by one of the other imams who escorted him to a cushion upon which he slowly sat. Several young men, including Major Thomas Patel of the British Royal Marines and Special Operations, came closer to hear what individual advice he might wish to give them. But one young man in particular seemed already to have been singled out for special consideration.

As he came to sit closer to the imam, the old man motioned for him to come forward. The imam leaned toward him and put his hands on both of the young man's shoulders and kissed him on each cheek and then placed a hand on his head and closed his eyes for a special blessing which he whispered to himself. The young man was dutifully humble and quiet, neither moving nor looking up as the blessing was bestowed. Moments later, the young man left without another word.

As others conversed with the old man, Patel bowed respectfully as he arose and walked out of the mosque where he was greeted by another broad-shouldered individual who was clean cut, blond, and who said something to him and handed him a folded sheet of paper. The major glanced at it, then turned away toward his home. Moments later, he made a phone call to NAS Key West. It was still early afternoon. He walked down a flight of stairs and got into his rented car, a gray Ford Galaxy, and turned down Wrightson Road and headed toward Piarco International Airport, a half an hour's drive through the city and out into the savanna and rural setting where the airport lay.

◆◆◆

Major Patel sat in his car watching through his binoculars as Mahtab sat beneath the veranda of the outdoor restaurant and tower talking with someone who looked very much like himself. The man was dark, perhaps Indian, and sported a beard longer than his own with gray streaks. Several times during their conversation, the older man reached out to pat Mahtab on the cheek or shoulder as if reassuring him of something. The older man's attire was businesslike, tan pants with a sharp crease in them. Black shoes, a collared white shirt, a loosely drawn tie with broad green and white stripes, and a sport coat that concealed an ascetic physique that bordered on emaciation. The man had a pair of heavy-rimmed black glasses that hung suspended around his neck and seemed curiously to bow the neck down with its otherwise nebulous weight.

After a half an hour, Mahtab rose from his chair. The older man did the same, kissed him on both cheeks, and handed him a string of prayer beads which the young man took in both hands. He then turned and walked out of the restaurant toward a hangar. Outside the hangar doors, a plane was already revved and ready to take off. A mechanic approached Mahtab as he walked toward the plane and motioned for someone else to come forward. Out of the shadow of the hangar itself, another young man of dark complexion, black hair, and clean shaven walked to meet them. They smiled as if they already knew one another. Major Patel recognized the other man as yet one more familiar face he had seen at several of the mosque services in previous weeks. First Mahtab entered the plane, a Cessna T303 Crusader, and then the other person. In several more minutes the plane was on the runway. Mahtab raised its flaps, and took off into the warm and very blue midafternoon sky. Major Patel picked up his satellite phone and again called NAS Key West.

As Mahtab piloted the plane across the blue water, his companion opened an envelope that provided a reminder of all the details of their flight. Mahtab was to fly the plane northwest for over six hundred miles to the island of Vieques off the coast of Puerto Rico. There he would be greeted in just several more hours by a man in his late twenties who represented a faction of Puerto Rican society disenchanted with the workings of the government of the Commonwealth of Puerto Rico and its status as something less than an independent nation and something less than a full-fledged state of the United States. He would have another plane waiting, which would be fully loaded with more than a thousand pounds of explosives and the necessary fuel capacity to fly the remaining six hundred plus miles to his target, United States Naval Base Guantanamo.

Although the facility itself at Vieques was run by the Federal Aviation Administration, it was lightly manned to do little to interfere in matters not of immediate significance and to do even less to consider nonessential matters. A plane departing shortly after its arrival, in order to get back to Trinidad, might be unusual but not particularly out of the ordinary. Since the United States Navy was forced by external pressure, wrought by anti-military publicity fanned in both Puerto Rico and the continental United States, to abandon its use of Vieques for amphibious assault training and naval bombardment exercises, it had become a haven for drug traffickers who loaded and unloaded their cargo in the shallow waters off its coast. No more Navy, a lot more drug runners.

Here, Mahtab Razak would immediately take to the air in another Cessna T303 Crusader for the final leg of his appointment with a warrior's destiny and with that of his heavenly father. A suspected illicit cargo of drugs would have been, in this instance, preferred by his liaison in Vieques as opposed to the explosives he now carried. As the Caribbean sun sank, Mahtab found himself measuring the distance to a rendezvous with the Americans. His flight companion who had facilitated the preparations for the plane's being turned into an instrument of destruction would stay on the island, preferring drug running to martyrdom.

RAPPORT BUILDING

Late Friday Morning

"Where?" asked Sanchez in Spanish.

The prisoner, still naked in his cell, looked up, red-eyed and pathetic. Neither rage nor hostility now emanated from his being, his shoulders slumped and his eyes puffy with black circles under them.

"I was not told, only that the equipment would be provided."

"Where did you get the passports?"

"They were given to us."

"By whom?"

"A Chinese man."

"Chinese?"

"We picked them up in Panama. We then went back to Nicaragua."

"But you clearly are not Nicaraguan. Your Spanish is terrible."

"May I have my clothes back?"

"Tell me more, then you can dress."

"What do you want to know?"

"Where did you learn to scuba dive?"

"In the Netherlands."

"The Netherlands? The Dutch are not known for their diving ability. Why there?"

"This is where I lived."

"Where in Netherlands?"

"Amsterdam."

"How long?"

"Fifteen years."

"I have read of divers from the Middle East there who called themselves the Al-Qaeda diving club. Were you part of this group?"

"It was a joke, at first."

"Then what?"

"I want my clothes back or I will not say anymore."

"You'll get your clothes back *when* you say more."

A long silence ensued. After several minutes, Sanchez rose and said, "You waste my time. We have no further use of you."

Alarmed, the prisoner looked up and said, "No, no, I have more. Just please, my clothes. Please, I have no dignity. Please."

Sanchez stopped with his back to the detainee, hesitated, and turned once to look at the prisoner. He then pounded on the door of the interrogation cell and yelled, "Guard, guard."

"No, no, I know what you are trying to do. I just want my clothes."

The guard, who was female, opened the door and stood before Sanchez holding the prisoner's clothes. As she handed them to him, she looked past him at the naked man huddled on the floor who attempted to cover himself.

"You are a bastard!" he shouted. "You humiliate me! You humiliate me! You are a pig!"

Sanchez walked up to the prisoner, stooped down, and handed him his clothes. "We even have cleaned them. Pigs are not so clean and kind as we are. Now put these on and remember that no one will hurt you if you talk to us. But if you fail to, there is nothing I can do for you.

"Now your friends. You will tell me if they are here with you. What mosque did you belong to?"

The prisoner took the clothes and put them on as Sanchez looked away. The guard remained at the door. Sanchez waved her away. She locked the door behind her and disappeared.

"I am hungry," whispered the prisoner.

"You try my patience. I too have not eaten for some time. You are a burden, but if you are hungry, we can eat together. Please, go on, tell me more. I am listening." Before the prisoner could say more Sanchez got up and again pounded on the door. Moments later, another guard appeared. Sanchez stepped out of the cell and whispered something to him. Within moments, four other guards appeared. Sanchez opened the door and motioned for the prisoner to stand.

"You will walk with me to dinner."

The four guards, two to either side of the doorway, waited as Sanchez and then the prisoner passed. They fell in silently behind the two men. Several minutes later, after walking through a labyrinth of empty cells and offices that seemed barely used and lightly attended, the group emerged into a courtyard that at one time had been an exercise area for the men detained in first the Batista regime, and then Castro's.

In the middle of the courtyard, under an arched blue-and-white canopy stretched between two palm trees, sat a large rectangular wooden table with place settings for two individuals. The place settings were on old wooden plates with carved flowers around their edges and shiny silver spoons, forks, knives, and bright blue cloth napkins. To the right of each plate was a large water glass already filled to the brim, ice and a lemon slice completing the effect of misplaced elegance in the old prison yard.

Sanchez motioned for one of the guards to pull out the chair for the prisoner who cautiously sat down with a discernible relief. Sanchez walked to the other side, both men now enveloped by the shade of the trees and the canopy. A moment later, another guard came out with an extension cord and an electric fan. The fan, an oddly shaped propeller-like device, was placed on the far end of the table where its low hum slightly vibrated the table and incessantly, but silently, shook the water glasses to a faint shimmer.

The prisoner looked around, quietly taking in the hacienda-type courtyard with its high concrete brick walls half covered in peeling plaster. Oddly, a garden of cactus and some shrub-like flowers had been planted and obviously maintained along one entire side of the yard. As the prisoner looked around, Sanchez snapped his fingers.

"You forget why you are here." He smiled. "Try to eat something before I take it all," he offered good-naturedly.

The prisoner watched as Sanchez reached with a fork and ladle to secure a helping of pulled pork and offered it. The prisoner squinted and asked, "Is it pig?"

"It's pork, of course it's pig."

"No, I may not eat it."

"Of course not, I was just checking to see what kind of Muslim you were. Not secular. Just a man of firm beliefs. Here, have some chicken. Also, the fruit is very good—mangoes, peaches, and coconut juice. You can have as much as you like."

"Why do you say I am Muslim?"

"Your face, your accent. The fact that you were doing something here that you should not have. You hate the Americans. Perhaps we can work together. But only if you share information with me."

The prisoner reached for the sliced chicken and drank some water, glancing now and again to either side to see where the guards were. As he began to eat, Sanchez smiled and said, "Cuba is a beautiful country with warm sun and warm people. You will like it here."

The veiled allusions to indefinite detention did not slip by the prisoner.

"Are you married?"

The prisoner looked up for a moment with a pained expression and then a tear formed in the corner of each eye and he went back to eating without saying a word.

The tears did not escape Sanchez. "So, then you have children as well. Perhaps they miss you already."

"Will I...will I see them again?"

"Do the Dutch even know you are here?"

"I did not come here for the Dutch. I came here because of the Americans."

"But you are on Cuban soil. If you harm the Americans, we will be blamed. They will think we conspired with you. Or maybe they will think that we allowed you to use our land as your base of operation. In either case, they will seek revenge against us."

"You said perhaps we could work together."

"First let me tell you a story about a slave, a runaway slave. You are not one of us. So in a sense, you are like a slave. But let me tell you. Do you like history?"

The prisoner continued looking at Sanchez but said nothing.

"A long time ago, a slave who was a gladiator ran away from his master and started a slave uprising against the Romans. He was very brave. But he led his uprising against the most formidable force in the ancient world. The Romans were determined to make him pay by killing him. But he was equally determined not to let them destroy him and his army of runaway slaves. To make his point both to the Romans and to his own men, he took one of the young Roman soldiers who had been captured. Then, in the very sight of the Romans, he had the young soldier crucified. They say he lingered on the cross for more than a day. The Romans watched one of their own die. The slaves watched as well. He meant nothing to the slaves and the Romans knew that this could happen to them."

"Is this the story of Isa?"

"You will let me finish. I think the Americans are like Romans. If they were to see someone crucified or even just punished for disturbing the peace between us, they would know that we are strong and that we will not tolerate anyone who harms us or brings difficulties to us. Do you agree?"

"The Americans?"

Sanchez looked at the prisoner who was now munching on a peach. "I tell you what I think. I think maybe you came to do us harm. You are like the Roman soldier who was crucified. But unlike him, you have no friends in the

Americans. They don't care for you. They don't even know you are here, do they?"

"I despise them."

"If I made a case for delivering you to them, what do you think they would do? I like you and so I do not wish to do that. They can be cruel as you know. You are no doubt aware of Abu Ghraib. You are Arab so first they would make you have sex with another man. They would waterboard you. But after that, then you may disappear. The Americans use the ocean to their advantage. Maybe you are someone they will punish to let the rest of the world know how they treat terrorists. To the slaves, the Roman was a terrorist. To the Romans, the slaves were terrorists. I wonder which you are. But I think you may have come to do Cuba harm and you did it with the help of bad people who despise not the Americans, but the Cubans."

Without another word, Sanchez rose and left the table. The prisoner sat alone with the guards at a distance while Sanchez disappeared through a doorway into a windowless office space. He then carried on a casual conversation with another officer, who periodically looked out the doorway and informed Sanchez of the prisoner. He sat alone in the middle of the courtyard, too upset to continue eating and befuddled by Sanchez's abrupt departure.

Over the next hour he drank the entire pitcher of water, waiting for Sanchez to return. After two hours, he motioned to one the guards that he needed to urinate. The guard pointed to a nearby wall where the prisoner relieved himself in the noonday heat. After three hours of sitting alone, he said, "I wish to speak to the gentleman soldier. Tell him I am his friend."

After letting the prisoner sit alone in the courtyard for four more hours, Sanchez walked out into the courtyard with two cigars and lit one for the prisoner and one for himself. Moments later, the same female guard who had seen him naked, walked out with a pitcher of coffee, sugar, and milk. As she put the items next to the prisoner, he looked away. Two cups were brought out by another guard who placed one in front of each of the men.

"I want to talk."

Sanchez sat and waited, smoking and enjoying the movement of shadows that played on the courtyard dust and desert. He smiled and the prisoner opened up to him.

ONE NIGHT

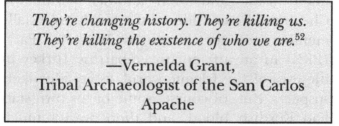

> *They're changing history. They're killing us.*
> *They're killing the existence of who we are.*[52]
>
> —Vernelda Grant,
> Tribal Archaeologist of the San Carlos
> Apache

Istanbul, Turkey—5:02 a.m., Saturday (9:02 p.m., Friday, Guantanamo Time)

For once in his life, he was flabbergasted. The chief of Turkish Police in Istanbul grabbed the edge of his desk with his left hand. An habitual early riser so that he could jump on problems and set the rudder for sailing through his daily activities, he now wished he had taken retirement two years earlier as he was entitled. Instead, he had stayed on at the behest of a wife who knew that the sedentary life of a retiree without purpose was beyond his capabilities. He would die. He cringed as the litany of missing items was relayed to him over his cell phone.

"How? How? How?" he screamed into the phone. "How can this happen? Who would do this? Chechens! Chechens! It must be! If it's illegal, it must be Chechens. They are the worst!"

Though he immediately let loose one invective-filled tirade and then another about the Chechens, he considered the Kurds, especially members of the Kurdistan Workers' Party (PKK) in an attempt to embarrass Turkey in the eyes of the Islamic world, as equally likely suspects. But, of course, some of his own staff had Kurdish blood, and there wasn't much point in antagonizing or embarrassing them.

"Shit! Shit!" he yelled. Before his assistant even entered his glassed-off area of the second floor of police headquarters, not yet knowing why his boss was in a fulmination, he stopped in consternation. "Get me the car! Damn it! Get the car or we'll both be dead!" He reached under his jacket and pulled out his SIG P220, opened his drawer, and pulled out a clip and smacked it into the gun. Not knowing what or whom he was up against, he raged at his assistant who was already on the phone. "Get the detachment—everyone that guards Topkapi. I want them all. All of them! Now!"

His assistant hesitated for a split second to see if his boss had further instructions. Chief Giray

Pasa was yelling, even as he still absentmindedly held his cell phone, through which the man at the other end attempted to ask and was hardly heard to say, "Sir, when will you be here?"

Ignoring the question, he shut his cell phone and cursed to himself as the morning call to prayer wafted through the interior of the police station. Its tenor of beauty and peace seemed to mock the frenetic pace of the chief and all others attempting to help or to get out of his way. Others froze in a panic, not knowing what had happened to unhinge a man whose reputation for self-control was unrivaled but for his toughness and courage in dealing with Kurdish separatists and would-be Al Qaeda.

As the chief rushed out the door, he ran into his secretary just coming in. He grabbed her by the left shoulder and spun her around, causing her to drop her cup of coffee on the floor and said, "You're coming with me!" As she stopped to protest, looking forlorn at her coffee, he responded, "To hell with your coffee!" Startled and nonplussed, she strode with him.

"What? What?" he yelled as she looked beseechingly at him for some sort of explanation as two others ran ahead, down the stairs to the lot where someone was already bringing his Fiat to the doorway. He approached the driver's side, and practically yanked the driver out by the collar as he seethed, "I'm driving! Get out!" His assistant barely got in on the passenger's side, as his secretary fell into the backseat of the car as it jerked forward with one of her feet still planted on the ground, causing her shoe to twist off and under the rear wheel.

"Shit! Shit! Shit!" he repeated as he sped off in the direction of the Topkapi Palace Museum. Then, in a stage whisper, he recited a phrase well known to certain elements of the Turkish Police. "How far can you see? How far can you see?" He answered himself, "Nowhere! For I have nothing and now I am blind..." He could not even finish as his breath was caught in his throat in an almost paralytic seizure. The morning air seemed condensed and voluminous as if it were too dense to be aspirated or even swallowed. He wanted to choke. He coughed in a futile attempt to exhale since his mind and body momentarily refused the reflex, causing him to nearly choke. He realized that he would prefer to be dead than ever be called to such a crime scene.

Minutes later, he pulled his car right up to where the Turkish gendarmes stood outside the courtyard of the Topkapi Palace Museum with machine guns, all in close proximity to one another. Two other cars filled with police and detectives immediately pulled up behind him, their sirens blaring and their flashing lights turning the early morning into a sickly disco scene with stags all about and a cherished female form hobbling from the backseat of the car with one high-heeled shoe still on. She walked back several paces and threw the shoe into the rear window of the car and ran after the chief in her bare feet. The chief strode toward the Gate of Salutation as he called out, "You have some explaining to do, Captain. You all do! You all do!" he repeated as he extended his arms toward the sleepy-eyed and barely dressed gendarme. Then he stopped and pointed at a gaggle of soldiers and police and said, "Why are you standing there? Huh? Spread out! Check the grounds! Look! Look! See things! Huh!"

Even as the sixty-four-year-old chief of police stomped forward, the captain of the gendarme who guarded the Topkapi Palace Museum fell into the chief's slipstream as he coursed through deferential military and police personnel who fell away from the charging chief as if they were negatively sparked ions. The chief was giving off a voltage that was about to knock them all down. Aloud he uttered, "Why are we here? What is special about this place, Captain?"

Hesitatingly, the captain responded, "Yes, the place is holy…" and then stopped at the chief's glare.

Entering the Chamber of the Sacred Relics, he found six soldiers standing around with the room completely illuminated and all pretense of the usual reverence gone. He walked right up to the empty casement which had previously held the objects of faith. The chief pushed aside one of the soldiers in his way and stopped abruptly as if what he already knew from the phone call earlier had been a hoax and that when he looked—somehow, someway—the Holy Relics would be revealed. As he looked upon the bulletproof plexiglass display case, his heart sank and a great pang of remorse followed as if over some long-forgotten sin that had been brought to the light of day and consciousness. It was as if the pained memory of some suppressed sin had gotten hold of his heart and shame was twisting it while squeezing the processes of his brain into a sieve that brought about its complete stoppage. His heart raced as he looked upon an empty casement that matched the abysmal emptiness of his own being from which he felt his very soul had been stolen.

The chief stared at the captain and said after a long delay, now recapturing his wits, "Really? And why is that, Captain? Tell me, why is that? Is that," and his voice began to rise, "is that because…because this place guards the Sacred Relics! Is it?" His voice was trembling and he threw his cigarette on the floor. "Is it? Because

I see nothing sacred here." Then he stopped as if abruptly coming to a sudden realization and said, "Yes, it is sacred." And uttered sarcastically, "For there we have the beard of ...Oh, no, that's not true, it must have been my imagination, but perhaps Mohammad had no beard."

"Ah, but no problems for here I see the tooth... oh, but no, no tooth either. So Mohammad was beardless and toothless and his seal..." Then, as if realizing for the first time what else might be missing, he gazed through the plexiglass into the adjoining room where he saw a golden throne and said aloud, "The mantle of the Prophet, the Prophet's mantle. Is it still here?"

Again, he bumped into a guard and then a curator who had made the mistake of standing too close to the chief. The chief, as he had with the others, snapped at him. "Access! Access! Open it! What else is missing?" Moments later, he and several others walked into the room and opened the gold box. Though they knew what to expect, they gasped and moaned in disbelief. His secretary began to cry and soldiers blanched and winced as if something were tugging at their hearts, even those who seldom attended mosque.

Then as the chief took one step backward, he bumped into the display that had held the swords of Mohammad—which had been mounted horizontally on teak wood racks. The chief slid his hand up and down in a slow-motion karate chop as if trying to ascertain that the swords were really gone. He repeated the motion in silence as he looked about him. Two more guards entered the room. He was inclined for a moment to speak softly when he caught sight of the captain of the guards once again. He exploded.

"Do you know what has been done here? Do you know the legacy that has been betrayed? Do you know the repercussions? Do you know what it is to be shamed by all the nations of the earth? Do you know what you—my—all our negligence has undone? Do you know our shame in all of Islam? Do you know of our shame in all of Christendom? For even the bones of John the Baptist, they are gone forever."

Then he breathed deeply and looked about the room as he said, "What the Mongols could not destroy and take from us, someone has. What the Romans could not take, someone has. What the Crusaders could not take, someone has. The Huns could not take this from us, but someone has. The Tartars and Greeks—even they."

As he looked across the room back into the other chamber, the broken pane that he had once noticed in the room of the Sacred Relics, but ignored, suddenly registered and he stepped briskly back into it and uttered again, "How can you see God? How far can you see? Even the Jews will now spit on us for the sword of David is missing. That which we would not sell to Israel, someone has taken. Even now the house of David must be cursing us."

Then, as if answering his own questions, he uttered, "I see. I see a life without redemption. We have betrayed Christendom, we have betrayed the house of David and Ibrahim, and we have failed Islam." He stood for an entire minute with his hands brought to his face in a gesture of unbearable fatigue. The light of day was only dawning and his hands remained in place now as a prayerful gesture to seek assistance for the job that would require all his skills. Bringing his hands down, he leveled his gaze at one of his lieutenants and said, "If I ask you to kill me, do not. Wait until we capture those who did this, then kill me!"

His self-deprecating remarks, his tirade, and even his quiet reverie on a life without redemption were brought to an end by yet another one of his detectives who entered the room. He had the good fortune to have little imagination and even less appreciation of the soulful eloquence of the chief's rant as he said, "I'm here, Chief, I'll decontaminate the scene.

Too many people here. Need to get them out. We'll check everything. We're already scouring the grounds inside and about the perimeter."

The chief then gently patted him on the shoulder as he passed him on his way out into the warm morning. He lit up a cigarette as he thought about the call he must now make to the prime minister and how he would have to explain all of this to the press. Then oddly, he wondered if the night's events would ostracize Turkey in the eyes of the Islamic world and simultaneously enhance the prospects of Turkey getting into the European Union. *How mundane*, he thought, *how mundane*. As he and his security detail drove back, leaving his assistant at the scene, he began to sing softly a silly American song he remembered from his youth. "Que sera, sera. . ." In a gesture of sympathy, his secretary lit her own cigarette and hummed along. Feeling the bulge of his revolver underneath his jacket, he began to sweat profusely at the thought of what he feared he might do. Thoughts of his wife and his grandchildren comforted him even as he imagined himself consoling them at the ridicule he feared they would endure. He asked then for Allah's blessing upon them. How unfair it was that He would allow the innocent to suffer.

THE MEETING

U.S. Intelligence Center, Guantanamo —9:06 p.m., Friday

"Sir, sir, you can't go in..." Before she could finish the sentence, Colonel Winston Bradley had already opened the door of Rusty Peppers' office. Peppers was on the phone. He held up one hand as if to keep the colonel at bay. Peppers' flustered secretary stood behind the colonel at the doorway, looking concerned and worried. Peppers motioned for the colonel to sit down and for his secretary to close the door. Peppers continued talking on the phone. As he leaned back, listening to the voice on the other end, he looked over at the colonel who had seated himself right next to Peppers' desk. The colonel then slid a 10x13-inch brown envelope over to Peppers. Even as he was speaking, Peppers undid the metal fastener with one hand, reached inside, and pulled out a handful

435

of 4x6-inch color photographs. What he saw momentarily stunned him. He then spread the photographs out like a large deck of cards.

"I'm afraid more is afoot than any of us realize, Commander," replied Peppers to the voice on the other end of the phone. "Colonel Bradley is in my office. Can you join us? The admiral's off island. We need to move on this."

Moments later, Chisolm knocked at the door.

"Jesus, come in. It's nine in the evening, who now?"

Chisolm entered.

"Hell's bells!" exclaimed Peppers. "I feel like this can't be good news, Grant. But, of course, I called you. We need to talk.

"Something's going on and I think…well, never mind. We just need to talk."

Chisolm continued standing. A moment later, Whiskers appeared behind him.

"Good evening, sir."

"Oh Christ! If the Christians in Action are here, this must be bad," said Peppers.

Moments later, the secretary appeared. "Sir, Commander DiPinta called. He's on his way over. He says he has to speak with you. He says it's urgent."

Peppers, who still held the landline phone in his right hand, invited everyone to sit down.

"Something wicked is coming our way, boys and girls," said Peppers. "Look at these."

He picked up the photographs spread across his desk, walked over to the circular table where everyone was seated, and spread them out for all to see.

"What did this?" gasped the colonel.

The color photographs were the remains of a man—a leg and the head were missing. The other leg was loosely attached as if someone or something had tried to wrench it off by twisting. The torso was enclosed in a black scuba vest with an array of flashlights and what at first was indecipherable. Chisolm leaned over the table to get a better look. Partially hanging out of one of the vest pockets was a plastic pack, the same kind, only smaller, he had found only days earlier in the bottom of the failed dry dock where Max had disappeared.

"It's C-4. At least that's what it looks like."

"Why?" asked Whiskers.

"Where was he found?" asked Chisolm.

"Our coasties found him early this morning on the east side of the GITMO River. Coincidentally, the SAT Corporation, which is responsible for the construction project on the leeward side, reported three of their Pakistani workers missing this morning.""Three Pakistanis?" asked Chisolm incredulously.

"I know, I know," replied Peppers. "The lowest bidder gets the contract."

After a slight pause, Peppers went on, "If this body in these lovely photographs had a head, we might know if he is one of them. The coasties found him in the shallows near the bridge as the sun was coming up."

Chisolm asked, "Does the construction company use any explosives?"

"None that I've ever heard of. Even if they did, they'd have to get permission from the HAZMAT people. But there's more. Take a look."

Peppers then reached into a canvas bag that the colonel had dropped next to his desk and pulled out a large dark green and black telephone. It was about eight inches in length with a large square keypad and a four-inch-wide digital display. Chisolm held out his hand. Peppers handed him the phone.

"This is hard to believe." Chisolm then looked at Peppers and then to Whiskers. "This is a rock phone. I used a prototype in Afghanistan. They can transmit through several hundred feet of dirt or rock. They're especially good in caves and mountainous terrain. But I didn't think anyone else had them. We were told only U.S. military personnel would have access, along with some of the Brits and Canadians."

"One of these was attached to what was left of him," added Peppers.

"I'd still like to know what did this," asked Whiskers.

"The coasties speculate that the man tried to cross the GITMO River at night near the bridge. It's shallow there, and he could cross virtually undetected. However, these same shallow waters are where some of our boys go to fish for sharks."

"Those aren't shark bites," insisted Chisolm.

"What else could they be?" asked Peppers.

Before anyone could answer, Peppers answered his own question. "The coasties have told us before about big creatures hidden among the mangroves. Anyone care to speculate as to what they saw?"

Chisolm offered, "Those are croc bites. Look at the teeth marks."

"I've heard about saltwater crocs, but I've never seen any before," offered Whiskers.

"The coasties have. Usually at night or early morning. Once they even saw one of the deer snatched by a croc when it came down to drink from the river."

"We have deer on the island?" asked Chisolm.

"Plenty of 'em," replied Peppers. "The legacy of one of the long-ago base commanders who was an avid hunter and wanted to have some whitetail in case he ever got the urge. He wanted..."

But before Peppers could finish his comment, the rock phone emitted a shrill but low volume beep. Then came a calm voice.

"Praise Allah before we strike. The moon is in our arms and we in those of Mohammad. The suq is destroyed."

After a ten-second pause, the voice continued, "I am the agent of Allah. My heart is already in paradise. In death I am reborn. Seize me and I shall recite."

Peppers looked at Chisolm and said, "Can you respond in the language? My Arabic is rusty."

"I don't think that's Arabic. I think it's Urdu. In fact, I know it is. I can translate though, some of it. "

But before another word was uttered, white noise flowed from the speaker. Then the static disappeared. The phone had been silenced at the other end. Moments later, there was another knock at the door and Peppers' secretary opened it.

"Sir, Commander DiPinta is here."

"Send him in."

As the commander walked in, dressed in a white T-shirt and blue jeans, he glanced at the others in the room. Peppers motioned to another chair. The commander remained standing, then said, "Rusty, I need to speak with you privately for a moment." He then lifted his left arm as a sort of signal. He held in it a large brown envelope. Peppers got up and walked out with the commander, closing the door behind him. Only a minute later, the two men re-entered the room.

"The commander has information I've asked him to share. It's essential to all of us. Colonel, be ready. This scares me."

The commander reached into the envelope, pulling out two white sheets of paper. One was a series of penciled notes. The other was a fax.

"Two hours ago," said the commander, "I received a fax on the dedicated line to Cuban military headquarters in Mirador Los Malones Barracks. This is the one we use to contact our Cuban counterpart, Colonel Sanchez. He asked me for a meeting at the Northeast Gate ASAP. I drove there to meet him. Sanchez said that his men have arrested a man in scuba equipment who they believe to be Pakistani. They caught him coming out of the water at Caimanera. They believe an attack of some sort is planned against our base. Oddly, interestingly, they're asking to help. They're willing to share information. They don't want an attack that can be blamed on them."

"Sir, may I interrupt?" asked Whiskers.

"Go on," injected Peppers.

The commander looked at Whiskers with annoyance.

"Sorry, Commander, for interrupting, but it is pertinent. Just a few days ago, for reasons that are not mine to divulge, we began to discuss plans for defending the base from a possible attack. I, well Max really, asked Grant to envision how and where he would attack. Grant can explain better than I…"

After a twenty-minute explanation, the commander called the Coast Guard.

In response, Peppers uttered, "Timing is everything."

The colonel pushed himself away from the table. "I think I need to call right now. I'll double the guard in the camp. Also, seems we need guards in Camp America."

"The MPs, Commander?"

"We'll be ready. We'll have them on the windward and leeward side."

Chisolm pointed back to the picture of the mangled remains of the person found that morning on the Guantanamo River. "This says to me that the attack is coming from water. It may already be in motion," said Grant. "We have six SEALs on base that I know of. They're here for additional training. I've already spoken with them and their commander, just in case. We've already worked out together—they're fit, just back from Iraq. They worked with the riverine boys. I need all of them."

The colonel offered, "I'm sending guards to each of the beach areas where a person could come ashore. Last night two men were picked up on Cable Beach. They floated in on a raft. They would have made it ashore undetected except for fishermen on the beach. They saw them coming in. We think it was a test of our perimeter. But they seemed to have been real Cubans. Our interrogators said they were fluent. They're genuine...still."

"Sir, we've mapped the weak points," said Whiskers as he pulled out a folding map from between the pages of a yellow legal pad.

"But, sir," added Chisolm, "this was before we knew about the rock phones. Supposedly, these were being handled by a firm in Canada and the UK exclusively for NATO personnel in the theater, Afghanistan."

Peppers frowned and said, "Well, to me that just means that they see themselves as using them. Tell me, are they watertight? Can they pick up signals underwater?"

"Supposedly, they can penetrate water. But you don't want to get them wet. Their signals are very powerful but the mechanism itself has durability issues. I used the prototype in combat." Chisolm glanced at Whiskers. He nodded in agreement.

"I used 'em a time myself. The prototype—they work."

"Gentlemen, details and action," responded Peppers. "We need to act but not provocatively." Peppers rubbed his chin as the others responded with silence, waiting for Peppers' suggestion. "Cubans, Pakistanis, and Yemenis—who the hell's next?" he added. "We've got to move—be prepared for anything. Does everybody know everybody else? Everybody here should have a base cell phone."

"But, Rusty," interrupted the colonel. "The phones, the rock phones. They must be planning at least one entry through a cave or some underground tunnel."

Peppers looked at the colonel and the commander and said, "No such entries exist, right, gentlemen?"

"Sir, I think we need a moment with you in private," said Whiskers.

"We?" asked Peppers.

"Grant and I need a moment of your time."

Peppers rose from his desk and headed toward the door as Chisolm and Whiskers followed. "Apparently, I'll be back shortly," said Peppers to the others as he left the room.

As Chisolm and Whiskers walked back into the room, they were immediately followed by a Navy lieutenant who breezed past the secretary to the door before Chisolm could close it behind him.

"Sir, I need to speak with Commander DiPinta. We have a message of urgency from Colonel Sanchez."

DiPinta stood up at hearing his name and walked to the door. "Sir, Colonel Sanchez is back at the Northeast Gate, requesting another meeting right now. He says it's urgent. He's waiting."

Peppers looked at the commander and said, "We'll be in touch—you have someone's attention. He may have more information for all of us."

"Maybe I should take someone from here with me."

Peppers looked at Chisolm. "He has combat experience. Send him back when you learn what we need to know."

Chisolm got up and followed Commander DiPinta and the lieutenant out.

As they left the room, Peppers and the colonel, along with Whiskers, went back to planning for what they suspected might happen, but for which they still felt inadequately prepared. Minutes later Chisolm, Commander DiPinta, and the lieutenant arrived in the lieutenant's SUV at the Northeast Gate. Sanchez was waiting along with one of his aides.

"Twice in one evening, Colonel Sanchez," said the commander.

"I enjoy your company," replied Sanchez with a half-smile.

The commander turned to Chisolm and said, "Lieutenant Commander, meet Colonel Sanchez. He's a very important figure, and he would not call us back so soon unless he had very important information." Sanchez took the hint and immediately began. Chisolm offered Sanchez his hand but not his name. Chisolm had already taken off the Velcro-attached name tag. The unspoken slight or the "no need to know" premise did not go unnoticed by Sanchez who replied with a slight smile and raised eyebrows as if to say, "As you wish it."

"Commander, we have no time for protocol this evening. Your countrymen, however much we disagree with their presence, are not despised by my people. We wish you no harm and neither do we wish to be blamed for any harm that comes to you. We believe that an attack is being planned against you, which may have the support of foreign elements within my own country." Sanchez paused and took a breath, feeling his own throat swelling shut for a moment. To divulge what he was about to could end his career and would certainly shed light on American-Cuban relations that seemingly defied what otherwise seemed apparent to the world. "Although we believe that the attack will certainly occur by water, we also believe that an attack is planned by land as well, using our own country as the base for the attack. Foreign elements have already entered Cuba. To do this, they must remain undetected or else our own border guards or your Marines would detect them. Their location must be within our immediate vicinity. We assume you yourselves may know of that location."

The commander returned a look of inquiry.

"Commander, you have long pretended not to know. We have also pretended not to know.

To do otherwise, at least on our part, would be to create a strain in American and Cuban relations, one greater than we already have."

"Colonel Sanchez," interrupted the commander, "what are you getting at?"

Sanchez took another deep breath and motioned for his aide to step back out of hearing distance.

"Commander, you and your countrymen have been building an underground facility on sovereign Cuban soil for more than four decades. This facility is intended as an underground submarine base. You have built it secretly, assuming we would never find out. We have pretended not to know in the event that our allies, the Russians, decided to stay too long or attempted to overthrow our government. As you and your own countrymen might say, we do not trust the Communists. As unlikely as it may seem, we assumed we might someday need your assistance."

Chisolm smiled at the last remark and marveled at the candor with which Sanchez spoke.

TIMING

9:38 p.m., Friday

In the hull of the *The Mustang Relent,* a Liberian registered freighter, Shakir looked at one of the vests that would be strapped onto each of the men who would attempt to penetrate the waters around Guantanamo. From a pocket on the back of the vest to another one on the front, a man with a small goatee and only three fingers on his right hand carefully wedded a series of wires to a detonating switch that was capable of being remotely activated or which would otherwise detonate at a prescribed time. One man onshore would have the detonating device in the event that any of the incursion team hesitated to fulfill their obligation as jihadists. The other was a timing device that was mounted in the back of the diving vest, which

451

could be detonated according to the time set by the one who wired the device.

The man constructing and inserting detonating devices had experienced all the satisfaction and the trauma that comes with designing destructive devices. He had made many which had left their imprint all over eastern Africa as well as Iraq and Afghanistan. A Saudi national who had been educated in Great Britain, he recognized no movement as one representing the purity of any cause with which he could identify. However, he succored the Islamic terrorists much as one aids and cheers for a particular athletic team. Those for whom he now worked paid him well and he considered them a kind of hometown favorite. Beyond that, he had no real interests in any movements. He regarded himself as an artist who had, like all great artists, suffered for his quest at perfection. His art was his mistress, and she had enticed him, even as a young man much as fire attracts the pyromaniac. An explosion was to him a singular manifestation of beauty, a blossom that penetrated the depths of human flesh—the layered metal, the shrapnel, the concentrically organized petals that were nothing less than orgasmic. He was a fiend who lived for his art and had surrendered one finger and one thumb in the process.

"Tell me again why you want the bombs to explode at 2 a.m."

"Because Guantanamo, where the Americans are, is in a different time zone. Look here in the Almanac. The Americans are on Eastern Daylight Time, the same as in Florida. But the rest of Cuba is one hour behind."

"You are sure?"

"Look, here you see the time zones are different."

"I can see that, but I want to know if you are sure."

In exasperation, Shakir threw the almanac on a hard metal desk fastened to the wall of the ship. "Do as you are told, you are paid enough not to ask too many questions."

"So, the vests detonate at two a.m. in Guantanamo, but the attack from the Cuban side begins at 1 a.m., 2 a.m. the American time—but the vests explode at 2 a.m. Cuban time."

"Yes, that gives us two hours to complete the attack. Now you understand. Everything is coordinated with the Cubans, not the Americans."

"I don't understand anything. I just know that the simpler an operation, the more likely it is to succeed. Yours frightens me. I do not wish to waste my art."

"Your art will not be wasted, only your concerns."

"I will be finished in one hour with the last of the vests. When you are ready, we will activate the timing devices."

Moments later, there was a knock on one of the bulkhead doors. Shakir opened it just enough to see the captain's face. Captain DeAngelo knew better than to try to force the door even an inch. Like the bomb maker, he too was well paid. He knew better than to ask many questions.

"We are there, on the boundary between Cuban and American waters. The Cubans may observe us but will not bother us. I will request entry into Guantanamo and move into position. They will ask for my manifest and give me a time to enter the harbor. But I may not proceed beyond a certain point or we may find ourselves being boarded by the Americans who think we are perhaps drug pushers."

The captain had a swarthy complexion with dark eyes that glowered. A native of Sicily, he had forsaken any concerns about the ultimate destination of his cargo and of the men who treated him so coldly but paid him so very well.

Shakir pushed the door open and motioned for the captain to lead the way. They immediately ascended a ladder that led to the sleeping quarters for the crew and then, beyond that, to the quarters where the dive team had been resting in anticipation of the night's assault. As they approached the hatchway together, Shakir gave the captain a stare as if to indicate that he should stay outside the hatchway. He entered the room where the men were already astir. Some were still lying in their bunks, but all of them were awake. Shakir approached each one with a smile and said, "My blessing upon you. You are an instrument of *jihad*, you are an instrument of Allah. He alone shall you worship."

He stood again at the doorway and asked, "You have washed?"

They nodded in assent. Though confident of their mission's importance, a couple of the men looked up at him from their bunks imploringly. The strain of their mission was now pushing against their natural impulse to live. Some kept their heads bowed as they contemplated the next several hours and their even greater desire to be in accord with the teachings of Mohammad, of their imam who now stood before them, their families, who would be so proud of them but whom they would not see again until the Day of Judgment, and of their own inner moral compass which told them that the decadence of the West must be destroyed. Without its destruction, its moral decay would infect the *umma* and undo what generations had sought to create in the name of the one true God.

"We are ready, we have rehearsed everything a hundred times," said one, the eldest among them. He had a face toughened by exposure to the desert, to the sea, and to the travails of life. Wounded once already in Iraq, he sought revenge upon the West with a persistence the others found admirable.

"Come with me," said Shakir.

When he opened the door, he found the captain leaning against the bulkhead with a cigar in his mouth, the lit match still in his hand. "When I smell tobacco, I can only think that it is another bad habit that infects the world, compliments of the Americans."

The captain now eyed him warily as he and the others passed by and said in a voice loud enough for others to hear, "But this is Cuban."

They descended into the cargo hull and each man took the vest assigned to him. Each was equipped with the two special compartments for explosives. Over this, they placed their BCD vests already connected to their Dräger breathing apparatus, which would enable them to breathe underwater for miles and even hours with a recyclable oxygen system that, although enduring, was also of decreasing value as the depth increased. Ideally, any swimmer using this would be at fifteen or twenty feet below the water's surface.

All of the men then assembled on deck and looked over the side where two Zodiacs were already inflated and moored alongside the freighter. The two teams of six men now dropped over the side into the boats. On each boat was a homing device that moved toward a beacon placed on the cliffs directly above the opening to the submarine pens. As the men assembled in the Zodiacs, they looked up at Shakir who now stood next to the captain, still puffing on his cigar. One of the men, in an attempt to lighten the somber and tense mood, said, "Come with us, it'll be a lot of fun." Even in the dim light of the bridge, they could make out his features as he smiled in reply.

"I have longed to do as you are doing, but my mission is to bring others to salvation through *jihad.* When I have no longer any purpose as an imam, then I will join you and others. We will gather hereafter in the embrace of Ibrahim, Moishe, Isa, and Mohammad. Yours is the test of true manhood. The virgins will be yours, for men such as yourselves are rare. Remember, our true home is not here but in heaven with Allah."

The motors were revved and the Zodiacs fled toward desolation, salvation, remembrance, and forgetfulness.

Alone on the cliffs overlooking the area immediately above the submarine pens stood one man. In his right hand, he held a transmitter that was sending out the signals the Zodiacs relied on to approach the area near Guantanamo without accidentally cruising into the area typically searched and guarded by the American Coast Guard vessels. Here in the Cuban waters, they could approach within two miles of the shoreline without the prospect of detection by even the Cuban border guards or the occasional boat patrol. Sergeant Juan Miguel scanned the black waters with his night vision binoculars hoping for a glimpse of the men whose destiny now lay in his hands. He thought of himself not merely as a soldier in quest of the Cuban revolution's true success but also, quite literally, as a stalwart lighthouse who would bring others to the fulfillment of the greatest quest, their greatest desire. Like

Jose Marti, he would become a hero to the Cuban people and all who valued the Cuban revolution, as he sought to bring down the Americans who continued to thwart the might of a once great socialist revolution. Those who had betrayed it with too great an accommodation of the American presence in Cuba and throughout the world— they would have to be punished.

As a youth in the one city in all of Cuba where the Muslim population approximated that of the non-Muslim, he had become enamored of the purity and ascetic joys of a monotheistic faith that could explain away his own faith, which at times seemed polytheistic to him. Father, Son, and Holy Spirit seemed like two too many gods. As one of his Muslim teenage friends had said to him, if Jesus is God, to whom did he pray? And in his latter teens, dissuaded by his very own teachers from considering the Revolution as practical and implementable any time soon, he felt the betrayal of his socialistic ideals. In Islam, the Revolution's call for equality was replaced by the *umma*, and the call to arms against imperialists had been replaced by a love of *jihad* and the sword of a god who would not be moved by the laziness and corruption of leaders defeated by the world. The god he now worshipped lived the Revolution in all its purity and maintained an ideological certitude that the truly pure of heart could follow. And like his god, this child of the Revolution would not be moved as he stood on a cliff overlooking the nighttime Caribbean, acting now as a true beacon of truth, liberty, and fixed geographic points of latitude, longitude, and the universal transverse meridians. Even if the satellites in the heavens should fail to transmit to the warriors coming his way, he would not. Sergeant Juan Miguel bin Nassir, the latter being the name of his boyhood friend who had introduced him to Islam, of the town of Playa del Rosario, now stood as a light in the darkness of the world. In the total darkness, he could not even see his own hands but he believed he knew that they were there. And like that belief, there were now others following his directions, even though they could not see him nor see the geographic coordinates that he transmitted through the ether of the universe to dark men in dark boats on dark water to their destiny.

DEATH BY WATER

1:03 a.m., Saturday

Chisolm backed into a niche along the coral wall next to the overhang below which he had seen a flash of light only moments before. Whiskers had followed, lingering above him. Not having seen the light himself, he momentarily lost sight of Chisolm, who had turned off his scooter and his flashlight. Only the bubbles ascending from below gave away Chisolm's position in the recess above the entry to the submarine pens.

As Whiskers descended, he stared as three black figures emerged below Chisolm, coming out from beneath the overhang that led into the submarine chambers. He had also turned off his flashlight several seconds after he noticed that Chisolm had turned off his. Grant had merely asked that he follow his lead.

Each of the three engaged their handheld scooters upon emerging from the pens. Grant and Whiskers did not know who these men were but could only surmise that they were part of the attack planned on Guantanamo. Only seconds after emerging, the three men formed a V with one figure leading and the other two a couple of body lengths behind him, one on either side. They immediately ascended to a mere fifteen feet below the surface. Still undetected, Chisolm and Whiskers hung suspended with their backs to the wall of coral and rock that descended from the cliffs above, past the opening of the submarine pens into the ocean depths below. They watched as the men headed west, the direction from which Chisolm and Whiskers had come.

Chisolm and Whiskers followed at a distance of more than fifty feet, the hum of their own scooters keeping pace with the three haloes in front of them, their adversaries' scooters' lights bouncing off the millennia of microscopic sea life to silhouette each man as if he were some artist's rendition of a saintly figure. Each of the three men carried over their shoulders a waterproof bag meant to protect something inside. Chisolm assumed it must be a weapon.

Seconds later, another three-man team emerged from the sub lair and began following Chisolm and Whiskers. At first, the three men thought they were following two of the three other men who had left only minutes ahead of them. Chisolm and Whiskers were slightly illuminated and cast a silhouette against the ocean in which the visibility was impaired by the night, but not by the water itself which possessed the usual clarity of the Caribbean seas. The dimness of the light behind him and Whiskers kept them unaware of their pursuers as they continued to focus on the three divers ahead of them.

But as the lead man scrutinized the pair, he wondered first at their not having their scooter lights turned on and the absence of a third diver. The second and third diver in turn noticed another peculiarity of the two divers in front. They were both diving with conventional dual tanks with the manifold connection, while this attack team, all six of them, were equipped with the long distance Dräger rebreathing apparatus. Both of them were also wearing flexible yellow night lights wrapped over their tanks unlike the other members of their own team, all of whom wore neon green lights.

The lead diver motioned for the other two to follow him as all three converged on Whiskers, who lagged behind Chisolm by two full body lengths. The rays from their scooter lamps brightened all around Whiskers, causing him to look over his left shoulder abruptly.

Simultaneously, Chisolm turned to his right as their lights illuminated the darkness, silhouetting Whiskers in a frightful glare.

Although all were encumbered by having to hold on to their scooters for propulsion, the lead diver reached for Whiskers' left flipper. Whiskers kicked viciously as he reached down with his right hand to unsheathe an ankle knife. But as he reached for it, Chisolm rammed his scooter directly into the converging attackers, causing Whiskers to drop his knife. The lead diver then pulled his own knife from his holster as Chisolm reached for the man's left hand, which still held his scooter. With his free hand, the assailant plunged his knife three inches deep into Whiskers' left hamstring. Whiskers twisted violently and attempted to rip the face mask off his assailant, even as Chisolm bashed one of the others in the face with his scooter, letting go of the man's hand as he did so. He bashed the head of one of the other assailants with the side of his scooter, causing the man to back away.

But one of the other divers attempted to yank the regulator from Chisolm's mouth. As he attempted to yank it out a second time, Chisolm let go of his scooter, gripping his assailant's hand with both his own, twisting it down hard and rotating it backwards until he felt a snap. He hung on tightly even as he continued twisting and then grabbed at yet another of the opponents as he twisted the man round and pressed his right arm around the man's neck. Realizing that the two men were wearing Dräger breathing devices, which are virtually useless at depths below forty feet, he clung tightly to both men as the other continued fighting with Whiskers. He reached round with one hand and pressed down on his vest valve and let air out of his BCD, causing him to sink lower. Twisting himself into a vertical position with his head down and his assailants beneath him, he kicked forcefully and repeatedly, attempting to pull them deeper and deeper as his own negative buoyancy caused him to sink. As he descended, his regulator now firmly back in his mouth, his assailants twisted and convulsed as the weight of ocean began to crush down on their chests, their breathing becoming more and more pained and their consciousness lessening. They now struggled to be free; harming Grant now seeming a useless proposition. Chisolm's own ears pained at the depths, and he swallowed hard repeatedly to equalize the pressure. He continued his descent, holding both men in a deathly embrace.

Chisolm glanced upward where one of the scooters still floated, apparently tethered to the lead assailant's hand. It cast enough light that Chisolm could see Whiskers held his opponent by the neck and was attempting to force him downward as he had seen Chisolm do. The assailant had had the knife pried from his hand but still fought, not to escape, but to kill Whiskers. He repeatedly attempted to rip the regulator from Whiskers' mouth. But Whiskers bit down hard on the regulator and squeezed even harder around his assailant's neck. After nearly a minute of kicking and punching and reaching to free himself from Whiskers' grip, the assailant began to flail about in a frenzy. Whiskers squeezed harder, embracing him, turning him round, and throttling him completely from behind until he stilled. Then, he depressed his regulator and slowly descended, following the glimmer of the flexible neon lights still faintly illuminating the depths beneath him.

At nearly one hundred feet, Chisolm was now perched on an overhang beyond which lay the fathomless abyss. There he held tightly to the two men who struggled faintly and spasmodically. After another minute, Whiskers, blood still trailing from his leg, joined him. His foe was now limp and apparently unconscious. Whiskers pulled the breathing apparatus from his adversary's face even as a trickle of bubbles parted his lips.

Chisolm had done the same to both of his assailants who were now quiet. Within moments, blood began to escape the nostrils of one and then the other. After a minute more, Chisolm, seeing blood from the noses of all three, tied a fishing wire around their necks and slowly began to ascend, the scooters still floating above with their lights on.

In the darkness beneath the waves, Chisolm now clicked on his overhead lamp and wrapped the fishing wire firmly around his weight belt. At sixty, forty, and twenty feet, he stopped for several minutes to decompress. Whiskers, though bleeding, continued to follow Chisolm to the surface, his trail of blood barely discernible in the dark water, something that marked the path of his ascent while creating a twinge of fear in him at the prospect of inciting saltwater denizens into a feeding frenzy.

At twenty feet, a large barracuda meandering through the depths approached the trail of bodies and, after circling for two minutes, nipped at the exposed fingers of one of the dead men. The barracuda backed away as if expecting a reaction and then converged again, this time twisting and turning its head until pulling away a piece of flesh from the pointer finger of the dead man's left hand.

But as it pulled away, two other barracudas, more than three quarters the length of a man, honed in on the man's flesh. Chisolm shined his flashlight at them, hoping to partially blind them or at least scare them off. Instead, he seemed only to be illuminating their meal. One of them turned from the corpse to Whiskers, flashed between his legs, and swiftly moved around him, coming between him and Chisolm. Chisolm reached for the still suspended scooter and attempted to butt the fish with it. Instead, the barracuda moved several feet away, turned, and converged on Chisolm where it lingered only an arm's length away, its jaws opening and closing in front of Chisolm's dive mask as if assessing his vulnerability. A large shadow passed overhead. The light from the scooter and Chisolm's flashlight picked up a white-bellied silhouette.

The barracudas, now four in number, continued to circle and then converge and nip at the exposed hands of the three corpses.

Chisolm and Whiskers watched their movements even as one continued to linger right in front of Chisolm, almost mimicking his motions. Chisolm and Whiskers slowly ascended to the surface. Chisolm could feel the tugging on the line as the barracudas bit at the exposed fingers. Finally, with increasing confidence and ferocity, the fish bit through the wetsuits of the three corpses, snapping and tearing at the thighs and arms of the dead.

Chisolm and Whiskers surfaced only thirty or so feet from a rocky ridge that extended parallel to the beach area, pulling themselves over the ridge and into an enclosed tidal basin where the two men could stand in chest-deep water cut off from the ocean.

Chisolm pulled on the line, drawing one corpse to the rocks. He dragged the body over the ridge even as he felt again the tug of a barracuda. It let go of a piece of the corpse's arm only after Grant smacked at its head, now above water and still attempting to tear off another piece of flesh. As he pulled the other two corpses in, Whiskers limped back to shore, still bleeding and wondering much blood he had already lost. He collapsed on the shore and was about to say something to Chisolm when he suddenly heard voices, calling out in the darkness.

Chisolm hesitated and then dragged the last of the three corpses into the tidal enclosure where the bodies sank a foot or two beneath the surface. He turned to Whiskers to ask if he too had heard a voice. The voice came again. Recognizing the language, Grant immediately turned off his headlamp. Whiskers had already done the same.

The voices came from an area just beyond several boulders nearby. Chisolm and Whiskers froze as three men, barely discernible in the darkness, continued talking to one another in Arabic. Quietly, Chisolm stepped out of the water, slipped off his flippers and moved behind one of the boulders. Despite the darkness, he twisted green fluorescent lights strapped to their backs gave away the approaching men's location.

BLOSSOMING DEATH

> *Brace yourselves, because the war with Muslims has just begun. Consider me the first droplet of the blood that will follow.*[56]
>
> —Faisal Shahzad, the Times Square Bomber

1:53 a.m., Saturday

Chisolm assumed that the three men were carrying weapons. He reached back to remove his own yellow-colored twist light and then moved over to Whiskers, patted him on the shoulder, and removed his as well. He whispered to him as he heard Whiskers gasp in pain. "Hold on, man, we have to get these three. We'll keep our tanks on for the moment. We may have to go back into the water."

As Chisolm looked again in the direction of the three men, he realized that they must be kneeling as the fluorescent lights were now only a couple of feet off the ground. All had their backs to Chisolm. But as he watched, he heard one of the men say again in Arabic, "Where are the others?"

"We have to move with or without them," translated Chisolm as one of the others spoke.

Their voices thereafter were muffled and indecipherable. Chisolm drifted over to one of the bodies of the three assailants. He quickly removed the Dräger from the largest of the three bodies. As he did so, he inspected the large waterproof bag strapped over the corpse's shoulder. Opening it, he reached in to find a fold-up composite stock and barrel. It was a Kalashnikov. Chisolm felt along the barrel and discovered a detachable cylinder, a silencer. He then felt the stock and action along with the banana clip to determine if it was fully loaded. It was.

As he reached back into the waterproof bag, he felt an odd semispherical protrusion on the man's back. He felt along its contour. He didn't know precisely what the shape was. It was relatively soft and almost pliable. His first thought was that it might be an explosive like C-4. But having it strapped to a man's back seemed odd unless…He continued to feel the protuberance, but as he did so, one of the men began walking in his direction.

Chisolm moved away from the body and backed against a large boulder that the man would have to walk past. As the man passed by, he turned on a low-intensity flashlight with a red bulb. He now stood alongside Whiskers who remained perfectly still, barely breathing. As the man flashed the light into the tidal basin, he uttered a universally understood one syllable profanity. He began to walk into the basin toward the one corpse that Chisolm had stripped of his Dräger. As he did so, Chisolm lifted the safety with a slight clicking sound muffled by the surf pounding against the rocks.

Chisolm pointed the Kalashnikov at the man's back and fired three rounds. The man fell face down, dead, into the water. The silencer worked, and the soundless death went undetected by his two compatriots.

Chisolm, whose black wetsuit was virtually the same as or at least indistinguishable from that of the man he had just killed, slid his own air tanks to the ground and threw on the other man's Dräger. He whispered to Whiskers, "Wait here. I'll take care of our two friends."

Whiskers moaned slightly in response. He was still bleeding despite a makeshift tourniquet made of his own weight belt strapped tightly around his thigh.

Chisolm grabbed the flashlight, which his victim had dropped in the water, and began walking toward the two men with the Kalashnikov in his right hand. As he approached, the green fluorescent lights on their backs still aglow, the men turned toward what they assumed to be the approaching sound of their own comrade. Chisolm flashed the light directly into the eyes of the man on his left. Suspicious, the man raised his own Kalashnikov when Chisolm fired once and then turned the light and gun directly on the other man. The other man put up one hand up to prevent the light from shining in his eyes. Chisolm saw that his Kalashnikov lay against a rock at his feet.

"Gif! Gif!" said Chisolm. "Hands up! Hands up!"

The man slowly raised his hands and whispered, "Achmed? Achmed?"

The beach was several hundred feet from the guard tower that overlooked the ocean on an elevation where a guard should have been able to see what was going on. But, if he were focused out toward the sea, all this activity might go unnoticed.

Chisolm continued speaking to the man in Arabic, "Come toward me."

As the man approached him, Chisolm moved aside and then behind the man and pointed the muzzle toward the small of his back.

"Taqdam! Taqdam!"

The man walked forward at Chisolm's command. As he approached the basin where Whiskers lay, Chisolm told him to kneel down. "Hands on head."

Chisolm then grabbed one hand and looped the fishing wire around it and then twisted it around the other wrist, as he brought the two hands together behind the man's back, and then pushed the man facedown into the sand. He then sat on the man's back as he grabbed one foot, tied it securely to the wrist, and then back again to the other foot. The fishing wire cut into the man's wrists and any attempt to break it or strain against it would only cause it to dig even deeper into his flesh.

Chisolm then walked back to the man's Kalashnikov and brought it over to Whiskers and handed it to him. He was grimacing in pain and still bleeding. Chisolm feared that the knife wound had nicked an artery.

"Look, keep the gun trained on him. I'm calling for help."

Chisolm picked up and reached into the waterproof side pocket of his BCD, pulled out his cell phone, and called Peppers. When he answered, Chisolm explained, "Whiskers is down. He needs medical attention now."

"Where are you?"

"Kittery Beach, sir. We need help now. Knife wound."

"Hold on, Grant." Several seconds later, Peppers was back on. "Grant, we have help on the way. I'm afraid the secrecy is blown—we have to send an ambulance. But we have someone there who is security conscious. He's a hospital commander. He understands. Two others will be with him. An ambulance, no sirens."

"The attack has started," replied Chisolm.

"We know. The sonar buoys in the harbor are detecting engineered noise. Fear is that they may be heading toward the desalinization plant. The coasties are alerted. All the boats are manned and ready."

"Sir, I need help. Send the SEAL team."

"We can't, they're working the harbor right now."

"Sir, then send me one man. They're using the sub pens. We have one captured. Others…"

Before he could finish, he heard another voice. "Lieutenant Commander Chisolm, this is Commander Briggs. I'm in charge of the SEAL training. I can send you one man. He's on a Coast Guard platform. We'll send the vessel to the beach area. He's my best man, but we have no weaponry with us."

"We have plenty of arms here," replied Chisolm, "compliments of our intruders."

Suddenly, a loud explosion occurred behind Chisolm. He fell involuntarily to the ground as several other explosions ripped the night air. A momentary pause was followed by another deafening blast. Chisolm covered his head with both arms as sand, rock, and other debris rained down on him.

Stunned, he lay waiting to see if there might be more explosions. After about a minute, Chisolm got up and sprinted in the direction of the first explosion. He flashed his light onto the body of Whiskers. He was covered in blood and pieces of flesh and black fiber from the wetsuits of the attackers. Chisolm then flashed his light to where the tied-up prisoner had been. What remained of his body was a smattering of flesh, guts, blood, and shredded wetsuit. His remains, like those of his comrades, were completely torn and scattered about. At his feet, Chisolm glimpsed something pliable and immediately drew his foot back. He flashed his light down and saw a human heart, blackened and moving spasmodically.

Chisolm thought to himself about the clay-like material he had felt on the back of one of the men he had killed. *C-4*, he thought. *They blew themselves up...even the dead. A suicide mission.* He looked again at the body of Whiskers and knew there would be a star carved in marble at CIA headquarters in Langley, Virginia, to honor this man's sacrifice.

Chisolm glanced again toward the guard tower on top of the hill that overlooked the ocean. He wondered why there had been no activity there. Surely someone had heard the explosions, despite the pounding of the surf. Just then, he heard two more explosions, but at a distance on the water. He saw nothing. In the blackness, he sensed the weirdness of the sound itself. It was as if it came not from the top of the water but from beneath, something muffled by the water itself. As Chisolm paused to consider what had happened, the ambulance pulled up to the beach area. He stumbled toward it and waved to the ambulance driver as well as two others, both of whom jumped out the passenger door before the vehicle even came to a complete stop. Seconds later, he thought he heard yet another and then three more muffled explosions. At such a distance, he was not entirely certain as to their direction. As the ambulance personnel approached with a collapsible stretcher, he walked forward and directed them to the body of Whiskers.

"Jesus!" one of the stretcher bearers exclaimed.

"This is inhuman," said the other.

The two men with the stretcher, as well as the driver who joined them, attempted to discern the reason for the condition of Whiskers' body. They then looked around the tidal pool, still awash in body parts. The head of one of the dead men was wedged between two rocks, the back of it completely missing. With each surge of the tide, the saltwater moved up several inches to touch the bottom of the head. One of the men wondered at the sting of the salt on already dead flesh.

FALSE SOUNDINGS

> *A lot of noise that's intentionally being put out there to keep you focused on the stuff that doesn't matter.*[57]
>
> —Adam Kmiec, "The Art of Misdirection"

3:00 a.m., Saturday

Chisolm looked at the shoreline of large concrete and steel blocks that acted like pylons and barriers to prevent anything resembling an amphibious assault. An attack from the sea was a concern that stretched all the way back to World War II. A large white light, on a vessel no more than one hundred feet offshore, moved its brightness from his left to directly at him, causing him to cover his eyes with his right arm.

"Sir, who are you, and what are you doing on the beach? Identify yourself."

The man hailing Chisolm, Petty Officer Grady, had a familiar voice even over the amplification of the bullhorn.

"Grady, is that you?"

Before anyone on the boat could answer, another muffled explosion occurred several hundred feet from the boat.

"Lieutenant Commander Chisolm?"

"Yes, get me on board."

The vessel moved closer to the shore, avoiding obstructions when Chisolm raised his hand to indicate stop.

"I'll come in…"

Chisolm flung his tanks over one shoulder. They still had twenty to thirty minutes of air left. With the Dräger equipment still on, he walked into the surf until waist deep and then splashed in, his tanks in front of him as a flotation device. He kicked hard to make his way out to the vessel. Moments later, Chisolm came alongside the starboard bow. One of the men on board reached down to grab the tanks while two others pulled Chisolm up onto the boat.

As he stood on board the softly rocking boat, Chisolm pointed over the port side toward two white lights in the distance off the shore on the Cuban side of the water. At first no one said anything and all of them merely watched as the boats drew closer. Then the boats stopped and turned out their lights.

"I actually hope they're Cuban," said Petty Officer Grady. "Things are tense tonight and something normal would be welcome."

"Sir, Petty Officer First Class Sean Spezzaferro. I'm the head of the SEAL Team here for a training exercise. Commander Briggs sent me. I'm at your disposal."

Chisolm, in the low light of the coast guard vessel's engine console, could see that he was smiling. The man's freckled face and reddish hair belied a darkly competitive nature and toughness. A quick handshake and Chisolm offered, "I hope you like the water because I think we'll be back in soon."

"I piss saltwater, sir."

"Good, as long as you don't drink it. I find the custom distasteful."

At that moment, Chisolm's cell phone rang. Moments later, he heard the voice of the base commander, Commander DiPinta.

"Lieutenant Commander, you and the coasties by the saltwater treatment facility pronto! One other boat already headed that way."

Chisolm looked at Grady, the captain of the boat and said, "Move to the saltwater treatment facility."

One of the other coast guard vessels was already floating in the waters immediately adjacent to the desalinization plant when Chisolm's boat arrived. Its searchlight was moving across the water in a slow back and forth motion, scanning the waters in a grid. The boat had its engine turned off and was floating quietly in the water while Chisolm's boat motored gently to its starboard. In a hushed voice, the captain of Chisolm's vessel asked, "See anything, sir?"

The captain of the other vessel overheard the question but did not answer. Instead, he only pointed in the direction of the beam from the search light, which one of the other coasties had stopped moving.

"Sir," whispered the petty officer handling the light, "there's something there." Everyone on board looked where the light focused on a large ripple that circled out. Then, in the darkness beyond the light's immediate illumination, a gasp and splash and then another of each to the stern of both vessels. Everyone spun abruptly toward the sound. The captain immediately turned the vessel in a slow spin, pivoting on the stern, its light now also scanning the water in an attempt to discern the source of the sound.

At that moment, Chisolm's cell phone vibrated again. He removed it once more from the waterproof vest pocket of his BCD.

"Sir," said Chisolm.

"This is Peppers. Hold on, I'm with the base commander."

"Lieutenant Commander Chisolm, the Coast Guard has orders to help you in any way you deem fit. Are you at the plant?"

"Yes, sir."

"We're getting sonar buoy reads within two hundred feet of the shoreline. They're mechanical disturbances. Could be underwater scooters. There's something there. GPS reads are being texted directly to your vessel. They should pop up on your vessel's LED."

Chisolm looked at the lit screen of the boat's console as the information was transmitted and then glanced at the GPS coordinates indicating the vessel's position.

"Sir, your coordinates are exactly the same as ours. We must be on top of them."

Another sound immediately to Chisolm's right and a large black hump appeared in the water.

"Jesus!" yelped the gunman, whose hands were clenched tightly on the .50 caliber mounted machine gun. "Made me jump!"

But as the men in both boats looked closely in front of the hump, two black and shiny eyes appeared. Temporarily blinded by the searchlight, they stared back blankly. Then a whiskered face came into focus adjacent to the hump. Then another gasp sounded as another hump surfaced.

"We're chasing manatees!" exclaimed Petty Officer Grady.

"How do you explain the mechanical disturbances, Mr. Chisolm?" asked the base commander.

"Don't know, sir, but we'll find out. Hang on, we may have answers."

As the manatees approached the craft, Chisolm noticed a small black box attached to the back of one of them as if impaled in the creature's thick blubbery hide. The docile creature, in a fit of playfulness and curiosity, continued staring and lounging in the light and moving itself gently to stay centered in its illumination.

"Move closer," ordered Chisolm.

Gently, the helmsman maneuvered the boat to within several feet of the still mesmerized manatees, while the other boat remained as motionless as possible, its motors cut, and quietly adrift. As one of the creatures moved sideways, closer to the boat, Chisolm reached over for the black box. He placed the fingers of his right hand underneath the black box, which was still giving off clearly audible sounds identical to those of an underwater scooter. He yanked hard. The device came off, two pinions with rotating hooks tearing off parts of the manatee's blubber. Still, the creature lingered as its mate came along side, rubbing its body against the boat's side as if examining its metal texture. Again, Chisolm reached down and tore loose another black box that, unlike the other, was silent but whose small flashing green light indicated its battery-powered package was still working. As Chisolm placed it on the deck next to him alongside the other, the green light on the other began to blink as the sound increased. Someone was manipulating the devices.

"Mr. Grady, search the shore. Someone's here."

Grady himself grabbed the searchlight and scanned the shoreline. While focusing on a cluster of trees near the shoreline, he suddenly detected movement. Someone was running alongside the road that curved around the plant and up onto an incline that led to several wooden buildings.

"Whoever it was has disappeared."

"Sir? Still there?" asked Chisolm as he again picked up his phone.

"This is Peppers. What the *hell* is going on?"

"Classic misdirection. Someone wants us here. I just pulled two sound amplifiers out of the backs of two manatees. Someone's playing with us. The real attack is somewhere else."

"Someone, somewhere—Grant, news for you. Two men were intercepted coming ashore near the airstrip—they were supposedly Cuban refugees, but they had wetsuits on and diving gear. Our boys surprised 'em. Said there was gear on them. Too much of it. They shouldn't have been able to carry it—unless they had an underwater sled. Their Spanish is nearly indecipherable. They're not natives of Cuba. Before they could be secured, they both went back into the water and disappeared."

Peppers paused and sighed. "I heard already about Whiskers. We'll miss 'im."

"Sir, I've no time for grief—an attack from the sea is difficult but imaginable. An attack by land is improbable but possible if the Cubans themselves orchestrate it."

"Commander DiPinta is in contact with Sanchez. He assures us that the Cubans are not behind this. We had to share certain things with him to get his full cooperation."

"Then who is? And where is the main attack to come from? Men are already dead. The Cubans have to know."

"Grant, here's something. I don't know all the answers. You may be right. An hour ago, two other men were seen jogging past Camp Delta. No one does that even late at night when the temperature is still nearly a hundred degrees. They jogged past the camp twice. But that's a restricted area. Only guards and intel personnel and interrogators are allowed in unaccompanied. And they're all on alert. But when the guards stepped out of the camp to question them, they sped off and disappeared in the vicinity of the HV, the High Value detention facility, Camp 7."

"I don't know exactly where that is, sir. So I'll take your word for it."

"Lieutenant Commander, this is Commander DiPinta again. You expect a land attack but where?"

"Sir, where do the tunnels and the electrical grids hook up? Do any of them have passageways a man could get through?"

"Shit! Who the hell knows? Do you know something?"

"Sir, the man whose body we picked up earlier had a rock phone on him. That tells me they expect to be communicating to one another from underground sites."

"All right. I hate to do this, but we may have to bring Sanchez into this more than we already have. In the meantime, we need you back in the water. Can you get back to the sub pens? Maybe there are points of egress that you don't know about. Reconnoiter and be careful. The boat you're on as well as the men on it are at your disposal. The other boat as well if you think you'll need it."

"Sir, I don't know how much our air tanks have left. But we'll see—we'll get back in one way or the other."

"Mr. Chisolm—one more thing. What haven't we considered? What haven't we prepared for?"

"Sir, there's always the unexpected."

CUTTER, CRUSADER, AND MiGS

Semper Paratus

—United States Coast Guard Motto

This is the history that turns otherwise rational heads in both Washington and Havana, as if the full moon had gotten to them.[58]

—Roger Cohen, "The End of the End of the Revolution"

4:14 a.m., Saturday

On board the U.S. Coast Guard cutter *Gallatin*, Chief Taylor blinked as he refocused on the computer screen. He blinked again as he put down his black coffee and looked at the sometime mesmerizing radar screen. An anomaly had appeared, disappeared, and reappeared—something was there. Nighttime low-flying objects were hardly unusual in this part of the world. Drug runners flew their aircraft as low to the ocean as possible to avoid radar detection as they headed toward the coast of Florida or to Puerto Rico, often dropping their illicit materials out of planes while their cargo handlers on shore waited in small craft to retrieve the floating parcels worth thousands and even hundreds of thousands of dollars each.

"Chief Taylor?"

"What is it?"

"Chief, we may have something. Seems to be a night rider—just above the waves. Telemetry on the screen indicates that he's maybe sixty miles from us—headed straight toward us."

"See if he stays on course. I doubt he knows we're here."

As the chief looked over the shoulder of the young Coast Guard sailor, the phone lit and buzzed softly.

"Chief Taylor here."

He nodded several times to the voice on the other end of the phone. "Yes, sir. Yes, sir. Yes, sir. We're here, ain't goin' nowhere, sir."

"Chief, he's on a beeline toward us."

"It can't be. But if he stays this low..."

While watching the screen, Taylor picked up the phone to call the captain. As he did so, the captain walked through the door into the radar room.

The chief was already standing and the others knew enough to continue their work despite the captain's presence.

"Gentlemen, we have special instructions. We are to move out of the anticipated trajectory of the incoming airplane. It appears to be on a heading directed toward the mainland of Cuba."

"Sir," said the chief, "it appears to be headed right toward Guantanamo."

The captain said nothing as he looked at the chief and held up an envelope with the words *TOP SECRET* printed across the top. The chief nodded knowingly and followed the captain as he motioned him toward the hatchway. Once outside, the captain said sternly, "This is highly classified and is not to be discussed with anyone other than me. You will monitor this plane acutely. No blinking. Keep your men on this at all cost. As far as they're concerned, it's another drug interdiction."

"I assume, sir, it's more than that."

"Much more, Chief. I'll be on the bridge. Keep me informed. I'll probably be buggin' you every several minutes. Remember, no blinking. We are to continue monitoring the flight's path but, from here on, NAS Key West will be directing. We are auxiliary. We help but do not interfere. The chopper stays in wraps. No flights. No nothin' except quiet and attentive observation. Any course changes by this bird and I want to know immediately."

"Yes, sir."

"Chief, sir, we have something," interrupted one of the sailors as he popped his head out the hatchway.

The captain motioned to head back inside. The chief and the captain entered.

"Sir," said one of the petty officers, "we have linkage with the P-3 operating out of Jacksonville. They're monitoring the same platform—the one headed our way." A maritime patrol aircraft of the U. S. Navy, the P-3 carried the most sophisticated surveillance and communication equipment of any aircraft in the world. It routinely reconnoitered the Atlantic Seaboard and the Caribbean Sea.

There was a squawk coming from one of the phones. The petty officer answered. "Chief, it's Key West, they've launched an intercept. They say its full bore. But they say there's a problem.

"They launched and apparently so did the Cubans. The P-3 has confirmed two MiG launches from Santiago. They're on a collision course with our intercept."

"Gimme the phone. Hello, Chief Taylor...We are monitoring...We...What the shit?..How ...We can't do that..." The captain caught the look of consternation on the chief's face and motioned for him to hand him the phone.

"This is Captain Sandoval. What's the problem?" He listened attentively and then a look of woe crossed his brow.

He put down the receiver and looked at the chief. "Message traffic indicates the Cubans may have misread our intentions. They apparently have launched to strike at our platform. Shit! Someone has to get to the Cubans. Damn it! Cubans, Americans, and a Trinidad drug runner—talk about triangulation."

"Chief, it looks like all three or four platforms are terrain mapping. Everyone's close enough to the floor to make a rooster tail. That means over the horizon communication has even less of a chance of calling back the MiGs unless we can link to them somehow."

The chief and the others grew silent and stared at the captain. He looked at the chief as he thought and then he raised his eyebrows. He peered anxiously at the secure phone hanging on the wall and picked it up. He punched in a coded sequence and waited. Someone answered at the other end at NSA Headquarters in Washington DC. "We're keyed secure. Highest importance. Get me to Cuban operations." There were several clicks and then a female voice answered. "This is MEMSAB, put me through to Mr. Triana."

"Mr. Triana here."

"Troy, I know you're watching all of this but we have a major problem. We need to either take out two Cuban MiGs about to attack one of our F-18s out of Key West or we have to communicate to the Cubans before we have an incident."

"What do you want done?"

"Someone has to get to the Cubans high enough up to pull back their planes and get them not to interfere."

"That'll take time."

"We don't have it. Our target's headed toward GITMO with hostile intent. We have to stop it. We can't let the Cubans interfere."

"Stay on the line." There was a buzzing sound and then silence followed by a series of invectives.

"Mr. Secretary, we need an answer immediately."

"Call back our plane? Ours? Incompetents! I'll get Key West on line. You stay on too!"

Moments later, the Secretary of Defense hollered into the phone. "The F-18 called off? Is that what you really want, Captain?" The irritation in the secretary's voice was enough for the captain to consider his own career before he answered.

"Mr. Secretary, there is still a plane headed for GITMO." There was a period of silence.

Then in a subdued voice, the Secretary of Defense uttered, "Let me get out of bed. I'm beat." After a period of silence again, he asked, "Captain, any ideas?"

"Yes, sir. Let our P-3 contact the Cuban aircraft directly. We have their codes. We broke them a while ago. We know their prescription. We can link directly to their aircraft."

"But, Captain, they don't know that we know their codes. That's way beyond top secret."

"Sir, time is running out."

"Troy, you got all this? What do you think?"

"It may be the only way, sir?"

"You got the personnel in place to do this there this time of night?"

"Got 'em, sir."

"Do it. I'll take the blame if anything else happens...I'm coming in. But I'll stay hooked to you. Our plane remains on course. We'll knock 'im out of the sky before he knows it."

Mahtab Razak continued to look at the instrument panel with his GPS for direction and miles to his destination. His altimeter indicated he was flying between twenty to thirty feet above the ocean. As he continued on a northwesterly course, the warmth of the cockpit began to chafe on his otherwise imperturbable demeanor. Soon he would be with his ancestors. He reached down in a prayerful gesture of ablution to touch his white cotton socks with the sweat of his own brow, as if washing his feet, and began to recite, "There is no god but God. Mohammad is his prophet." Then he touched his right hand to his head, to his lips, and then to his heart, and again uttered, "There is no god but God. Mohammad is his prophet."

Mahtab looked out the cockpit windows, where the night remained unabated and the stars shone with a luster as the Milky Way continued to unfold in the total darkness above the sea. As he again looked to the altimeter, he wondered at the heavens and considered whether or not the afterlife would enable him to see clearly the crack in the moon left by Mohammad.

In the darkness, he already felt the warmth of Allah's embrace, even as he imagined his momentary suffering as the plane destroyed the infidel's cradle of evil where the liars polluted the minds of the world and the sons of Islam who lived like animals in cages. But Allah would soon send a great wind to lift them up out of the prison camp to dwell with him in the heavens. There in the heavens he was sure he would meet them and Salahuddin, Nur al-Din, and of course, Mohammad and the trusted companions who were righteous and taught the wisdom of Islam with the sword.

His wits sharpened and the smell of the sea in all its saltiness blew into the cockpit and the odor of his own breath and body mingled with it, slightly distasteful and almost ponderous. For a moment he wondered if Allah would protect his body from the devourers of human flesh that lived in the sea. Would he be delivered piecemeal onto the throne of the heavens where He dwelt? Or would he be reassembled in lasting carnality that would enable him to embrace the eternal blessings of the virgins forever at his disposal? He warmed at the prospect and then turned again to prayerful and lasting jubilation at the prospect of executing *jihad.*

"I am the man, I am the sword, I am the child of wisdom, I lift the sword of Allah. I am the man, I am the sword, I am the child..." His prayer beads hung on the latch to the door, next to his right hand, and vibrated with the plane's movement. As he continued to pray, he spotted the lights of a distant ship off to his right. He began again, with the ninety-nine names of Allah, "You are Allah and there is no other, You are Al-Rahma, the compassionate, and there is no other, You are Al-Rahim, the merciful, and there is no other, You are Al-Malik, the king, and there is no other..."

"We have a visual, sir." The petty officer standing on the bow of the ship with his night vision binoculars watched as the barely lit cockpit and the tail lights of the plane came into view.

"Non comprende, non comprende," repeated the pilot.

"This the United States Navy—P-3 Orion—Cease and desist. Call off your attack. Do not attack..."

"Sir, it's no use. They think it's a ruse...Uh-oh, uh-oh, it's getting worse. Indications are the first MiG just launched. Our aircraft is only minutes away from target but on course to intercept with Cubans. Cubans have launched one missile...now two."

"Sir, it's worse than that. Target destroyed!"

"Which target?" uttered the captain on board the *Gallatin*.

"Did our guy launch?" screamed the secretary.

"This is confusing, Troy. We have a launch but it's coming from the Cubans. Our guy still hasn't launched."

"Then what the hell are you guys talking about? What target was destroyed?" screamed the Secretary of Defense.

On the bow of the cutter *Gallatin* a coast guardsman had watched until suddenly the night sky lit into a fireball. The force of the explosion had sent vibrations across the waters. For a moment several pieces of debris remained burning on the ocean's surface and then disappeared beneath the darkness and the waves.

"Man, that was spectacular...," uttered the petty officer on the bow. A mate standing next to him looked on with shock and admiration at the beauty of a seeming supernova being born over Caribbean waters. If it hadn't been for the burning debris, he might have thought it to be a lightning bolt.

In the onboard intelligence facilities, the *Gallatin* staff watched as the U.S. Navy's pilot continued on course toward a target that he could no longer find on his radar.

THE LEGACY OF
DIGGERS AND MOLES

> *Some move earth and heaven;*
> *the Seabees move dirt.*
> —Chief Charles Wentz, Jr., USN (Retired)

5:13 a.m., Saturday

Chisolm and Spezzaferro emerged from the holding and decompression tank of the submarine pen. To their surprise and Chisolm's consternation, they found the entire facility lit up. When Chisolm had left the facility only a day earlier, he had secured the pen by turning out the lights with the exception of the constantly glowing red lights, which give minimal glare and allowed for rotating crews to sleep with minimal disturbance even in a work area. Now everything was aglow.

Chisolm and Spezzaferro took off their tanks and flippers and shouldered their Kalashnikovs. As they approached the area where Chisolm had been only a day earlier, he noticed that the locks on one of the large panel-like doors had been removed and that the doors were partially open. He and Spezzaferro looked in to find an armory filled with exact duplicates of the rifles they were holding. They examined the room, which still housed weaponry apparently left behind by the U.S. Navy, including two Berettas holstered and hanging from hooks. He examined closely the rifles along one entire wall and then the abundance of ammunition.

"Look at this," said Chisolm. "The markings on these guns…"

"They must belong to the Cubans, they have to know about this place," replied Spezzaferro.

"No, there's something strange."

"Border guards, they could be storing their weaponry here for an assault by the Cubans against GITMO."

"No, look here." He pointed to the action on his own Kalashnikov and said, "These are the guns we took from the dead invaders. They have distinctive markings. These were made in Bulgaria. Now look at this." He took one of the Kalashnikovs from the wall and said, "The Cubans don't use these any longer. At least their border guards don't. Instead, they use the Kalashnikov upgrade with the metal stock, which makes it lighter. Besides, see this, it's a Chinese marking. The Russians and the Venezuelans have supplied the Cubans for years. They don't normally get their stuff from China."

"But why would they suddenly get a new supplier?"

"That's what I'd like to know. Something's not right. I'm wondering if the Cubans are even in on this."

"You mean…"

"I don't mean anything yet. We'd better look around."

As they left the armory, Chisolm followed the curve of one of the alleyways that led from the large open bay area of the submarine pen into a shaft or tunnel that had a steel door on rollers. The door was open and the tunnel was lit from overhead by incandescent bulbs that hung from the ceiling and were connected by cords that ran in all directions. But the cords ultimately gathered like a coil of snakes near an entrance to yet another passageway. Here the area grew smaller. The lighting of the passageway was poor and had little in the way of metallic beams or flooring to support anything more than human foot traffic. As they entered the space, Chisolm stepped on a large poster size sheet of paper covered with dust. He reached down, picked it up, and held it up to the light and half smiled as he read the poster: "This is Ivan. He follows orders unquestioningly. Think what he will do when he is told to kill you." Chisolm looked at the grim-faced soldier of the Soviet Union staring back at him and said, "Something left over from the Cold War." As they walked a little farther, they ran across the remnants of a poster that had been plastered repeatedly along one side of the passageway that showed a large fish sporting a beard and smoking a cigar. Beneath it were the words, "Let's mount Fidel, one way or the other."

They continued walking for several minutes. The earthen walls were surprisingly cool to the touch given the heat of the Cuban summer. But as the path ascended gradually, almost imperceptibly, the heat rose accordingly. After several minutes of walking, they came to a metal door with ventilation screens at the top and bottom. Chisolm leaned quietly against the door, listening for anything that might be on the other side. After half a minute, Chisolm attempted to push the door open. At first it would not budge. But then he and Spezzaferro leaned hard against it and gradually the door opened until first Chisolm and then Spezzaferro squeezed through. Lying next to the door was the obstruction, the body of a Cuban soldier, a sergeant in the Border Guards. Chisolm reached down to touch the man's throat. He was dead and still warm. Chisolm looked more closely and noticed rope burns around the man's neck. He had apparently been strangled. He pulled the body away from the door a little and in the dim light he saw the man's name tag: Menendez.

"Why?" asked Spezzaferro in a whisper.

Chisolm merely shook his head slowly in response.

The room itself was something like a large locker room. Shelves were filled with everything from military boots, T-shirts, several boxes of cigars, and C rations to medical equipment. The large amount of what appeared to be freshly supplied medical equipment suggested an infirmary that may have recently been or was about to be used. On one of the walls hung a Cuban flag, while on the others were pictures of Fidel Castro, another of his brother Raul, still another of Che Guevara, and a faded movie-size poster of Marilyn Monroe.

"By the looks of this room and the cleanliness, sir, I'd say this place is still being used. Are we in a Cuban..."

Before Spezzaferro could finish his sentence, the sound of footsteps leading into the space became louder and louder. At first, Chisolm and Spezzaferro wanted to step back into the tunnel. Before they could move, the door opened and immediately three men walked in, followed by seven or eight others. Everyone froze as Chisolm pointed his rifle at the head of the man who first walked into the room. All of them were wearing black ninja-type outfits, fitted with vests similar to those a suicide bomber might wear but, as yet, none had been wired, hooked up, or laden with explosives.

"Americans," whispered one of the men standing next to the man at whom Chisolm's rifle was pointed. Spezzaferro took two steps forward, glanced at Chisolm and then motioned for them to kneel down. Each of the men wore a green scarf around his neck. None of them appeared to be armed. Based solely upon their appearance, Chisolm spoke to them in Arabic.

"Who are you?"

No response.

"Who are you?"

Again, no response.

The door behind the men was still open and one of them nearest to it began to inch his way backward out of the room. As he did so, Chisolm stepped forward and raised his rifle menacingly and cautioned him by shaking his head *no* and looking right at him. The man stopped moving.

Finally, the lead man smiled slightly and said in English, "We are the sons of Allah, and we know you are not supposed to be here. You are American and you are trespassing on Cuban soil. We are here by invitation of the Cuban government. I am certain that you are not. Leave."

Chisolm stepped forward another pace as he quickly considered his options. He neither anticipated nor expected to be burdened with prisoners. He also could not shoot unarmed men. Therefore, he motioned for the men to go back out the door. As soon as all of them were out, he slammed his body against it and bolted the heavy door from within. He heard hurried footsteps outside as the men disappeared. Immediately, he and Spezzaferro ran to the opposite door and descended again through the passageway through which they had come. As they ran, Chisolm spoke haltingly between strides, saying, "They were dressed for intrusion—but no diving equipment—there has to be another tunnel leading directly onto GITMO."

After several minutes of running, Chisolm and Spezzaferro slowed as they approached the original point of entrance. As they exited the area, they listened for a moment to see if they were being followed. Grant took out the rock phone and attempted to speak to Peppers.

"Let's hope this thing works," he said.

Moments later, Peppers voice came on. "Sir, Chisolm here. We're in the pens. But there are complications. The enemy must have an attack plan. They're trying to penetrate we think through underground passageways. I swear its Arabs. Not Cuban…"

The connection dropped before Chisolm could finish. He tried again, and as Peppers' voice momentarily came through, Chisolm attempted to speak. The connection again dropped. In frustration, Chisolm tried again. This time he couldn't even get a signal. But he hoped Peppers had heard enough.

While Chisolm had attempted to make contact with Peppers, Spezzaferro had looked about and found an oddity on the markings of the various panels that housed what looked to be an enormous ventilation and cooling system. All but one of them had warnings and instructions written in English. In one pane, someone had scrawled the words, "Prohibito." He noticed that the lock on the exterior of this one panel was severed as if by wire cutters. He pulled the door open and looked inside. As Chisolm approached, he looked back at him and smiled.

"Señor Chisolm, habla Español?"

"Find something?"

"Sir, listen, hear that?" whispered Spezzaferro.

"It's Arabic."

Chisolm then turned and touched Spezzaferro on the shoulder to signal the need to advance on their bellies. The passageway widened and was broad enough for both of them to move side by side. As they advanced at a snail's pace, the voices grew louder and somewhat animated as if they were arguing. One of the men had voiced his displeasure at being condemned to die without any certitude that he would actually get to kill an American. Another tried to reassure him that it was necessary to be positive. The Americans did not know that the attacks were coming and therefore would not be unable to fight back immediately. There would be time to kill them. Each was also reminded by yet the voice of another, perhaps the team leader, that they were on a mission ordained by God himself and that they would be praised hereafter as they sacrificed themselves in the name of virtue. For all good Muslims are men of virtue. Their mission could not fail. As he finished his remarks, one of the men uttered, "Allah Akbar, Allah Akbar." The others repeated the words much as one would repeat the cheers of "We're number one." From the sound of the various voices, Chisolm discerned that there were no more than six men.

Once they were within thirty feet of the men, Chisolm, with his heart pounding in his throat, tapped Spezzaferro on the shoulder to indicate "attack." This time Chisolm would not hesitate to shoot. Surely these men were armed and, surely, they meant harm. Chisolm turned on his flashlight and shined it directly into the eyes of the startled men. Before they could respond, Spezzaferro let loose a barrage and Chisolm did the same. They kept firing even as they moved forward. When they reached the six men, three were still moving. Three others were sufficiently ventilated from the chest to the head to be without the prospect of recovery. They already appeared dead. One of the three moving men attempted to lift his hand toward a button on his chest. Chisolm fired twice into the man's head and then did the same to each of the other still-moving men. Spezzaferro said nothing. He understood. Chisolm reached down and pulled the green scarf from around the neck of the last man he shot. Spezzaferro took one of the scarves as well from another.

Chisolm flashed his light all around. This was the end of the tunnel. But as he flashed the light above him, he discovered a pull-down ladder connected to a side of a concrete and steel cylinder. He yanked on the ladder several times before it descended. He climbed up the hatch to a wheel lock, which he had to grasp with both hands to turn. He turned the hatch wheel several times before he was able to push it open. He was immediately hit by the heat of the nighttime Cuban air. As he looked around, his flashlight now off, he discerned the lights of Camp Delta. He scanned about, attempting to get his bearings. "I'll be," he said to himself. In the distance, to his right, was Wind Mill Hill. He was within several hundred feet of the main gate to the secured facilities surrounding the prison camp. He understood that anyone approaching the gate from this direction would be immediately suspect and subject to possible fire by the guards, all of whom were on high alert. He looked back down the tunnel and turned on his flashlight where Spezzaferro awaited him expectantly with no sense of where they had come out.

"I'll come down. Look at this," said Chisolm.

Spezzaferro climbed the ladder immediately after Chisolm and looked in disbelief at the surroundings. They realized that the enemy had gotten both within range of the guard posts to Camp Delta, and within striking distance of the camp and its adjoining facilities. Not knowing the full extent of the enemy forces, Chisolm decided to make one more check of the passageways and the pen facilities. But before they left, Chisolm and Spezzaferro checked the pockets of the dead for any bits of information that might be of use to the intelligence office. All of their pockets were empty. Chisolm and Spezzaferro each took another Kalashnikov and strapped them over their shoulders.

DARKNESS AND LIGHT

> *Only your voice*
> *spelling the tempest may compel our good.*[59]
>
> —John Berryman, "Canto Amor"

5:38 a.m., Saturday

Ten minutes after turning back to make one more inspection of the pen facilities, Chisolm and Spezzaferro found themselves emerging from a faintly lit tunnel into the cavernous submarine complex. This time, the entire facility was dark. Someone had been here. As they emerged from the tunnel, they realized the sound of the opening door would alert any others present to their arrival. Chisolm ducked as he emerged. Spezzaferro did the same. They stopped to listen for a minute. There was no sound. If others were still here, they were suspiciously quiet. As he moved forward, he heard a snap and several clicks. Chisolm and Spezzaferro both dropped to the ground but still saw nothing. Then a voice boomed out of the darkness.

"Lieutenant Commander Chisolm, we know you are here and we know why." The English was spoken with a Spanish accent and the voice sounded familiar. "In a moment we will turn on the lights. Right now, we can see you but you cannot see us. We are using night vision goggles. We need a moment to adjust our eyes and then we will illuminate the darkness. Do not be concerned. In this instance, I think we are working together."

"Who are you?"

"I am disappointed, Mr. Chisolm, that you do not recognize my voice from our recent meeting."

"Colonel Sanchez," responded Chisolm.

"Cover your eyes, we are turning the lights back on."

Several loud clicks from the wall of switches turned on rows of overhead lighting. Chisolm, Spezzaferro, and a dozen Cuban soldiers standing opposite them, on either side of Colonel Sanchez, blinked and shielded their eyes. Sanchez was dressed in a desert camouflage uniform similar to that worn by U.S. personnel. Chisolm and Spezzaferro now saw that all of them, including Colonel Sanchez, had their night vision equipment propped up on their foreheads. Colonel Sanchez immediately stepped forward and extended his hand to Grant and nodded formally to Spezzaferro.

"Who is your companion?"

"This, sir, is a fellow warrior," replied Chisolm, not seeing any need to give away Spezzaferro's name nor the fact that he was a SEAL.

Sanchez smiled knowingly at Chisolm and said, "I appreciate your caution." He then stepped forward, yet again, and extended his hand to Spezzaferro.

"Mr. Chisolm, things are most grave."

"It appears that way."

"Walk with me."

Colonel Sanchez then moved away from the others with Chisolm now alongside him. Once outside the hearing of the others, he turned to Grant and said, "First of all, I outrank you and I would appreciate a salute. My men need to be properly educated. So, please, as we depart, do not forget to render a salute."

"Sorry, Colonel, in the Navy, we don't typically salute indoors."

"Perhaps. But you are on Cuban soil. What has come of the other team of insurgents?"

"If you mean those we just secured in the tunnel—"

"Secured is a strange choice of words. What did you do with them? You came from the tunnel, and we have questioned others who told us about the other team."

"They're dead."

"I like your brevity, Mr. Chisolm. However, we have a delicate situation here. You now know that we know and, indeed, have known about this facility for some time. It always amazes me that you could think to build something like this on Cuban soil while your country was still employing several thousand of my countrymen at Guantanamo, and still not expect us to know about it."

Chisolm eyed Sanchez suspiciously and then asked, "What else do you know?"

"I know that you are the liaison officer from your Central Command and I know—." Here he paused for dramatic effect and said, "*Vi pani myetya Paruski, nyet?*"

Chisolm remained quiet and waited. Sanchez continued, "I also know that you speak Arabic. You are a valuable asset to your country."

Chisolm merely smiled slightly and asked, "Where is this headed, sir?"

"Are the bodies in the tunnel?"

"Yes."

"We will dispose of them with a proper burial, one that keeps their existence a secret. And now, Mr. Chisolm, your presence here is an embarrassment to my country although I admire your work."

"Sir, where are the men we ran into at the end of the other passageway, the one which you came through, to get here?"

"You have your own interrogation methods and we have ours. We will question them. We have already begun the process. But my point, Mr. Chisolm, is this. You and your people are like some other people. We like you and we admire you, but we don't quite trust you. I spoke only a short while ago with your base commander as well as Mr. Peppers. We believe your facilities remain 'secure.' The intruders have been killed or apprehended. However, we can no longer pretend not to know about this facility.

And, of course, you can no longer continue in this impudent display of gunboat diplomacy whereby you violate Cuban sovereignty on a daily basis. This facility, you shall pretend, does not exist. You have not been here. You must also make certain that your 'fellow warrior' forgets that he, too, was ever here."

"Sir, were the Cubans completely unaware of this intrusion by the attackers?"

Sanchez paused and looked away for a moment before saying, "You don't speak for your country, I assume, but I do speak for mine when I say that there is a traitor in our midst, or this attack could not have been planned as it was and no one could have gotten into my country without the cooperation of a member of my own staff. Of course, you would be shocked to learn of such a thing but we will find him out. Someone had to provide access to Cuba for these individuals to get here. Somehow they were able to obtain the appropriate passports and pass themselves off as Nicaraguans. The clearance required to enter my country had to come from a fellow Cuban. I will find him out. We are even now checking the logs of all flights in and out of my country. There will be more considered later. But the matter of this incursion onto Cuban soil by terrorists cannot easily be kept from the public. However, we are more capable of discretion on this matter than the American press. If you say nothing, we shall say nothing. I would normally suggest that you leave the way you came but that may be difficult. Have you enough air?"

"I'm certain we can make it last. But we have to pressurize a bit first. We'll be popping out at about sixty feet below sea level. We'll need a little time."

"I did not mean to hurry you. But you need to explain all of this to your superiors. We will need to meet again concerning these matters before our next scheduled routine meeting at the North East Gate. Perhaps you will have some more prisoners to turn over to us. People who do not share the appreciation of the delights of a socialist paradise."

Chisolm managed a slight smile, despite his having been up all night, at a touch of sarcasm in the colonel's last remark. Colonel Sanchez then turned around, Chisolm did the same and waved Spezzaferro over to him. Colonel Sanchez then looked at Chisolm again as if assessing him and said, "You have something. I think you are like me. I'm sure we will talk again soon. I will make certain that the Ministry of Interior observes whatever your country and mine agree to."

Chisolm then rendered a salute to Colonel Sanchez who smiled and returned it. Spezzaferro followed Chisolm's lead.

RETRIBUTION

5:39 a.m., Saturday

Shakir lifted his tired head from his hands as the weight of his endeavor came down upon him as it never had before. Without explanation, he began to sweat profusely and a vise seemed to be crushing his very skull. With eyes that flickered in pain, he told the captain, "Assemble all of the crew in the galley if they wish to be paid. You will be there too."

Ten minutes later, the entire crew of nine men and the captain sat at the table in the galley as Shakir entered. The Cuban sun was just up over the horizon, and most of the crew had been awake much if not all of the night. They did not know the details of the activities in which they were now participating, but they did know that all of this was highly irregular but something for which their pay would enable most of them to retire in luxury for the rest of their lives. Shakir walked in with two duffle bags that appeared to be fully loaded. He opened the first and handed each man a stack of one hundred dollar bills several inches thick. To the captain he handed two such stacks. He instructed each man to count the number of bills to make certain that the amount was correct. Then he took a deep breath to quiet his fast-beating heart and, while the men counted, he reached into the other duffle bag. Without even pulling the weapon out, he pointed the Uzi from within the bag directly at the man nearest him and pulled the trigger. The room exploded in gunfire. Each man fell according to his nearness to him, the captain falling last as he attempted to flee out the hatch leading to the ship's deck. Within seconds, all nine crewmen and the captain lay slaughtered, their flesh and blood splattered around the room. Shakir shook uncontrollably all over. For the first time in his life, he had done what he had sent others to do. He had taken ten lives and now must take that of the only other person completely familiar with his plans. As he paused to pick up the bills that lay scattered about the galley, he considered this next victim, the man who lay sleeping in the hull, awaiting word of the success of his endeavor to create a most violent and beautiful work of art. His hands still shook as he exited the galley. Before descending, he decided to look once more over the side of the ship to consider the distant lights of Guantanamo. He wanted to pray as he stood on the port bow but knew that Allah would understand his haste. With the Uzi in his right hand, he descended the steps and completed the task he had assigned himself.

Ten minutes later, he stood once more on the port bow, fully clothed in a black diving suit, a double tank of air with the appropriate manifold on his back. He prepared to now head toward the beacon that had guided the two teams toward their destiny, toward their historic rendezvous with evil. Moored to the port stern trailed the last Zodiac, the one he would now use to follow toward the same beacon. But as he looked again at the twinkling lights of Guantanamo, he saw two specs, what he thought were boats, coming over the water in a hellish pace directly toward the ship.

Before he could prepare himself to enter the water, an explosion rocked the ship to port, throwing him overboard into the sea. Five seconds later, the side of the ship blew up as another explosion sent a blinding spray of debris coursing out across the water. A wave buried him beneath the sea. He fought to surface, choking with water and surrounded by debris. As he emerged, blood from a cut on his forehead trickled into his mouth and more gushed from his nose. His own chest felt compressed and pained.

The ship he had been standing on only moments earlier was nearly broken in two, its bow now pointed skyward and the stern listing to one side, its metal garishly twisted above the water line and the cargo slipping and splashing into the sea. As the ship rolled to port, the propellers flashed above the water line, sucking and pulling him into their vortex. He swam in a panic to escape but was pulled under until the last of the ship's stern dropped off into the depths, letting him go. When he emerged, he saw the bow still partially exposed. Off to his right, two Cuban MiG-21s flew overhead at no more than one hundred feet above the water.

Pained and bloodied, he floated on his back, his dive mask still wrapped around one wrist and his regulator dangling alongside him. As he slowly realized his predicament, his eyes followed the MiGs into the morning sun just now peering above the horizon. Bruised and battered, he continued looking east and began to recite his morning prayers and, within minutes, he floated sleepily on the water, unable to fathom any longer where he might be.

A NEWS DAY

6:58 a.m., Saturday

Rusty Peppers assembled his intelligence team along with Commander DiPinta, the base commander, and several others who were already privy to the full import of what had transpired in the past several hours. All had been awake the entire night. They waited for Grant and Petty Officer Sean Spezzaferro, along with several members of the CIA who also had knowledge of the events. All were tired but mentally alert; the night's events had pumped them full of adrenalin.

Chisolm walked in along with the SEAL who had been given temporary clearance to view and hear all, since he had been so closely linked to the night's extraordinary events. Both Chisolm and Spezzaferro were pale with exhaustion. Peppers offered each of the men a cup of black coffee, which several others were already drinking.

"What happened last night was unbelievable and yet not unexpected. The colonel and Sanchez have been in close contact all night. But some of you may not yet know the full extent of all that transpired. Over the last several hours, this base has been invaded by land, by air, and by sea. There have been attempts to do all three in a coordinated attack. As far as we know, all such efforts have been thwarted. All of them have failed and there are, I am happy to say, a lot of dead bad guys. Our base appears to be secure and even the Cubans may have been instrumental in thwarting this damnable Al-Qaeda operation. Based upon what I have heard and seen on the satellite hookups and this morning's television programs, as well as the internet news service, not a word of this has leaked out, at least not yet. You may have noticed already that not all branches of the intelligence community are represented here this morning. That is by design. I don't want anybody to know anything about what happened last night unless it is absolutely necessary. That means I don't want you explaining to anyone anything. In good time, I'm sure this will leak out. Someone'll write a book about it or something. Now, I can't tell other agencies represented here what to do, but you who are here by invitation may assume that I've got your back. I hope you've got mine."

As he made the last statement, Peppers looked over at two of the CIA people whose identity he had yet to provide to the others present.

"I've had an opportunity to gather pieces of information from our own branches of Homeland Security as well as from Colonel Sanchez. He assures me that this matter is being contained and that his personnel are reliable. The Cubans, for reasons I am not cognizant of, do not wish for word of this attack to leak out. However, I think I know at least part of that reason. You see, in the last several hours, the Cubans have, according to our own agents, destroyed one airplane which they and we believe was headed to this base on a suicide mission. They have also attacked and sunk a freighter off our coast in international waters which they will, of course, deny. Our agents also tell us that they have registered a complaint this morning with the Chinese government and that of Nicaragua for complicity in some of these events. I suppose that what has happened in the past few hours could be enough to strain their relations with their Communist allies. Given the amount of oil which the Chinese hope to suck out of the ocean off the coast of Cuba, I also don't think that they would be pleased to have this information leaked. The Nicaraguans—their involvement is something we haven't pieced together yet."

Peppers sighed deeply as the lack of sleep momentarily clouded his mind. He rubbed his eyes and offered, "This feels like Vietnam, hot, sweaty, and extraordinarily complicated. But bad guys are bad guys wherever they are. The good thing is they're dead. And speaking of the dead, we lost a comrade in arms last night. His name is already known to a few of you. I hope you remember the sacrifice some have made for our great nation, not just for us but for our children and grandchildren, as well. However, his absence is not to be noted. As far as others are concerned, he is merely away on another mission, one for which he was perfectly suited and therefore had to be transported back to the mainland immediately. Our dead friends are always with us. We remember them in our continued exertions to bring our heel down on Al-Qaeda and its likes all over the world."

The entire group was exhausted and remained respectfully quiet.

"However, there are other events transpiring around the world which have an element about them that makes me wonder. I picked this up this morning. Some extraordinary occurrences in other parts of the world. I've run off copies." He passed around a copy of a report he had found early in the morning on MSN. All read quietly.

> (Nicosia, Cypress)—The curators of a shrine sacred to the Muslim world report that it was vandalized late last night. The shrine, which houses the remains of the Prophet Mohammad's aunt, is the fourth most frequently visited site in the Islamic world. Thousands of pilgrims from around the world come to it each year.
>
> According to the curators of the site, the doors of the mosque remain unlocked throughout the year. The amount of human traffic in and out of the location is normally thought of as a deterrent to any kind of desecration. However, in the heat of the summer, the site is less frequently visited, which may have given looters or others easy access to the mosque's interior.
>
> Nothing was disturbed except the tomb of Umm Haram. She died when she fell

off her horse in the year AD 649, shortly after the Muslims invaded the island. The curator and two guards who are on duty only during daylight hours found the tomb itself had been broken open and the remains removed. The imam who lives on the grounds next to the shrine was not home at the time of the vandalism and is reportedly on vacation. The site is situated on the outskirts of Larnaca, one of the busiest tourist locations in Cypress.

When all had finished reading the news account, the colonel said, "I'm sure the Turks on the island will blame the Greeks for this. More tension." "Well, speaking of Turks," said Peppers. "I took the liberty of preparing yet another news report." He then passed out copies.

(Istanbul, Turkey)—The Topkapi Palace, home to the leaders of the Ottoman Turkish Empire for over five hundred years, was burglarized sometime in the late hours of the night by individuals who removed some of its most treasured possessions. An early inventory of the stolen items includes several that are sacred to Islam. The head of Istanbul's police indicated that there had been extensive damage to several of the rooms at the world-famous museum. Among the items missing are the reputed strands from the beard of the Prophet Mohammad along with a sword which he carried into battle. A full investigation of the items missing or damaged is underway.

"Why would anyone steal part of a man's beard?" asked the colonel.

"You wouldn't do something like this unless you had a clear motive—there has to be something to this—the selection of items. And why on the same night as someone breaking into the tomb on Cypress?" added Peppers.

"Any thoughts?" asked the base commander as he looked at bleary-eyed Chisolm.

"Not much I can conjure at the moment, sir," replied Grant. "But I'm inclined to agree—this has to have been coordinated. Two major sites in one night, the same night in which our base is attacked. Everything points to an Al-Qaeda plot, the planning, the details, the sophistication."

"And let's not forget that we have someone here on base who may well be a factor in all of this. His timing is suspect. Former detainee coming back to GITMO as a member of the

International Red Cross. Some of the attorneys here seem to be nothing but whores for hire—the money coming from dirty sources," added Peppers.

For a long period of time, the entire room was silent. Finally, Peppers rubbed his temples with both hands, sat up briskly, and smiled. "Gentlemen, we need to get some sleep. Grant, you have a source in the camp itself who seems to desire your company. Who knows, he may be able to add some insights about the museum caper. Maybe he can even tell us why someone would steal part of a man's beard. Let's return this evening to see if we can get some measure of all that's transpired—this ordeal is giving me a headache. And at least for one day, all attorney visits, all interrogations, all Red Cross visits are delayed. Nothing more until tomorrow."

BREAKING ICONS

10:02 a.m., Saturday

Exhausted, physically and mentally, Colonel Sanchez yearned for just a few moments of silence. He wanted the opportunity to sit down and close his eyes without the prospect of being addressed by yet another of his men seeking directions about the Arab prisoners in their possession or about the handling of the information concerning the night's events. He looked around outside his office door for a moment as if to assure himself that he might actually escape for a brief respite from the night's turmoil. He walked up two steps in the late morning heat, seeking to enter his office through a backdoor.

As he entered the recessed area, he noticed that the usually locked door was open. He knew that he himself was scrupulous about security;

he housed his weapons in his office and it was unlikely that he could have left it open. But in the turmoil of the night's activities, he surmised that one of his own aides might have come looking for him or some article or some piece of information. As he entered, he took off his holster with his sidearm and, for the first time, felt the full weight of the evening's activities. His uniform was soaked in sweat. He leaned over a small sink and turned on the water, but even it was warm. Still he splashed some on his face and wiped it with a small white towel as he looked at his face in a mirror. For a moment he wondered at the import of last night's events and how he would report it all to Fidel Castro and his brother Raul. It was stranger than anything any of them might have conjured up. The Cubans and Americans working together to thwart an attack on an illegal American military base on Cuban soil that housed prisoners from the Islamic world who may have been helped in this endeavor by a fellow socialistic state of China. Even the Nicaraguans may have been involved.

As he looked in the mirror, he caught a glimpse of movement in the office behind him. His office door had a window with a venetian blind, so he was not entirely certain if he had seen movement or not. His eyes were slightly irritated with his own sweat and drops from the water he had just thrown on his face. Perhaps one of his aides, he thought. He walked three steps to the door and opened it. As he did so, a startled Sergeant Juan Miguel turned abruptly, holding in his hands papers he had just lifted from a file drawer.

"Juan Miguel, what are you doing?"

"I just came back to get some papers, sir, some things to consider."

"What do you mean *consider*?"

"Last night, I understand, many things happened. I am confused by it all—I, I, want to understand it, sir."

Sanchez paused as he eased himself over toward his own desk. He looked down questioningly and an involuntary sigh of exhaustion escaped him. Without saying another word, while still looking down at his desk, he considered its contents: a lamp with a flexible neck, a large piece of glass that covered most of the desk and under which he had several papers, and a picture of himself as a much younger man taken in Angola. Standing next to him were several comrades in jungle fatigues with their arms around one another. Their arms wrapped over each other's shoulders, they appeared in good spirits and represented his fondest memories of the comradeship born of combat.

The only other item was a baseball. It sat in a small porcelain ashtray shaped like a human hand, only with three fingers instead of four and a large thumb. The baseball had been given to him years earlier from a game in the Cuban Industrial League in which he had struck out seventeen batters in nine innings, one of the best pitching performances of his career.

Sergeant Juan Miguel remained standing apprehensively and then put down the papers.

"Sergeant Juan Miguel, where were you last night?"

"I was all over but…" His hand moved away from the filing cabinet on which he had laid the papers and rested on the holstered firearm on his right hip. "I have always respected you, sir, as a soldier."

"But?" responded Sanchez.

"You know that the world is stupid," he blabbered.

"You know this?"

Looking confused and almost faint, Sergeant Miguel was about to speak again when he caught himself. He then summoned from the depths of his soul not a lie which he had been prepared to tell to exonerate himself in the eyes of a man who was as good a soldier as any, but the words he had been steeped in by his boyhood friend and the imam who had helped purge his soul of sin. "You know, of course, that you should not meet with the Americans. If you talk often with them, you too become corrupt. You help them defeat the soul of socialism…" He paused.

"Excuse me, sir, but you yourself have told me that socialism is good in some ways but that it is wrong in that it has no room for the spirit. You said that to me on one of our trips to the American base.

"You talk with them. You drink coffee with them. You are becoming like them. You are betraying the ideals of socialism. I have even heard you laugh with them. You have betrayed the ideals of a classless society with mere atheism and materialism. But I have learned other things, other ways to create the ideals of socialism but to do it with a soul."

As Sanchez nonchalantly moved a step closer to his desk, Sergeant Miguel unfastened his leather gun strap holding his firearm securely in his holster and placed his hand upon its grip.

"So how will you create this socialistic utopia, Sergeant Miguel?" asked Sanchez as he looked squarely into the face of a man whom he had helped to train.

"The ideals of socialism are…" He stopped and started again, "The ideals are not always bad but they are corrupted. The collective may be good, but it must be replaced by the *umma* so that men can still profess their faith to God."

"You are free to do that here in Cuba."

"It is a lie. No one can worship and follow his heart and soul. The socialists here are corrupt like the Americans, and unfortunately, sir, you are one like them and…"

Before he could continue, Sanchez picked up the baseball, knocking the holder onto the tiled floor and threw it straight at Sergeant Miguel. The ball hit him squarely in the face just above the nose and he fell to the floor with his gun still in the holster. Sanchez ran to grab it before he could respond. But the figure did not move. As Sanchez knelt by his side, he placed a finger on the supine figure's neck. There was no pulse. For a moment, Sanchez placed a hand on his own forehead. He looked down at the face of his former aide and one-time driver. The eyes were still open. He reached out with his right hand and closed them. Then, as he had done several times in the battlefield, he blessed the man and asked, "Keep him, Lord." And then to himself he whispered, "I am sorry for all our souls. We are so many falling on one another to be at peace." He sighed again deeply and reached for the baseball. He looked at the signature of which he had been so proud.

ANGELS AND SHARKS

> *There are no angels yet here*
> *comes an angel...I am the plumed*
> *serpent the beast with fangs of fire....*[63]
> —Adrienne Rich, "Gabriel"

7:00 a.m., Sunday

The United States Coast Guard cutter *Gallatin* continued to monitor and coordinate with the U.S. P-3 Orion aircraft that traversed the Caribbean attempting to surmise the full extent of the explosions that had registered on both sonar and the eyes in the sky. The navigator on board continued to coordinate the ship's path to intersect the site of the Liberian freighter's explosion only the day before. With no explanation or even a threat of possible retaliation from the Cuban government, the ship slowed its powerful engines as it began to drift through pieces of debris from a ship whose disappearance mystified the Americans. On the border between international and Cuban waters, the tensions in the region merited caution and extreme diligence as the cutter looked for possible survivors. Moving at a mere three knots per hour and following the currents in anticipation of the direction in which any survivors were likely to have been carried, the ship's crew, from the bridge to the fantail to the bow and the starboard and port, looked for any sign of life. Oddly, the Cubans reported nothing amiss to their American counterparts, despite frequent exchanges in the past as they coordinated efforts to stem the flow of illegal drugs through or near Cuba itself.

Using powerful stationary binoculars from the bridge, one of the watch petty officers constantly scanned the sea hoping to find some sign of life. At precisely 7:07 a.m. he called out, "I have a contact. Debris and possible survivor, two o'clock off the starboard bow."

The captain ordered the ship turned on the information and continued scanning for other signs of life around them. As they approached the blistered figure, the ship slowed even more as the watch spotted two other figures, both apparently dead, and one surrounded by a reef of sharks already tugging and nipping at the body and swimming off with chunks of flesh. The body's head appeared to be missing. Another body, as yet untouched by the sharks, was floating slightly below the surface. It was already puffy with decomposition and on the verge of bursting from internal gases. The grimness of the scene silenced the crew as they steadied the ship to retrieve the remains. They set one of the lifeboats into the water with a crew of four.

They bypassed both bodies, hoping to save the one figure who still appeared alive. Shakir saw first the Coast Guard vessel itself and then the rescue boat approaching him. One of the men on board was equipped with a rifle to kill sharks that were already circling in the waters nearby. But as the boat drew closer, Shakir attempted to swim away, pushing himself in the direction of several bull sharks that circled in a decreasingly small radius. As if he feared the rescue boat more than the sharks, he lifted his arms and kicked his feet to move away from them.

He still felt the tightness in his chest. Only now it seemed even more compressed. The agony of waiting for deliverance from God, whom he served so well, would soon be relieved. He drifted yet in the water alongside several pieces of debris from the ship. His air tanks had kept him afloat without his having to exert any effort and for a while at least he had slept in the water and awakened to find himself floating in the beauty of blue water that seemed clear and absent of malice. But after a day and night without fresh water, his face blistered from the heat and his lips were parched and cracking from the saltwater and dry air.

He turned toward the large black chip that speared the water and, because he knew that he was God's chosen, he began to swim toward it, assured of his own protection despite the menace. As he swam, the fin in the water turned toward him. He kicked vigorously, unafraid and assured of deliverance. Delusional, suffering from heat and thirst, he placed the regulator instinctively into his mouth and began to recite the names of the fish of the sea, the creatures of the land, and the birds of the air. For like the first man, he too had spoken with God and knew that he would be protected and he must give things their true name. The shark, the length of three men, sped toward him and opened his jaws and came down hard upon his torso, the teeth scraping on his tanks and the teeth at the back of his mouth cracking down on his head. As the shark clamped down even harder, Shakir felt the embrace of Gabrielle and began to recite, for he was of the Quraysh and he knew that "There is no God…" But his tanks wedged into the jaws of the beast, and it could not shake him loose nor could Shakir be frightened.

As the shark shook its head from side to side just beneath the surface, gashes on Shakir's chest and arms primed the water with a ribbon of blood as if waiting for the ultra-blue of the ocean to finish its decoration of the surface. The creature swam forward, the tanks and shoulders still wedged into its jaws. It surged violently to the surface attempting to disgorge its meal that was now grinding against its jaw bones. As it did, Shakir's blood blossomed into a miraculous red rose that lingered in the blue water as the shark circled again near the Coast Guard cutter. Shakir was not afraid and, as he was released by the shark, he pulled out his regulator and unbuckled his diving vest and, with great difficulty, he dropped the tanks and vest from his shoulders and pushed them away.

"Over here, sir, over here," cried one of the crewmen on board the rescue boat. He held out a pole with a safety hook on it to try and pull him to the boat but, as he did so, Shakir looked again at the black chip turning and diving before him with its precise grin. Then it opened its jaws and he willingly entered its mouth and he again began to recite, "There is no God..." The shark took him into itself and, like Jonah before him, he descended into the depths as he entered the belly of the beast.

THE DEPARTURE

> *They are ready again to do us in, as soon as an opening presents itself—which will be immediately after hostilities cease.*[64]
>
> —E. B. White, "No Crackpots?"

11:02 a.m., Wednesday

Machmood sat in the leeward terminal of Guantanamo Bay. He walked distractedly from one picture to another—the walls of the facility's interior were covered with pictures from the 1920s through the recent past of aircraft landings, departures, or still shots of planes parked on the runway at Guantanamo Bay. Pictures from the distant past showed battleships throughout the harbor in the aftermath of the Spanish-American War. The photographs provided a welcome relief from the constant barrage of mindless soaps and perennially talking heads of the various news programs that assaulted a person's ears and mind from the televisions placed in every corner of the passenger waiting room.

As he paced the room, his colleagues from the International Red Cross watched him, attempting to figure out the cause of his anxiety which had for the past two days alternated between fits of moroseness and a sour attitude toward visiting the camps to speak with various detainees. His ruddy complexion seemed strained and his eyes had bags underneath them as if he had not slept soundly for several days. At last his pacing stopped and he slipped outside the passenger terminal where he pulled out a cigarette and lit it. He contemplated his disappointment in what he now perceived to be the failure of the mission with which he had been tasked even as he carried out the requisite visits of a concerned citizen of the International Red Cross. There had been nothing more than a one-day delay or cancellation of the usual visits to suggest that anything unusual had occurred at Guantanamo. He was all but certain that the raid had been called off or had failed miserably, or had been postponed without his knowing anything more about it.

Minutes later, he watched as a small aircraft took off from the runway and began its trip to wherever. He pointed his lit cigarette at the plane as if he were aiming a gun and then said softly to himself, "Boom. You will be my own target. Where others have failed, I will not." He watched until a hangar interrupted his view, then threw down his cigarette and walked back inside to await the departure of the Continental Airlines flight 737 for Jacksonville, Florida.

Rather than sit with the other members of the International Red Cross, he sat alone in a remote area of the passenger terminal where he pulled out a detailed map of Camp Delta that he had drawn while working at Guantanamo for the past six days. He wondered when he would next be able to return to the camp and how different things would be. Taking out his pen, he began to color in some of the spaces on the map, and he wrote down several dimensions of the camp as if the added detail would make the difference in the next attempted raid. Then, abruptly, he crumpled up the piece of paper and stuck it back into his lightweight summer sport coat. He looked across the room to his colleagues, one of whom was still watching him, as if attempting to discern the cause of his anxiety. Machmood then got up with a smile and approached the others and said, "I love Cuba. I will come back again and then maybe we will have better luck next time. The prisoners here need us."

The others smiled in return and then sat in silence as they awaited the instructions to begin boarding the now refueled aircraft that had come in from Florida several hours before. After the flight to Jacksonville, Florida, they would overnight there and then leave the next morning for Spain and then Geneva, Switzerland. Now seated next to his colleagues, Machmood contemplated the flight and wondered if there might be someone else in the crowd of passengers who was like himself and who might have found a way to put a bomb on the plane. He wondered at the prospect of his death in such a circumstance and considered an old adage, "When man thinks, God laughs." He was certain that God was laughing now, and he decided to think no more about such matters.

THE MIRACULOUS
MEDALLION

> *By the North Gate, the wind blows full of sand,*
> *Lonely from the beginning of time until now!...*
> *No longer the men for offence and defence.*[65]
>
> —Rihaku, "Lament of the Frontier Guard"

The Northeast Gate, Guantanamo

Two weeks after the events which had forced
an unlikely alliance of American and Cuban
military personnel to thwart an attack on the
Guantanamo facilities, Colonel Sanchez had
requested a special meeting at the Northeast
Gate. In this instance, it would be Cuba's turn
to play host, especially since it had requested
a meeting well in advance of those routinely
scheduled. There were no Cuban refugees to
repatriate and there would be no discussions,
as in the past, to consider how the two nations
could help one another if there were a hurricane
in the vicinity. No discussions on the usual
workings of the rights of passage for ocean-

going ships entering Guantanamo Bay on their way to the adjoining Cuban city of Caimanera. No discussions on the prospect of augmenting the retirement checks issued by the United States Government to former Cuban workers at the Navy base. No, instead Colonel Sanchez had called the meeting in which he specified those whom he preferred to see in attendance: Base Commander DiPinta, Rusty Peppers, and Grant Chisolm, no one else.

On this particular morning, since he was to host the session, and since he had become accustomed to always arriving first, to teach the American lions whose territory they were on—his, not theirs—he was conflicted by a genuine desire to host them as if they were now friends and not merely representatives of their governments. For his part, Sanchez had even considered coming into the meeting less formally attired, as if to say that things had somehow changed. But as he sat waiting in the hacienda-like abode that was 16x16-foot former guardhouse for this particular gate, he opened up a book on America's great baseball players. He read with particular interest the story of Ted Williams who, despite the accolades and devotion of his many fans, could never bring himself to tip his hat to them. This morning he felt like Ted Williams. Like him, he could not bring himself to tip his hat to the Americans despite the fact that he wanted to. The rigor of his military bearing, he told himself, had to be maintained. Still, he hoped there was some way.

His aide came in and sat next to him, holding a leather attaché case along with a box, not bigger than a four-inch cube. As they sat awaiting the Americans, Sanchez asked his aide what he thought about the activities of two weeks ago—did he think word would get out, and did it bother him that he and the Americans had actually worked well together? Were there any lessons to be drawn from this?

His aide was silent for a minute and said, "I have a brother who played baseball who once threatened to leave everyone and everything behind if his family did not come and watch him play ball. We all thought he was just complaining. We all like baseball and we had all played it. We just didn't think he would actually do it until one day he disappeared. None of us had a chance to say goodbye. We cried because we knew that he had left the country. He went to Florida—illegally—now we have heard he has signed a contract to play minor league baseball with the Florida Marlins."

"I did not know that. Why didn't you say anything before this?"

"I was afraid that there would be consequences. I did not want you to mistrust me because I have a brother playing baseball in America. Still, I wish we had said goodbye to him."

Sanchez paused before speaking and said, "Regret, it is a terrible thing. We live to learn, I think, and we learn too late."

At that point, their conversation was interrupted as the door opened and two U.S. Marines entered, followed by DiPinta, Peppers, and Chisolm. DiPinta was in his usual desert camouflage. Peppers was casually dressed in a dark green dress shirt with the sleeves rolled up and a pair of black pants and black dress shoes. Chisolm was in street clothes, a white Banlon shirt, tan pants, and tan loafers. His one camouflage uniform was still at the cleaners after two weeks of wear and tear.

As they greeted Sanchez and his aide, whom they also knew from previous meetings over the past few weeks and months, Sanchez stood erect in his usual impeccable attire and, for a moment, hesitated to say anything. He had called the meeting, but his brain seemed to stop working. The usual array of cordialities and weather-related banalities seemed to have escaped him. He wanted to say something for which there was no precedent in any of his meetings with the Americans. They sat at the table. Sanchez blinked several times as if trying to force the appropriate thoughts to the forefront of his mind. After a long pause, his aide shifted in his chair uncomfortably. Then Sanchez, without thought, reached across the table, gesturing toward Chisolm and said, "You are a soldier whom I can admire."

Chisolm smiled in response but said nothing, somewhat embarrassed by the compliment. Then Sanchez cleared his throat and said, "Commander, Mr. Peppers, and Mr. Chisolm, thank you for coming here today. As you see, we have prepared some fine Cuban coffee, the kind Columbus would have wanted if he had stayed longer at Guantanamo when he came here. The recent events have, of course, come to the attention of our president who has informed me that he is pleased to work so well with the Americans in defeating terrorism. He thanks you for your efforts and assures you that the prisoners we have taken will be justly dealt with. However, he also wishes to keep these events most quiet as he fears that talking about them will jeopardize Cuba's relations with other nations, not least of which is America itself."

Commander DiPinta replied, "And we too appreciate all his cooperation in this matter. We hope to exercise sufficient discretion so that these events are not given undue treatment, if any treatment, by the American press."

Finally, Sanchez was able to compose himself enough to say what he was feeling. "Gentlemen, I consider you the type of individuals that anyone would be glad to go into battle with. I propose a toast."

He then poured five cups of coffee, one for each of the Americans, as well as one for his aide and one for himself. They each sipped at the very dark and very strong coffee, just the way Sanchez liked it. With the break in decorum that Sanchez afforded, there was an affability that was less polished, less calculated, and less strained than that of any previous meetings. The conversation flowed and flowered about small and inconsequential details of life that insinuated themselves into each person's memory.

Finally, Sanchez paused amidst the trivialities and friendly banalities and asked, "Do any of you know why the enemy failed?"

All were silent as they waited for Sanchez to explain.

"As you know, we have interrogation methods that are most effective. And one of the men we have arrested explained something. He told us that the attack was to be in full force at 2 a.m.—2 a.m. your time. In other words, he assumed that time for you would be different for the time for us; 2 a.m. for you was assumed to be 1 a.m. for us. In fact, he failed to note that we abandoned the daylight savings time at a different date each year. They used almanacs that are two years old to make their plans. The men who blew up did so because they had timing devices preset to allow them one hour to do damage. However, they started one hour too late. The person who set the timing devices could not have known this. They were operating by our time, and not yours, or so they thought. In fact, on the day of the attack, we were operating on the same time. The devices were to detonate at 2 a.m. our time, which was, in fact, the same as your time. The devices..."

"Colonel Sanchez," interrupted Peppers, "if I hadn't been aware of all the suicide bombings myself, I might not believe it. We got lucky this time."

"Sir," said Chisolm, "I recall a few years ago NASA attempted to put a satellite in a particular orbit and failed because half of the team was working with miles and the other half was working on the metric system, something that neither side knew until they ran into problems with the satellite's orbit. It is hard to believe, but if NASA can make that mistake with people sitting in the same room together..."

"Well said," replied Sanchez as he shrugged his shoulders.

"What will you do with the men you are now holding as prisoners?" asked Peppers.

Sanchez smiled and offered, "We were thinking of putting them in small boats and letting them escape to Florida, or maybe we will let them escape to Guantanamo—of course, they might just keep swimming to Jamaica. But for the moment, they are—how shall I say—they are enjoying the benefits of Cuba's justice."

Peppers smiled in response and said, "I would truly like an opportunity to talk with them."

"I'm certain," said Sanchez.

After half an hour, Sanchez then rose and said, "Thank you. Now if you gentlemen don't mind, I would like to have a few moments alone with Mr. Chisolm. I have something I would like to tell him."

Slightly perplexed but nonetheless accommodating, DiPinta and Peppers shook hands with Sanchez and his aide and left the building to wait outside. Sanchez's aide walked out the doorway to the Cuban side and waited. Chisolm remained standing as the others left.

"Mr. Chisolm, I have been a fighting man all my life, and I can appreciate a fellow warrior like yourself. I know of your exploits and know that it is doubtful we shall meet again. Therefore, I want to tell you a brief story related to my family.

"My mother's side of my family is pure Spanish, no mestizo, no nothing, except pure Spanish. They came from Spain over three hundred years ago. They too were warriors, and they settled in the city of Santiago. Now you may not know why, so I shall tell you. They were Castilians and, like the Castilians of old, they went into battle against the Moors, the Muslim warriors who had conquered Spain. And in their fervor, in their galloping into battle against them, these men who were of the house of St. James Compostella, they would shout out their battle cry, "Santiago!" which as you may know, in Spanish, means "St. James." I hope you will therefore accept this token of my esteem for all that you have done." With that, Sanchez reached around the back of his own neck and unlatched a silver chain which was otherwise hidden beneath his crisp white T-shirt. At the end of the chain was a silver medallion, on one side of which were engraved scallop shells. He handed it to Chisolm who turned it over and saw the words "*De Profundis*" engraved on the back side. "This word also, *de profundis*, was part of their battle cry. For in their fight against the

Moors, they called out for God's help from the depths of their souls.

"This medallion is quite old and has been in my family for some time."

Chisolm's eyes glistened in appreciation and he again shook Sanchez's hand. He placed the medallion around his own neck. Sanchez smiled approvingly. His aide glanced through the window where he stood outside at a respectful distance. Then Sanchez reached down for the box on the table and handed it to Chisolm. Chisolm opened the top and reached inside. As he did so, Sanchez smiled and said, "I know you are an athlete, and I hope you like baseball."

"I love it as a matter of fact."

"Good, then you will appreciate this, I think."

Grant took a baseball from the box and looked at the writing on it. "Fidel Castro, El Hombre Huracan."

"Mr. Chisolm, he loves baseball too and this ball is special to me. It once saved my life, a story which I will tell you another time if we are permitted."

"You must have been quite a player."

"I love the game."

"Sir, I am honored."

"So am I, to meet such a fine soldier. I hope that we shall never meet opposite one another on the field of battle."

"Likewise, sir."

"De Profundis," my friend.

REPATRIATION

*To exhale a breath of long forgotten
And legendary things.*[66]

—Blok, "The Stranger"

Bagram, Afghanistan—Three Weeks Later

Six Afghan officials sat in a Mine Resistant Ambush Protected All-Terrain Vehicle (M-ATV) just off the runway awaiting the arrival of a C-130 cargo plane. The day was deafeningly silent, despite the fact that the airfield itself was usually a hub of activity for planes arriving with supplies and military equipment for NATO troops still fighting the Taliban. The C-130 was making, what for it was, a routine entry into the dangerous air space above and near Kabul, the Afghan capital. Whenever a detainee was being repatriated to Afghanistan, all other flights were temporarily delayed or cancelled to accommodate a high priority "package." The clear blue skies above Bagram Air Base, just outside of Kabul, were seemingly portentous. As if in anticipation of a particularly joyous present, three men in polo shirts and a petite woman in military desert fatigues leaned against another M-ATV, their eyes covered with sunglasses and their attire, appropriately Western and glaringly non-Afghan, identifying them as CIA and U.S. military personnel.

The C-130 began a fast spiraling descent intended to make any attempts to shoot it down very difficult. The crewmen aboard made ready as the plane propelled itself into a shortening gyre, a full-bellied beast, its landing come round at last. Minutes later, the plane's engines slowed as it moved toward the tarmac and the waiting Afghan and American officials. Ten minutes later, the plane's entourage of officials exited the large rear ramp: several sergeants-at-arms, one medical official, one JAG representative, and two crew members in charge of cargo deliveries. Immediately, a squad of United States Army personnel formed an armed perimeter around the plane as Chisolm and two detainees followed, escorted on either side by yet another sergeant-at-arms. Chisolm stood at the bottom of the ramp as two bearded warriors slowly walked down with their leg irons dragging on the metal ramp. As the detainees reached the bottom of the ramp, they were escorted into another windowless van which pulled over behind the awaiting Afghan officials. A number of photographs were taken by a combat photographer as evidence of the physical condition and the actual repatriation of these two individuals to their homeland. Several sheets of paper were signed by the attendant American officials while they yet awaited the departure of the last "package."

Detainee 9696, or Ibrahim Saroyan, or Moustafa as he preferred to be called, was escorted down the ramp by yet another twosome of sergeants-at-arms. But as he stood next to Chisolm while the various papers were signed, the CIA personnel stepped through the perimeter and approached Chisolm, one of them addressing him only as "Sir." Chisolm and the prisoner followed as the personnel led the way to their vehicle, the petite soldier now behind the wheel of the oversized and heavily armored M-ATV. Before the detainee was formally turned over to the CIA, Chisolm instructed the sergeant-at-arms to unshackle the prisoner.

Two of the men helped pull Ibrahim Saroyan into the rear of the vehicle. Chisolm followed, pulling himself in and sitting next to the detainee on the long bench seat. The interior was cooled by air conditioning and offered as much protection as any vehicle in the world which could still be expected to actually move at a reasonable speed with its heavy armor plating and triceratops bulkiness.

After sitting in silence for several minutes, Detainee 9696 said to all present, "I am the plot, you are the plotters. Together we make history."

He then looked at Chisolm and said, "Even if I had no eyes, I would yearn to see the unraveling of a great mystery like the one we are about to go on."

Chisolm straightened himself and smiled. "I am a lucky man and, if, as you say, there is a mystery to be solved, then I think we shall have yet another great adventure."

As the personnel were about to close the rear hatch of the vehicle, another man approached and handed the driver an envelope which she immediately opened. The man stood alongside the door and waited. When she was through reading, she said, "Sir, go around back. We'll let you in."

Major Thomas Patel climbed into the rear of the vehicle and shook hands all around, no one mentioning their names, no one acknowledging the fact that they had already been informed that Patel had just spent three days on various commercial and military hops flying from Trinidad, to Guantanamo, to Jacksonville, Florida, to Rota, Spain, to Bahrain, and finally to Afghanistan. Chisolm and Patel glanced at one another, silently acknowledging what each felt about the presence of the other.

No matter the challenge, each would have picked the other as the best of men to assume the greatest risk against the greatest peril that one could confront in the hostile environment into which they soon would be thrust.

EPILOGUE
AT THE BIRTH OF A
NEW WORLD

> *To fight against the infidels is Jihad; but to fight against your evil self is greater Jihad.* [67]
>
> —Abu Bakr

Riyadh, Saudi Arabia, Two Months After the Attack on Guantanamo

In the bleached white attire of traditional Saudi dress, Haban al-Amur, the reluctant warrior who had abandoned the quest and the diving team organized by Shakir Amir, stepped into the foyer of the Sheraton Hotel in the center of Riyadh, the capital city of Saudi Arabia. Using a purloined passport and presenting a new identity that was as obscure and unrevealing as his dark sunglasses, Haban checked into the hotel with a new name as a single business traveler. Then, after only several minutes of seemingly mindless wandering about the various hallways and doorways of the hotel, he rode each of the four elevators all the way up and all the way down, checking his watch for the time required for each ascent and descent. He then checked each of the doorways at the end of the hallways on several different floors to make certain that they were unlocked.

An hour later, he sat in his hotel room where he logged on to a computer with an encryption device and sent a brief message to someone in London. He then waited several minutes for a reply. When it came, he was relieved. The period of waiting was over.

He looked at the floor plan of the hotel he had pulled from his briefcase and once again checked the location of certain rooms and the best points of entering and exiting.

He then wandered back to the restaurant area. He kept his sunglasses on even as he drank lemonade and watched two individuals at a nearby table who were engaged in an animated conversation. Confirming the identities of the two men was easy, as he had gotten to know them while on Farasan Island. One of them, and his real interest, was the man known to him only as Ishmael, the same man who had helped plan the very attack which he had abandoned after he witnessed the destruction at the cemetery. Trained in the Shia tradition, but passing himself off as a Sunni, he had moved into the inner circles of the Sunni brotherhood that sponsored international mischief and terrorism. Now he would avenge the losses of a thousand-plus years. He watched the man whose face he knew so well.

Four hours later, he emerged from beneath the bed of the man who had helped train him in the art of destruction. He looked down at the sleeping figure and then at his watch, which read 2 a.m. He slid his razor-sharp knife across the throat of the sleeping figure whose eyes opened as the knife cut him from ear to ear. Ishmael attempted to sit up but began to choke. He fell backward with his eyes open and gasped once for air and then succumbed. A slight spray of blood fell across the bed and onto Haban's clothing, a black cloak which was draped over his white robe. He removed the black cloak and dropped it to the floor. Next to the head and partially across the chest of Ishmael he left a red cloth.

"May your death be long, and your life forgotten. Praise unto Allah."

Haban walked out into the hallway and took the nearest elevator down to the hotel lobby, called a friend, and waited. Ten minutes later, a silver Mercedes-Benz pulled up and Haban got into the backseat. As he did so, he shook hands with Mr. Shamar Khan and looked ahead as Major Patel, dressed in the livery of the hordes of taxi drivers from the nearby airport, sped off into the night and an awaiting charter to London's Heathrow Airport.

◆◆◆

Ferry Landing at Guantanamo Bay, Windward Side

Despite her frustration and disappointment at the realization of the fate that had befallen her, Blanche DeNegris maintained her professionalism even at the moment when she received the e-mail from Chisolm explaining that he was soon to return to Afghanistan. She, as a former graduate student in archaeological studies at the University of Cincinnati, had parlayed her connections there into being brought on board at the last minute as part of a team of archaeologists and environmentalists sent to Guantanamo under the auspices of the Department of Defense. The role of the archaeologist was to investigate rumors that had persisted over the years of archaeological relics supposedly buried or abandoned over the years by the Americans, the Cubans, the British, the French, pirates and, of course, the Spanish. Having arrived at the base several days after Grant's departure, she buried herself in the painstakingly slow and sometimes fruitless endeavor of filtering shovel loads of dirt, sand, and rock in hopes of finding a diamond in the rough, an artifact from the past that painted the world of the dead in colors that the living could actually see.

Three weeks after arriving on the island, she awoke from a startling dream in which she envisioned herself looking at a film negative of the location at which the dig site was established. In the dream, she was digging when three crosses floated up out of the water of Guantanamo Bay and landed near the site of the dig. All the crosses were red, very large, and upside down while the rest of the environs of the dream were simply black and white as in a negative. At first, she dismissed the dream and wanted to go back to sleep. But then it struck her that the dreamscape was the actual site of their archaeological endeavors and the dream might be trying to tell her something. But what? She took out a notebook and jotted down the key elements of the dream and attempted to go back to sleep.

An hour later, at the first glimmer of sun, she made herself some coffee and then hopped in the white two-door Chevy from Guantanamo's lone car rental agency and rattled all the way down to Ferry Landing at the precise location of the dig. The dig site was on one side of the monument erected several years earlier to commemorate Columbus's landing at

Guantanamo Bay on his second voyage to the New World in 1494. Considering the significance of the negative in the dream, Blanche moved to the other side of the monument and began to dig with a pickax and shovel.

Two hours later, exhausted and sweating profusely from the rising Cuban sun, her shovel hit something hard but slightly malleable that clinked as she tapped at it again with the blade. Reaching with a garden shovel, she cleared the dirt and pebbles away, even as she reached around with her other hand and attempted to lift the container from the soil. The size of a shoebox, it was oddly shaped, with six uneven sides and a depth of no more than three inches, with encrustations of rust and dirt that constrained her attempt to lift the lid from its base. She struggled with the lid until a few taps from the garden shovel loosened the debris, and she was able to pry it open. Inside was a velvety smooth purple cloth wrapped around an object. She gently unwrapped the object with trembling hands and found a cross made of pure silver covered with engraved scallops. She turned it over and on the back saw a series of inscribed oddly shaped cursive m's in various angles, some of them upside-down and others with what looked like m's with an extra loop or two. Placing the cross back in the box, she covered up the site and walked with the container to her car where she pulled out a thermos of coffee and drank another cup. She knew.

◆◆◆

Yerevan, Armenia

Grant Chisolm and Moustafa sat in the quiet of a family house in the suburbs of the capital city of Armenia. The widow, still dressed in black after more than three years of mourning, brought out a tray of tea and sat it down on the dark brown coffee table. She offered a cup to Moustafa and then to Chisolm. She spoke in halting English.

"He has been gone for several years now and yet the children and I still miss him. We always knew that one day it could happen. Not because he was a priest but because he was a good man that knew a secret that the whole world wants. I cry for him every day." She unfolded a yellow sheet of paper and said to Moustafa, "This is what they wanted. He told me about it years before he died. He would want you to have it. Someone must know how to interpret it."

She handed the sheet to him. He looked at it for a minute and then handed it to Chisolm and said, "Do you recognize this?"

"I think so—we studied this in a cryptography class I took. No one has been able to decipher it."

"We will," replied Moustafa.

Chisolm placed it delicately on the coffee table for all to see.

GLOSSARY OF TERMS

BDU—Battle Dress Uniform. The standard combat or military fatigues of various branches of the United States military which have recently been replaced in most locales by a digitalized camouflage uniform.

CENTCOM—Central Command. The United States military's command for all of its affairs in parts of the Horn of Africa, most of the Middle East, including Iraq, and parts of Central Asia, including Afghanistan.

EUCOM—European Command. The United States military's command for all of its affairs in Europe and, until recently, most of Africa and parts of Southwest Asia.

Hosay—An annual procession particularly in Trinidad in which Muslims, largely Shia, commemorate the Battle of Karbala and the deaths of Mohammad's grandsons, Hussein and Hassan.

HVD—High-Value Detainee. This is a term applied by the United States military and its allies to individuals captured in the Global War on Terrorism who are considered important figures.

IED—Improvised Explosive Device. A term applied to any number of explosive devices which can be set off through a variety of means to include pressure sensitivity, trip wires, timing mechanisms, or manual switches.

Infidel—A term used by Christians and Muslims to describe those who are not of their faith. The term literally means "non faithful."

Jannat Al-Baqi Cemetery—A cemetery in Medina, Saudi Arabia, in which Mohammad and many of his relatives are buried. Shrines and commemorative placards on the sites of various graves were destroyed in 1925 by the House of Saud at the request of Wahhabist scholars who argued that no markers should be placed at grave sites. Many Muslims, especially Shia, are opposed to the Saudi government's interpretation of Mohammad's remarks concerning burial practices and think the site should have been preserved out of respect to the Prophet's family and friends. The site is largely covered up by a mosque situated on the site.

Jihad—An Arabic term derived from the Koran referencing every Muslim's obligation to fight against evil through military or personal obstruction of those who represent it. From the perspective of certain Muslims, this may require violence against those who do not submit to any or even just a few of the tenets of Islam.

JWICS—An abbreviation for Joint Worldwide Intelligence Communications System. A highly classified U. S. Department of Defense worldwide communications system.

Magna Ecclesia—The great church of Constantinople commissioned by Justinian the Great. At one time the largest church in the world. Upon conquest of Constantinople by the Turks in 1453, it was turned into a mosque. However, neither Muslims nor Christians were allowed to worship in it after the collapse of the Ottoman Empire in 1917. It was turned into a museum and archaeological site and remained so until 2020 when it was again turned into a mosque. It is also known as the Church of Hagia Sophia.

Shaheed—An Arabic term referencing a Muslim who lays down his life as a *witness* or *martyr* for Islam.

Takfiri—A Muslim, whether of the Shia or Sunni sect, who takes it upon himself to declare other Muslims guilty of impiety, blasphemy, or apostasy and who can therefore excommunicate those individuals. Certain takfiri also deem it appropriate to carry out acts of violence against such individuals.

Taqiyya—An Arabic term referencing a Muslim who conceals his faith through actions that might be termed blasphemous or in some way inconsistent with the teachings of the Koran. The concept of *taqiyya* is intended to keep Muslims safe from persecution by allowing them to hide their true identity.

Umma—A term in Islam which references those parts of the world inhabited and ruled by Muslims. Among Muslims the term conveys the belief that any portion of the world once Muslim is eternally Muslim and must eventually return forcefully, if not peacefully, to its rule. Among many Muslims this requires jihad whereby countries like Spain and Portugal who were once ruled by Islamic leaders must eventually submit again to the authority of what some refer to as the Caliphate, the one-time ruling body of Islam. It is the Muslim counterpart to the term Christendom.

END NOTES

[1] Bible, New International Version. (Grant Rapids, MI: Zondervan, 2005), page 696 Psalm 130: 1.

[2] Kristophorn, Mamoa. "From Mohammad to 9/11; does the West get it?" Lecture delivered in Stuttgart, Germany, defense strategy session, August, 2005.

[3] Hersch, Marc. Three Sigma Systems, "Allahu Akbar." Last modified February 12, 2011. Accessed September 28, 2012. http://www.3sigma.com/allahu-akbar/.

[4] Blake, William. "Creatures." The Premier Book of Major Poets, ed. Anita Dore (New York: Fawcett Premier, 1993), 60.

[5] Katz, Steve. Sourcebooks, Inc., "Lion Taming." Accessed September 25, 2012. http://www.liontaming.com.

[6] Tally, M. "Religious Conflicts in the Age of Reason." Lecture, Cleveland, Ohio 2006.

[7] Columbus, Christopher. The American Spectator, "Cuba's Hidden Heroes" as quoted from his journals. Last modified 12/30/2008. Accessed September 24, 2008.

[8] Limbaugh, Rush. "The Rush Limbaugh Show." Performed August 13, 2007. The EIB Network. Radio Broadcast.

[9] Wilde, Alistaire. "The Culinary Cupid." (London: self-published, 2010).

[10] Dunham, Jeff. "Achmed the Dead Terrorist." http: //www. grindtv. com/mo re/video/ achmed_the_dead_terrorist/#25455.

[11] Josephus, Flavius. *Antiquities of the Jews*, Book 20, Chapter 9, 1 text at Wikisource.

[12] Koran. (Dallas: Darrusalam, 1999), 58 4:157.

[13] Khalidi, Tarif. *The Muslim Jesus: Sayings and Stories in Islamic Literature*, (Boston: Harvard University Press, April 20, 2003), 186.

[14] Muhammad, al-Bukhari. "Sahih al-Bukhari." Last modified April 30, 2004. Accessed September 25, 2012. http://www.paklinks. com/gs/religion-and-scripture/151663-the-prophets-saw-grave.

[15] Naipaul. *Among the Believers* (New York: Vintage Books, 1982), 19.

[16] ThUmP, LyRics. Full Sail University, "Creative Writing for Entertainment." Last modified March 29, 2011. (Accessed September 25, 2012). http://www.gspoetry.com/war-wounds-spokenword-poems-481331.html.

[17] Cacoyannis, Michael. "Zorba the Greek." Film adaptation of Nikos Kazantzakis's book Zorba the Greek, VHS.

[18] Lawrence, D. H. .Ad Council, "Poetry X: Poetry Archives." Last modified September 13, 2011. (Accessed September 25, 2012). http://poetry.poetryx.com/poems/5787/.

[19] Hastings, Mark. "The Poet of the Sphere." Last modified 2012. (Accessed September 25, 2012). http://poetofthesphere.com/2011/04/13/my-poem-the-sphere/.

[20] Chin, Thomas. (Poet), Interview by Eric Wentz, South Korea "Buddhism and the Soul," A and B=C, December 2005.

[21] Sterling, Liz. "A Wary Interview." The Sun Sentinel. com, on-line edition, sec. Feature, March 10, 2007. http://articles.sun-sentinel.com/2007-03-10/features/0703080547_1_intuition-gut-reactions-insights (Accessed September 25, 2012).

[22] Hinckley, Jr., John. "Think exist.com." (Accessed September 26, 2012). http://thinkexist.com/quotation/your_prodigal_son_has_left_again_to_exorcise_some/211195.html.

[23] Hardy, Thomas. "oldpoetry.com." (Accessed September 26, 2012). http://oldpoetry.com/Thomas_Hardy/The_Voice.

[24] J.H.D., (Poet), Interview by Eric Wentz, Orlando, Florida" "Speaking of Angels"," "Poems of the ***", October 2009.

[25] Tan, Amy. "The Language of Discretion." One World Many Cultures, ed. Stuart and Terry Hirschberg (Newark: Longman, 2007), 38.

[26] Heaney, Seamus. Faber and Faber, "Seamus Heaney: Collected Poems." Last modified 2009. (Accessed September 26, 2012). http://www.rte.ie/heaneyat70/media/CD_Boxset_Listings.pdf.

[27] Lenormant, Francois. Chaldean Magic: Its Origin and Development, (Boston: Red Wheel/Weiser, LLC, 1999), 18.

[28] De Lamartine, Alphonse. Istanbul Travel Advisor, "Istanbul." Last modified October 21, 2011. Accessed September 26, 2012. http://istanbultraveladvisor. com/?p=86.

[29] Rougeau, Steve, (SFC). "Honor, Valor, Courage." JTF Guantanamo Public Affairs, August 7 (2009).

[30] Muir, John. The Yosemite, (1911) http://www.cherylkanenwisher.com/2011/05/remnants-of-spring.html (Accessed September 26, 2012), Chapter 5.

[31] Gluzinski, Thomas. "Brotherhood of Silence." De Opresso Liber: A Poetry and Prose Anthology of Special Forces Soldiers, (Fayetteville, North Carolina: Old Mountain Press,)http://www.oldmp.com/anthology/war.htm (Accessed September 26, 2012).

[32] Stork, Charles Wharton. Poets.org, (Accessed September 26, 2012). https://www.poets.org/m/dsp_poem.php?prmMID=20880.

[33] Carmine S., (Poet recited this line in a public presentation.), Interview by Eric Wentz, Madison, Wisconsin "Poetry." Utopia, April 2011.

[34] Berry, Wendell. gratefulness.org, "The Peace of Wild Things." Last modified 1985. (Accessed September 26, 2012). http://www.gratefulness.org/poetry/peace_of_wild_things.htm.

[35] 786, Kibzy. Wattpad, "Ripples in the Water." (Accessed September 26, 2012). http://www.wattpad.com/432397-poems-by-kibzy786-coming-back-soon.

[36] M.T., "The Water Witch." Poem read by M.T., April,2007, compact disc.

[37] Sorkin, Alan. "A Few Good Men." Script adaptation from drama to film, DVD.

[38] Homer. *The Odyssey*. (Oxford, England: Oxford University Press, 1991), Chap. lines 181-182.

[39] Lucas, George. "Star Wars." 1977, VHS.

[40] Collins, Billy. "The Brooklyn Museum of Art." *New York*, May 18, 1987, 109.

[41] Wikipedia. "Blind man's buff." (Accessed October 9, 2012). http://en.wikipedia.org/wiki/Blind_man's_buff.

[42] Kipling, Rudyard. "The Ballad of East and West." *A Victorian Anthology*, ed. Edmund Clarence Stedman (Cambridge: Riverside Press,1895)http://www.bartleby.com/246/1129.html (Accessed September 26, 2012).

[43] The New Jerusalem Bible. Judges 12:5-6.

44 St. Anthony Press, "The Hail Mary in Arabic." (Accessed September 26, 2012). http://www. stanthonysparish.com/prayers/hailmary.htm.

[45] Given to the author at a poetry reading in Chicago, Illinois, fall of 2010.

[46] al-Bukari, *110 Ahadith Qudsi,* (Houston, Texas: Darrusalam, 1996), 62.

[47] Larkin, Phillip. "Deceptions." *oldpoetry.com.*

[48] "Pygmalion," Musical adaptation by Alan Learner and Frederick Loewe, 1938, compact disc.

[49] Koenig, A.T. "Teasing Life." Accessed September 26, 2012. No longer available.

[50] Lewis, C. S. *The Problem of Pain.* (MacMillan and Company,1940) http://voices.yahoo. com/gods-megaphone-ourpain-1008223. html?cat=10 (accessed September 26, 2012).

[51] *110 Ahadith Qudsi,* (Houston, Texas: Darrusalam, 1996), 113.

[52] Grant, Verelda. Native Village. "January 1,2009,Issue 174,Volume 1." (Accessed September 26, 2012). http://www. nativevillage.org/Archives/2007/Jan 1 News I 174B/Jan 107 News Issue 174 V1.htm.

[53] Emmerson, Les. "Signs." Good-byes and Butterflies, Performed by Five Man Electric Band, compact disc.

[54] Tobias, Fred. "Timing." Sung by Jimmy Jones, compact disc.

[55] Neruda, Pablo. The Heights of Macchu Picchu. (Stanford: Stanford University Press, 1980), 81.

[56] Shahzad, Faisal. "Faisal Shahzad Gets life for Times Square Bomb Plot." New York Post, . http://www.nypost.com/p/news/local/manhattan/proud_to_be_terrorist_DBtc5U2eAYhWzacVpxK24K (Accessed September 26, 2012).

[57] Kmiec, Adam. "The Art of Misdirection: Kmiec Ramblings" online forum, April 22, 2011, Misdirection—its definition and consequences, http://www.thekmiecs.com/misc/the-art-of-misdirection/.1.

[58] Cohen, Roger. "The End of the End of the Revolution." New York Times, December 5, 2008. http://www.nytimes.com/2008/12/07/magazine/07cuba-t.html?pagewanted=3&_r=moc.semityn.www (Accessed September 26, 2012).

59 Berryman, John. "Canto Amor," http://www. mattlogelin.com/archives/2010/09/07/ words-stolen-from-another/(Accessed September 26, 2012).

60 King James Bible. (Cambridge, England: Cambridge University Press, 1611)http:// kingjbible.com/psalms/69.htm (Accessed September 27, 2012), Psalm 69:22.

61 Tennyson, Alfred. "The Brook." http://www. wussu.com/poems/alttb.htm (Accessed September 27, 2012).

62 Anonymous to Teachers of Plato online forum, "Idealism." No longer available.

63 Rich, Adrienne. "Gabriel." Poetry Tuesday, ed. Debbie Millman (2006) http:// debbiemillman.blogspot.com/2006/07/ poetry-tuesday-gabriel.html (Accessed September 27, 2012).

64 White, E. B. "No Crackpots?" New Yorker, September 12, 1942, 137.

65 Rihaku, "Lament of the Frontier Guard." ed. Ezra Pound (The Atlantic, 2005) http://www.theatlantic.com/magazine/ archive/2005/01/ezra-pound-lament-of-the-frontier-guard/303714/ (Accessed September 27, 2012).

[66] Blok, Alexander. "The Stranger." Famous Inspirational Poems, http://www.inspirationalstories.com/poems/thestranger-aleksandr-blok-poem/ (Accessed September 27, 2012).

[67] Bakr, Abu. Brainy Quote. "Jihad." (Accessed September 27, 2012). http://www.brainyquote.com/quotes/keywords/jihad.html.

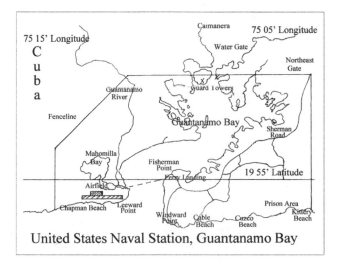

Cuba

75 15' Longitude

75 05' Longitude

Camanera

Water Gate

Northeast Gate

Guantanamo River

Guard Towers

Fenceline

Guantanamo Bay

Sherman Road

Mahomilla Bay

Fisherman Point

Perry Landing

19 55' Latitude

Airfield

Leeward Point

Chapman Beach

Windward Point

Cable Beach

Cuzco Beach

Prison Area

Kittery Beach

United States Naval Station, Guantanamo Bay

ABOUT THE AUTHOR

Eric Wentz is a twenty-six-year veteran of the U. S. Navy and Navy Reserves, in which capacity, he has served as an intelligence officer, an interrogator, and a linguist. His real-life experiences which contribute so heavily to the making of his books are augmented by a bachelor's degree in history and English literature, a master's degree in linguistics, and a Master of Science degree and doctorate in educational administration. His first novel, *Piercing the Veil*, was published in 2009 and praised by *USA Today* as a "novel of intrigue" and "hidden best seller."

In addition to numerous military awards and decorations, he is the recipient of teaching awards from the Departments of Commerce and Defense, as well as Homeland Security.

He is also a certified SCUBA diver who has plumbed the depths of the Mediterranean and the Caribbean , as well as an experienced canoeist who has traversed the rivers of the Yukon and the Northwest Territories.

He is a member of the Civil Air Patrol and Coast Guard Auxiliary and an amateur archaeologist. He recently completed another advanced degree in Criminal Justice through the Department of Homeland Security.

Check out further details on Amazon.com as well as his website, ericwentz.com.